Echoes

A HARP SECURITY NOVEL

Laura K. Curtis

RHP

BY LAURA K. CURTIS

THE HARP SECURITY SERIES
Twisted
Lost
Echoes
Mind Games

THE GOODY'S GOODIES SERIES
Toying with His Affections
Gaming the System

To the people of St. Martin/Sint Maarten who have welcomed me for more than thirty years and proven time and time again that it really is "the friendly island."

PROLOGUE

St. Martin, French West Indies

Nicole Lewis Brody made a beautiful corpse. But then, being long on looks and short on life came with her genes. Her killer chuckled at his own wit even as he forced down the faint acid flavor of panic rising to the back of his throat. He hadn't planned to kill her just yet. The minute she'd started making noises about trying to find her biological father the end had been inevitable, but he'd hoped to be able to finish her off in a manner that would keep the police out of it, as he had with her mother.

Nikki liked drugs and parties, and he didn't want to pollute her system more than she'd managed on her own, so an overdose was out of the question. He'd made mistakes early on, corrupted the bodies of his first attempts, and lost any chance of benefit. And he couldn't kill her from a distance; he'd learned that from earlier attempts as well. He'd had a few ideas about how to proceed, so he'd laid a solid foundation, thank Father in Heaven, but he hadn't settled on a perfect method yet.

And then she'd found a picture of that damned writer, Calliope Pearson, and the situation had become urgent. Panic threatened once more, and he pushed it away. Once complete, he'd never again have to endure that horrible pressure, as if some alien being were eating through his chest while compressing his head. His doctor could stop warning him about acid reflux, too, because he'd be too strong to worry. Even now, in his imperfect state and under threat of discovery, he had come up with a new plan. He could keep this one on ice until he could take what he needed. He'd been in her basement plenty of times, and admired her chest freezer, but he couldn't very well leave her in her own home. Too many variables, too much potential for disaster. Plus, tonight he was free to move her, and that might not be the case again for some time.

He duct-taped her ankles together and wrapped them in a cashmere stole from her closet. He was going to have to drag her down the hall, and he didn't want to leave scuff marks on the polished wooden floors. There could be no signs of struggle should the gendarmes choose to visit.

He hefted her, feeling the strain in his back, his arms. Damn. He couldn't afford to cripple himself here. The bitch was heavy for being so skinny. He hadn't had to move any of the others, and the logistics of the situation gave him pause. He dropped her to the floor, her head landing on the woven cotton area rug with a dull thud, and reconsidered his plan. Maybe he should return her clothes to their drawers, her suitcases to the closet, and leave her for her husband to find, as had been his original design.

After all, there were still a few others out there who could help him, though he'd thinned the herd by more than half.

The idea of watching the ants scuttle around after finding this one's dead body brought a thin smile to his lips, as it had the moment he'd conceived it. Hell, Nikki Lewis owned half the hotel where Calliope Pearson was planning to stay; maybe management would shut the place down for a couple of weeks for a proper mourning period. Talk about two birds with one stone. Even if the resort stayed open, he had an associate who could probably get rid of Pearson before she ever set foot on the island. He'd call the man in the morning and put him to work.

But the timing concerned him. If he could rely on his connection to rid him of the final difficult woman in his life, he could leave this one to rot where she lay. But what if the man failed? They had only a week, so he had to plan for all contingencies, and if Pearson did make it to St. Martin, her appearance would raise questions he'd prefer Nicole's corpse not be available to answer.

And then, he was almost sure Nikki had what he needed. He'd caught her breath, her soul, when he'd strangled her, but he hadn't finished with her body. He had neither the time nor the instruments to complete the process, and he couldn't just leave his future lying in a heap on her own living room floor.

Without a body, and with her toiletries and jewelry missing, people would likely believe Nicole had simply taken a long vacation, postponing—if not entirely eliminating—any investigation, which would make his life easier.

Unfortunately, her husband was unlikely to let such an explanation stand for long. Aidan Macmillan Brody was another little complication, another rock Nicole had tossed into the smooth waters of his life. If she'd chosen anyone but an ex-cop to marry, he could have framed her husband and been done with it. But pointing a finger at a cop, even an American cop, even a former American cop, was a risky proposition. No, as much of a pain in the ass as removing her corpse might be, having Nicole disappear was safer and smarter.

Once again, he lifted the bitch's upper body and began dragging her toward the kitchen.

CHAPTER ONE

HEAT AND HUMIDITY knocked Callie Pearson back a step as she ventured out of the modern, well-cooled terminal building at Princess Juliana airport on the Dutch side of the island of Sint Maarten. She'd spent the previous week at a hiking resort in Scotland, and even after two days at home in New York, the island's late-afternoon temperature came as a shock. August was hardly the ideal time to visit the Caribbean, being brutally hot as well as smack in the middle of hurricane season, but it was the only time she could get a reservation at Paradis de la Mer, the exclusive, five-star resort she hoped held answers to her own past.

A rickety van doing double duty as a Heineken delivery truck took her to the rental-car lot, where she got her first taste of "island time." Although only one man preceded her in line, it was a full half hour before she was under way, her little Toyota plugging valiantly along despite an engine obviously overtaxed by the air-conditioning system. After a few minutes, she cranked open the driver's side window, letting in the scent of the island. With the vents off, the car picked up speed.

Her route wound through the Dutch side of the island, down a rutted, potholed road bisecting the desolate ghost town of a once-elegant property. In her research, she'd found pictures of the place before Hurricane Luis in 1995, when it had been the largest of Sint Maarten's many resorts, but the damage had been extreme and the owners had absconded with the insurance money, leaving a blighted and rotting landscape.

Past the permanently open gate marking the property's exit, however, the island's lush beauty reasserted itself, and she was so fascinated by the view that—even having studied every map she could find—Callie missed the Paradis's entrance at first. The e-mail confirmation she'd received had instructed her to begin looking for it on the left soon after she passed from the Dutch to the French side of the island, but it hadn't mentioned the lack of demarcation between the two.

A small stone marker at the foot of what appeared to be a private road said merely "Paradis," startling a small laugh out of her. Clearly the hotel's owners didn't lack for arrogance. She turned carefully up the narrow lane, hugging the edge as it wound toward the sea in a series of blind S-curves. A couple hundred feet up the drive, just before a turnoff to the right that seemed to lead to an even narrower road, a guard stepped out of a tree-shaded gatehouse and waved her down. He gave her a decidedly peculiar look, examined her ID, then stepped back inside and reached for the phone. The call lasted less than a minute, but his frown deepened and he shook his head before he raised the heavy metal pole serving as a barrier and pointed straight ahead.

Callie drove through slowly, flicking glances backward at the guard as she did. He had checked her driver's license against a clipboard, leading her to assume he had a list of guests and approved visitors, but if she hadn't been on it, he hadn't said so. Could he tell, just by looking, that she was more than a simple travel writer looking for a story? A little shiver ran up her spine as she realized he hadn't closed the gate. Instead, he stood in the center of the road, speaking into a walkie-talkie she hadn't noticed when she drove up and watching her as she parked and approached the sprawling mansion of a hotel.

A plump woman standing behind a mahogany desk just inside the entrance greeted Callie with a smile that didn't quite reach her eyes. And those eyes didn't blink. She never even looked down at the reservation book open on the desk. Callie resisted the urge to look down and see whether she'd spilled something on her clothes.

"Madame Pearson. Welcome to Paradis de la Mer."

"Thank you. And please, call me Callie."

"I am Claudine." The woman paused as if debating what to say next. "I see you have suitcases. Let me call Ben to take them upstairs for you."

"That would be great."

But the woman didn't pick up the phone on her desk. Instead, her gaze shifted over Callie's shoulder.

"Christ," said a deep voice to her left, tinged with accusation beneath the distinctive thickness of the American southeast, "where did Nikki find you?"

"Excuse me?" Callie turned to give the stranger a piece of her mind but momentarily lost her train of thought. The man was too close, too big. He stood with his back to the door, so that her first impression was of an impenetrable void rimmed in bright light. Closer examination proved no more comforting.

A gun rode in a holster threaded onto his belt, a silent, matte black threat. In a separate holster, the man wore a walkie-talkie, which probably meant the gate guard had called him. But why? What threat could she possibly pose? Ragged ebony hair and stubble the same color contrasted with an almost military posture, and a vicious, ropy scar running from just above one cold, green eye down his cheek and angling toward the corner of his mouth gave the harsh planes of his face a dangerous cast. But the worn jeans covering his slim hips and molded to his muscular thighs were present-able, and the charcoal gray T-shirt stretched across his broad shoulders sported a Paradis de la Mer logo embroidered in red and gold over his heart. He belonged. Still, Callie took an involuntary step back, which brought her up against the desk without placing nearly enough space between the new-comer and herself.

"Maybe it's a coincidence," said Claudine in French.

"Not on your life," said the stranger. "This is one of Nikki's games. She found a fatter, plainer version of herself and brought her to stay here while we were all worried sick."

Callie balled her hands into fists at her sides and grit-ted her teeth against the words of outrage threatening to pour forth. She'd decided long before her arrival her purposes would be better served by pretending to speak only English. Sure, she could stand to lose five or ten pounds, but she wasn't fat. And she'd never cultivated a dramatic appearance because it didn't fit her lifestyle. Middle of the road, that was her: average height; average weight for her height; medium length, medium brown hair; and perfectly happy with her position smack in the center of the bell curve, thank you very much.

Breathing in for four beats and out for eight, she achieved a modicum of control. The byplay had been quick, so much so it wouldn't have been offensive to someone who didn't understand the content. Whatever was going on, it couldn't be related to a riddle almost three decades old, so her best bet was to continue as planned.

"Is this how you welcome all your guests? Speaking to one another instead of to them? It's a wonder St. Martin dares call itself 'the friendly island.'"

The man ignored the touch of sarcasm she'd allowed to creep into her words. Instead of taking the easy out and backing off, pretending the exchange was meaningless, he moved even closer. "Do you have a sister, Miss Pearson?"

Never let them see you sweat. It was the defining rule by which her father taught her to live. She drew herself up and gave him her best superior glare. "Not that it's any of your business, but no. Maybe I just have one of those faces. People often think they know me."

"Not likely. You have fairly distinctive features. And you share them with Nicole Lewis." Those jade eyes, opaque, shadowed, and unreadable, pinned her like a specimen fastened to a display board. "Or, more accurately, Nicole Lewis Brody. My wife."

Nicole Lewis, half owner of the Paradis? Nicole Lewis, his wife? Not some casual acquaintance with a vague resemblance, then. The slight sheen of sweat Callie had acquired on the drive from the airport cooled abruptly, leaving goose bumps in its wake. She'd come to St. Martin to solve a mystery, but she hadn't anticipated being forced to dive into a second one.

"I don't know what to say."

The man snorted in disbelief.

"Mac." The woman came out from behind the desk, shaking her head, then addressed Callie. "I am terribly sorry. Mac is our head of security. His wife, one of the resort's owners, vanished nine days ago. We are all distressed by her disappearance."

"Naturally," Callie replied. "And if I could help you, I would. But I don't know her. I recognize the name, of course, because when she and her brother inherited the Paradis, the trade papers had articles front to back. But I don't think there were any pictures. I had no idea we looked alike. And I've been out of touch for the last week; I didn't even realize she was missing."

A slight exaggeration. She had heard rumors, but she'd spent most of the two days she'd been at home recovering from jet lag and coping with the fact that her gas fireplace—turned off for the summer—had developed a leak, which might have killed both her and her roommate had Erin not detected the peculiar odor. Even hard news had taken a back-seat to personal drama, and Nicole's disappearance had been treated more as gossip than tragedy by the press.

On the flight down, she'd recalled the story and wondered whether the woman had turned up, but had assumed she'd hear further—and more accurate—details when she got to the island. Now she wished she'd paid closer attention to the early stories.

"Of course not." Brody nodded abruptly and left without further comment. Callie rubbed her hands over the pebbled flesh of her arms, almost cold.

"I must apologize again, Miss Pearson. Mac is terribly upset about Nikki. We all are. But we have been looking forward to your arrival. It has been such a long time since anyone's written about Paradis de la Mer. Dr. and Mrs. Lewis preferred not to have the publicity, but since Nikki and her brother took over running the hotel, we are becoming more modern, yes?" Her round, brown face creased into a smile, but her eyes remained watchful and worried.

"I'm certain everything will be wonderful. The Paradis has an excellent reputation."

A tall, thin, Caribe gentleman dressed in red and gold, the colors of the Paradis, appeared from behind a heavy wooden door to carry Callie's luggage. Although he looked as if a tropical breeze could blow him away, he hefted the bags effortlessly.

"Ben will help you with your belongings. Your suite is on

the third floor. Sadly, our elevator is not working. The repairmen on the island are no better than repairmen anywhere, but they assure me all will be in order tomorrow."

"It's fine. From what I hear about the food on the island, I'll need the exercise."

"Oh, yes. St. Martin has the best food in the world. Even better than Paris!"

Callie thanked her and followed Ben up a winding stone staircase to the third floor. As they turned down the long hallway toward her suite, she marked the position of the elevator, its stainless steel doors baldly modern yet somehow appropriate, and seamlessly set into the whitewashed stone walls. The promotional material the Paradis had sent when she had made her reservation explained that the rambling building had been a private home before being remodeled into a hotel in the 1940s by César and Hélène Charbonnet. Over the next twenty years, the French couple had acquired considerable acreage around the original building, including half a mile of private beach.

As the story went—though Callie suspected the tale to be more romance than reality—the Charbonnets' happiness was marred only by the fact that their son, Andre, and his wife could provide them with no grandchildren. In desperation, Andre and Marie turned to an American fertility specialist, Dr. Mark Lewis, who had often vacationed at the Paradis. Three years before Hélène's death, Lewis performed a miracle, and Hélène had the grandchild she so desperately wanted. As a gesture of gratitude, Andre, who had no talent for running a hotel and was quickly heading for bankruptcy, sold the Paradis to Lewis for far below market value in the mid-1970s. The fifty-something Lewis and his wife, Ava, a thirty-something model, had transformed the hotel into an intensely private resort, a haven for politicians, sports figures, and celebrities of all stripes who wished to disappear for a week or two.

Mark Lewis had died of heart failure in 2004, and six years later his wife had wrecked her car, crashing through the guardrail on a road in Alto Adige, high in the Italian Alps, and tumbling nearly three hundred meters to her death. That had not been in the promotional literature, which merely stated that Nicole Lewis and her brother, John, had taken over the running of the Paradis in 2010, opening it to a wider audience.

Whatever the truth of the matter, the Charbonnets and Lewises had created a world-class resort.

Callie had traveled extensively, and had stayed in more than one five-star resort, but when Ben opened the door to her suite, she drew a breath at the sheer, luxurious beauty.

Diaphanous sheers hung in front of a sliding glass door that opened onto a wide balcony overlooking the pool. Two white rattan armchairs and a couch, all decorated in shades of burgundy, clustered about a marble-topped coffee table on which rested a huge fruit basket. Would she receive such treatment if the owners didn't know she planned to feature the hotel in her next article? Then again, given the room rates, they could afford to treat all their guests like royalty.

Ben opened louvered doors to reveal the bedroom. Despite her professional mandate to remain objective, Callie's first reaction to the Paradis's bedroom was entirely emotional: she wished she'd brought a lover. The walls, like those of the living area, had been painted a creamy butter yellow, the floor covered in deep terracotta tiles. The king-sized mahogany sleigh bed could have overwhelmed the small space, but it merely dominated, seducing with promises of long, lazy days and hot nights spent between crisp linen sheets.

Callie thanked Ben and tipped him generously. Once he had left and she had locked the door behind him, she unzipped her computer bag and set her laptop on the teak desk in the living area. In many of the places she'd stayed over the years, finding Internet access had been a challenge, but the younger Lewises had added wireless access to the list of the Paradis's amenities. While the computer booted up, she took a quick, cool shower.

She'd laid out linen shorts and her favorite cap-sleeved tee for the afternoon, but when she emerged from the bathroom wrapped in the enormous, Egyptian cotton bath sheet, she couldn't resist testing the huge bed. A thick, fluffy duvet enveloped her, caressing her skin as she sank onto the firm mattress. Yes, this would be the perfect spot for romance.

She tried to imagine sharing the bed with any of the few lovers she'd chosen in her life, and failed. Too self-involved, too intellectual, too critical . . . None of them would appreciate the simple beauty of the space. None would suit the plush sensuality.

She shook off the depressing parade of less-than-satisfactory images, rolled off the seductive bed, and dressed. By the time she sat down at the little desk, her parents' photo shone out from the screen of her laptop. The picture had been taken in the main square in Milan, a fabulous cathedral as a backdrop. They were laughing. If Callie had one memory of her mother, who had died when she was eight, it was her laughter. Much later, when Callie realized how long Sharon Pearson had suffered from the cancer that eventually stole her life, she wondered how her mother could have maintained such a cheerful disposition. Her father's smiles were rarer even early on, and had disappeared completely the painfully sunny afternoon Callie had helped him scatter her mother's ashes from a cliff overlooking the Atlantic. For nearly twenty years, he'd focused solely on his work and his daughter, homeschooling her all over the world as they traveled together.

Until he died, she had believed they had no secrets from one another.

Callie checked her e-mail and dashed off notes to both her housemate and her editor so they'd know she'd arrived safely. She had closed her mail program and was starting to write down her impressions of the island and the hotel when a knock interrupted the process. Expecting turndown service or something similar, she was unprepared to find Mac Brody on the other side. Startled, she stepped back, an action he chose to interpret as an invitation.

"I have a few questions for you." Keeping his eyes on her face, he shut the door behind him. Callie pushed away the nervous tremor that simple action engendered, but couldn't prevent herself from shuffling backward a few more paces. He had to be close to a foot taller than she was—six one or six two would be her guess—and she rationalized her movement as way to look him in the face without craning her neck.

"Mr. Brody," she said, determined to be polite—no point in alienating a potentially valuable source on her first day—"I'm terribly sorry about your wife, but I've told you everything I know, which is precisely nothing."

"You'll understand if I don't believe you."

"Actually—"

He ignored her attempt at denial, speaking over her. "I had a chat with Tom Ingalls."

"Then you know I was telling you the truth. I'm here on a story."

"Maybe. But he explained you don't work for the magazine.

You specifically asked to come here. Your use of their name is a courtesy."

"Travel writers freelance. I've written for *Travel/Style* many times. It's true that I proposed this article before writing it, and it's also true I'd usually have the story in hand before I contacted Tom. But the Paradis isn't exactly cheap, and before I spent the money to stay here, I wanted to be certain he'd be interested in the article. *Travel/Style* has right of first refusal, and Tom allowed me to use their name because doing so often nets me lower rates than the norm and reservations where I might not be able to get them otherwise."

"So it's just coincidence, your arrival just after Nikki, who could be your twin, vanishes."

"I've had my reservation for months." Five, to be precise. She'd taken the first room she could get once she'd recognized the setting of the mysterious photograph she'd found among her father's belongings. "And my picture and résumé are on my website. My appearance is not exactly a state secret."

"He also informed me you speak fluent French." Callie waited for Mac to apologize for his earlier rudeness. He didn't. "Would you care to explain why you didn't reveal that little fact?"

She shrugged, deliberately casual. "I find I get a better feel for the experience of most of our readers that way. The majority of them don't speak any foreign languages."

"Why did you choose the Paradis?"

"Aside from the opportunity to stay at a fancy resort and be able to write it off?" She tried a smile, but his grim expression didn't lighten and she sighed loudly, allowing her irritation to show. "The Paradis hasn't been done. Many of our readers can afford to stay here, but they won't spend the money for a room without a recommendation from someone they trust. They'll opt for the known elegance and comfort of La Samanna, instead."

"So you've never been here before?"

"Surely you can check the records and see I haven't."

"Not the hotel. The island."

"No." Evasion she could handle; outright lying wasn't in her nature, and she paused before answering. A split second, but he caught it. His eyes narrowed, pulling the scar tight. How had he gotten it? Surely not in his job at a five-star resort.

"This is a small island, Miss Pearson."

"Thirty-four square miles. I do my homework."

"Thirty-four square miles, much of which is uninhabited. Sooner or later, someone's going to recognize you."

The sound of another knock saved her having to deny his assertion. Brody didn't step aside, forcing her to brush by him to get to the door. She refused to look at him as she did so, but she could feel both the heat and the vibrating tension of his body. Both provoked reactions in her own body she refused to consider.

Callie recognized her visitor immediately. Businessman handsome, John Lewis was the public face of the Paradis. He gave interviews, talked up the resort at every turn, and was rarely seen off the island without a gorgeous woman hanging on his arm.

He introduced himself, clasping her right hand in both of his. "Excuse me for staring. I thought Claudine must be imagining things when she told me how like Nicole you looked. But the similarity is amazing." Laugh lines fanned out beside his gray eyes as he grinned at her.

"So I've been told." And it was beginning to grate. Seriously, what was it with these people? Did they really believe she was connected to a woman as rich and famous as Nikki Lewis? And Mac, what had he said, that Nikki had *hired* her? Did he think so little of his own wife that he imagined she would do such a thing?

He peered over her shoulder and the smile disappeared. "I see you've met Mac."

"Oh, yes. And I am sorry to be so rude. Won't you come in?"

He stepped into the room and shook hands with Brody. "Miss Pearson here must have given you quite a shock."

"You could say that." Brody's heated gaze met hers, promising a continuation of his interrogation at some future time.

"Of course, if you look closely, you can see the resemblance is superficial. Your eyes are dark brown; hers are hazel." John reached out and brushed a lock of Callie's hair away from her face, an intimacy she might have protested had they been alone. But pride would not allow her to fuss over such a trivial thing in front of Brody. "Your hair is wavy; Nicole's is straight."

"Wavy is too kind." Callie knew exactly what the humidity did to her hair, and "wavy" didn't begin to describe it. She never dared cut it above her shoulder blades for fear of morphing into a poodle in New York's summer humidity. She'd restrained it in a French braid for her flight, but stubborn strands were wiggling free, frizzing around her face from climate and the shower. Her mother had always called her heart-shaped face and curly locks throwbacks to previous generations of Gruene women, but Callie had never seen pictures of her mother's family, who had cast her out for marrying outside their faith.

John laughed. "Well, it's not straight, like my sister's, anyway. And although her color depends on a series of very expensive treatments, I am pretty sure it's a bit lighter than yours is when in its natural state." His gaze dropped to her mouth. Lingered. "And I doubt your lips owe their shape to collagen injections."

Callie blinked. If she didn't know better, she'd believe the man was making a pass at her. Not that such a thing hadn't happened before, but here? Now? When even Nicole Lewis's husband had commented on how much alike they looked? Her shoulder blades twitched before she tuned back in to what John was saying.

"In fact, any one of your features, taken individually, is substantially different from my sister's. But the overall effect is quite astonishing. Perhaps the two of you are distant cousins."

"The two of us? But not you?"

"Nicole is my half sister. If you're related to her, it's definitely through Ava. Our father's family isn't nearly as attractive." He winked, but she glanced away. He had a point beyond a simple comparison of her features with his sister's, but she couldn't imagine what it might be.

"Then again," said Mac, "maybe you two were twins separated at birth. Maybe you came here looking for your biological parents. An inheritance."

"Now, really. That's going a bit far, don't you think? Besides, I'll happily show you my birth certificate—travel as much as I do and you always know where it is." She kept her tone as light as she could, dismissed Mac, and turned back toward John. "How old is your sister?"

"She'll be twenty-nine at the end of next month." Callie hadn't realized Nicole Lewis was so young. John was in his early forties—the PR package she'd read had included the information that he'd become a full partner in the hotel at the age of thirty—and she'd never considered there could be so many years between them. If the articles on Nicole's disappearance had mentioned her age, Callie hadn't noticed. A hotel like the Paradis would be a great deal of responsibility for someone not yet thirty. No wonder John handled all the PR work.

"So much for your theory, Mr. Brody. I won't be twenty-eight until October."

"She's got you there, Mac." Though John spoke lightly, a thread of tension wove through the words. It vanished when he turned his attention back to her. "I'm afraid I have to go. But I hope we can get together before you leave. *Travel/Style's* readers are just the kind of clientele we're hoping to attract. I'd love to get your input on some ideas I have for the future of the Paradis."

"I'm sure we can arrange something. After I leave here, I'll be staying at Port de Plaisance for a week."

"Why?" John's expression of horror was almost comical.

"Because two nights here are all I can afford. My friend Marlon has a time-share over there he's letting me use."

"Don't be ridiculous. You can stay here as long as you want. Let me just make sure this room is available and we don't have to move you." Before Callie could protest, he was out the door, leaving her alone with Brody.

"Is he always like that?" If she could focus the conversation on John Lewis, perhaps she could distract Brody from his suspicions about her. Plus, a profile of the hotel's young owner would make a nice addition to her article. "Bulldozing over objections?"

"He's used to getting what he wants."

"Why would he want me to stay here?" Not that she'd complain, given how prominently the Paradis figured in the mystery she was trying to unravel. But the invitation was almost too convenient, and the situation — the two men, the missing woman, the strange undercurrents — gave her the willies. Brody quirked an eyebrow, the expression a challenge.

"Oh, please. You can't think he has anything romantic in mind. He must be twenty years older than I am."

"Fifteen. And I wouldn't call what he has in mind 'romance.'"

"Romance, sex, whatever. We only just met."

Brody's gaze did a slow crawl down her body and back up. Callie felt her face heat, along with several other areas she'd have preferred stay cool.

"Believe me, sugar, it only takes one look for a man to know what he wants." The image of the suite's bedroom, its seductive, king-sized bed, popped into Callie's head. She squelched it, but not before her breath hitched in her chest. Damn the man; he'd as much as told Claudine he considered Callie fat and boring. He had no right to pretend she was some kind of sex goddess. And where had her self-respect run off to?

"I still say you're being ridiculous." She turned her back on him and walked to the small galley kitchen, where she pulled a bottle of water out of the under-counter refrigerator. Bone-bred courtesy forced her to offer one to Brody. His refusal left an awkward silence, broken by the ring of his cell phone.

He listened to the voice on the other end for the moment, then rubbed a hand through the waves of his coarse, black hair, making parts of it stand straight up. "Again? I swear, Lewis needs to throw them out. I don't care how much they pay." He took a deep breath, let it out slowly. "Just hold on to her. I'll be right there."

He flipped the phone shut. "We're not finished," he said as he moved to the door.

"I guess you're lucky I'll be staying here for a while, then."

Brody paused, hand on the knob. "You're taking Lewis up on his offer?" He infused the words with so much innuendo they washed over Callie like a slimy current. She stopped herself from protesting just in time. What difference did it make if he believed her promiscuous as well as dull? Maybe if he found her contemptible enough, he'd leave her alone to pursue her investigation.

"Look at this place." She tossed her head. "Who wouldn't want to stay here for free?"

"Certainly not you." He paused to examine her a final time, giving nothing away, then left without another word.

As the door swung shut, Callie's muscles all relaxed at once, leaving her weak and limp. Mac Brody put her on edge and kept her there. She'd be wise to avoid him as much as possible.

⌒

MAC GRUNTED IN displeasure as he set the barbell into its cradle with a clang. His concentration was shot. Maybe he ought to go for a swim; at least he wouldn't injure himself if his form was off in the water the way he might on the weights. But he had no desire to head for the pool. Not when he'd just hauled April Matthews out of it, wrestling a towel around her and explaining—for the third time in less than two weeks—why she couldn't strip naked poolside no matter how famous she was or how much money her husband had. Then he'd been forced to wait with her in her room with one of the female bartenders as a chaperone while Andy, one of his assistants, dug up Clayton Matthews and brought him back to take control of his wife.

The first time April had pulled her little stunt, Mac had assumed that dropping her at the door to her room would suffice to teach her a lesson. She'd been back at the pool in twenty minutes. The second time, he'd made the mistake of accompanying her inside her suite, only to find her plastered to him almost before he cleared the threshold, her hand halfway down his pants. The woman was a viper.

Nowadays, he always brought one of the female staffers with him when he had to deal with April. So he and Maris had sat in the living area of the suite, watching April fling herself around the room, ranting about getting them both fired—all the time naked as a jaybird—for more than an hour. Mac didn't think he'd ever been as happy to see anyone as he had been to see Clayton Matthews, and he'd left the hotel as soon as Matthews took over, heading back to his cottage. While still on Lewis-owned ground, the home he shared with Nikki wasn't part of the hotel proper. It was fenced and gated; no one could enter without his permission or knowledge. He'd remodeled one of the three bays of the cottage's garage almost the moment he'd moved in, converting it into a bare-bones gym, and most of the time a hard sweat sufficed to calm him no matter what he had to deal with up at the hotel.

But the usual tactics weren't working. And, much as he wanted to blame April Matthews or his missing wife, another woman entirely was at fault.

Calliope Pearson.

Who was she? He'd checked her website before going to see her, but he hadn't been able to learn much. Given the list of credits on her site, she probably did plan to write an article. But if that was all she planned, he'd eat his barbells.

And like hell was her resemblance to Nikki, or the timing of her arrival, coincidental.

Mac poured himself a glass of water and headed upstairs for a shower, letting his mind drift, hoping it would snag on something important. The technique had served him well in his years with the Atlanta Police Department.

In some ways, Lewis had been right: feature for feature, Callie and Nikki weren't so much identical as similar. The two women were much of a height, though he'd only rarely seen Nikki without heels—by the pool, she chose clear-topped, Lucite-heeled slip-ons; fresh out of the shower, she wore feather-topped suede-heeled mules—so it was hard to say for certain. It was also hard to say whether their skin tones would match, given that Nikki loved sunbathing almost as much as she loved her stiletto heels. John hadn't commented on the shape of Callie's face—the hair coming to a delicate widow's peak to create a heart emphasized by high cheek-bones—but that, too, she shared with Nikki. Callie's chin, however, was decidedly her own, less pointy and more stubborn than Nikki's, which didn't bode well for making her see reason and reveal the truth about her intentions.

He'd remarked to Claudine on the weight difference between the two women, and when he'd talked to Ingalls and realized Callie had understood every word, he'd seen another variance: no matter what game she played, Nikki would never have been able to control her outrage if she'd heard him say such a thing. She'd have launched herself at him and tried to claw his eyes out. Truth be told, Mac preferred the softer curves, but he'd once made the mistake of telling Nicole she didn't need to work so hard at maintaining her figure. He'd been cut off from said figure for two weeks until he learned an appropriate appreciation for it.

Although Callie's were darker, both women's eyes shared a slight, almost exotic tilt. Nikki emphasized hers with black liner and dark shadow. And lies. Nikki's eyes were filled with them, though it had taken him too damned long to figure that out. Calliope Pearson, on the other hand, didn't seem able to lie worth a damn, though she was giving it the old college try.

And those lips . . . He understood why Lewis had had trouble looking away from Callie's mouth. He'd had a problem with it himself. She wore some kind of transparent gloss that made her lips slick and shiny and led a man to imagine them on him. Around him.

He turned the shower to full cold.

CHAPTER TWO

A RESTLESS NIGHT DID nothing to improve Mac's mood, and seeing Callie sharing a table with John at breakfast didn't help. True, she was taking notes as they spoke, and the conversation appeared more business than pleasure for the moment, but Mac had little doubt where it would lead. As he strolled over to their table, he told himself he was only interrupting them to irritate John.

"You have to do something about the Matthewses," he said, forgoing a greeting. "I realize they have two weeks left on their reservation, but she's pissing off the rest of the guests. Especially the Dunlaps, who don't want their seven-year-old twins exposed to April Matthews's . . . twins."

He saw Callie's lips twitch, but she repressed her smile as she rose. "I'll go. You two have things to discuss. Thanks so much for taking the time to chat, John."

Lewis stood, also, laying a proprietary hand on Callie's arm. "Stay. The Matthewses can wait until after breakfast."

"I have a feeling breakfast is over." Mac nodded toward the doorway, where he'd noticed Claudine escorting two men dressed in the uniforms of the gendarmes, the French police, in their direction.

Mac knew the younger of the two relatively well, but had never seen him so grim-faced. The first time they had met, Michel Vichy had been dragging away a drunk who had managed to vomit all over his impeccably pressed uniform. Even then, he had maintained the aloof air Mac had found common among the gendarmerie. Until, of course, one shared a few bottles of good French wine with them off duty, at which point they became some of the friendliest and most expansive people Mac had ever met. Not so different from the police he'd worked with in Atlanta, though the gendarmes dressed better.

"Monsieur Lewis." John inclined his head. "And Monsieur Brody. *Pourrions-nous avoir quelque compte rendu de votre temps?*" The French police were more polite, too. No American cop would request a few minutes of a suspect's time. And from the look on Michel's face, Mac had a pretty good idea that both he and John had landed on a list of "persons of interest."

"I was just leaving." For the first time, the policemen turned their attention on Callie. The older one put out a hand to stop her.

"A moment, mademoiselle." The French had been a power play, a way of putting Mac and John in their places. The gendarme spoke to Callie in English. "You are related to Madame Brody?"

"No. I'm not."

"This is difficult to believe."

Mac watched Callie draw herself up to her full five-foot-four-inch height, leaving her a good half a foot shorter than the man questioning her. Despite the height difference, she managed to look down her slightly freckled nose at him and, as much as he mistrusted her, Mac felt like laughing. "Difficult or not, monsieur, it is the truth."

Michel took a notebook and pen from his pocket. "Your name, mademoiselle?"

"Callie Pearson."

"Callie?" He said it with a disdain only a Frenchman could achieve, as if he found her unusual name offensive.

"Calliope Elizabeth Pearson."

"And what is your business here?"

Mac watched her carefully, but she didn't flinch or hesitate. Apparently, she had told the lie often enough to be comfortable with it. "I'm writing an article for an American travel magazine about the island and the resort."

"You are a friend of the Lewis family?"

"No. Just a writer."

"*Bien.* You may go." Michel watched as Callie took her plate of fruit and cheese and settled a few tables away. Then he turned back to Mac. "It is as she says? She is not family to your wife?"

"So she claims."

Michel raised an eyebrow at the noncommittal answer. "But it is so easy to know. Some from you"—he jerked his chin at John—"and some from her, and voila! DNA tells all." Of course, it was not nearly so simple, but apparently French police were as curious, as impatient, and as suspicious as their American counterparts. As far as Mac was concerned, the French cop's suspicions had a side benefit: they forced Lewis into a grudging admission.

"If she's related to my sister, she won't have genes in common with me."

"No? But why?"

Mac watched John shift in his chair. The fact that Nicole Lewis was illegitimate, that her conception had almost ended the Lewis marriage one short year after it had begun, was an open secret on the island. The gendarmes, however, worked in three-year rotations, and Michel had been in St. Martin only five months. Either he had not heard the gossip about Nicole's birth, or he'd adopted the naïve facade to watch John's reaction. The gendarmes were not casual hotel guests; what John had glossed over with Callie he had to detail for them.

"Nicole isn't my blood sister. She was born in Paris. My father and Ava were separated at the time."

"Ah." Michel lifted his shoulders in a typically Gallic shrug. "A shame." He seemed to collect himself, to remember the reason for his visit, though Mac was certain it had never left his mind. "Is there a place we might speak privately?"

"All of us?"

"If you please." Again the deferential tone, a thin veneer over shrewd evaluation.

"I suppose we can use the office." John dropped his napkin on the table and led the small procession out of the dining room and down the hall behind the reception area. Once the four men had seated themselves around the desk, Michel introduced his partner, Alec Saint-Simone. Saint-Simone withdrew a small bag from his pocket and dumped out its contents.

"You recognize this, yes?"

Mac reached for the slender gold circlet set all around with perfect baguette-cut diamonds, but withdrew his hand before touching it. "It's Nikki's ring."

"You gave it to her?"

"No, actually. It was Ava's. Nikki chose it as her wedding ring for sentimental reasons." And because he couldn't afford anything half as nice. "Where did you find it?"

"Sadly, it was on the finger of a young woman who had, how do you say . . . *lavée vers le haut sur la plage* . . . washed ashore."

Mac closed his eyes against the sorrow, guilt and anger threatening to swamp him. He'd suspected she was dead, but he hadn't wanted to believe it. She — or someone using her phone—had texted the day of her disappearance to say she'd gone to St. Barths with friends and Mac could damned well entertain himself until she got home. And since he'd served her with divorce papers the day before, the texted message, along with the disappearance of a suitcase full of clothes and all her hairbrushes and cosmetics, wasn't entirely unexpected. But he didn't like the fact that neither she nor any of her friends had contacted him since then.

And Calliope Pearson's arrival had given him renewed hope for a moment that it was all one of Nikki's games, that she was off at a spa somewhere laughing at him.

"Of course, it is possible that she sold the ring," said Vichy, "or gave it away. We cannot be certain this young woman is your wife. Fingerprints are not so reliable when the victim has spent considerable time in the sea, and in this case there are additional difficulties." Again, the gendarme shrugged. "We could be certain with DNA, but when you made your first report, you informed us she had taken with her all her cosmetics, brushes, earrings, anything that might provide for us her own DNA to compare."

"And isn't that convenient." John glared at Mac. "If you couldn't find proof that my sister was dead, you couldn't start a murder investigation."

"For Christ's sake, Lewis. I'm the one who insisted on filing the report. The rest of you kept saying she just needed a break."

"A break from you."

"If she wanted a break from me, all she had to do was sign the divorce papers."

Vichy interrupted before the argument blew up into battle. "You and Madame Brody were divorcing?"

Mac had been a cop long enough to know how the

gendarmes would interpret that information. But his relationship with Nikki had been public in both its swift rise and
its spectacular fall, and however much his desire for a divorce
might damage him in the eyes of the investigators, trying to
hide it would only exacerbate the problem.

"I asked for one, even filed the papers. She hadn't signed
them yet."

"You failed to mention this when you came to us last week."

"It would only have confused the issue. I wanted her considered a missing person, not a runaway wife."

Vichy nodded briefly. "You were married in the United
States?"

"In Florida. Yes."

"And Madame Brody, did she have provisions for a
divorce?"

"You mean a prenup? Yes." They'd married in the cham-
bers of a federal judge who had been a friend of Mark Lewis's.
He'd had the prenuptial agreement waiting alongside their
marriage license on his desk when they arrived. Not the most
romantic of circumstances, but Mac hadn't been thinking
about romance at the time. Hadn't, truth be told, been thinking much at all.

"So you wouldn't get a damned thing if the two of you
divorced." John's flat, angry statement spiked Mac's blood
pressure, bringing him back to the present.

"I didn't have a damned thing before we got married, and
I was doing just fine."

"You had a job here, which I can assure you, you would
have lost. Will lose the minute we leave this room."

"Monsieur Lewis. Restrain yourself, if you please. We have
not ascertained even that the woman from the sea is your
sister."

"What are we waiting for? I don't need DNA or finger-prints to recognize my own sister. Just take me to her. I'll identify her and we can get the investigation moving."

"I am afraid it is not so easy. The young lady who was wearing the ring had been much damaged. You would not recognize her."

"Dental records, then. Nicole's dentist in Miami can fax them to you."

"I am afraid such records will not suffice."

John stared blankly, his mouth moving without sound for several seconds. "Jesus Christ," he finally choked out, "what the hell happened?"

"*Les requins* . . . the sharks. She had been in the water for some time." John's face washed green, and Mac knew his own mirrored it. *Oh, Nikki, I'm so fucking sorry.* He'd seen a body pulled from the Chattahoochee once; the image would be with him the rest of his life.

He shook off the memory. "So what's next?"

"For you? Nothing. We will be in touch."

"You expect us to sit around like it's any other day when you've just found my sister's body?"

"Perhaps we have. Perhaps not."

"So we just twiddle our thumbs until you get the finger-prints matched?"

"Unless you have an avenue you believe we should explore."

"What about Callie Pearson?" Three pairs of eyes turned on Mac. "I can't be the only one who finds her turning up here just now suspicious. I mean, look at her! John, you yourself said she could be related to Ava." John shook his head. "I'll admit, it's strange. But maybe it's irrelevant, or connected in some completely innocent way."

"Give me one possible innocent explanation."

"Maybe the timing isn't entirely coincidental. Possibly, Nicole knew Miss Pearson was coming and didn't want to face her, so she took off." Lewis warmed to his theory. "I mean, think about it. Nicole only likes to be the center of attention when she can control it. She probably saw a picture of Calliope and knew the minute the woman showed up here, all the old gossip about Ava's lover would be resurrected. Being a Lewis is important to Nicole."

That much was certainly true. Nikki had refused to take his name when they married, calling the tradition outdated. Mac rubbed a hand along his scar, which tended to itch when he got tense. The doctors insisted the phenomenon was entirely psychological, that no medical reason for it existed, but what did they know?

And what did he? He'd been married to Nicole Lewis only three months, all of which had been fraught with arguments, prevarications, and outright lies. He'd been too angry at the end, hadn't paid enough attention to Nicole's mood. Not that he'd have been able to interpret it even if he had, but perhaps he could have gotten her to talk to him, and his guilt might not have assumed such crippling proportions. John's explanation deserved consideration.

"You really believe she gave her ring to some stranger and took off?"

John sighed. "No, I don't. But I also don't see any point in trying to figure out whether Calliope Pearson and my sister are somehow related. Even if they were, what difference would it make?"

"I have no idea." And it frustrated the hell out of him. "But Michel asked about avenues to explore, and Calliope Pearson is one hell of an avenue. Even if she doesn't mean to be. Maybe you're right. Maybe Nikki got a load of the woman's website and freaked. Could be she asked someone—the wrong someone—to help her, and that's how she ended up in Plum Bay." Something flitted along the edge of his vision, but he didn't turn. Another medically impossible stress reaction, the hallucination would fade soon enough. He focused on Vichy.

"Michel, surely you could at least question Miss Pearson. Ask her if she knows anyone here on the island. Has any relatives here. Because if she does, that could be who Nicole turned to for help."

"*Mais oui*, we can ask Mademoiselle Pearson any number of things. But we cannot compel her to give us her saliva in order to determine whether she and Madame Brody are related, or whether she is related to the body we found, and if she tells us she knows no one here in St. Martin, who will contradict her?"

"It couldn't hurt to ask," Mac insisted. He knew what he would have done in Atlanta. He'd have had Calliope Pearson sweating in an interrogation room for so long she'd be forced to ask for a drink. And when she tossed the soda can, he'd have had her DNA without asking. But maybe the gendarmes didn't operate the same way.

"DNA testing takes a long time," said John. "And I imagine the gendarmes are no more interested in paying for a test that won't tell them anything useful than your own department in Atlanta would have been."

"The gendarmes don't have to pay for it or even request it. Michel could just ask her who she and Nikki might know in common. You can ask her about the DNA as a personal favor, as Nicole's brother. A private lab can have paternity results in twenty-four hours, full profiles in less than seventy-two if you're willing to pony up the cash. They aren't backed up with casework the way government labs are, at least in the US." Mac watched John struggle, cheapskate versus brother.

"Fine. Not that Miss Pearson is likely to agree."

"Unsure of your powers of persuasion?"

"Dammit, Brody—"

"Gentlemen! Saint-Simone, would you be so kind as to check the dining room for Mademoiselle Pearson?"

But Callie was gone.

A SINGLE MAIN ROAD circled the island, and Callie had set aside her first full day to drive it. Her tape recorder rested in the passenger seat, ready to capture her impressions, but she couldn't concentrate on the sights, sounds, or smells. Even the unlikely sight of a parade of goats running through a strip mall at the edge of Marigot, the capital of the French side, as if intent on an afternoon of shopping, failed to overcome the memory of the grim-faced gendarmes at breakfast.

They had to have come about Brody's missing wife. Where could Nicole Lewis Brody have gone? Had the police found her? And if so, was she well? Had she made accusations against her brother or her husband? Was she even alive?

After leaving the dining room, Callie had returned to her room to see if she could find a picture of Nicole on the web, to judge for herself the similarities in their looks. She'd found several articles about the missing heiress, all carefully worded. Without a ransom demand or a body, none of the journalists seemed willing to commit to calling her absence a crime. None wanted egg on their faces should she be discovered on a party boat or in a rehab center. Only a few photographs were available, none particularly sharp or close-up. Nicole preferred the European party scene and hadn't attained enough celebrity status to attract paparazzi interest, so she was never the focus of the photographers' attention, merely one of the "beautiful people" in the background.

And she was beautiful, no question about that. Callie had forced herself to admit the validity of Mac's assessment: Nicole's silky blond hair, almost breakably slender figure, and impeccably made-up face far outshone her own. Nicole Lewis Brody was the kind of woman other women hated—never a hair out of place or a run in her hose. She and Brody must have made a striking couple. His shaggy, unkempt black hair, the menacing scar slashed across his face, and his broad, muscular frame perfectly complemented Nicole's brand of delicate femininity. Callie caught herself wondering whether the woman had planned it that way, then castigated herself for the catty thought. Brody's reaction to Callie had painted his wife in a less-than-flattering light, as had the articles about her wild lifestyle and the mystery surrounding her disappearance, but Callie wasn't given to accepting others' opinions as her own.

She pulled into a small parking lot having driven the Dutch side and most of the French side, and ended up in the tiny village of Grand Case. Of course, she'd have to do the whole thing over again, preoccupied as she'd been, but for the moment her stomach was reminding her of her interrupted breakfast. Across from the parking lot, a cheerfully painted building boasted a sign for "Calmos Café." Both "calm" and "café" sounded pretty good, and her friend Marlon had recommended the spot, so Callie draped a beach towel around her neck, slung her tote bag over her shoulder, and followed the sign's arrow down a shady pathway.

No more than thirty feet from the sidewalk, the passage widened to reveal a typical beach bar. The space had no walls other than the one created by the tiny clothing shop facing the street. The beamed roof rested on poles and palm trees, and the floor was nothing more than hard-packed sand. Should a hurricane destroy it, the bar could be rebuilt in a matter of days.

"Bonjour!" A slim young man behind the bar—or inside it, really, given that it formed a rectangle in the center of the covered space—waved Callie toward the beachfront area. "Take a spot anywhere. I will be right there."

Callie did as ordered, passing beyond the roofed area to the white-sand beach. A dozen faded umbrellas shaded lounge chairs, only a few of which were occupied. Two topless women lay at the water's edge, letting the tide, swells rather than waves, cool the lower halves of their bodies. Both were tobacco brown, and Callie's pale, sun-sensitive skin shrank in painful protest. Didn't they worry about skin cancer?

When the waiter arrived, she ordered a grilled seafood plate for lunch, opting for a mango daiquiri rather than coffee. So what if she had a puzzle to solve and an article to write? She was on vacation, too. Positioning her chair for maximum shade, she pulled out the Frommer's guide to St. Martin and settled down to learn about the island's colorful history.

Half-asleep from the sun, the food, and a second daiquiri, she jerked awake when she overheard a young man talking to two women under the umbrella next to hers. She closed her eyes and pretended to doze, letting her mind translate the conversation into English.

"They say a water-skier found her at Plum Bay." He drew out the story, relishing his position as gossip-bearer. "He got near the rocks, and, poof! There she was. The gendarmes cannot identify her. They say that she is terribly damaged, that she was in the sea a long time and fish and sharks ate parts of her. Still, they believe it is Nikki Lewis." Lewis, Callie noted, not Brody. However long Nicole and Mac had been married, it wasn't long enough to alter the locals' perception of her as a Lewis of Paradis de la Mer rather than as Mac's wife.

"Did she fall from a boat?"

"No. My friend in the gendarmerie says she was murdered." He dropped his voice so low Callie almost missed the next word. "Strangled."

Both women gasped, luckily loudly enough to cover Callie's own startled inhalation. "No!"

"Yes! According to my friend, they suspect the husband or the brother killed her."

"But why?"

Out of the corner of her eye, Callie saw him shrug. "Only God knows. My friend says the gendarmes are almost certain it was a man who killed her. Strangulation is rare between strangers, and the two men closest to her are John Lewis and Mac Brody."

"Unless she had a lover," offered one of the women.

"Pah!" The second woman practically spat. "You have obviously never seen her husband. No woman with a man like him at home would shop for something else." And oh, boy, did Callie agree on that point. Brody rubbed her the wrong way—and the feeling was obviously mutual—but even so, she had to admit that the irksome personality came wrapped in a hell of a hot physical package.

The man had evidently imparted all his gossip, so he shifted away to pass it along to another group farther down the beach. The two women speculated for a while on Nikki Lewis's fate, revealing she'd been known on the island as a party girl, even after her marriage. Callie tried to imagine Mac Brody by Nikki's side in any of the photographs she'd found on the web, and failed. He would never have fit into Nicole Lewis's social set. What had possessed the woman to marry him? The memory of his green gaze sweeping her body intruded, and she shook it off. So what if he reeked of sex? No one in the modern era got married for that.

Suddenly, the sun seemed unbearably hot. Definitely time for a swim.

EXHAUSTED, AND LIBERALLY crusted with sand and salt, Callie thanked the gods of contractors when she arrived back at the resort to find she didn't have to climb the stairs. The elevator doors parted onto the third floor, and a fan-driven breeze cooled her overheated skin. She staggered down the hall, tugged along by the anticipation of getting clean and taking a nice nap before dinner. But when she opened the door to her suite, her hopes for a relaxing evening took a fatal dive.

Her computer was gone. The little desk sat almost directly opposite the doorway, so she noticed the empty surface before she set foot over the threshold. Could the thief still be inside? But no, he would have done his work while his victim was likely to be at the beach or the pool, having lunch, or shopping in Marigot or Philipsburg. Still, she listened for several seconds before proceeding slowly and cautiously into the room.

A brief search revealed the thief had taken the few pieces of jewelry she'd brought with her as well as her laptop. That fact should have reassured her—proving the guy to be a regular burglar who took whatever he could carry—but she couldn't shake the idea the theft was somehow tied to her investigation. With a longing glance at the bathroom's multi-jet shower and fluffy towels, she took the elevator back down to the lobby and explained the situation to Claudine, who quickly ushered her into the business office and urged her into one of the leather chairs before rushing out to find Mac and John. Callie could hear the two men arguing even before they entered the room.

"You're supposed to keep this place secure! How did a thief manage to sneak in?" John's voice was a low roar, imparting rage without alerting the whole hotel to the crime. *Impressive.*

"Who says he snuck in? Maybe he's always been here, or maybe he made a reservation."

"Our guests don't need to steal. And you're supposed to vet all our employees."

"I've only worked here eight months. In that time, you've hired four people. Three of them are seasonal—they aren't here at the moment. The other one is Giselle, Alexandre's niece. If someone who works for you took Miss Pearson's things, you hired them before you hired me."

The door opened and John hurried across the room to kneel in front of Callie and clasp her hands in his own.

"Are you all right?" As John questioned her, Mac turned away to confer quietly with Claudine.

"I'm fine. Pissed, but fine." She extracted her fingers from John's and tucked them beneath her thighs. She hadn't stopped to get a jacket from her room, and the air-conditioning in the office felt far too cold against clothes damp from her swim.

"Claudine says you got back from the beach and found

your belongings had been taken?" Mac tossed the last words of the question over his shoulder as he answered a sharp rap at the door. Claudine handed him a blanket, which he brought over and draped across Callie's shoulders. With brisk, impersonal motions, he rubbed her arms, then folded the blanket around her like a cocoon.

"Yes." Callie had to crane her head backward to see him because he had remained behind her, while John still knelt in front. "I'm afraid I was at the beach all day, so I can't narrow down the time frame at all. I left at ten thirty and only just got back."

"It's not your job to concern yourself with timing," John assured her.

"Nope," Mac agreed with a half smile, "that's my job, but it sure would have been nice if you could have given me a hand with it." Humor with a hint of sarcasm laced his voice, and Callie wasn't certain whether to be amused or offended. Amusement won, and she laughed.

"It's good that you can laugh." John rose, both voice and posture somewhat stiff. "If any of our other guests have been robbed, I hope they'll be as relaxed."

"This hasn't happened to anyone else?" Before John could answer, Callie waved at two of the other leather desk chairs. "And would the two of you please sit down?"

Both men rolled their chairs near to her, forming a tight triangle, before Mac spoke.

"So far, only you have reported anything missing." His tone indicated he found the singularity as suspicious as she did.

"First the gendarmes at breakfast," John said, "now this. What you must think of us. I assure you, Paradis de la Mer is not usually in such disarray."

"I'm sure it's not. I promise, these occurrences won't taint my article." An easy promise since she doubted she'd manage to write it at all.

"That's very kind of you. We'll find another room for you; you won't be comfortable in your current one."

Callie considered. "Actually, I don't need to move. It's only one more night." She could feel Mac's eyes, sharp and evaluative, but kept her own on John.

"I thought we had agreed you would stay at the Paradis!"

"We didn't, really." Although keeping her room would make her investigation easier, John's insistence and increasingly obvious flirtation were beginning to wear on her nerves.

"I'll put you in one of the bungalows."

Mac's choke precisely echoed Callie's own reaction. She knew to the penny how much the Paradis charged for a single night in one of their seven beachfront cabins, especially since the dollar's plummet relative to the euro.

"Don't be ridiculous."

"No, seriously. We never fill the bungalows in the off-season, and you'd have plenty of privacy there to work on your writing." The offer was too tempting to refuse. "Wonderful," John gushed when she accepted. "I'll have Ben move your things as soon as I see which one is empty."

"Don't trouble Ben; I'll do it myself. And please, no maid service. I'd rather not have someone in every day."

"I'll tell Ayida," said Mac. "I want to talk to her about Miss Pearson's computer anyway."

"Ayida's been with us for ages! You can't imagine she had anything to do with the theft!"

"I don't. It occurred to me she might have noticed whether Miss Pearson's computer was on the desk when she tidied the room. But, hey, you don't want me to work out the weekend, it's fine with me. I should pack anyway."

Callie looked from one man to the other. "Pack?"

"As of Monday, I'm out of a job and out of my house," said Mac.

"You say that as if it's unwarranted!" John turned to Callie. "You saw the gendarmes this morning! He probably killed my sister!"

"You don't even know the woman they found is your sister." If asked that morning, Callie could not have conceived a scenario in which she would defend Mac Brody, but since her father's death she had found herself in more than one previously unimaginable situation. "And from what I hear, the police are just as interested in you as they are in him."

"Where did you hear such a thing?"

"On the beach in Grand Case, same place I heard they couldn't identify the woman. In all probability, the gossip has spread all over the island. At the very least it's saturated the French side." "Dammit, I—" "It's all right," Mac broke in, his voice oddly gentle. He touched the back of Callie's hand with one long finger, creating a tiny electrical current that raised all the fine hairs along her forearm. "John's made his opinion more than clear, and I have no desire to work where I'm not wanted."

"Look—"

"You gave me until Monday to get my things together, so I figured to keep doing my job for the next forty-eight hours or so. But if you don't want my help, like I said, it's no skin off my nose. I still think you should talk to Ayida. And deal with that other matter we discussed at breakfast."

"What matter?" asked Callie.

"The security chief here," said John, voice rich with disdain, "recommended asking you for a DNA sample to compare with the woman found on the beach."

Callie studied Mac, who offered no apology, excuse, or explanation.

"Why?"

"Because my wife is dead, or at the very least missing. And you're here, you look like her, and you just became the first guest in the history of the Paradis to have her room burglarized. Even if I believed in coincidence, which I don't, I'd have a hard time accepting all those things as unconnected."

"And if it turns out I am related to the woman on the beach? How would that help? Doesn't it make more sense for John to get tested? Or have you already identified her?"

It was John who answered. "No, we aren't certain of her identity. But I haven't been completely open with you about Nicole. She is—was—the product of an affair my step-mother had, so testing me won't help. But you look so much like Nicole that if you shared DNA with the woman they found, it would be one more confirmation. I don't know who her father was, so I can't ask for his help, but perhaps your father . . . one of your parents was related to him?"

"My father did not have an affair with Nicole's mother, if that's what you're implying." Callie wiggled her shoulders, trying to release the instinctive defensive tension. John was trying to make sense of an unimaginable situation—if anyone could understand that, she could. And what, really, did she know about her father? He'd obviously kept secrets. "It's possible, I suppose, that one of them was related to either Ava or her lover."

"Could you ask them?"

"My mother died when I was a child, and my father died six months ago. So no, I can't ask. But it doesn't matter. Without Ava's lover's name, I'd have had nothing specific enough to ask anyway. And, as to the other, my parents were devoted to each other. My mother was ill for years. If their relationship had any weaknesses, it would have self-destructed."

"I'm sorry," said Mac.

"That must have been dreadful for you."

Callie acknowledged both men's sympathy with a single nod. "But you still haven't explained why my relationship to the dead woman, or lack thereof, matters."

Mac shrugged. "Maybe it doesn't. But all practical considerations aside, aren't you curious?"

Was she? Absolutely. Being related to Nikki Lewis, Nikki Brody, would raise more questions than it answered, but it would also give her license to ask them without appearing suspicious.

"Of course I am. My mother was estranged from her family, and my father's only brother had no children, so I have no family—I'd love to find some." She examined the two men, but both wore matching poker faces. "How do we go about it?"

"Do you care whether we involve the gendarmes?" Mac turned to pace as if developing his ideas on the spot, but Callie had the feeling he'd planned well in advance. She curled her fingers into fists at the deception, the desire to fight back rising in her breast. But she needed to play the game, not call him on his bullshit if she wanted answers.

"Not at all. Why?"

"Because they have the equipment, the sample cards, and the procedures to keep track of the chain of evidence." "Sample cards?" "DNA deteriorates over time. There are a number of collection systems. The gendarmerie uses samples cards. They're chemically treated to stabilize and preserve the DNA for transport. John's offered to pay a private lab to expedite the analysis, but without the gendarmes, we'd have to order a collection kit and have it sent here.

"The thing is, if the sample is collected officially, the gendarmes can use it for their own purposes later on down the road."

"Not a problem. They won't be finding my DNA at any crime scenes." She hoped.

"I'll drive you over in the morning, then."

His peremptory tone set Callie's teeth on edge. She could certainly drive herself to the police station—how hard could it be to find? But protesting would be pointless. Mac clearly knew the gendarmes; his presence would doubtless make the whole process run more smoothly.

"Let me just see where we can put you." John's interruption jerked her attention from Mac. Intentional? Certainly, his dislike of Mac—which the other man returned in spades—seemed both deep and longstanding. Callie had the impression the gendarmes' scrutiny had merely provided an excuse, that John had been itching to fire Mac for a long time.

"Bungalow five is open. It's not made up yet, though. So if you really don't mind staying where you are tonight, we can move you in the morning."

"Sounds like a plan."

⌇

A SINGLE LIGHT ILLUMINATED the oversized mahogany desk. Fingers scrabbling inside the pen drawer, he found the button and released the false back of the file drawer on the bottom right side. He pulled out the leather-bound journal to enter the results of his latest experiments.

Not good. The small piece of Nicole's body he'd removed hadn't defrosted well, and swallowing it had provided no surcease. Of course, he hadn't expected something so external to be important, but he'd given it a shot in the name of science and because, with her body still frozen, he couldn't get to his primary goal. Research, it seemed, must continue. The women had been left to help him, and each death brought him closer to understanding how. Unfortunately, there weren't enough left to keep at it in such a haphazard fashion. He cursed his faulty brain; he should have taken a more clinical approach from the beginning.

Instead, he'd assumed the problem was metaphysical. He'd hired a guy to kill the first two, the twins, believing that the cessation of their lives would suffice to effect his cure. And when his agent had informed him it was done, he had felt strong, renewed, a whole man for the first time in years. It didn't last, however. Within days, the nagging fears, the accusations, all detailed in her whining voice, returned. He was sick. He was wrong. He was doomed. He would lose everything.

He had almost sunk, then almost given in. But the women, the knowledge that they were out there and could help him, had saved him. He'd read up on spiritual healing and found his first mistake: no action taken by another on his behalf could help him. He had to help himself.

So he'd begun to record his observations and research. The third had been a gift from Father, a sign he was on the right track. He'd called her office on a pretext, giving a false name, hoping to lure her to him, only to find she was already on her way. No time for an elaborate plan, but he'd managed well enough. One day, her remains might turn up, but no one would recognize them. Unfortunately, he'd had to scramble at the end, and though he'd felt stronger the minute her heart ceased to beat, he never believed her murder to be a cure.

Clear of mind, he'd returned to his studies, and had immediately begun planning the fourth. He had carefully seduced her into his trap. The risk had a healing quality of its own, and during the pursuit he hardly ever felt the blade of panic against his throat. He'd slept with her first, because some of the books claimed sex held restorative powers. It didn't. But the murder did. He flipped back to the description in his journal, though he didn't need the words to evoke it for him.

> I had placed the knife in the crevice where the seat bench met its back before I picked her up. She wanted to be bad, to do the things she'd never been allowed as a child, and I was more than happy to oblige. I took her to a seedy part of town, got naked with her, and just as she cried out her pleasure into my mouth, I shoved the blade up beneath her sternum and into her heart. I swallowed her air, her cries, her soul as it left her body. I licked the blood from her breasts and I was renewed.

The feeling had lasted for weeks. And even when the voice had returned, it had been weak, annoying rather than fearsome. But experience taught him it would gather strength, so he'd outfitted the little lab that now housed Nicole's body in the hidden room of his home, added studies in biology to those in metaphysics, and prepared to take his cure from Nicole Lewis.

He just hadn't quite figured out how. And now he wondered whether freezing her might have destroyed something vital. Or whether her party-hearty lifestyle had corrupted her beyond help.

Either way, it was a good thing Calliope Pearson hadn't died before getting to the island. She could serve as plan B. Perhaps even plan A.

CHAPTER THREE

By eleven that night, Callie wished she'd insisted on moving right away. She had returned to her room, packed the few items she'd hung in the closet, and luxuriated in a long, hot shower. After dinner from room service—delicious, fast, and hot on arrival, she noted for the article she might or might not write—she'd crawled into bed, certain sleep would take her under immediately.

It didn't. Instead, her mind brought up images of the gendarmes, of Mac's face—angry and hard when first they met, disgusted when she led him to believe she would seduce John to keep her room, half-amused when she had defended him—and of Nikki's smiling image in the web photos. Every sound in the room made her twitch, her mind conjuring shadowy images of the thief returning for something he'd forgotten. Under normal circumstances, Callie surfed the web when she couldn't sleep. But her computer was gone.

She flipped on the light and picked up the photograph she'd set on the bedside table upon arrival. Using her fingernail, she unscrewed the thin, plywood backing from the frame and pried it off. Between her parents' wedding picture and the plywood lay the object that had started her quest.

Unlike the formal black-and-white portrait hiding it, the second photograph had been taken with an inexpensive camera, likely an Instamatic. Enlarged to five by seven, it had become grainy, the colors harsh. Even so, Sharon Pearson's joy beamed out, outshining even the bright Caribbean day. She stood barefoot on the beach, a drooling baby cuddled in her arms. A palatial hotel loomed in the background. Although the sun shone from behind the photographer—her father, Callie assumed—the building seemed in some way shadowed, as if from within. That her father had hidden the photograph inside the framed wedding picture he kept on his various desks as long as Callie could remember would have aroused her curiosity even without the notation on the back: *Sharon and Calliope, PdlM StM, September, 1987.*

The identification, scrawled in her father's bold, distinctive hand, was faded, clearly written at or near the time the snapshot had been taken, not so long afterward that he could have confused the dates. Besides, her father had nicknamed her "Pumpkin" because her birthday was so close to Halloween. They'd watched the Charlie Brown specials every year, and he'd teased her about being the "Great Pumpkin." He wouldn't have accidentally written the wrong month on the back of a picture he obviously considered important.

And if he had, he would have corrected his mistake immediately. Frank Pearson had been meticulously, almost fanatically organized. He kept voluminous records, all of which Callie had surveyed as executor of his will. He'd documented every trip he'd ever taken, kept journals describing the people he'd met and the places he'd seen, both before and after his marriage, but nowhere did information about a Caribbean vacation appear. And although he had been an avid photographer, the picture Callie held was the only evidence she'd found that her parents had traveled at all during her infancy.

She had rejected a dozen possible explanations. Her birth certificate proved she'd been born in New York and hadn't been adopted. The child in the picture couldn't be an older, since-deceased sister because there wasn't enough time between the date of the photograph and Callie's own birth. Sharon Pearson had lost touch with her family long before her daughter was born, so the "Calliope" in the picture couldn't be a relative.

For all her concentration and focus, the image provided no answers; it hadn't since she had discovered it while changing the frame from her father's modernistic ebony and chrome to one suiting her own, more traditional taste. Her recognition of the Paradis remained the only clue it had surrendered, and that tidbit divulged grudgingly, given the angle of the photograph and the distance of the hotel from the subject.

Callie had determined at breakfast that even as early as thirty years past, the Paradis had owned all of its current half-mile-long stretch of private beach, which meant the shot had been taken on hotel property. Her parents might have stayed in the very room in which Callie sat, a fact that did nothing to help her sleep. Muttering to herself in frustration, she slid the snapshot back into its hiding place, retightened the screws, and stood the frame back on the table. Then she padded across the room to the French doors and let herself out onto the balcony. Directly beneath her lay the poolside bar, hidden by the orange tiles of the balcony. In front of her, a series of underwater spotlights illuminated the pool's aqua depths. The hotel discouraged swimming after dark but did not expressly forbid it. The printed sheet of policies Callie had found on the desk in her suite explained that day or night, swimming in the pool or at the beach was at the guest's own risk.

Beyond the pool, the reflection of the moon gleamed against the rippling onyx sea. It called to her, and she pulled on a pair of cropped pants, an old T-shirt, and her flip-flops, then took the stairs down to the lobby. No one sat at the desk, but Callie had no doubt ringing the little silver bell would bring a night attendant in record time. She didn't test the theory. The lounge chairs by the pool had been neatly stacked to one side, and the canvas umbrellas in their over-sized, sand-filled planters were closed, as was the bar. She made a mental note to ask John whether it stayed open later during the high season.

The slap of her flip-flops echoed as she descended the winding, bowered path to the beach, sending a little shiver up her spine. She felt like a character in a *Twilight Zone* episode, wandering a strange and deserted land, alone, surrounded by oppressive beauty.

The stone pavers of the path gave way abruptly to sand, and the front of Callie's shoe caught, sending her sprawling. She checked reflexively to be sure no one had noticed the embarrassing slip, then shook her head at her own foolishness. Who could have seen her? Plucking off her sandals, she curled her toes in the sand, which had gone slightly cool despite the warmth remaining in the air. She meandered along the water's edge, letting the tiny waves lap over her feet, occa-sionally glancing back to judge her distance from the Paradis, until she considered herself positioned in much the same spot where her mother stood in the mystery photograph.

She plunked herself down on the sand and drew her knees up beneath her chin. What had Sharon Pearson been thinking that day? Callie didn't have much experience with children, but if she'd had to choose an adjective to describe the baby in her mother's arms, she would have chosen "new." Tiny, wrinkled fingers grasped the edge of the blanket wrap-ping her, and her face, equally wrinkled, was blotchy and red. A dozen times, Callie had tried to see herself in that baby. A dozen times, she had failed.

"I'd expect you to be asleep."

Callie's heart stuttered and her muscles froze before she recognized the honeyed drawl with its sandpaper edge.

"I needed to unwind. I didn't realize having my things stolen had affected me so much."

Uninvited, Mac settled beside her, close enough that the heat radiating off his body caressed her skin. "You handled it well. Better, as John mentioned, than most of our guests would."

Distracted by his nearness, it took her a minute to interpret the comment. "Is there a question in there somewhere, Mr. Brody?"

"Mac. And, yeah, it occurred to me you might have expected something similar, and it might not have come as such a surprise."

"I assure you, I expected nothing of the kind. If, as you claim, my shock didn't show, it's because I'm a tad less sheltered than your standard clientele."

"You're not exactly poverty-stricken."

She should have realized he'd pry into her background, but the sense of violation the simple comment engendered was as strong as that from the burglary. Her response sounded stilted and prudish, but she couldn't soften it.

"I've lived all over the world, including places where money attracts undesirable attention."

"You traveled with your father?"

"Yes."

"According to the press, he was a businessman." Another question couched as a statement. It seemed Brody's preferred method of interrogation. She would go with it, at least for the moment. Nothing about her father's life could hurt her, and perhaps talking about him might spark hitherto hidden memories.

"Half businessman. The other half diplomat."

"Diplomat." The word rolled across Mac's tongue. "Another word for 'spy'?"

Callie laughed, her first spontaneous outburst since her arrival. "For a while, in my early teens, I imagined him as James Bond. But no, he wasn't some undercover hero. I meant 'diplomat' in the most literal sense. Let's say you owned a big corporation"—Mac snorted—"and you wanted to open an overseas branch. You'd hire my father and he'd go first to find all the contacts you'd need. He'd pave the way with individuals and government entities, find you security personnel, work on community relations, and clean up messes your predecessors might have left behind. Sometimes, the trips we took were short. Not much in Europe, for example, took very long to arrange. A couple of months here, a couple of months there. But we spent a year in Greece when one of his employers got tangled up with some unsavory types, and two in Indonesia while he tried to mediate between various factions in and out of government."

"Sounds like quite a life for a child."

"It was. And it prepared me for upheavals, for things like having my belongings taken." Wow. She'd just revealed more about her childhood to Mac than she had to anyone else in the ten years since she'd moved out of her father's house. Time to turn the tables.

"And you? Where did you grow up?"

"In the slums in Atlanta."

"I never thought about Atlanta having slums. It seems so clean and pretty."

He chuckled, a low rumble of sound that heated her blood despite the soft breeze off the ocean. "The board of tourism would be happy to hear it. But in reality, Atlanta's just like any other city."

"How did you get out?"

"The same way as any other kid in my neighborhood with an iota of ambition. I joined the Army straight out of high school. Learned a lot about the world and myself in my six years in, one thing being I have little talent for—and less patience with—politics. And I'm not good with rules. So I left. Came home and joined the Atlanta PD." Callie could hear the warning: he knew how to investigate. She chose to focus on another aspect of his story.

"I can't imagine the police department being any less political or rule-oriented than the military."

"It's not. But if you don't care about rank, and you're good at your job, you can fudge the rules and avoid the politics."

"I don't understand."

"There are two tracks in most police departments. In one, you go from foot patrol to radio car and so on up to detective in Vice, Homicide, or wherever you want to end up. That one is based on talent, drive, and determination. On the other hand, you also take a series of civil-service exams that take you from sergeant to lieutenant to captain and so on. You pass the exam, you gain the rank. But if you want that rank to mean something, you want to be able to take advantage of it, you have to make nice with the powers that be. Me, I didn't care about that."

"Then why did you leave?"

"I lost my peripheral vision." He touched the scar slashing down his face. "Knife fight. I didn't want to spend my life doing paperwork, so I took partial disability. An Army buddy had retired and opened a charter fishing service down here, so I joined him. It was supposed to be temporary, but it didn't turn out that way."

"And you got married." She hadn't meant to say it, to bring

the missing woman into their conversation, but she could feel herself getting sucked into his story. His regret and longing for his old life sat beside them in the sand, and she needed to push them away before they became part of her own sadness. Adding Nikki's presence reminded her of all the reasons not to sympathize with him.

"Yeah." They sat in companionable silence, listening to the swish of the waves. "You should go back. It's not safe here."

"Back to the hotel, or back to New York?"

"To New York. Barring that, upstairs."

"Why? What's so dangerous?"

He gestured at the inky water. "The island is like the sea. Beautiful on the surface, even clear down to the sandy bottom. But beauty isn't innocence. Sea urchins, lionfish, even man-o'-war jellyfish are gorgeous but deadly."

"Cynical."

"Realistic."

Callie yawned. "I guess I could head back to bed."

"Good idea. What time should I pick you up to go to the station?"

The station. Right. Somehow, in the susurrant darkness of the beach, she'd forgotten about that. Despite their discussion of danger—and her own, deliberate prodding of the open wound Nikki must represent for him—the gendarmes, the DNA, the dead body, even the mysterious photograph that had started her whole journey had seemed very far away. For a few minutes, she'd been a tourist, sharing the sand with a sexy stranger. She let the fantasy go with a sigh. "After breakfast? Say ten thirty?"

"Eating with the boss again?"

"He's helping me with a history of the Paradis." Again she wondered about the tension between the two men.

"Sure." Mac walked her back up to the hotel and watched until the door closed behind her.

⸻

WHAT WAS SHE up to? No way did the theft alone drive her down to the beach in the middle of the night. And it wasn't some damned article, either. She'd seemed so straightforward, so honest out there in the night, just a woman sitting on the sand, reminiscing about a lost parent, that she'd drawn him in for a few minutes. He'd almost fallen for the act, but Mac had never had any patience with liars, and his marriage had only served to strengthen his disgust. It had taken the whole trip back to his cottage, but he'd shaken off the brief sense of camaraderie. Whatever Calliope Pearson was hiding, he'd dig it out.

He crawled out of bed at five, unable to sleep, and spent the morning packing and fuming. He didn't touch anything of Nikki's, or even the items they'd bought together. In ten months on the island, he'd acquired three boxes of books; a few clothes; climbing, sailing, and snorkel gear; and a darkly stained teak chest of drawers into which he folded all his clothes, including the two suits Nikki had insisted he buy. The only thing he intended to keep from their marriage was the Jeep. In the unlikely event of Nikki's return, he'd give it to her, but his motorcycle just wasn't practical for everyday use.

At ten, he locked up the house and set out. Because he planned to take Callie into Marigot, he drove rather than walked, cutting the travel time from fifteen minutes to five. He could have left later, but he wanted to observe Callie and John together, strictly for investigative purposes.

They sat closer than they had the previous day, their elbows almost touching. Dark hair spilled over Callie's shoulder and brushed her breast in a chaos of curls as she leaned over her pad to make notes, and Mac felt an unwelcome tug of desire. She looked up, catching his eye, and blushed. He raised an eyebrow, and she shifted her attention back to John, who covered her hand with his own and spoke to her for a few seconds before letting her gather her possessions to leave.

When she stood, Mac saw she'd donned a loose, sand-colored, knee-length linen dress rather than the shorts she'd worn the day before. She probably thought the straight line hid her curves, lent her a professional appearance. *Wrong.* As she approached, the dress shifted slightly with each step, each swing of her toned arms, and his body reacted as if the nubby material were caressing his skin rather than hers.

He reminded himself not to underestimate her. How many times had he watched Nikki hold up various outfits against her body, judging the effect they'd have on those she met? Of course, Nikki usually had only one goal, but a few subdued, conservative outfits did hang in her walk-in closet. She liked to wear them for her martyr appearances, after a particularly long night or a blowout argument, to prove people had misjudged her. So perhaps Callie was aware to precisely what degree that demure little dress raised his blood pressure.

His thoughts must have shown on his face, because Callie faltered, then stopped a few feet from him.

"Mac?"

"Ready to go?"

"Of course. But is everything okay? You look . . ." He raised an eyebrow, watching her struggle for the right word. "Nothing happened?"

"Not a thing." He held open the hotel's door and let her out into the blazing heat. She squinted against the glare, reaching into her bag for sunglasses, and he wondered whether she'd slept any more than he had.

He led the way to the Jeep, opened the passenger door, and held out a hand to help her in.

She pushed the sunglasses down and looked at him over the top with skeptical astonishment. "Southern gentleman?"

Seldom-used muscles quirked his lips into a grin. "I'll give you the Southern part."

"Oh, dear." Her dark eyes sparkled as she rested her small hand in his and hopped into the car. "I'll try to keep that in mind."

Without forethought, he tightened his fingers on hers, trapping them. She stilled but didn't pull away, her eyes—no longer sparkling with humor, but deep and shadowed—never leaving his.

"There are no gentlemen," he said, remembering the way she'd sat so close to Lewis. "Never trust anyone who claims to be one."

She swallowed before she spoke, and he watched the movement of the muscles in her throat. Her voice sounded hoarse. "But I should trust you?"

He let go of her hand and pushed the door closed without answering. As he rounded the front of the vehicle, he worked to regain control over his reaction to her. The attraction was too strong, almost violent. Every time he thought he had it contained with logic, it escaped the cage. *You're an ass,* he told himself. *You know damned well she can't be trusted.* But still, his unruly body responded to her the minute he slid into his seat and saw her knotting her hair up.

SHE WAS IN trouble. Callie bent her head to gather her hair, taking the time to hide the warmth rising in her face. Though she ran her fingers and palms through her curls, she could still feel the burning heat of Mac's hand grasping hers. What was wrong with her? Less than forty-eight hours before, she'd admonished herself to steer clear of the man, but she'd willingly climbed into his car, the fly to his spider. She should have insisted on driving herself to the station.

She secured the knot of hair with a pair of intricately carved chopsticks she'd inherited from her mother as Mac buckled himself into his seat.

"A/C or windows?" he asked, inserting the key into the ignition.

"I'd prefer air conditioning, if you don't mind. I'm usually not such a wimp about the heat, but this trip is killing me." She regretted the words immediately. "I'm sorry, I shouldn't have put it that way. I didn't mean to be so insensitive."

He flicked a glance at her as he put the car in gear. "Don't worry about it."

But she did. She'd taken well to heart her father's lessons in diplomacy, in speaking carefully and acting even more so, and in always considering the feelings of others. Mac's wife was missing at best. At worst, the gendarmes had recovered her body. Callie's careless words doubtless reminded him of the sad situation. But she couldn't withdraw them, and anything she might add would only exacerbate the problem. So she changed the subject.

"How much did you know about St. Martin before you moved here?"

He huffed a brief laugh. "Not a damned thing. Travis, the Army buddy I told you about, he's been here for a couple of years, and started harassing me about coming to visit maybe a year ago. He'd tell me how the booze was good, the food was better, and the women were easy, but I just couldn't get a week free of work, or so it seemed at the time."

"Did you tell him what happened? Or did you just show up?"

Mac went silent for so long Callie began to wonder whether she'd said something wrong.

"Neither. He called me. Two days after I was released from the hospital. Told me the island was a great place to retire, and he had a spare boat I could sleep on if I wanted it."

"How did he know?"

"I have no idea. At the time, I was dealing with the disability paperwork and hearings, and the fallout from the knife fight. I was on painkillers and antibiotics, and every day it seemed like someone new wanted a piece of me, so I never even asked how Travis found out."

"Was the fight, the arrest in the papers? Maybe he was keeping track of you online."

"Nope. I was undercover at the time. Since we'd hoped I would be able to go back to work, the only name the press ever got was my cover."

His voice had lost some of its intensity, and when Callie looked at him, he didn't turn his head. She assumed he'd divided his attention between the road and his memories, trying to figure out how his friend had become aware of his injury.

"Do you have friends in common? Maybe from your days in the Army?"

"No one who should have been keeping track."

And wasn't that just the closemouthed answer she could have expected from him. But she had to admit that his private life, his friends, they weren't any of her business. She switched back to the original topic, thankful Marigot was close to the hotel.

"So what did you think of St. Martin when you got here?"

One side of his mouth tipped up, and her throat dried as it had when he'd grasped her hand. God, the man simply oozed sex appeal without even trying.

"Hot," he said, and for a minute, she thought he was echoing her own thoughts. She felt a blush rise into her face, then realized he had merely answered her question.

"Surely it was hot in Georgia."

"Yup. And in Afghanistan, too. But you asked what I thought of the island." He shot her an unreadable look. "Everything about this place is hot. And wet."

Callie tensed to keep from squirming in her seat. The way he said the words, he couldn't be unaware of the double entendre. Her blood suddenly pulsed very close to the surface of her skin.

"Well," she said, striving for a lighter note. "It certainly is beautiful."

"Oh, yeah." He took his eyes from the road long enough to sweep over her body. "It certainly is."

Which effectively put an end to her ability to speak.

⌒

MAC HAD NO idea why he felt compelled to tease Callie. Maybe just because he hadn't seen a woman blush in such a long time. Maybe because her reaction assured him the sexual charges running along his nerves every time he looked at her weren't entirely one-sided. Either way, by the time they reached the village, his mood had improved.

He'd arranged with Michel Vichy to meet them at the station. The gendarme welcomed them, but examined Callie with eyes both curious and critical.

"I understand some items were removed from your room yesterday."

Callie glared at Mac, who threw up his hands in mock surrender. "Don't blame me. I didn't make the call."

"*Non.* Monsieur Lewis telephoned. May I ask why you did not?"

"It wasn't important, and I probably won't be here long enough for you to catch the thief."

"You have very little faith in our abilities." Mac wondered whether Michel had added the hint of defensiveness to try to get a rise out of Callie, or whether he really was offended. Either way, it immediately set Callie aflutter. She didn't, apparently, enjoy making people feel small. She kept surprising him; he'd have to stop judging her by Nicole's yardstick.

"No, no. That's not it at all. But surely more serious cases occupy your attention."

"Every case is serious. The island relies on tourists. We cannot have them robbed at every turn. But the choice is yours, of course, if you choose to ignore the theft."

"Either way works for me. I'm happy to fill out the paperwork to make the report, but replacing the laptop and the jewelry won't cost more than flying back here and finding a hotel for the duration of the trial. And whether you'd need me here for that or not, I'd want to come."

Michel nodded, accepting her explanation far more

readily than Mac did. DNA collection took all of ten minutes, including the time Callie spent filling in the permission forms that required her address and phone number, both of which Mac memorized on the spot.

Michel engaged Callie in casual conversation during the process, slipping in questions about whether she had any friends or acquaintances on the island, whether this was her first trip, whether—aside from the theft—she was enjoying herself. He kept the whole discussion light and innocuous, eliciting the information he needed without Callie becoming aware of the interrogation. Unfortunately, none of her answers—which Mac judged honest despite his reservations—exposed any connection to Nikki.

When they left the station, Callie insisted Mac drop her back at the Paradis so she could get her car. As he couldn't follow her from the hotel inconspicuously, he took the afternoon to check the feelers he'd put out about Nikki's whereabouts, updating them to include requests for information about Callie. His description of her as his wife's virtual double raised some eyebrows but conveniently explained his curiosity.

Rumors of the body on the beach had multiplied, and Mac found himself spending more time giving answers than getting them. Especially once word got out he'd rented an apartment overlooking the marina in Marigot. He stocked the kitchen in the new apartment and hauled the three boxes of books he'd packed up from his old house to the new place, then wandered down to his favorite bar and settled in a corner where he could see every one of the restaurants that lined the marina. If Callie planned to write about the island, chances were good she'd show up sooner or later, as the open-air eateries along the lagoon in Marina Royale attracted more casual diners than did any others. Having ordered a beer, he opened a book and kicked back to wait.

A few people stopped by his table as the night wore on, but his mood must have been evident; for the most part, they left him alone.

At seven, Mac ordered a pizza. At eight, his quarry approached. He tensed, afraid she'd choose his restaurant for dinner, but she stepped into one two doors down instead. Finally, something was going his way. From his position he could watch her without her being aware of him.

She'd changed clothes, this time dressing down in khaki walking shorts and a boatneck tee, and he wondered how she'd occupied herself during the day. She'd switched rooms at some point, down to one of the fancy bungalows. Lewis's offer had set every alarm ringing in Mac's skull. What the hell did the man want with her? Not sex, despite the goading insinuations Mac had made, because Lewis always kept his women away from the hotel.

And what did Callie want with Lewis? Having spent a little more time with her, he was pretty sure she wouldn't trade her body for a five-star room, as she'd let him believe that first day. Which made liars out of both of them.

She chatted with her waiter, flirting a little, laughing a lot, drawing a fair amount of attention and more than one double take. He'd hear soon enough from friends of Nikki's. Full dark fell while Callie ate, but she didn't immediately head back toward the parking lot when she left the restaurant. Rather, she passed directly in front of his position, strolling in an unhurried fashion toward the main shopping street.

Marigot's business district was well lit, and Mac kept several yards back as he tracked Callie's progress. Once in a while she'd stop and make notes on a pad she pulled from her black tote. When she hesitated a moment and then turned down an alley, Mac picked up his pace, not wanting to lose her. He couldn't imagine what had drawn her attention; no stores or tourist attractions lay down the dark lane. Could she be meeting someone? Five feet from the corner he paused. Adopting a nonchalant manner, he sauntered past the narrow opening, glancing into the shadows as he did.

Callie wasn't alone, but she clearly hadn't arranged the situation. At first glance, Mac counted three young men wearing dark clothing and baseball caps pulled low over their brows. Backing up and slipping into the shadows at the mouth of the alley to evaluate the situation, he saw a fourth youth, smaller and younger. A decoy. He'd seen the move plenty of times in Atlanta: the younger kid would call for help, appearing to suffer at the hands of a bully, to draw in a good Samaritan who would, in short order, find himself—or herself—the victim.

Mac wouldn't have believed such a ruse would work on Callie. God knew, Nikki wouldn't have been affected by the kid's plight, but then the evidence of fundamental differences between the two women was mounting. Mac moved closer with careful, quiet steps, keeping out of sight. Not that Callie's tormentors seemed particularly concerned about being seen.

"C'mon, lady, give it up."

"I don't think so." Callie sounded calm and controlled, but from his vantage point Mac could see her muscles tighten. His own followed suit, and, as the largest of the men moved to take Callie's purse by force, Mac prepared to spring to her rescue. But she surprised him yet again.

He couldn't follow the exact movement in the dark, but it was quick and clean and resulted in the thug who'd approached her doubling over, then falling to his knees.

"Shit," said one of his companions in the Creole patois

Mac had learned to understand, though he couldn't speak it, "he didn't say she would fight back!" He pulled the big man—still gasping for air—to his feet, and the group took off down the alley.

Mac was torn between following them, checking on Callie, and holding his position to observe her next moves. Concern won, and he moved forward, deliberately making plenty of noise and calling out so as not to startle her.

When she turned her coffee-colored eyes on him, he recognized the wildness of adrenaline overload in them.

"What are you doing here?" Aggression, too, commonly succeeded adrenaline, especially when fear prompted the rush.

"I followed you."

"Nice of you to help out."

"I would have, but you seemed to have the situation well in hand and I figured you'd rather take care of it yourself."

She acknowledged the truth of the statement with a nod. Reaction had begun to set in, though, and when she rubbed her hands up and down her arms, he pulled off the button-down shirt he wore over his black T-shirt and wrapped it around her. He counted it a measure of how disturbed she was that she didn't object. He hated to worry her further, but she needed to know the truth.

"They followed you, too."

"You saw them?"

"No, but I wasn't looking for them, either. Chances are they tracked you from across the street until they got a sense of your direction. There's just the one main street on this side of the marina, so it wouldn't be hard. Then they got ahead of you to set you up."

"They couldn't have known I'd walk after dinner. What if I'd just gone back to the car?"

"They'd probably have snatched your purse, knocked you into the lagoon, and run. That would be more dangerous for them, though, because the gendarmes patrol regularly around the water and the marina has private security as well."

"But why?" Even in the darkness, Mac could see her shiver. He took her hand.

"Let's get out of here. I'll take you for crepes and coffee."

"No . . ."

"Sugar and caffeine are what you need right now. Trust me on this."

Visibly reluctant, she let him lead her through the dark streets to a bright little open-air restaurant and settle her into a seat in the corner. Two men sat at the bar, arguing over the best way to care for a boat's engine, and several younger ones sat with notebook computers at tables, accessing the restaurant's wireless network. The bustle, as much as the food, would calm her, and as much as it went against the grain for him to leave his own back unprotected, she needed the security more than he did.

"What makes you so certain those guys singled me out?"

"Think about it. First someone steals your computer and your jewelry. Then you're assaulted."

"They didn't hurt me."

"They weren't meant to." He repeated what he'd heard as the men had scuttled away.

"Who's 'he'?"

"No idea. If I thought for a minute those guys knew who'd hired them, I'd have gone after them. But whoever 'he' is, he wants you to leave the island, preferably of your own accord. The idea is to make your stay so unpleasant you'll cut it short, but not to physically harm you, which might bring the cops down on him."

"Then taking my purse would be exceptionally stupid. My passport, all my ID is in it. I didn't want to leave anything important in my room after the burglary."

"I doubt he realized that. He probably thought you'd give up your purse without a fight."

"Surprise." She grinned weakly, impressing him with her grit. "But you still haven't explained why someone would want me gone."

"I won't be able to until you let me in on what you're doing here." For a moment, he thought she'd open up, but the waitress arrived with their food, and by the time she left Callie's defenses were once more in place.

"How do I know you weren't the one who sent them after me?"

"You don't. But I haven't made any secret of the fact I'd rather you leave, so I'd be the first person you'd suspect. You may not believe it, but I'm actually smarter than that."

Callie stayed quiet a long time, steadily eating her way through the thin French pancake filled with bananas and chocolate-hazelnut cream. Mac wondered what was going on behind the dark eyes that would not meet his own. About two-thirds of the way through her crepe, she put down her fork and nodded decisively.

"Will you come back to the Paradis with me? There's something in the bungalow I'd like to show you."

"Now?"

"If you don't mind."

In answer, he dropped a twenty-dollar bill on the table and reached for her hand. "We'll take my car."

CHAPTER FOUR

As the Jeep rolled through the night, Callie studied Mac through half-lidded eyes, still unsure showing him the old photograph was the right thing to do. She'd come to the island without a plan, with merely a vague sense that if there were anything to be found it would be at the Paradis rather than in New York.

And boy, had she found something. Starting with Nikki Lewis, a woman so like herself in appearance even her husband and brother had noticed the resemblance; a woman who had disappeared just before her arrival; a woman who had quite possibly been murdered. And then, before she could come to terms with Nicole, there had been the computer-stealing thief and a group of thugs hired to drive her away.

Not to mention the man beside her. Tough, straightforward, and attractive despite the violent scar, he confused the hell out of her. Had he murdered his wife? She didn't believe so, but she'd begun to doubt her judgment after finding the photograph that proved her father had lied to her—implicitly or explicitly—all her life. Plus, common sense told her not to discount the twin effects of fear and hormones: Mac was big, strong, and solid, and she was scared. Leaning on him would be easy.

She picked at the sleeve of his shirt she still wore over her own, suddenly remembering that he'd also wrapped her in a blanket when her computer had been stolen. The blanket, though, had smelled fresh and vaguely floral, scented with whatever they used on the sheets at the Paradis. Mac's shirt smelled rich, and earthy despite the tang of salt that overlay everything on the island.

So not going down that road. To distract herself, she asked the first question that came to mind.

"What will you do now that you can't work at the Paradis? Will you stay on the island?"

"I haven't exactly had time to consider my options. But, like Trav said, this is as good a place as any to retire."

"You're too young to retire."

He slanted a glance in her direction. "Yeah? So what kind of job am I suited for, in your opinion?"

"What did you do in the Army?"

"Grunt," he said, and Callie felt her molars grinding at the deliberately monosyllabic answer. He was baiting her. She narrowed her eyes on his profile, hoping he could feel her glare.

"Even if I believed that, and I don't, you weren't a grunt on the police force. You had the brains and ambition to make detective, so you could probably get any job you wanted."

"Yeah? You'd hire me?" The teasing humor surprised her even more than the little half grin that went with it, and she almost went for a flip response. He'd probably have preferred it. She suspected he didn't like to talk about work. At a guess, he'd defined himself by his position for years, and losing it would have decimated the most vital piece of his self-image. How peculiar to imagine such an intimidating man in any way insecure, but once the idea took hold, Callie couldn't shake it. So she gave him a serious answer instead.

"If I had any reason to hire anyone, yes. My father would have taken you on in a heartbeat. Surely there are companies, other people who do now what he did." Callie studied him. He had a couple outstanding attributes she so wasn't going to mention. Because, really, they didn't qualify him for a job. At least not a respectable one. She allowed herself a small, private smile before returning to the topic at hand. "You understood those men at the marina tonight, and I heard you talking to Claudine when I arrived. How many languages do you speak?"

"I'm good with languages," he admitted with a shrug "I can function in French and Spanish, and I picked up the local slang wherever the government stationed me within a couple months."

"So all of that—the investigative experience, the combat experience, the languages, God knows what else—and retirement is the best option you can come up with?"

He let the silence grow again before answering, the teasing note back in his voice. "Retirement doesn't mean living a life of ease, you know. Fishing is hard work." Despite herself, Callie laughed.

⌒

THE GATE GUARD at the Paradis waved them through with barely a glance, and Mac took the narrow, sandy drive that led to the lot behind the bungalows. He pulled into the space marked with an elaborately scrolled number five, unsnapped his seat belt, and fixed his eyes on her.

"Ready?"

"Not really. But I don't suppose that matters."

"It matters. But there's not much we can do about it at the moment." If she hadn't known better, she might have thought he was apologizing.

"I'll get over it." She climbed from the car, taking the large metal skeleton key that opened the bungalow's back gate from her pocket. Each of the hotel's seven beachfront cabins had a fenced and gated garden behind it containing a few trees, frangipani, hibiscus, and various tropical creepers to protect guests from the eyes of anyone who might wander into the parking area. In the center of bungalow five's garden, a fountain that doubled as a birdbath burbled cheerfully. Callie wished she could shut it off.

Following the crushed shell path around the fountain, she led Mac to the back door. She unlocked it, but before she could turn the knob, he covered her hand with his own.

"Let me." Halogen-harsh illumination from the parking area behind them combined with the dappled moonlight to cast his features into a forbidding mask, and Callie stepped back without argument.

The door creaked slightly, its hinges rough from exposure to the damp and salty air, but Mac moved silently, all predator in the night. The back door of the cottage led into the kitchen, and as Callie followed Mac inside, her gaze went to the knife block on the counter. All six blades rested in their slots.

Mac slipped on into the living room, and she paused at the knife block, choosing a weapon and then toeing off her shoes to move more quietly.

She had left the front curtains open, and the moonlight coming in the windows shifted and rippled as it reflected off the water, setting shadows fluttering. Every movement caught her attention, tripped her nerves, twisted her stomach, but Mac hardly seemed to notice them. Because of his lack of peripheral vision? It was possible, she supposed, but he walked with total self-assurance, apparently not bothered by his disability. No, more likely he didn't track the shifting shadows because he sorted the innocuous from the danger-ous automatically.

Each bungalow had three bedrooms. Mac cleared the smaller ones first, stopping into each for only seconds before reemerging. She'd propped the door to the master bedroom ajar so air could circulate while she was gone, but he paused at the threshold to glance back over his shoulder at her. There was nothing submissive in the action. He wasn't asking per-mission, simply evaluating her reaction. She chose to give him none, though a dark corner of her psyche, some vestigial instinct of a more primitive time, sent shivers of heat through her as she watched him slide into her private space.

A moment later the spell snapped as he switched on the light.

"I take it everything's the way you left it?"

Her mouth had gone dry, and she had to swallow twice before she could answer. "It looks that way."

"Okay, then. What did you want me to see?"

She laid the kitchen knife on the dresser and gestured for him to sit on the bed. She took the photograph from the nightstand and settled beside him. She turned the frame over, then found herself staring at the back of it, unable to remem-ber why she'd picked it up.

"Callie?"

"Sorry." She opened the frame and handed over the snap-shot. Mac held it up to the light, tilting it to see the details.

"So you have been here before." He gave Callie a small smile, which she appreciated but could not return. It was too late for humor.

"Look at the note on the back."

She could see him process the date, connecting it with what she'd told him about her birthday, but a sudden, sharp pounding on the cabin's front door precluded speech. He stuffed the picture—along with the framed wedding photograph—beneath the pillows on her bed with one hand, shoving her to the floor with the other.

"Callie! Are you in there? Callie!"

"It's John." Callie started to rise, but Mac laid a warning hand on her shoulder, holding her down.

"What does he want with you?"

"I have no idea, but he's making enough noise to attract everyone within miles. He'd hardly do that if he intended to hurt me." With obvious reluctance, Mac released her and she called out to let John know she was on the way.

"Thank God," John said when she opened the door. His face was pale, his dress shirt wrinkled, a far cry from his usual suave appearance. "Your roommate called from New York. She's been trying to reach you on your cell but couldn't get through. And your car wasn't here. I told Billy at the gate to keep an eye out for you, but he didn't expect you to come back in a different vehicle. Andy here saw the Jeep parked in your spot and called me."

The young man wore a Paradis security uniform—khaki pants, a maroon shirt, and a gun belt—and he didn't meet Callie's eyes the whole time John was speaking. He kept glancing off to one side or another, or staring down at his feet, until Mac addressed him.

"Good eye, Andy."

"Thank you, sir." The boy's relief made his previous dilemma clear: he felt caught between John and Mac. The Jeep would have been a dead giveaway as to who had brought her home, and no doubt Andy worried about ratting out one of his bosses to the other.

"What did Erin want?"

"She said your house had been broken into."

"What?" Erin Campbell shared a house with Callie in Chappaqua, an hour north of New York City. The house was bigger than Callie needed, especially since she traveled so much, but she loved the feeling of permanence the property gave her. When home, she spent a great deal of time in the yard, trying her hand at gardening and generally enjoying the sensation of rootedness she'd never gotten from apartment living. Erin, on the other hand, never traveled. Head chef at an upscale restaurant, all she wanted from a place to live was peace and quiet, a stress-free environment she couldn't find in the city.

"Was anything taken?"

"I don't know." John handed her a cell phone. "You should call her. She called here about two hours ago. She sounded very upset. The police were there."

Waving John's proffered phone away, Callie dug through her handbag and pulled out her own. "I never hear the damned thing," she explained as she dialed. "I don't even know why I carry it."

Erin's boyfriend, Tommy Lowell, answered her cell and explained that Erin was in the shower.

"The place is a wreck," he said. "It's really strange. They took some obvious stuff—the jar of change in the kitchen, the TV from the living room, stuff that was laying out in the open— but they didn't go through Erin's closet, so they didn't find her jewelry box. Same thing in your room. The dresser drawers hadn't even been opened. It's the kind of thing I'd expect my students to do. Lots of vandalism, not a lot of profit."

"Erin's computer?"

"She had it at my place. We went up to Vermont for the weekend."

"Oh, that's right! I forgot she'd taken the weekend off."

"I'm just glad she wasn't home."

"Me, too. Do the police have any idea when it happened?"

"Probably late last night. One of the planters outside the front door was knocked over and Marianne, from next door, says it wasn't like that yesterday."

"I'll come home tomorrow. Erin should stay with you for a couple of days."

"She won't do that, Callie. You know her."

"Yeah." Erin had grown up on the proverbial wrong side of the tracks in Chicago. She considered herself invincible. "You'll stay there, then?"

"Of course. I already got a sub for tomorrow. If you let us know when you're coming in, we can pick you up at the airport."

"I'll just call a car service. You guys have enough to worry about. I'll see you sometime tomorrow afternoon or evening."

"Good deal. I'll tell Erin."

When she hung up, Andy had disappeared but both John and Mac were staring at her. Self-conscious, she invited them to sit. They each took one of the chintz-covered rattan chairs, and she was suddenly struck by how out of place Mac appeared in the sophisticated, somehow feminine setting. The furniture seemed too flimsy to contain the energy radiating from him. How could he believe he was cut out to spend his life here? Or had he been so in love with Nikki Lewis that he hadn't even considered that marrying her might force him into a lifestyle he couldn't tolerate? She pushed the question away and filled the men in on what she'd learned from Tommy.

"He has no idea what they were after?" John asked when she finished.

The lie sprang to her lips so easily it frightened her: "He

teaches at a pretty violent school. He didn't say so specifically, but he seemed to be hinting that some of his students might have done it. Summer school isn't where they want to be, and they've been known to take out their frustrations on their teachers."

Mac's expression didn't change, but disbelief radiated from his tense body. Callie could almost smell it. John, however, appeared to take her statement at face value. "At least no one was hurt. Are you sure you have to go home, though? If your friend's students did the damage, there's no reason for you to rush back."

"The police will want to talk to me. And I want to be certain nothing else was taken. The house is in my name, too, so all the insurance issues will fall on me."

"That's terrible. Maybe we can arrange for you to come back sometime?"

She forced herself to return John's smile. "Maybe. Right now, I need to call the airlines and see if I can get a flight out tomorrow."

"It shouldn't be too hard. Most of the time-shares start on Fridays, Saturdays, or Sundays, so those are the big fly-in and fly-out days. You shouldn't have too much trouble on a Monday. I'll leave you to it." John stood. "You coming, Brody?"

"Miss Pearson and I have unfinished business."

John looked as if he might say more, but then shrugged. Callie walked him to the door. He pressed a business card into her hand and told her to call or e-mail him and let him know how she was getting on. From the corner of her eye, she saw Mac walking back toward the bedroom, and by the time she joined him there, he had pulled the snapshot back out of its hiding place and was sitting on the bed examining it under the light from the reading lamp.

"What do you know about this so far?"

"Nothing. There's no record of my parents ever taking a trip here, they never mentioned it, and I have a birth certificate from the state of New York showing I was born October twenty-sixth."

"Did you have anything on your computer about this? Like a digital copy?"

Callie shifted and picked at the hem of her shorts, not meeting Mac's eye. "Yes. I shouldn't have brought the original with me, but it's habit. My father always had the wedding photograph on his desk, and I've kept it close since his death."

"Did you post the digital copy anywhere? Adoption boards, anything like that?"

"No. I told you I wasn't adopted. And given that my father hid the picture all these years, it didn't seem to me I ought to broadcast its location."

"Is your computer password protected, or would whoever took it be able to find this on it?"

"They'd find it. The confidential files—financial stuff, things like that—have passwords to open them, but I've never worried about the computer itself. Does it matter? They took the computer; they probably already knew about the picture."

"Maybe. Maybe they were flying blind. The fact that you look so much like Nikki can't be coincidental." He tapped the photo against his fingers. "This is an old secret. Whoever wants to keep it hidden may have taken one look at you, scented danger, and taken the computer to see what they could find out about what you're doing here."

"Do you think they were looking for the original at my house?"

"I don't know. It's more likely the break-in was intended

to serve the same purpose as the mugging: to send you home. Finding the picture would have been a bonus, but not vital. You've seen it, scanned it at least once, possibly shown it around. Now he's doing damage control, trying to keep you away from the darkest parts of the story."

"He's going to win. I have to go home. If the secret is here, I won't find it."

"Maybe. I doubt the whole story is here. I've said it before: it's hard to keep something quiet on such a small island. And thirty years ago it would have been damned near impossible. Since your parents were obviously living in the States at the time this was taken, chances are good that's where the bulk of the secret is buried. It's just harder to unravel from that end, so whoever's orchestrating this thinks he's safer with you there."

"Well, there's not much I can do now. I have to call the airlines and try to find a flight home." She pulled her suitcase from the closet, not even noticing when he came up behind her until she turned around and practically bumped into him. He took the bag from her hand and laid it on the bed.

"Do you really want to know what's behind this picture? No matter how ugly it might be?" His voice was soft, even gentle, but when she glanced up at his face, his features had settled into an unreadable mask.

"If I stop looking now, do you think whoever is behind this will leave me alone?" He didn't answer.

"Then I don't have much choice, do I?"

"In my opinion? No." He paused, examining her. "Do you trust me?"

"I don't know." He'd certainly behaved as if he had her best interests at heart, but she was swimming in murky waters and he could be one of the circling sharks. "Why?"

"I still have friends on the Atlanta PD. I'd like to have them run the DNA we sent off to the lab against a couple of databases. It wouldn't be official — without the proper chain of custody it couldn't be — but whatever is going on, I can't shake the feeling it has something to do with your heritage, yours and Nikki's. And if there are two of you, maybe there are more."

She sat on the edge of the bed and dropped her head into her hands. Why had she started this? There had been nothing wrong with her childhood. Her mother's death had hurt, but her father had done everything in his power to make sure she never felt deprived. So why had she thrown it all away just because of a photograph? Why couldn't she have let it go?

"I don't see how you expect it to help, but how could it hurt?"

"Again, that depends on how much you can accept."

"Worried about me?" She aimed for flippancy but missed the mark, and when he put one long, calloused finger under her chin and forced her eyes to meet his, she trembled under the impact of the impenetrable darkness of his gaze.

"Yeah. I'm worried. I don't need fingerprints to tell me Nikki's dead. And I don't need DNA to tell me you're related to her." He stepped out of the room and returned with a pad and pen from the desk in the living room. "I'm going to write a note to Michel asking him to add Vince's information — that's my partner — to the DNA request. It has to come from him. If that's okay with you, you can sign the note and I'll drop it by the station for Michel."

He scribbled the information onto the paper, then held it out to her. After a brief hesitation, she took it and signed. *In for a penny, in for a pound.* She handed it back to him, and he ripped off the top sheet, folded it in quarters, and jammed it into the back pocket of his jeans.

"Do you want me to stay for the rest of the night?"

There was a loaded question if ever she'd heard one, but he didn't seem to notice the double entendre.

"Thanks, but I'll be fine. As you say, the objective is to get me to leave, not draw attention to me with violence."

He nodded. "If you give me your keys, I'll get your car returned to the rental company."

Damn, she'd completely forgotten she'd left the little Toyota in the lot in Marigot.

"That would be great. I got it from Budget at the airport." She dug out the keys and handed them over. "It'll save me the hassle of returning it before the flight, too."

"Call me if you need a ride."

"Oh, no, thanks, I'll just take a cab."

"Let me give you my number anyway." He held out a hand and she gave him her cell. He punched in his number quickly and passed it back. "I put myself at speed dial three. Call if anything comes up."

"I will. Mac . . . thanks." Why did she suddenly feel like a teenager after a prom date, unable to make up her mind about what kind of send-off she wanted to give her escort? This was not a man she wanted anything to do with on a personal level, and she'd do well to remember it. She walked with him through the kitchen to the back door.

"I'll be in touch," he said, before fading into the swaying shadows of the back garden. She heard the iron gate creak open, then swing shut, and she closed and locked the door against the night.

THE EARLIEST FLIGHT Callie could get a guaranteed seat on didn't leave until three in the afternoon, but she'd put herself on a standby list for one at eleven, so at nine thirty the next morning she plunked herself and her bags into a seat in the snack area at Princess Juliana airport, with a cup of abominable coffee, and focused blearily on CNN playing on the overhead television. The perky, dark-haired anchorwoman shook her head sorrowfully as she informed viewers that incidences of animal cruelty were on the rise in the United States. In exactly the same tone, she went on to read a list of fourteen new children's toys that had been recalled because they contained lead paint.

"Tell me something I don't know," Callie muttered.

"After the break," the announcer said, as if in reply, "our own Christina Sargo has a live interview with millionaire hotelier John Lewis, whose sister, Nicole, disappeared eleven days ago. Police on the tiny Caribbean island of St. Martin, where the Lewises run the world-famous Paradis de la Mer resort, believe they have found Ms. Lewis's body. After the interview, we'll be talking to a forensics expert about how bodies are identified when traditional methods cannot be employed."

A live interview? When had he arranged that? Callie tapped her foot and shredded her napkin as the commercials went on and on.

John looked even worse, more disheveled than he had the night before, and Callie wondered whether he'd slept at all. She'd expected a videophone interview, but the news station had apparently sprung for a flight, because Ms. Sargo sat opposite John in the business office of the Paradis. She opened with a few remarks for anyone who hadn't heard about the missing heiress, then segued into the actual interview with a few softball questions. Callie was ready to scream before the reporter got around to asking the question she wanted answered.

"The police can't conclusively determine the woman they found on Plum Bay Beach to be your sister. Why are you so certain it's her?"

"She was wearing Nicole's ring. The police have to take into account that someone might have stolen it or Nicole could have sold it or given it away. But that ring was Ava's, and Ava had little hands. In the summer, Nicole couldn't get it off her finger. She talked about having it resized, but she was afraid she'd lose it when the weather turned cold if it became too loose."

"But the police don't consider that strong enough evidence of her identity?"

"No. It's not their fault. Under normal circumstances, I'd be with them one hundred percent, too, because you don't want people being misidentified. But . . ."

"But?"

"Well, until the police confirm that the woman they found is my sister, they don't have any reason to investigate her disappearance as a murder. So her killer has more time to cover his tracks."

"Do you think he deliberately obscured her identity, then?"

"I doubt he expected her to be found at all. The police say there are indications she may have been weighed down, had something tied around her ankle." He shook his head. "My sister was a bit of a wild child. I'm ashamed to admit it, but when she first disappeared, even I didn't consider anything serious might have happened. The man who murdered her more than likely hoped to take advantage of that as long as no body was recovered."

Mac. John won't say his name, but he has to mean Mac.

Only Nicole's husband would benefit from her being believed alive. He'd admitted to growing up poor. Depending on Nicole's will, he'd either become immensely wealthy upon her death—which would put him squarely in the police spotlight—or he would go right back to having nothing. Either way, he was better off if people thought Nikki had run out on him.

The sound of her own name over the loudspeaker jerked Callie's attention back to her surroundings. She physically shook her head to clear it, and the airline again paged her to the gate for the early flight to New York. She looked down at the suitcase by her feet, then back up at the television, where the anchorwoman was promising further details the moment they were released. Could she really go home now? If Mac were arrested, he'd hardly be in a position to call her with the DNA results. Would the gendarmes call? She had no experience with the French legal system, but she was sure Mac's former partner wouldn't bother to inform her.

Mac would tell her to go home. Hell, he *had* told her to do so more than once. But she'd set out to find out who she was, and going home felt an awful lot like giving up. Someone, presumably someone in St. Martin, wanted her gone, and whoever it was had long-enough reach to have her house in New York broken into. So going home wouldn't make her safer.

They called her name over the public address system again. *Make up your mind, Callie. Stay or go.* But it wasn't really a choice. All that waited for her at home were insurance forms and hassles beyond measure. Erin could check to be sure nothing else had been taken, and the insurance company could wait until she went back. She'd phone and explain the situation.

And then there was Mac. Didn't she owe it to him to stay, to be sure he was okay? He'd helped her out, looked after her.

She called Erin and left a message, then walked to the ticketing area and switched her flight home back to its original date. The man behind the Budget rental counter was a little confused by the fact that she wanted to rent another car when her friend had dropped her first one off only two hours before, but he was accommodating. Doubtless he'd be telling his friends about the "crazy American woman" for weeks.

Instead of returning to the Paradis, however, Callie followed the directions her friend Marlon had given her to get to the Princess Port de Plaisance, where he had his time-share.

"The French side is beaches and bistros," he had explained, "and the Dutch side is time-shares, casinos, and bargain shopping. Most of the Dutch hotels don't have great beachfront property—unless you count some so close to the airport the beach has warnings about the blast from departing jets causing injury—but who cares? The hotel's a place to sleep. And they have a breakfast spot at the Princess called Zee Best that's to die for, which is more than most of the time-share resorts boast."

Callie noted the differences between the Princess and the Paradis immediately. Instead of a subtle, easily overlooked stone marker, a huge sign surrounded by flashing bulbs announced the presence of a casino, a beauty salon, and a spa. No guard asked for her identification. In fact, the guardhouse stood empty, the barrier raised to allow free entry and exit, which made sense given that casino patrons would likely go elsewhere if they had to show ID to get onto the property. The grounds were neatly tended but without the lush excess that characterized the Paradis.

The man behind the reservations counter took her day-late arrival in stride but told her she would still have to leave on Sunday. He called a bellman, explaining that Marlon's unit was in building twelve, quite some distance away. Neither the clerk nor the bellman introduced themselves, nor did they wear name tags. Not unusual in her experience, but so removed from what she'd found at the Paradis that Callie forced the issue by holding out a hand to the young bellman as she climbed aboard the golf cart onto which he'd loaded her suitcase.

"Hi," she said. "I'm Callie."

"Baptiste," he replied. "Is this your first time staying with us?"

"Yes, it is. I'm borrowing a friend's week."

Baptiste nodded. "You will come back. Everyone does." They rounded the building and Callie could see why. Port de Plaisance, too, had suffered at the hands of Hurricane Luis and owners more interested in taking insurance pay-outs for themselves than revitalizing their properties. In fact, Marlon had bought his week during the five years the dec-imated resort had been shut down after the hurricane. The new owner, a man Marlon referred to only as "the Turk," had bought the property for the marina and the casino and had invested heavily in renovating those.

The marina investment had certainly paid off. Every slip was filled with graceful boats ranging in size from two-seater fishing boats with high-end fishing rigs to full-on yachts.

The time-share buildings were on an oval island, bor-dered by the marina on one side and Simpson Bay Lagoon on the other, and many of them appeared to be undergo-ing extensive renovation. A guard stood to the side of the little bridge leading to the island and wrote down the room number Baptiste gave him before lifting the barrier to allow them across. Token security at best. Building twelve stood almost at the tip of the residential island, and Marlon's third-floor suite had a view of the entire marina as well as across the lagoon to Simpson Bay and out to the sea. It also had a full kitchen, two bedrooms with private baths and a big living area. So maybe it wasn't the Paradis, but Callie could definitely see spending one week a year at the Princess. Maybe once she got back to her normal life, she should consider a piece, or a series of pieces, on time-shares.

She put away her clothes, then packed a few things into her satchel to take with her to Marigot, where she planned to sit at one of the restaurants and figure out her next move. She opened the door to leave and found Mac on the other side, hand raised as if to knock.

"What are you doing here?"

"I should be the one asking that. You were supposed to fly home today."

"How did you find out I hadn't?"

"I asked around about you when you first arrived. When you checked in here, Carl from the front desk called me." Mac sighed and rubbed a hand across his face, drawing Callie's eyes to the thick, black stubble shadowing his jaw. He appeared even more ragged than John had on television that morning. According to the time stamp on the rental company's papers, Mac had returned her car to the airport at 7:23, so if he hadn't been to bed, where had he gone after he'd left her at her bungalow the night before? "Look, I'm tired and hungry, so how about you let me buy you lunch and you can explain why you changed your mind about heading home."

He took her back to the marina in Marigot to eat. Waiters from every restaurant they passed on the boardwalk along the water stepped out to talk to Mac and introduce themselves to her. No wonder he had found her so effortlessly—he had connections. He took her to a spot next door to the one she'd chosen the night before, explaining that he liked it for both the food and the view. At first, she didn't understand, as all the bistros looked out over the water, but when the waiter gestured for them to take what she assumed must be Mac's "regular" table, his meaning became clear.

At the southeast corner of the U-shaped boardwalk, the restaurant offered no indoor seating, but Mac sat them with their backs to the small building housing the bar, the kitchen, and the restroom. From their vantage point they could watch all the comings and goings along the waterfront.

"This is where you were last night, how you found me."

He nodded. "Choosing tactically advantageous spots becomes second nature after a while. If you'd decided to go to Grand Case or Philipsburg for dinner, I'd have had to wait for someone to call me."

"Like they did today."

"Exactly." The waiter came over with menus and took their drink orders—coffee for Mac, diet soda for Callie—and the moment he left, Mac began questioning her.

"Why did you change your mind about leaving the island?"

She answered with a question of her own. "Did you see John on TV this morning?"

Mac grimaced. "Yeah. Slow news day in the US, I guess. And it didn't endear him to the gendarmes any. But why does it make any difference to you?"

"It's true what he said about how she'd been anchored to something?"

"Yeah. The gendarmes think whoever tied her used twine or something and didn't realize how tight they would have to tie it for her not to . . . You don't want to hear this."

"Just say it."

"You tend to think of a body bloating in the water. And it does. But once that happens, the skin, the flesh become loose, tearable. Hers tore and she came . . . unmoored. Floated."

The waiter came back with their drinks, but Mac sent him away without ordering food.

"Do you think her murderer wanted her to stay hidden?"

"It's not as black and white as it sounds. The guy's smart enough to kill a woman and get her out into the water without anyone noticing. So we can't afford to consider him an idiot. But she washed up in Plum Bay. Do you know how the island is shaped?" "Not really, but I have a map." She dug through her purse and pulled it out, along with a ballpoint pen.

"Okay." He took the map of the heart-shaped island and circled a spot at the top left, almost due west of the marina where they sat. "That's Plum Bay. Sticks out into the middle of the Caribbean, so on the face of it you'd think it wasn't such an unlikely spot for a body to wash ashore. But this island isn't just half-French and half-Dutch; it's half-Caribbean and half-Atlantic. Why would you dump a body you were trying to hide into the Caribbean, where it's likely to get far less damaged, and where people scuba dive all over the place, when the Atlantic is just around the other side of the island? There would be some logic to it if you believed Nikki had been killed at the Paradis, because Plum Bay is the closest publicly accessible beach. But it didn't go down that way. For all the privacy the Paradis offers, no one takes one of the boats from there without someone noticing."

"Except you or John. Which is why the police suspect one or both of you."

"Pretty much."

"Okay, then, what if there was no boat? The beach at the Paradis has cliffs above it. What about if someone lured her up there and killed her, then tossed her over?" Even as she asked, she marveled at her own ability to be dispassionate. She should have been sickened, and maybe she would be. Later. When she had time to think things over. But right now, she craved knowledge, information to help her find her footing in the landscape that had begun to shift the moment she first found her father's picture.

"The gendarmes went over that area when Nikki first disappeared. So did I." Mac's coldness matched hers. She could almost rationalize his lack of emotion—he'd been a cop, after all—but he was talking about his wife, and his detached tone gave her chills. "There aren't any signs of a struggle, and he'd have to give her a hell of a push to get her far enough out to actually hit deep water. Plus, the body didn't appear damaged enough to have tumbled like that. No, he took her body out in a boat, probably no more than a few miles, and dumped her over the side."

"Why?"

"The only thing that makes sense to me is that he wanted her found. He tied her loosely so she'd . . . decay . . . for a while, but left her close enough to shore that the current wouldn't sweep her out to sea entirely when the ropes came off."

Okay, that officially freaked her out despite her preoccupation with her own situation. "That's unthinkable."

"To you, to me, to any normal person, yeah." He seemed about to say more, but the ringing of his cell phone, sitting on the table between them, cut him off.

CHAPTER FIVE

MAC GLANCED DOWN at the phone's display, the caller ID showing his partner's personal number. Mac had dropped the note Callie had signed the night before at the station first thing that morning, and, apparently, Michel had already contacted the lab about adding Vince's name to the report request. Whatever had turned up, it wouldn't be good. If Callie's DNA hadn't rung any bells, Vince would just have e-mailed him an aggravated note about wasting department time and resources.

"What the hell have you stepped in this time, Brody?" Vince didn't bother with a greeting.

"Why don't you tell me?"

"You want me to tell you? I'll tell you. The captain wants your ass back in Georgia, pronto. He's pissed. Your friend the French cop apparently chose to go the paternity-test route for quick results on the DNA, so we got the profile you told me about this morning rather than tomorrow. We ran your little request about an hour ago, and it brought the fucking feds down on us."

The feds? He looked over at Callie, whose eyes were fixed on him as she tried to hear what his partner was saying. "Shit," Mac said into the phone. "What do they want?"

"They want to know why we're running DNA belonging to someone who has three dead half sisters, possibly victims of a serial killer, and a half brother in jail for rape."

"Whoa. Back up. That's all one family?"

"No. It's three families, but all parties have the same father. Don't ask how, since no one is owning up to affairs or adoption. Girls one and two were thirty-five-year-old fraternal twin sisters, both disappeared from Virginia almost three months ago, presumed dead. Their DNA came from Missing Persons. Dead girl three's body was found five weeks back in an abandoned rental car in DC. Vehicle rented with phony ID needless to say. No ID on the body. Plenty of blood, though, so they ran her through the databases. No complete matches, but the vehicle had been set on fire, too, so they went for partial matches as well, and Missing Persons came back with the twins — same paternity. Running paternity, CODIS found someone, too, another half sibling: Ed Steele. You might recognize his father: the televangelist named Ephraim Steele, who went down for embezzling twenty years or so ago.

"Anyway, Ed's a real piece of work. Been in prison in Florida for five years so far. He was a federal case — rapes in three states — so pinging his DNA brought them back. Plus, dead girl three was eventually identified as Robin Cory, who has international ties, which fucks the whole thing up even worse. And then there's your girl. Feds want to know who she is and where they can find her. Since I don't happen to have that information, life's not too pleasant around here at the moment."

"The report Michel sent, does it show just one profile, or two?"

"Just one. There's a notation at the bottom that says 'no match to second sample,' and indicates that further tests will be done, but we didn't get anything on another sample."

What the hell? "No match?"

"That's what I said."

"But he only called for a straight paternity test."

"Yeah. Looks like he went for speed, with full profile to

follow." Mac would probably have taken the same route. After all, no one knew who Nikki's father was, which made him the most likely point of connection between her and Callie. And whatever the genetic testing might show, Mac refused to believe the connection didn't exist. Could that possibly mean the dead woman wasn't Nikki? But then how did she get hold of Nikki's ring?

"Thanks, Vince. I'll get back to you."

"Like hell! You gotta give me something. I can't stall these guys forever. I'm going to have to tell them how my name happened to end up on a DNA request from a French cop on a minuscule Caribbean island. Especially since not one of the connected cases come under our jurisdiction."

"Do it. Give them my name and Michel's, but leave Callie's out of it."

"Who?" He could practically hear his former partner's smirk. "You mean Subject AXP8834201? The unnamed female whose saliva the French cop sent in for testing?"

"Yeah. Her. Michel will give her up soon enough, but I need some time to stash her. Tell the chief I'm sorry about the feds."

"You got it. Listen, I sent all the files to your e-mail address. Don't know that they'll help much, and if it comes back on me I'll fucking kill you. But I figure you need all the help you can get. Keep in touch."

"Thanks. Will do." Mac snapped the phone shut and looked at Callie, who was watching him expectantly.

"I'll be right back," he said. "I have to run down the street to the Internet café and print out some e-mails my partner in Atlanta sent me."

"What did he say? I heard something about a family? And 'no match'—does that mean between me and Nicole?"

"Not now, okay? Let me get the files, and we can go over them together." For a moment he thought she would insist on accompanying him to the Internet café, but at last she let him go. On his way out, he stopped and asked their waiter to bring them a couple of pizzas.

Vince had sent reams of paperwork. All the crimes had taken place in urban areas with well-computerized police departments, so he'd been able to get whole case files transferred to Atlanta, much of which he'd copied and pasted into e-mail-ready documents. He'd also included links to publicly accessible newspaper articles. Somehow, the feds had kept the blood relationship between the three cases out of the press—Mac figured that wouldn't last long—but the three women had been high-profile victims, and Ed Steele, the serial rapist, had garnered more than a few inches of newsprint himself. By the time Mac had finished printing everything, he had an inch-thick stack of paper.

He cut through one of the many alleys leading from Rue de la Liberté to the marina, then took a step back out of sight when he realized Callie was no longer alone at the table.

CALLIE HOPED MAC'S errand would keep him away until John left, but doubted she'd be so lucky, especially since John didn't seem in any rush to go. He claimed he was just having lunch, getting away from the hotel, where he felt scrutinized at every turn, but his appearance on the heels of Mac's departure raised the hairs at the back of her neck. And his surprise at seeing her in town rang false. If Mac had connections who told him she was there, surely John had even more. But she didn't call him on it. If he turned out to be the keeper of her family's secrets, she needed him on her side.

"The interview probably wasn't the smartest thing I've ever done," he admitted ruefully as she scanned the boardwalk. "But I felt helpless. I'm in an odd position here on the island. Nicole and I inherited the hotel, which is a good chunk of real estate, but I'm not a French citizen. Nicole is—was—but my father and Ava didn't move here until I was eleven. I had to learn French as a foreign language, and it shows. Even though I've lived here most of my life, I'm not considered a native. I'm still an American, an outsider, and since they're going to treat me that way no matter what I do, I decided I might as well take advantage of the press contacts I've made over the years. Let the American media put a bit of pressure on and see what happens."

He paused, waiting for her reaction, and she couldn't prevent herself from asking. "The other day you as much as said you believed Mac had killed her. Is that still the case?"

"The police thought he did. Or at least, that's what I assumed from their visit, until you told me about all the other gossip. For myself, I don't know what to think. Dad and Ava kept the Paradis so private they never needed much in the way of security. But the resort never operated at capacity, either, and didn't bring in the kind of money Nicole and I needed for the modernization we envisioned. I worried the old system wouldn't suffice once Nicole and I got the place running the way it should, though, and Dad's old head of security had no tech savvy at all. So when Nicole picked Brody up one night and brought him home, he seemed like the answer to a prayer. Five months later, they got married, and three months after that, she disappeared. What would you think?"

"Tough call." But she could appreciate John's point.

"Besides," he continued, "there's the trust."

"Trust?"

He rubbed his head. "French inheritance law is a mess, and my father wasn't as careful as he should have been about his assets. But the one thing he did protect was the hotel. Nicole didn't inherit her portion of it outright. It's in trust until her thirty-fifth birthday. My father didn't have a great deal of respect for women's financial acumen, I'm afraid. And since she died before thirty-five, her half of the resort and the vast majority of her personal fortune, which she also inherited from my father, reverts back to the trust. Despite the fact that she died intestate, it doesn't, in fact, go to her husband because it was never hers to will away. So, you see, Brody would have good reason to hide the fact that she was dead. Nobody else would."

She did see. But Mac didn't seem the kind of guy who put a whole lot of emphasis on material goods. She doubted he'd marry for money, let alone kill for it.

"Who controls the trust?"

"There are three trustees. My father made me a full partner in the resort when I turned thirty, so my half of the property isn't in a trust. I'm the primary trustee on Nicole's portion, along with my father's old medical partners, and since she died before it was dissolved, the whole resort will come to me, which is another reason the police suspect me of having something to do with her death. But it's ridiculous. The hotel is doing wonderfully, and being a trustee meant I had control over the money anyway. Nicole never disagreed with my proposals. I had the degrees; she was content to let me run the place. So I had no reason to want to hurt her."

The waiter approached. "Madame," he said, after nodding briefly to John, "your friend ordered some pizzas before he left. Shall I bring them now, or wait for him to return?"

"Why don't you wait. In the meantime, do you think I could get another soda?"

"But of course." With a little half bow, he moved away toward the entrance, where a group of six waited to be seated.

"I didn't realize you were here with someone." John studied her. "Damn. It's Brody, isn't it? He's why you stayed."

"No. I meant what I said earlier: I decided against going home because there's nothing there that can't wait. I have Marlon's time-share week, which would be a shame to waste, and I promised *Travel/Style* an article. Besides, I want to know what Detective — is it Detective? Or do the gendarmes use some other term? I want to know what Vichy discovers about any relationship I might have to Nicole. Assuming, that is, the woman he found on Plum Bay is your sister."

John pushed back his chair and rose. "Right. Of course that's what's keeping you here. Just do me a favor and be careful with Brody. Whatever the DNA test shows, when I look at you I can't help being reminded of Nicole. She was rich and beautiful and very much alive. Now, she's not. She trusted the wrong person somewhere along the line, and it got her killed."

John started to walk away, but paused after a few steps and returned. "I realize I'm coming on a bit strong, and I apologize. If you find yourself in a jam, I hope you'll remember I have your best interests at heart and call me. You have my number."

"I will," Callie promised. She watched him stride down the boardwalk and caught the movement when Mac stepped out of a passageway only seconds after John had passed it. John, moving quickly, didn't notice. Mac watched until he came to the end of the marina and turned for the parking lot; then he headed back to the restaurant.

When he reached their table, Mac dropped a stack of papers on it, and Callie was surprised to recognize the face smiling out of the top sheet. "That's Robin Cory. Her murder was still at the top of the news in Scotland when I was there last week. What does she have to do with this?"

"You know her?"

"No, but her blue-blood, American mother married a blue-collar Scot, sort of a reverse Princess Diana thing, and Robin is a Scottish citizen. Or she was. She was killed, what, a month ago in DC? I went over to Scotland to review a company that does hiking and camping vacations before I came here, and the story of Robin's murder was inescapable."

"She's your sister."

"What?" Callie's mind spun in a half dozen directions. First, a possible relationship to Nicole Lewis, now one to Robin Cory. Both rich, well connected, and dead. She narrowed her eyes at Mac, willing him to continue.

"To be more precise," he said, "she's your half sister." He flipped through the sheaf of papers and found another photograph, this one clearly a publicity shot of two women accepting some kind of award. "Deborah and Diane Masters also share your blood." Another picture, a mug shot this time. "As does Ed Steele."

"What do you mean, they share my blood?"

"According to the DNA lab, all of you have the same father."

"You're lying." But he wasn't. She could see the truth on his face. "How is that possible?"

"Let's take it slowly. You have a pad?" She pulled her notebook from her bag and passed it across the table. He sifted through the papers for a few minutes, making notes. The waiter stopped by and laid two steaming pizzas on the table, along with another soda for Callie. When he departed, Mac pushed the pad back toward her.

"Ed Steele is the youngest. Robin was born in April of '80, Deborah and Diane four months later. Then you. Steele was born January of '88, so your mother would have been pregnant with you when he was conceived."

"My father didn't have an affair with Ed Steele's mother any more than he did with Nikki's. Speaking of which, did I understand your partner to say I wasn't related to her?"

"He said the test showed you didn't share paternity with whoever washed up on Plum Bay Beach."

"I thought you were certain it was Nikki?"

"John is. I'm certain Nikki's dead—I agree with him on that—so until all this came to light, it made sense that the body the gendarmes found was hers. Now, things have changed."

"How so?"

"Maybe whoever killed her didn't want her connected to the rest of these cases, connected to you. So he gave us another body, someone whose DNA wouldn't ring any bells.

"That's insane."

"Is it? More insane than the fact that whoever fathered you also fathered three, possibly four, murdered women and a convicted rapist?"

"I told you, my father didn't stray even once, let alone multiple times."

"It's the most logical explanation."

"Only because you didn't know him, didn't see him with my mother."

"Which is the same thing you're going to say when I broach the possibility that Ephraim Steele might be your father, the father of all of you."

A memory pushed forward. She'd been six or seven at the time, old enough to be interested in her parents' conversation, but not mature enough to understand it. Ephraim Steele had been on the television, his ministry under investigation, and her mother had practically spat, calling him a venial, hypocritical ass. Her tone, as much as the words themselves, had caught Callie's attention; Sharon Pearson rarely had a negative word for anyone.

"My mother absolutely did not have an affair with Steele, but I think she knew him. Her family is Jewish, and as I recall, the Steeles were, too, until Ephraim climbed aboard the televangelist money train, changed his name from Steinmetz to Steele, and became a Pentacostal."

"It's possible the sex wasn't consensual."

Callie's skin went cold, almost numb. "You think Ed Steele learned to be a sexual predator — or inherited the desire — from his father?" Was such a thing even possible?

"His parents are dead, so we have no way of knowing that Ephraim was his biological father." Mac reached across the table and unfolded her fingers that had clenched into fists. "According to the case file, Robin Cory's mother insists she wasn't assaulted — the FBI got to that question fairly quickly when the blood relationships came to light — but she can't, or won't, explain Robin's genetic abnormality. Will Cory is also mum on the subject. Frank Masters, Deborah and Diane's father, claims to have had no idea the women weren't his daughters, and says that if his wife was raped thirty years ago, he never knew about it."

"Thirty years ago the stigma would have been intolerable." Callie let the idea sink in. Why would all these women have kept the children conceived through violence? The joy on her mother's face in the photograph was real — would she feel that for a child of rape? But what other explanation could there be? Her father had not had affairs. They might have lied to her about everything else in her life, but nothing could convince her that her parents' love had not been deep and true.

"Sexual assault would explain a lot of the inconsistencies. If my father was out of the country nine months before my real birthday, they could have fudged the date to protect my mother's name."

"It's possible."

"But you don't think that's the answer."

"I don't think it's enough. What kind of rapist follows his victims for more than thirty years, then one day decides to go out and kill his own offspring?"

"The Steeles, the Corys, my parents . . . We don't travel in the same circles, but the families are all well off. Are the Masterses?" "Oil money going back generations. And if we include Nikki, we have another family in the same class." Callie considered the circumstances that might have brought one man into the lives of all the families whose files lay before her. "These weren't women he could have snatched off the street. He had to be part of their circles."

"That's my take on it, yeah."

"He knows us. That's how he's kept track all these years."

"Possible. But none of your families are low profile, and since the advent of Google Alerts and other Internet technologies, it's become much easier to keep an eye on someone. So maybe he only started looking for you recently."

"But the murders still don't make sense. They attracted attention, brought our genetic peculiarities to light."

"Ed Steele's DNA went into the system after the first rape, close to seven years ago. His conviction, which publicly and irrevocably linked his name to that DNA, came down just over five years ago. Until then, our boy had nothing to worry about. Maybe he didn't kill the Masters women at all. But if he's been keeping tabs on his progeny, he's got to have realized the minute the cops ran Debbie and Diane, they'd find the connection to Steele."

"And he panicked? Killed Robin Cory and Nikki? And then another woman to hide the fact that Nikki's death was tied to the others?"

"It's a theory."

"But why?"

"Not a clue. But I have to ask why your father hid that picture, didn't want anyone to know he'd stayed at the Paradis. I wonder whether Ephraim Steele—under either of his names—vacationed with the Lewises. The computerized records only go back into the mid-nineties. That's what I looked at when you first showed up, and there was no record of your family. But there are older records, paper, in the file cabinets. Part of being a good hotelier is tracking your clients' tastes and preferences."

"You think they go back that far? Thirty years?"

"Won't know until I get a look."

"But you don't work there anymore."

"Nope. But no one would think twice about me being on the grounds. It's not hard to bypass the gate on foot if you know where to go and don't mind a few nettles."

"John would have a fit if he saw you."

"I was hoping you'd give me a hand with that. Invite the guy to dinner. Tell him it's for the magazine, that you want to go to Le Tastevin or one of the other Grand Case restaurants so you can review it. Have a few glasses of wine; keep him off the property as long as possible. Hell, show him the picture. The killer knows you have it, so you're not tipping your hand even if Lewis is involved somehow, or lets slip to someone who is. Ask him if he ever remembers meeting your parents."

He meant to break into the hotel? And make her an accessory? Somehow, she hadn't envisioned criminal activities when she set out to discover the truth behind the photograph. *Naïve, Callie. Very naïve.* "Why can't I just ask him to let me look at the files?"

"Because he might not agree, and then he'd be on guard, which would make it considerably more difficult to get a peek inside."

"John was just a kid when the rest of us were conceived. You can't think he has anything to do with these murders."

"He was a teenager. But no, I don't think he's the root of the problem. There's a distinct possibility the Paradis is involved, though, and the Lewis family fortune—John's fortune—is tied to the resort. His first instinct, for better or worse, will be to protect it."

"Then why should I ask him about the picture?"

"I didn't say you had to believe what he told you. Just watch his reaction. Or don't." Mac shrugged. "See where the conversation leads."

"And you'll do the rest?"

"I know what to look for. And I know the property." But he didn't meet her eyes. What was he planning to do while she kept John busy?

CHAPTER SIX

JOHN HAD ACCEPTED Callie's invitation to dinner, though he'd evinced no small surprise at it. She'd had to bring up his offer of help and tell him she needed assistance only he could provide before the suspicion left his voice. Although she'd made it clear the dinner was about business and information, not romance, he insisted on picking her up, and they met in the lobby of the Princess Port de Plaisance at seven that night.

"I wish you'd come back to the Paradis," John groused as they walked to his Fiat. "This place is so . . . touristy."

Callie couldn't help laughing. "I am a tourist, John. You're the one who lives here." She thought about the role the Paradis might have played in her past and sobered. "Besides, once you see the thing I want to talk to you about, you'll understand why I'm not comfortable at the Paradis."

John drove fast, whipping the little car around curves Callie would never have dreamt of taking without brakes, though even he had to slow down going through the more populated areas. Like most islands—indeed, like most places with economies based on tourism, whether islands or not— the contrast between rich and poor areas was striking, but unlike some spots Callie had visited, there seemed little antagonism on either side. As they drove along the back side of the marina, kids on bikes wove in and out of traffic, popping wheelies and tossing objects back and forth between them. Adults hung out on the sidewalks, drinking and eating barbeque from miniscule storefront bars. Callie laughed aloud at the sign for one such spot, called Skanki Shampoo Bar and Restaurant. She made John stop the car so she could take a quick cell phone picture.

John took the same route she'd used to get to Calmos Café to get to Le Tastevin, but once there the similarities ended. Le Tastevin was anything but casual. The intimate restaurant faced out over the ocean, white tablecloths covered the tables, and flickering candles provided romantic ambiance. If Callie really had come to write an article, this was a spot she'd be reviewing, though she would rather be there on an actual date.

John waited until the waiter had taken their orders and brought them a bottle of white wine and a tiny amuse-bouche of cold carrot soup before asking the reason for her invitation.

She withdrew the photo from her purse and passed it across the table to him. "You recognize the spot?"

"Of course." He studied the picture in the flickering candle-light, then flipped it over, read the inscription, and frowned. "I thought your birthday was in October?"

"That's what my birth certificate says, so you can understand why the photo made me curious. I found it among my father's things after he died, and made my reservation at the Paradis as soon as I figured out where it had been taken. Were you living at the hotel in those days?"

"During the summer, yes, but this says it was taken in September. I would have been in boarding school. Massachusetts. Both my father and Ava enjoyed the island lifestyle, but they didn't want their children educated here. I was eleven when they bought the Paradis, and I stayed in the States with my mother's sister until I could go to boarding school at the beginning of eighth grade. With Nicole, they went for tutors and homeschooling until she was thirteen, at which point she went to boarding school, too, but in France."

"That must have been difficult for you."

"Not really. My school friends were insanely jealous of my life here, and came to visit frequently during vacations. I went to Cornell for college, to the School of Hotel Administration, so it was actually more difficult to come home after that when my father was still in charge and refused to modernize or expand."

"Do you remember any of the people who stayed here in those days?"

"Not really. A couple big-name tennis stars who impressed the hell out of me." He smiled. "I was always a nerd, never had much coordination. I don't remember your mother, if that's what you mean."

"No, I was thinking of a television preacher named Ephraim Steele."

"Steele . . . The name sounds very familiar. Wait, didn't he go to prison for embezzlement or something in the late eighties?"

"He was about to, but he had a heart attack."

"That's right. I don't think he ever stayed at the Paradis, but I could check for you. Does he have something to do with this?"

"Maybe," she hedged. "My mother knew him."

"What makes you think he stayed with us?"

"Nothing, really. But he was the most famous of all my parents' acquaintances, and back in the day the Paradis mostly hosted celebrities. I wondered how my parents ended up on your beach, and thought they might have been guests of the reverend's." She'd practiced the lie while she dressed for dinner, and was proud of how smoothly it came out.

John laughed. "Yes, I am afraid my father was a bit of a name-dropper. He liked to surround himself with famous movie stars, politicians, athletes. It made him feel important.

You should see all the photographs we have of him with this politician, that talk show host. I'll go through them—if Steele stayed at the Paradis, we'll have photos."

"Steele's real name was Steinmetz. I doubt he'd have been using it, but if he wanted to remain anonymous, he might have."

"I'll check them both," John promised. "But tell me, why do you think your parents got you a false birth certificate? If, indeed, this is you in the picture." He passed it back to her, and she slid it into the zippered compartment inside her bag.

"I don't know. I'm not sure I care, really." Sweat popped out along her hairline, and she took a long sip of water before continuing. "It was all such a long time ago. I was curious, and I'm a travel writer, so coming to the Paradis made sense."

"But staying at the hotel doesn't?"

"As I said, whatever my parents were doing here, it was thirty years ago. I'm hardly going to find traces of them now. And it's a little weird, staying there without knowing why. Port de Plaisance wasn't built back then; there aren't any ghosts hanging around."

The waiter arrived with bowls of lobster bisque, and by unspoken agreement Callie and John kept the conversation light as they ate, steering clear of anything involving either his family or hers. Over cappuccino, however, John returned to the subject of the mysterious picture.

"If you'd like," he offered, "we can go back to my place for a couple of hours and go through some of my father's scrapbooks. We hung the framed photos at the hotel, but Ava clipped every article written about either herself, my father, or the Paradis, and put them in big albums at my house, along with hundreds of photographs of parties and events we had at the Paradis through the years."

Callie didn't have to fake the enthusiasm of her response. "What a wonderful invitation. But I always assumed you lived at the hotel. In retrospect, that seems silly."

"Not silly at all. In fact, both my house and Nicole's are on property owned by the corporation set up to run the hotel, so technically I suppose we do live there. But we're down the road a little ways, not on the beach. From home to the hotel is about a ten-minute walk for me, so I am close enough to deal with emergencies, but not so close people assume I'm available for every little thing."

"Sounds perfect."

"It is. You'll see."

LEWIS'S SECURITY HAD been pathetically easy to bypass. Mac had arranged for the new system's installation at the same time as he'd updated the ones at the resort and at the house he and Nikki shared, and John had never bothered to change the original code. Sloppy.

The original house had been built in the 1940s, the property annexed to the hotel by the Charbonnets in 1952. Mark and Ava Lewis had demolished most of the place, leaving only the large, farm-style kitchen. Nikki, who couldn't tell a bell pepper from a serrano, raved about the AGA stove and granite countertops and had imitated the look on a smaller scale for her own house. After the doctor's death his wife had taken a suite at the hotel and left the house, and its fabulous kitchen, to John.

Ava had traveled extensively, even more so after her husband's death, so the move made sense for her, but the first time Mac and Nikki had visited, he'd been shocked by the manner in which John lived. The place was enormous. Four bedrooms upstairs; living room, kitchen, dining room, office, and sunporch downstairs. It was a house for a family, not for a bachelor.

In the master bedroom closet, Mac brushed aside silk and linen shirts in search of a hidden wall safe or other compartment. He'd considered going through the home office first, but years as a cop had taught him that people tended to keep their valuables in their bedrooms. He always advised women to keep their jewelry in a stockpot in their kitchen cabinet, but to the best of his knowledge none of them did so.

The master bedroom revealed no secrets, and the other three second-floor rooms took only seconds each to search, as they were practically empty. Leaving the main floor for last, Mac headed for the basement. The moonlight had provided enough illumination for most of his search, but as Mac descended the stairs from the kitchen, he flipped on his flashlight. The bright LED beam revealed a setup similar to the one in Nikki's house.

To the left of the stairs, a large, glass-doored wine refrigerator hummed quietly. A beer guy, Mac had never paid much attention to the one in his own cellar, though Nikki had always kept the top half, where the temperature was set for white wine, well stocked. John Lewis, from the look of his unit, preferred reds. Beside the refrigerator sat a chest freezer. Mac had periodically filled theirs with mahi, tuna, and wahoo after fishing trips with Travis, but he couldn't imagine John doing the same, so he checked to be certain the freezer wasn't being used to store information rather than food. The beam bounced off the shiny, quilted-metal interior. The freezer was utterly bare, the air stale. At some point, John had unplugged it but left the lid closed. Rookie mistake—the man probably cooked no more often than his sister.

Stacks of boxes lined the back wall, neatly handwritten labels proclaiming them Ava Lewis's belongings. Nikki had kept her mother's jewelry, and her clothing had gone to charity, but a moving service had evidently packed her suite and removed the knickknacks and personal items to John's house. She must have been a collector as well as a traveler, Mac thought, running the light over the labels. "Art Glass—French." "Art Glass—Czech." "Switzerland." "Spain." "Italy." The boxes might have been a good hiding place, but anything in them would be hard to access, and they didn't appear to have been opened and resealed at any time. A heavy layer of sandy dust coated them.

Mac climbed the stairs, scanned the kitchen briefly, then moved to the office. He'd just stepped inside when lights flashed through the window as a car pulled into the drive. He pushed the door almost closed, the same way he had found it, and crouched to the side of the window, watching as John's Fiat slowed to a stop and he and Callie stepped out.

What the hell was she doing?

The sidelights on either side of the front door opened directly onto the hall leading to the office, making it impossible for Mac to leave the room without being spotted, so he slipped into the office closet he knew from previous visits was used for coats. As the temperature hovered in the eighties even at night, John should have no reason to open the louvered door.

"That's odd," Mac heard John say when the front door opened. "I could have sworn I set the alarm."

"I do that all the time," Callie replied.

For a moment John didn't speak and Mac held his breath,

hoping he wouldn't insist on searching the house. Luckily, he seemed to shake off his suspicions. "I guess I'm not functioning at top performance these days. Can I get you something to drink? Coffee? Wine?"

"A glass of red wine would be lovely."

"Fine. I've got a very nice pinot noir; let me just run downstairs and get it. Make yourself at home."

John's departure for the basement gave Mac the perfect opportunity to escape, but he found himself reluctant to take it. Not only would he have to reveal his presence to Callie, but if he took off he would be leaving her alone in a place he instinctively considered enemy territory. And at some point, he'd accepted that whatever else she might be, Calliope Pearson wasn't his enemy.

So he resigned himself to staying and tried to find a comfortable position in the small closet. He'd been in tighter quarters more than once, but he didn't like not being able to see Callie and John. He was debating deserting the closet and taking a position behind the couch against the opposite wall when his quarry solved the problem for him.

"Most of the photographs are in the office," he heard John say. "Let's take the wine in there and see what we can find."

A minute later, Mac watched through the slatted door as John escorted Callie in, seated her on the couch, and set a glass of red wine on the coffee table in front of her. He stepped toward the closet and Mac tensed, heart speeding. But just before John touched the door, he turned aside and reached for something on one of the built-in bookshelves lining the wall next to the closet.

"She kept them by year," he said, and Mac had the peculiar sensation that John was speaking directly to him there in the closet. "She was away a lot in the early eighties because of the problems she and my father were having, but she still kept track of what was going on with the hotel. She came back right after Nicole was born."

John shifted back into Mac's view, carrying three heavy, leather-bound photo albums toward the couch. He laid them on the table and settled next to Callie. He lifted the top book and set it so it rested on Callie's lap, then shifted close to her so he could turn the pages. The move didn't appear to disturb Callie, but Mac found his hands clenching into fists. Lewis was too smooth by half.

"This book is from 1982. That's my father, there," John said, pointing to a photograph, "with Pierre Mauroy, Prime Minister of France at the time. We didn't get many American politicians, but we had more than a few European ones." He skipped a few pages. "This is the kind of thing you're probably looking for, though. This was one of the bigger parties I remember ever seeing at the hotel, and it was my first summer on the island. Greek oil tycoon weds American pop star; they took over the hotel. Actually, they took over the whole island, as I recall."

They looked through the pictures, Callie laughing aloud a couple of times over the fashions in evidence, but if she recognized any of the families involved in the murders, she gave no sign. They made it through the 1982 and 1983 albums, but when John reached for the 1984 one, Callie excused herself to use the bathroom. John rose, too, to show her the way, and to refill their wineglasses, and Mac wondered whether he could take the chance to slip out of the house, but decided it was too risky. Lewis had brought Callie; he'd have to take her back to her hotel, leaving the house unguarded, which would be far safer. Unless, of course, she decided to spend the night.

IN THE TINY half bathroom off the kitchen, Callie took a deep breath and let it out slowly. She'd laughed off Mac's assertion that John Lewis was interested in her sexually, but the past several hours had, infuriatingly, proved the man correct. There was no mistaking the signs. And although she was undeniably flattered, given the kind of women John had been photographed with over the years, she was also a bit creeped out. After all, people kept telling her how much she looked like his sister.

Or, according to him, not his sister. If he'd never grown up thinking of Nicole as a blood relation, maybe the attraction wasn't so out of bounds. But although he was handsome, urbane, and obviously intelligent, Callie felt not in the least drawn to him. And she had a sneaky feeling that the real problem for John was that he didn't show well compared to Mac Brody. Not the direction she particularly wanted her mind traveling, but she was too honest not to acknowledge the situation for what it was.

Should she cut the visit short? There had been nothing of importance in the albums they'd seen so far. Would staying to flip through more give John the wrong idea about her desires? But the longer she kept John occupied, the better chance Mac had of finding something in the Paradis files, if anything existed to be found. In the end, she resolved to compromise by suggesting skipping forward to the one from 1987, when her parents had visited the island.

When she returned to the office, John was reshelving the albums they'd looked through. As he reached for 1984, she stopped him.

"I'm getting tired. I thought we could just stick to the one that would show my parents, if they ever stayed at the hotel."

"Of course. I'm sorry."

"Don't be silly. I'm just fried—too much travel and excitement in the past couple of weeks. And good food, wine, the ocean . . . It's all catching up with me."

"Completely understandable. Let's just have a look at 1987, then." He led her back to the sofa and opened the last book. The first few pages were taken up with photographs of a New Year's Eve party held at the Paradis.

"Ava looks great. Nicole was born in September, you said? She must have worked out like a fiend to get back in shape for this party."

"That was Ava," John conceded. "All about appearances. The first construction my father did on the hotel when he got it was to put in the gym and spa building. He claimed he did it to attract athletes who needed to work out while on vacation, and it certainly served that purpose, but even though I was just a teenager, I knew he was building it for Ava."

John pointed out a woman holding an infant. The child held a tiny silver rattle up as if in victory. "There's Nicole. Life of the party and only three months old."

"She was born in France, right? How long did it take your parents to reconcile?"

"Oh, that happened as soon as she was born. Their separation kept Ava out of the public eye during her pregnancy, kept gossip to a minimum, but Ava came back to the island pretty much the minute Nicole was old enough to travel. A child, illegitimate or not, is far less provocative meat for the gossips than pregnancy."

"Your father must have loved Ava very much to take Nicole for his own."

"He probably did. But it's equally true that he had no patience with failure, and since my mother left him in the rudest way possible, he probably wasn't going to give up on his second marriage so easily. He wouldn't like the picture it painted of him."

"Your parents were divorced?" She'd assumed, when he said he'd lived with his aunt, that his mother had died.

"No. My mother committed suicide."

"Oh, no! I'm so sorry."

He shrugged off her condolences. "I was nine when she did it, and had lived with her mood swings and alcoholism for years; it made me sad, but it was also a relief. My aunt had a kid almost exactly my age, and she raised us together until my father sent for me."

He turned one of the pages in the photo album, dismissing the subject. "There's one of the tennis stars I told you about who stayed here that year."

"I can see how she might have made an impression!"

They flipped through the book, but Callie saw none of the families whose pictures she'd studied in the papers Mac had printed out. None of the Steeles, Masterses, Corys, or Pearsons had been guests at the Paradis, if the albums were anything to go by.

John drove Callie back to her hotel. She wanted him to leave her at the lobby, but he insisted on walking her across the little footbridge and all the way to her room. The security guard at the bridge noted her room number as he had earlier but once again did not ask for any kind of verification. At the door, John pressed a kiss to Callie's cheek and promised to call the next day once he'd been through the Paradis files to see whether her parents or the Steeles had been registered at the resort.

Callie bolted the door behind her, took a bottle of water out of the refrigerator, and stepped out onto the balcony overlooking the marina. Although exhausted, she was too keyed up to sleep. She hoped John didn't take it into his head to go check the files at the Paradis right away or that, if he did, Mac had had time to go through them and get out.

Boats bobbed in the bay, their lights reflecting off the black mirror of the water. Her father had loved the water and had always been happiest when his assignments took him to places near the ocean. He'd arranged for them to live on a boat during his tenure in Greece, cruising from island to island on weekends he didn't have to work and throughout her childhood, he'd maintained a house and a small fishing boat on Montauk Point, out at the end of Long Island. They'd gone on many a deep-sea fishing expedition together.

Leaving the sliding glass doors open to the night, Callie went back inside. She would close them before she went to bed, more to keep out mosquitoes than because she worried about anyone breaking into her third-floor suite, but the sounds and scents of the tropical evening drifting across the bay were soothing.

The bathroom — done up in shades of seashell pink, both marble and synthetic composites — verged on tacky, but the tub was huge and the water pressure strong. Callie twisted her hair up in a clip, turned the water almost all the way to hot, and stepped under the spray to work out some of the knots in her back and neck. She stood beneath the water until the whole bathroom had filled with steam, then wrapped herself in the robe the hotel had provided and opened the door.

If not for the smell, she might have fallen into the trap. But the door opened inward, and she took a deep breath to clear the steam from her lungs, so she noticed the chemical odor before stepping into the bedroom. Without taking her eyes off the doorway, she backed up and snatched her sharply pointed tweezers from the sink, then waited for whoever had invaded her room to realize he'd lost the element of surprise and attack.

It didn't take long.

He came at her fast. She had an impression of wiry grace, smooth strength, dark skin and muscle, before all her concentration was taken up by self-defense. She slashed out with the tweezers, felt the drag, and heard him grunt as they connected, slicing into his skin. His leg caught hers, sending her to the ground, and she rolled, taking him down with her. For a moment, she had the upper hand, and felt a tiny surge of triumph, but he squirmed free and got an arm around her neck. She tried to knock him back with her head, but he was ready for her.

Callie gasped for breath as black spots obscured her vision. On the edge of passing out, she heard a tremendous crash. Her captor cursed and released her, but it was too late; the world faded into darkness.

She woke to the sound of Mac's voice as he spoke urgently into his cell phone. He had pulled the blackout curtains, but the dim light of his phone's display illuminated her room at the Princess. She was lying on top of the bed, still dressed in the robe she'd put on after her shower. Her body ached and her throat throbbed.

"Check there first. Call when you get here and we'll come aboard." He switched on the bedside lamp, then snapped the phone shut and settled next to her.

"How do you feel?"

"Like shit." Callie tried to smile and was horrified to feel tears gathering in the corners of her eyes. She sat up quickly, brushing them away, and drew her knees beneath her chin. "What happened?"

"You had a visitor."

"I got that much. I also got that he didn't want to kill me, just knock me out. I smelled something."

"Chloroform. He probably hoped to carry you off somewhere so his boss could find out what you know and who you've told. He didn't count on you fighting back. And he didn't count on me. Unfortunately, by the time I got in, he was out the window and on the ground."

"Who were you talking to on the phone?"

"Travis Moreland. He's the Army buddy I told you about, the one who charters out fishing boats. He's coming to pick us up. It's fairly evident that you're no longer safe here." "I guess it's a good thing I didn't unpack."

"In this case, yes. But under normal circumstances, it's better if you do."

"What do you mean?"

He rubbed his forehead. "If the guy had succeeded tonight, he could just have picked up your suitcase, grabbed whatever you left in the bathroom, and he'd be done. In a matter of seconds, there'd be nothing for the police to go on, no way for them to track you. When you get to a hotel, if you spread your possessions out, you make it harder for criminals to eliminate their tracks."

"I never thought of it that way."

He grimaced. "Most people don't. Luckily, they don't have to. But when a guy goes to the police saying his wife disappeared on a business trip, and her hotel room is empty of personal belongings, it's damned hard to determine whether she left of her own accord or not. If she unpacks, there's a chance whoever abducts her will leave something behind—shoes in the closet, a watch in the safe, an address book in the desk drawer—that will lend credence to her husband's claims."

"From now on, I'll unpack." She scooted to the edge of the bed, then stood. "Let me get dressed, and I'll be ready to go. I gather your friend is picking us up by boat?"

"Yeah. He'll call when he's found a spot to pull up in the marina. We're safer on the water at the moment, though we should probably report tonight's incident." He rubbed the scar on his face with one finger in a thoughtful gesture, and Callie realized that at some point it had become invisible to her, just part of the man. "The question is, do we really want to involve the Dutch police? The gendarmes are already in because of Nikki, and the feds want to chat because of the murders in the US, so I'd like to avoid muddying the waters even further if at all possible. I had to break your door to get in, but no doubt we can come to terms with the hotel so that they don't report it." He glared at her. "You didn't bolt it."

"I most certainly did!"

"Ah, then your little friend must have unlocked it after he let himself in via the balcony. That's what I would have done. He probably intended to take you out that way—he couldn't very well carry you down the rope he hooked to the balcony—and had an accomplice waiting to help. We got lucky; the door would have been a lot more trouble for me if the bolt had been on."

Glancing at him as she headed into the bathroom to change, Callie doubted the security lock would have caused Mac much difficulty. The man's muscles had muscles, for which she was immensely grateful at the moment.

"I'll have Marlon phone the hotel in the morning," she called through the door. "This is his timeshare week, and he's good at getting what he wants. He's a lawyer. He can explain that he won't mention his friend being attacked on their property if they won't file a police report. I somehow doubt the resort is anxious for the bad publicity an incident like this could generate."

Callie stripped off the robe and examined herself in the full-length mirror on the back of the bathroom door. Her neck was a bit red, but there was surprisingly little bruising. Her hip, where she'd landed when her assailant had tripped her, was another matter. Already darkening, it promised to become a Technicolor extravaganza, and when she pulled her jeans on she could feel the whole area beginning to swell. But at least the drops of blood spattered on the floor weren't hers.

She pulled on a bra and a clean T-shirt, brushed her hair, then rejoined Mac in the bedroom.

"You know, I stabbed the guy with a pair of tweezers, and looking at the amount of blood in there, I must have gotten him better than I realized. Maybe we should go to the police—if they put out a bulletin, maybe someone would remember seeing an injured guy in the area."

"I wondered what you'd used. Unfortunately, I doubt he stayed on the island after the attack. He was probably hired from somewhere else specifically so he wouldn't be recognized, came in by boat, and planned to take you out the same way. Unless you think you got his face, in which case he might have had to get patched up quickly."

"No. I was hoping to, but he was too fast. I got his collarbone area, I think. My many and varied self-defense teachers would be disappointed."

"I doubt it. You're alive and free; that's a pretty damned good job, if you ask me." His green eyes held approval and something more, something hotter and darker that had her stumbling backward.

"Oh! Let me get my toothbrush. It will just take me a second to throw all this junk in my suitcase, and then I'll be ready to go."

On cue, his cell phone rang, and he turned away, striding toward the window. By the time she had stuffed her toiletries into her suitcase, he'd spotted Travis's boat, *The Tramp*, out the window.

"We're on the way," he said. "See you in a minute." He shut the phone. "Can you carry the bag? I doubt your friend is still hanging around, but I'd like to keep my hands free just in case."

"No problem." Callie hoisted the bag up onto her shoulder.

Mac hustled Callie down the stairs, refusing to take the elevator. She understood his logic — in the small, blind space, they would be vulnerable the moment the doors opened — but resented it nonetheless with every throb of her hip.

Under the marina lights, *The Tramp* gleamed. Although it was clearly a working boat, and not a new one, the perfectly maintained sport cruiser close to thirty feet long bore little resemblance to the beat-up fishing charter Callie had imagined. The man piloting was little more than a shadow beneath the canvas cockpit cover until he stepped to the rear of the boat and held out his hand to help her aboard, at which point she realized her assumptions about him had missed the mark by an even wider margin than had those about his boat.

Mac's description of Travis as an old Army buddy who'd opened a charter service had prompted a mental image of an aging beach bum living out his last years on the water, but Travis Moreland couldn't have been more than thirty-five, and, in a previous age, might have posed for Michelangelo. Steel-blue eyes glinted in a sharply sculpted face softened only marginally by a mop of dirty blond hair. But if his features had been stolen from heaven, the arm Travis held out to her had reached into the fires of hell itself. The scar tissue began at his wrist and continued up to disappear beneath the sleeve of his black T-shirt.

"Firebomb," he said as she took his hand and stepped onto the boat. "I was lucky. I had gloves on."

What was the proper reply? Callie swallowed. "While you were in the Army?"

He nodded. "Afghanistan."

The boat rocked slightly as Mac joined them. Travis produced a gun from the small of his back and handed it over. "I wasn't the only one at your place tonight," Travis told Mac. "Whoever beat me there doesn't know you, didn't look for the traps, and didn't find the e-kit."

"Traps? E-kit?" she asked.

Both men looked at her, but it was Mac who answered.

"I use markers so I know if my doors or windows have been opened. Hairs, tape, threads. Trav recognized them, saw they'd been disturbed. An e-kit is an exit kit, an emergency kit. Passports, weapons, cash, first aid. You may hear it referred to as a 'go bag.' Things you might need to get out, and get out fast."

"Normal people don't live that way."

"Then I guess you're lucky Mac here isn't normal." Travis unlooped the line holding them to the dock. "I'm going to take her around to the port and drop you two at the *Lady*. You can take her out for a few days. You should think about Miami."

Mac nodded, and Travis ducked into the cockpit.

"Miami?"

"Trav thinks we should head for the States. The *Lady* can

make Miami quick enough, and he knows a harbormaster there."

"I can't believe he owns boats called *Lady* and *The Tramp*."

"Believe it. *Lady* is a fifty-two-foot sedan bridge. Custom job. A real beaut. He must like you, because he'd never give her up and volunteer to sleep on *The Tramp* for however long this takes otherwise."

"He only just met me," Callie protested.

The engine caught and the boat jerked slightly. Mac steadied Callie with a hand on her arm and flashed her a quick grin. "Take it as a compliment. Trav doesn't like many people."

Callie looked toward the cockpit. If *Lady* was as well maintained as *The Tramp*, Travis Moreland owned boat real estate worth millions of dollars. A twitch skittered up her spine.

"What happened to him?"

"He's never told me more than he did you. Firebomb."

They passed a tower and Travis gave two short blasts to the horn, leaning out of the cockpit and waving to an invisible watcher. After five years, he'd know everyone on the island. Whoever tracked traffic in and out of the marina was probably used to him coming and going. Though possibly not at — she checked her watch — one in the morning. No wonder she was so tired.

"We'll be in the port in twenty minutes." Mac shoved the gun into the waistband of his jeans and lifted her bag. "I'm going to stash the suitcase below, where it won't get wet. You want to sit out here, or below?"

"Out here." The boat was picking up speed, and she raised her voice against the wind. "It's a beautiful night."

Mac grinned again, his eyes darkening once more with the expression that made her stomach tighten. "That it is."

They were pulling into a slip next to *Lady*—whose graceful lines and striking beauty suited her name—when Mac's cell phone rang. He passed the rope he'd been holding to Callie and pulled it out of his pocket.

"That can't be good news," Travis said. He cut the engine and dropped bumper buoys over each side of *The Tramp*, then jumped lightly down from the cockpit, took the rope from Callie, and tied the boat in.

"No," Mac agreed, recognizing the Atlanta area code on the caller ID, "it can't."

MAC'S PARTNER'S WORDS confirmed his fears.

"Ed Steele is dead. Took a shiv to the gut in the yard this afternoon."

"Hell, Vince, and you're just finding out now?"

"Not my problem, as has been made abundantly clear to me by *los federales*. And not yours, either. But just in case you were thinking of maybe paying the man a social call, I figured you should know there was no point."

Which, of course, was exactly why Steele had been killed. "They see who did it?"

"Nope. Working theory is racial. Steele was tight with the neo-Nazi set."

"Bull. It was a hit, bought and paid for." He felt, rather than saw, both Callie and Travis staring at him.

"No argument from me. For the record, I am calling to convince you to reach out to the feds because you're in danger. And so is the Pearson woman." Mac understood: Vince's phone calls were being monitored.

"They know about Callie?"

"Your pal in the gendarmerie down there gave her up. If I talk to you, I'm supposed to pass along the message that he'd like a word with you. Apparently, they've been calling you and you haven't answered."

"I must have left that cell phone at home."

Vince coughed a laugh. "Don't you hate it when that happens? Don't they know about this one?"

"They'll get it in the morning. Vichy has the one I got when I took the job at the Paradis, but this one's old, still with a provider in the States rather than down here. I keep it around for a-holes like you to call me on. The gendarmes will have to contact the wireless companies to get the number. It was on my personnel file at the Paradis, but that has ... um ... probably been misplaced."

"You know, man, I miss working with you. I really do."

"Yeah, yeah. You got a pen? I'll give you a dispose-a-phone number." The prepaid cell was something else Mac kept in his e-kit. When Vince was ready, Mac read the number off to him.

"I'll pick one up myself in the morning, and call you when—if—I hear anything. In the meantime, watch your back."

"Thanks for the heads up."

"Who's dead?" asked Callie as Mac disconnected.

"Ed Steele. Shanked in prison."

"One less reason to go to Miami," Travis observed. "But it does give you a clearer picture of what you're dealing with."

"What do you mean?" Callie was fraying, and Mac could hear it. The hollow tone edged with desperation made him want to reach for her, but he held himself away, letting Travis answer.

"People kill for all kinds of reasons, Miss Pearson. When they do it for thrills or to fulfill some kind of fantasy, we call them serial killers. The FBI, they're used to that. They have their profilers to tell them all about some guys' sicknesses. But the man who's after you, he's your garden-variety murderer. No fantasy. At least, not as a compulsion, not as the thing in and of itself that drives him to kill. He may enjoy killing people, and there may be misfiring brain cells behind his actions, but he's also willing to forgo the thrill and pay a con to knife a guy in prison if that's what it takes to get the job done."

"I see."

Mac doubted she did. For all her talk about having lived in rough places, and for all her self-defense classes, Callie had never knowingly sat across a table from a murderer. In Narcotics, he'd done it on a regular basis.

Travis dug a set of keys out of his pocket and handed them to Mac. "Take the *Lady*. Get her out on the open water." His cell rang, and he checked the readout. "Fuck. I wondered how long it would take." He held out the phone. "It's not for me, buddy; it's for you."

Mac looked at the display, which listed an unfamiliar number with a 212 area code and an all-too-familiar name: Nash. Mac backed away as if the ringing cell carried a disease. "I had no idea you were still in touch with Nash."

Dwight "Nashville" Harper had been their XO. He'd taken four bullets during a mission gone disastrously wrong the year before Mac left the unit, lost a kidney, and taken a medical discharge. A week after the shooting, while Nash was recovering at Walter Reed, their CO, Al Thomas, had been assassinated. Two bullets to the back of his head. The timing had always bothered Mac.

Nash had called a couple of times when he'd come through Atlanta working for the Drug Enforcement Agency, but Mac had always managed to be too busy to see the man. If Nash and Travis had kept in contact, it explained how Travis had heard about the knife fight that ended Mac's career. Nash never left anything to chance. He would have kept an eye on anyone he considered useful, and cops were always useful.

"I wouldn't say we're in touch. He left the DEA four years ago, started a private firm. He's been bugging me to join up. Says I'm wasting my talents out here." Well, on that point, Mac would have to agree. But who was he to judge? "He's still got plenty of federal contacts, though, so it was only a matter of time until he caught onto the fact that they want to chat with you." The phone quieted momentarily as voice mail kicked in, then began to ring again. Clearly, Nash wasn't ready to talk to a machine.

"He could be useful." Travis held out the cell once more.

"Fine." Mac flipped the phone open and held it to his ear. "This is Brody."

There was a moment of silence.

"Is Travis okay?"

"Yeah, Nash, he's fine. He figured you wanted me, and he didn't want to play middleman."

Another quiet period, then Nash's twangy drawl, still familiar after so many years. "He was right. I have some information. I'd have given it to him if I had to, but I'd rather pass it straight to you."

"What do you want in return?"

"Nothing. No, I take that back. I want you to promise to call if I can help."

Mac wanted to make a different promise, that it would be a cold day in hell before he asked his former XO for anything.

But he couldn't. Travis was right about Nash having resources, and Callie might need them.

"I'll think about it."

The man had the nerve to laugh. "Good enough. When your ... situation ... came across my desk earlier today, I did some digging. Called in some favors. Did you know that your wife was in a car wreck when she was sixteen?"

"She was?"

"Indeed. Broke her left arm in two places. I had a lovely chat with a source who tells me the body the gendarmes found on the shore there had no healed fractures."

"It's not Nikki."

"No."

"Christ." He'd considered the possibility, but only as a theoretical. He glanced at Callie, watching him with a concerned frown. "I wonder why her brother didn't mention anything about it."

"Now, I found that rather curious myself, especially after I watched the man on television spouting off about his beloved sister. So I checked him out, too. It's possible—not probable, but possible—that he didn't know. Nicole Lewis was in boarding school in Switzerland at the time of the accident. It was 2002, a year John Lewis spent primarily in the US."

"Still, I can't believe he wasn't aware his sister had been in an accident."

"You always did rush to judgment." Only the faintest reproof tinted the words. "But let's leave John Lewis alone for a minute. I'd rather talk about something else. Were you aware that Calliope Pearson and Edward Steele both have birth certificates signed by the same midwife, a woman named Cherie Marshall? I find that odd, especially since Cherie presided over the birth of Miss Pearson in Montauk, New York, and Mr. Steele in Miami, Florida. I haven't managed to get my hands on birth certificates for Robin Cory or Deborah or Diane Masters yet, but I am confident I will in time."

Mac believed him. Nash Harper had always excelled at gathering intel. At twenty-three, Mac had placed the blame for his CO's death squarely at his XO's door. Eleven years later, he wondered whether the assassination, and Nash's shooting, might have been the result of something Nash had uncovered rather than something he'd done. "I have to go. I'll call you back. But I'm giving this phone back to Travis, and we're splitting up."

"So don't call us, we'll call you? Be sure you do, Brody."

"Yeah." He hung up and tossed the phone back to Travis, who'd taken the time while Mac was talking to retrieve Callie's suitcase and set it on the dock.

"Get going," he said as he clipped the phone to the waistband of his jeans. "The *Lady* is fully gassed and ready. Even the galley's stocked. I don't have any charters until Friday, so I'm headed for Guadeloupe. Give me a call if you need me."

"Will do." Mac stepped off the boat, then helped Callie onto the dock. Trav was already pulling in the fenders and casting off, clearly anxious to be gone. As *The Tramp* rumbled to life and pulled away, Mac raised an arm in farewell. For a moment on deck, coordinating information between Trav, Vince, and Nash, he'd been part of a team again; he hadn't realized how much he missed the experience.

Shaking off the uncomfortable awareness, he slung Callie's bag onto the aft deck of the *Lady*, then stepped aboard himself and held out a hand.

"C'mon."

Callie laid a hand lightly in his, and he tried to ignore the anticipatory spark it caused. He had always been the same—when his system was in gear, as it was now, he fired on all cylinders. Sex, violence, danger . . . For Mac it was ready for one, ready for all. He'd do well to remember that his reaction to the woman beside him had less to do with her than with the situation. He let go of her the minute she seemed steady on her feet.

"You spent much time on the water?"

"A fair amount. When my father worked in Greece, we lived aboard a fifty-eight-footer that was similar to this one, but it's been ten years since I went out on anything bigger than a sport fisherman."

"Trav bought this and the little Sea Ray off the same guy. Bought out his whole business, in fact. The really big motor yachts around here have full-time staff, but the guy who built this one was a loner. No family even, which made this yacht hard to sell despite the level of luxury, because he designed it with a single stateroom. The dinette folds out into a sleeper, but most people who buy a boat this size want two bedrooms."

He led her down the center aisle, where the saloon and dinette were to their left and the open, U-shaped galley to their right, toward the stairs leading down to the stateroom.

"Whoa. This is something else."

He laughed. All the crap she'd had thrown at her, and this was the first actual evidence of surprise he'd seen. But he could relate.

"Yeah. That was my reaction. The wood here is as nice as anything at the Paradis, and Travis replaced all the brass with oil-rubbed bronze by himself."

Callie paused to finger one of the woven throws tossed over the white leatherette sofas.

"Those he brought back from the Middle East, I think, though he might have had someone send them to him later on," Mac explained. "He told me the boat was too sterile when he moved in."

When they reached the stairs down to the stateroom, Mac stepped aside so Callie could precede him. The bedroom was another kind of rustic altogether, a faded French provincial style. Suddenly, despite its size, Mac felt stifled. He dropped Callie's bag on the blue and yellow quilt that covered the king-sized bed.

"You should get some rest. I'm going up to take us out. I'll be back in a bit." With a quick wave, he bolted from the room and back up the stairs.

CHAPTER SEVEN

Either Travis or Mac must have set the coffee machine to come on automatically, because the final drops were hissing into the carafe when Callie staggered out of the stateroom the next morning. The clock read 8:07. Her head and hip ached in tandem, and she wanted nothing more than to crawl back beneath the covers.

Mac lay stretched out on the sofa, an arm beneath his head and one of the throws pulled over his legs like a blanket. The dark hair, tanned skin, heavy growth of stubble . . . He was a long, black, exhausted shadow on the white leatherette, and the sight pinched her heart. Why hadn't he joined her in the stateroom? The bed was enormous. Did he think she was such a prude she would have kicked up a fuss? Or did her heritage — possibly his wife's heritage — freak him out as badly as it did her?

On the counter in the galley rested a stack of papers Callie recognized as the information Mac had printed out at the marina the previous day. Travis must have retrieved them when he'd gone to Mac's apartment for the "e-kit," the whole idea of which she found both frightening and almost unbearably sad. What kind of life trained a person to keep an escape kit at hand at all times?

Callie poured herself a mug of the steaming brew, took the printouts and her sunglasses, and went above to the small outdoor seating area. Storm clouds lowered, and the air was close, already overheating. Mac had anchored them about a half mile offshore. She could see the beach, its white sand bordered by what appeared to be hotels and restaurants rather than private residences. After examining the shoreline, she concluded the beach was Grand Case, where she'd sat and listened to strangers discuss the possibility that Mac might have murdered his wife.

Could that really have been only three days before? No wonder exhaustion dragged at her. In less than a week, her whole life had gone to hell. Her roommate, Erin, had told her to let go of the picture and hang on to the memories instead, but she hadn't listened. Tears welled in her eyes and she blinked them back.

No use crying over spilt milk. They were her father's words, and she heard them in his voice. He'd always been practical, and honest. He'd shared everything with her. Why not this?

She settled on the white vinyl bench seat and began looking through the files. At some point, probably while she'd been getting ready for dinner with John, Mac had sorted the information into four paper-clipped sections. The top contained general background, and then there was a section for each of the blood-linked families. Callie started with Ed Steele's, and was forcing herself to read through the reports of the rapes he had committed when she felt Mac come up behind her.

"You'd be safer inside."

He'd obviously come to find her the moment he woke, because stubble still obscured his jawline, and he had the worst case of bed head Callie had seen in quite some time. Despite whatever sleep he'd managed to get, his jade eyes remained shadowed. Callie looked away, appalled by her own desire to ease the trouble she saw lurking behind them.

"There's no one for miles." *Keep it together, Callie. Just the facts. He doesn't need your sympathy.*

"Not at the moment. Do it for me, okay? I need to shower, and I'd rather you were out of sight while I do. Let anyone passing by assume Trav's aboard by himself, as usual."

"Yeah, okay." She gathered the papers and her coffee, and stood.

"We have a breakfast date in an hour," Mac said as he led the way back down the stairs. "Vichy called."

"We're going to Marigot? Is that safe?"

"No. Which is why we're meeting him on the beach just over there. The restaurant opens at ten. We'll take the inflatable. It's not safe—nothing is—but it's better than driving or walking through town. And even if the gendarmerie weren't in the middle of Marigot, I'd prefer meeting on more neutral ground."

"Why does he want to talk to us? Is it about Nikki, about whatever your friend Nash told you? The body they found— it wasn't her, was it?"

"No."

"How did he know? Nash, I mean. Who is he?"

"Nash is . . ." He shook his head. "We're going to have to talk about some of the things he said. But let me shower first."

Reluctantly, she agreed, returning to her examination of the case files. Ed Steele showed absolutely no remorse during his trial. He'd plead not guilty, but once DNA connected him to all the rapes, he gave in and made a deal. Although the pages were nothing more than toner and paper, they felt dirty, made *Callie* feel dirty, especially when she remembered that the man was her half brother. A kind of pleasure and pride shone through Steele's words that fouled the taste of her coffee, soured her stomach, and made her skin crawl.

By the time Mac returned, she was more than ready to push the papers aside in favor of talking about something—anything—else, but when she asked about the mysterious Nash, Mac answered with a question of his own.

"Do you know a woman named Cherie Marshall?"

It took her a moment to place the name. "That's the midwife who signed my birth certificate. But I never met her, at least that I remember. Why?"

"Because Nash says she was also midwife at Ed Steele's birth."

She stared at him. "Ed Steele and I had the same midwife as well as the same father?"

"So it seems."

"There has to be some kind of mistake. None of this makes any sense."

"I've been considering the fact that both your mother and Ephraim Steele were Jewish. What if all this has something to do with religion? Did you come across anything about religion in the files you were looking at?"

"No, but I haven't gotten that far. You take the information on the Masterses; I'll check out Robin Cory." She handed him a sheaf of papers.

After a few minutes of reading, Mac grunted. "Nothing specific, but the names Deborah and Diane do crop up in the Jewish community regularly."

"But Robin's family was Episcopalian. They held the funeral at her church, and these reports are full of quotes from various members of the religious community about her volunteer work. There is one thing, though. . . ."

"Yeah?"

"The PR photo in the Masters file was from an award ceremony in Brazil or something, wasn't it?"

Mac nodded. "For a campaign on women's rights they spearheaded there."

"Well, Robin and her family traveled extensively, too. As did we when I was growing up. My mother hated Ephraim Steele and called him greedy. I remember the exact moment we talked about it. There was a newscaster talking about the scandal that brought down his ministry and showing photographs and receipts that proved he'd stayed in five-star hotels while supposedly doing 'missionary work.'"

"That's right. It was a huge part of the end of his career." Mac checked his watch. "I have to get the inflatable ready. I'll be right back. Can you make a list of the countries you went to and the approximate times? Maybe something will pop if Nash can get hold of everyone else's schedules."

"You still haven't told me who Nash is and why he has access to that kind of information."

He hesitated, and she thought he might refuse to answer. Finally, he said, "Nash was in the same unit with me and Trav a long time ago. I'm not sure who he is now, but if there's intel to be gotten, he'll get it."

Which was completely unsatisfactory, but before she could protest, Mac was gone, heading for the cockpit and the two-person inflatable that would carry them to the beach. Callie dug through her satchel for a pen and began making a list of the places her father had taken them when she was a child. She'd barely started when she had to go back through the bag looking for the cell phone she could hear ringing.

"Miss Pearson," said an unfamiliar voice when she answered, "my name is Nash Harper. It's imperative that I speak with Mac Brody immediately. Can you put him on the line?"

"Why don't you call his number?"

"I don't have it on hand. Yours was easier to find, and time is of the essence."

Someone had Mac's number, Callie thought, because above her head she could hear it ringing.

"I'll see if I can find him."

"You're on a fifty-two-foot yacht, Miss Pearson. You're currently anchored off Grand Case. There aren't that many places for him to hide, which is exactly why I need to speak to him. Right now."

When she climbed the stairs, she saw Mac with his cell wedged between his shoulder and ear as his hands flew over the controls. The *Lady* lurched in the water as her engines came to life and her anchor began to retract.

"I'll call you back in ten," Mac said into his phone when he realized Callie had come up the stairs. He flipped his own phone shut, shoved it into his pocket, and held out a hand for hers.

"That Nash?" He answered her unasked question. "Trav said he'd be calling."

⌒

"Wʜᴀᴛ ᴛʜᴇ ꜰᴜᴄᴋ happened?" Mac asked without preamble as soon as Callie passed him the cell.

"The cleaning crew went by your old house this morning and found your wife in the kitchen. Strangled. Missing, of all things, her left hand, where she would have worn the ring that was found on the other woman. Mutilated in other ways as well. Autopsy pending, but my sources tell me certain things indicate she's been dead since she disappeared. Probably stored in a meat locker somewhere, since there's virtually no decomp."

Mac flashed back to his visit to John Lewis's house. "There's a chest freezer in our basement, and another in her brother's."

"Yes. Working theory is that you kept her in yours for a while. No reason yet proposed for why you'd have taken her out of her hiding place and left her to be found, let alone why you'd have chopped off a piece of her body, or where that piece might turn up."

"Fuck."

"Are you moving?"

"A yacht isn't a damn motorcycle. It takes a few minutes to get going. I'm working on it. I have to put the phone down; you'll be on speaker." He dropped the cell into the cup holder next to the wheel.

"Good." Distorted by the cell's tiny speaker, Nash's voice was barely audible over the *thrum* of the engine. "I have a chopper on the way. ETA nine minutes."

"Nine minutes? Where the hell are you?"

"We left Puerto Rico almost an hour ago."

Mac felt the anchor settle home, and got the *Lady* moving. With less cabin space, she had greater potential speed than most cruisers her length, but no motor yacht could outrun the speedboats the gendarmes were apt to send after them. He wanted out of Grand Case. Preferably yesterday.

"When you get the *Lady* in gear, head northwest. That cuts down the time till we meet, and puts you as far from land as possible. The further you are out of the casual cruisers' seaways, the less possibility anyone will notice when the Jayhawk drops four people onto the *Lady*, complete with paperwork showing they rented her for a week from Travis, and picks you two up. The new 'renters' will set course for Guadeloupe. Travis is already working on that end."

Nash had always been efficient. Obviously, some things hadn't changed.

But the distinctive *roar-and-slap* sound of an approaching

speedboat warned Nash's efficiency might have been over-matched by that of the French police. Or someone else.

"We have company," he said.

"Five minutes out," replied Nash.

"You said nine."

"I lied." He hadn't, Mac felt certain. A favorite for Coast Guard search-and-rescue ops, Sikorsky Jayhawks were built for distance, not speed. He figured Nash had calculated the nine minutes when the Hawk was moving at standard speed, about 140 knots. But he was willing to bet the pilot was pushing the thing to top speed—listed as 180 knots—before Callie had even handed him the phone.

The boat came into view around the tip of Happy Bay at the same time as Mac heard another familiar sound, that of a helicopter closing in rapidly.

"You did say you had a Jayhawk?"

"Yeah, and that's not us."

"No shit." At his best guess, the thing coming up no more than fifty feet off the water behind the French powerboat was a Huey. Light, fast, and lethal. Seconds later, the speedboat was engulfed in flames.

"Mac!"

"I see it."

"Two minutes," said Nash in his ear, and Mac wondered how the hell hard he was pushing the Jayhawk.

"Take the wheel," he said to Callie. When he was sure she had the boat under control, he reached into the cabinet hidden behind a sliding panel and pulled out the rifle Travis always kept at hand. Long-range shooting wasn't his forte, and firing at a helicopter wasn't the smartest thing in the world to do, even if action-movie heroes made it seem to be, but he didn't have to hit the Huey, just make the pilot cautious, hold him back for a minute until Nash could get to them. If the Huey pilot were smart, he would take one look at the Jayhawk and head for the hills. Mac took careful aim, the scope showing him all too clearly the gunner leaning out of the chopper, and fired.

The shooter would have seen him, too. The pilot swerved, heading slightly away to recalculate, and Mac heard the heavy thump of the Jayhawk's rotors. So did the Huey's occupants. The smaller chopper dipped and turned, racing back the way it had come.

⸺

Oh. My. God. What had happened to her life? When had she become the person the police chased and strange men shot at?

The big helicopter hovered over them, kicking up water all around, and Callie slowed the *Lady* to a halt. Mac reached over her shoulder and activated the control to drop the anchor. At the same moment, she heard a thud behind her, and turned to see a rope ladder fall from the open helicopter door. Two men dressed in Hawaiian shirts and cutoffs jumped to the aft deck, followed by a pair of big duffel bags and two casually attired women.

"Come on," said Mac, leading her down the cockpit steps. "We're out of here."

Callie had brought her handbag up with her, but when she started inside to grab her suitcase as well, Mac stopped her.

"No time. This place is going to be swarming with cops any minute. The chopper has to be gone before they get here."

When in strange seas, listen to the captain. Another of her father's maxims and never more apt. Callie changed direction. One of the young men gave her a hand up the first few rungs of the ladder, which swayed despite his efforts to steady it. At the top, another man reached out to help her inside. The second her knee made contact with the Jayhawk's deck, the copter lurched into motion. Alarmed, she looked over her shoulder. The ladder, Mac halfway up it, swung wildly as the aircraft headed back the way it had come. He didn't seem to mind, climbing steadily until he joined her inside.

"You okay?" He was practically shouting to be heard over the steady *hup-hup-hup* of the rotors.

"Yes." She thought for a second. "No. They blew up a police boat!" She'd seen the fires herself, yet still couldn't quite believe it.

"Yeah." Mac laid a large, rough hand along the side of her face in a strangely reassuring gesture. "You're doing great. Just hang in there a little longer. Let me talk to Nash." He turned to the young man who still knelt at the open door, a hand on the grab bar. "He flying?"

"Yes, sir."

Callie forced herself to her feet, steadying herself with a hand on Mac's shoulder. The rumbling dips and sways of the aircraft didn't seem to impact him at all. "I'm coming, too."

"No need." The man standing in the open cockpit door flashed a brilliant white smile at her. "Trey doesn't need my help; he just humors me by letting me sit copilot." He held out a hand and she took it. "Dwight Harper, Miss Pearson. Everyone calls me Nash."

"Calliope Pearson," she replied. "Call me Callie."

He let go of her hand and gestured to seats bolted to the cabin walls. When she took one, he sat across from her, then indicated the young man who had helped her aboard. "And this is Joseph."

"Ma'am." Joseph flicked his eyes in her direction, then returned his concentration to the open panel door, beyond which she could see the *Lady*, rapidly vanishing into the distance.

"Thank you for your help, Joseph," she called, wondering why he didn't shut the door and cut out at least a little of the noise.

"What is all this, Nash?" The harsh tone of Mac's voice caught Callie's attention, and she twisted in her seat to see him examining some kind of oversized gun snapped into a holder built into the wall.

"This is part of Harp Security Enterprises. Usually we keep the Jayhawk in Miami, but when I got off the phone with you last night, I asked Trey to take her to San Juan, and I flew down to meet it."

"And what, exactly, does Harp Security Enterprises do?"

Nash flashed that white grin again. "A little of this, a little of that. You might consider working for HSE when all this is over. We could use you. And I think you'd like it." A muscle jumped in Mac's jaw, and Callie interrupted before he could say whatever he was thinking.

"Not that I don't appreciate the rescue, Mr. Harper —"

"Nash."

"Nash. Really, it was great. But where are you taking us?"

"First to San Juan. Then on to HSE headquarters in New York."

"Just like that? Surely, between the fact that the FBI seems interested in me and the fact that someone chasing us just blew up a boat belonging to a foreign government's military, there will be flags on both my passport and Mac's.

"I doubt Nash plans to go through immigration." Mac ceased his prowling and took the seat next to Callie's.

"No," Nash agreed. "I'm afraid we have to use somewhat unorthodox methods, especially with Nikki Lewis's body raising more questions."

"They found her?"

Nash outlined the situation, and Callie, unable to think of appropriate words, reached for Mac's hand to comfort him. Oddly, the contact soothed her as well. Mac squeezed briefly before letting her go.

"Dollars to doughnuts once they test her blood they'll find she's part of whatever Callie's tangled up in."

"No bet." Nash looked over at the open side panel. "You can close her up, Joseph; Trey will keep an eye on radar, but it appears we're clear."

"Yes, sir." The young man did as ordered, then disappeared into the cockpit. Relative quiet followed.

"The flight to the airstrip in Puerto Rico takes about an hour. The plane will be waiting, and after that it's another four hours to New York." Nash glanced at his watch. "We filed our flight plan last night. Barring unforeseen problems, we should be back in Manhattan early this evening."

"And then what?" asked Callie.

"We have an apartment for the two of you at headquarters. A safe house, if you will. You'll stay there while we track down the who and why of these attacks."

"And just how do you plan to do that?" Callie could hear the anger in Mac's voice. He'd told her himself he wasn't good at rules or politics. She suspected he didn't take orders well, either. And he wouldn't just wait around to see what Nash came up with; he'd want to make things happen. There was something else, too: despite the fact Nash had rescued them, and they appeared to have quite a long history, Callie got the feeling Mac didn't trust the man.

"My people are doing a thorough search into the backgrounds of all parties. I told them to start with Ephraim Steele. His downfall was quite public, and his financials were thoroughly examined at the time. All those records are available to the right person."

"And you're the right person?" Wow, that hardly did her father's diplomatic training credit. Mac's aggressiveness must be rubbing off on her.

"Nash has always been the right person. No matter the situation."

"No," Nash corrected him. "Not always, not in every situation. But in this one, I know the right people and I've set them the goal of putting Ephraim Steele's life under a microscope."

"Steele's wife was very vocal about his prosecution being persecution, as I recall," Mac said. "Has anyone spoken to her?"

"Polly Steele died in a one-car accident two months after her husband's heart attack."

"Another loose end snipped off." Mac's flat statement sent a shiver over Callie's skin that skittered up her spine. Her shoulders twitched in response. "Someone likes to keep everything nice and tidy."

"Yes," Nash agreed. "I think Ephraim Steele's heart attack may have been the first of the killings. Steele was going down. If he knew something that could get him a shorter sentence, there's not a doubt in my mind he'd have given it up. Someone got to him before that could happen. And just in case Polly got curious, they took her out of the picture, too."

"But left Ed?"

"He was a kid at the time. Doubtful his parents would have shared anything criminal with him, and while it wasn't unlikely that Ephraim, faced with jail time, might have a heart attack, or that Polly, a well-known drunk, would have a fatal wreck, killing their kid could have made the cops look a little harder." Callie noticed it didn't occur to Nash—or, seemingly, Mac, who was nodding at the analysis—that the killer left Ed alone just because he didn't want to kill a child.

Nash touched her knee. "Callie, I hate to ask this of you, but how would you feel about having your father's body exhumed? I know the original exam found he had died of an aneurism, but given how many sudden deaths we seem to have here, I'd like my own people to be able to check him out."

Callie had to swallow twice before she could answer. "My father was cremated. Both he and my mother. That's what they wanted. I scattered his ashes the same place we'd taken hers."

CHAPTER EIGHT

BY THE TIME the town car that had met them at the charter
gate at New York's JFK airport pulled up in front of a building on the lower west side of Manhattan and waited for the
metal garage gate to roll up, Mac could see the exhaustion in
every drooping line of Callie's body. On the ground in Puerto
Rico, they'd hustled from the chopper straight into a private jet.
The opulence had impressed Mac—though he'd die before he
said so—but Callie seemed to take it in stride. He supposed
with her background, she'd been on more than a few.

They'd used the flight time to thoroughly reexamine
the information Vince had passed along. Callie had stuffed the
papers into her oversized handbag before coming to find
him on the *Lady*. He found her presence of mind admirable.
Actually, he found a number of things about her admirable.

Like the fact that she'd noticed Ephraim and Polly Steele
had died the same way Mark and Ava Lewis had. Even Nash
had been impressed with that observation.

The car rolled slowly forward down a ramp, and the steel
door began to descend. At the bottom, a second gate, this
one in steel lattice, waited until their driver, whom Nash had
introduced as Dylan, entered a code into a box before it slid
smoothly to the left. Past the gate, two cars were parked to
the left and two to the right. Dylan backed into the single
remaining spot on the right.

"Home, sweet home," said Nash, hopping out and offering
a hand to Callie. "Welcome to Harp Security."

"Quite a place," Mac remarked as he followed her out of the vehicle. Cement and steel loomed around them. Judging by the ramp's length, he estimated they were ten feet underground, but the ceiling was twenty feet above them, and his voice bounced off the walls a bit.

"There's a street-level entrance around the front of the building. Two-story lobby, with an elevator that takes you to the public offices of HSE the floor above. From here, you can get to both the public and private floors." He patted the car's hood. "Go on home, Dylan. I'll see you in the morning."

"Yes, sir." The driver waited until they'd crossed the garage and punched the elevator button before heading back to the ramp. He stopped at the bottom, entering a code and waiting for the gate to open again before proceeding.

"Different codes to come and go?"

"Of course. We're also being watched." Nash pointed out several cameras. "If Dylan had entered the wrong numbers, or anything unexpected had occurred, he wouldn't be able to get out and we wouldn't be able to get in." The elevator doors opened. "But all is well, so up we go."

The elevator stopped on the second floor. As they stepped out into a spacious antechamber, a perfectly groomed blonde woman shifted position from behind a large desk to greet them. She smiled as they approached, but the expression never touched her level gray eyes. Not a receptionist, then. An agent.

"Any problems, Lexie?"

"None. Seventh floor is still working on the project you assigned."

"Seventh floor is computers and intel," Nash explained. "This is Lexie Morton. She was good enough to come with me when I left the DEA. She runs the office and all our internal security. If anyone's scheduled to come in or out of the office, either Lexie is here or I am. Usually, we both are.

"Lexie, this is Calliope Pearson and Mac Brody. They'll need ninth-floor access."

The woman withdrew two sets of keys from the desk and handed them over. "The smaller keys work in the elevator. This is the third floor. All you have to do to get here is push a button. Same for four, which is the gym. Every other floor requires a specific key, and some an additional combination. If you wanted to go visit the geek squad on seven, you'd come here and I'd open the elevator for seven for one trip and punch in the right code."

"And if you weren't here?"

"Then someone with a seven key and the correct code would have to come down and pick you up. You're on nine, which has the guest apartments. We've put you both in A. The larger key will open the front door. We keep it available in case someone needs to stay overnight."

"How many floors are there?" Callie asked.

"Twelve."

"I live on twelve," Nash explained. "Nine, ten, and eleven have two apartments each, occupied by HSE operatives between assignments or clients needing a safe place to stay. Eight is the lab."

"Nice setup." Mac had never been to New York, but even in Atlanta a building like this one wouldn't come cheap.

Nash shrugged. "My mother's family owned the building, turned it from a factory warehouse into retail and rental apartments in the sixties. It was fully leased in 2001, but after 9/11, we lost both galleries that took up the bottom floors, and even once the area was cleared, people didn't want to come back. I'd been with the DEA for a couple of years and was already thinking of getting out. I let anyone who wanted to terminate a lease do so without penalties, then waited for the two who didn't want to leave to run out their leases, and began renovating. We officially opened our doors in January of 2010.

"Give me a few minutes to get them settled, Lexie, and I'll be back." He led them back to the elevator, taking a key from his pocket and slipping it into the spot next to the button for the ninth floor. The button lit up and he pressed it.

"I had Lexie stock your apartment. There should be clothes for both of you and plenty of food. We'll talk in the morning; with a little luck, my guys will have come up with something by then. The phone lines in the apartment are completely secure, and there's an office with Internet access, also secure." Mac wasn't keen on waiting, but he accepted Nash's ruling because Callie needed the rest. He'd use the time to call Vince and do some of his own research. He might not have the same quality of insider information Nash did, but he was good enough at connecting the dots.

The front door to the apartment opened into a large living room with an oversized galley kitchen separated by a marble-topped counter. Nash opened a door on the left to show them the bedroom and bathroom.

"The couch in the living room folds out into a queen-sized bed," he explained. "It's fully made up. Pillows, extra sheets, blankets, things like that are all in the closet."

"You said the phones were secure?" Callie asked.

"Absolutely."

"So I can call my roommate, tell her I'm okay?"

"Yes. But keep it short, and don't tell her where you are. In fact, it's better you don't even mention leaving the island. Chances are good that her phone is being monitored, at least by the FBI if not by whoever tried to take you out of the game this morning. She should go stay with a friend for the duration."

"She won't."

"When we were only concerned with simple robbery and vandalism, she wouldn't." Mac had understood Callie's explanation of Erin's feelings on the matter. He and Erin appeared to come from the same background, one that dictated you didn't give up your place to the first guy who tried to chase you off. But the explosion that morning had upped the ante. "It's not safe anymore."

"If someone wanted to hurt her, all they'd have to do is go to the restaurant." "I'll send someone up to keep an eye on her," Nash offered. "I doubt she's in any real danger, but if someone thought they could get to you through her, they might try."

"I don't know how to thank you. For any of this." Callie gave Tommy's full name and address to Nash, though she didn't really expect Erin to be willing to leave the Chappaqua house for Tommy's studio apartment in Yonkers.

"I'm sure we can think of something." Not even the slightest hint of anything sexual colored Nash's reply, but Mac bristled just the same.

"Nash enjoys having people owe him," he said.

"Is that what this is all about? Creating favors?" Callie cocked her head to one side, examining Nash. Damned if he hadn't been wondering the same thing. He couldn't figure out Nash's agenda. Not that that was anything new, but it bugged him.

"Favors make the world go around. So, yeah, I like having people owe me. I can call them when I need information. I'm expending more than one finding out about Ephraim Steele, so I'm not sorry to be gathering a few more in return. But, as Mac can tell you, I need more than one reason to take any action."

"And your other reasons?"

"Ah, I prefer to keep those to myself. Although I admit, I've been trying to get Travis to join HSE for years, and involving him and Mac in an op makes that more likely. Which reminds me, I do have to get back downstairs and make certain everything with his 'renters' went off smoothly. Sooner or later, their cover will fall apart. Someone will go through the records and discover they didn't actually pass through St. Barths last week, the way their passport stamps and the paperwork they signed with Travis indicate. They never took a ferry from St. Barths to St. Martin, couldn't have met with Trav and boarded the *Lady* in Marigot and taken her out last night. We need to have this situation cleared up before that happens.

"Since I haven't heard otherwise, I suspect everything's fine for the time being, but I do want to be positive. I'll arrange for your roommate's protection at the same time. Her full name is Erin Campbell?" Callie nodded. "Shall we agree to meet at eight tomorrow morning in reception?"

Callie and Mac agreed, and Nash left them alone. Callie immediately went into the office to call her friend, and Mac stepped toward the wall of windows overlooking the West Side Highway and the Hudson River. A mirror film had been applied to the inside, preventing prying eyes from seeing into the apartment, and he suspected the glass was bulletproof. Still, the huge expanse of it made him feel unprotected.

But the view was magnificent. Across the river, an enormous clock sat on a promontory, glowing red in the fading light, and boats and helicopters lined the river on both banks. A flock of pigeons strutted self-importantly around an all-but-empty parking lot, while seagulls bombed the Hudson.

"She's not answering." Callie came up behind him. "She's probably at work. I left her a message, told her to go stay with Tommy, that I was fine and would call her." She fidgeted. "Can I make you some dinner? We didn't eat much on the flight, and I need to be doing something."

"Great idea. Let's go see what Nash has given us to work with."

They settled on steaks, which Callie slid into the broiler while she washed, diced, and stir-fried fresh baby broccoli and asparagus spears. Though the kitchen was large for its style, it only accommodated one person, so he went into the bedroom while she worked and called Vince, who'd texted Mac's disposable cell with his own new number at some point while they were en route to New York.

"Good to hear your voice," Vince said when Mac identified himself.

"Same here."

"Where the hell are you?"

"Can't tell you."

"How did I know you were going to say that? You're all over the news. You know your friend Vichy wasn't aboard the launch that got blown up, right?" Mac did. Nash had received a radio call while they were in flight to tell him that the boat, which belonged to the Gendarmerie Maritime, had come from Guadeloupe at Vichy's request the previous evening. Vichy himself had headed to their meeting in a car; the launch had been backup, in case Mac and Callie had tried to get away by water.

"I'm all but locked out," Vince continued. "The feds only

humor me because they think I can lead them to you. They've got boots on the ground in the Caribbean, now, too."

"Which will serve no other purpose than to irritate the locals, who just lost their brothers. It doesn't pay to forget that the gendarmes aren't American police. They're the law-enforcement branch of the French military, and will be even less appreciative of outside interference than you or I would be."

"Yeah, well, no one ever said those guys were smart."

Mac laughed. "You got anything else?"

"One thing. And I don't know how reliable it is, so take it with a grain of salt."

"Gotcha."

"A week before her death, Robin Cory attended a fund-raiser in support of an organization devoted to fighting AIDS in Africa. So did your brother-in-law. That part is fact, backed up by photographs of the event. But none of those pictures show them together, so the gossip about the two of them possibly hooking up is unsubstantiated. It may also be completely meaningless, since he was at another well-photographed event—with a different woman, in a different country—the night the Masters women disappeared."

"Still, an oddity."

"I thought so. I guess there's no point in asking whether there's anything new on your end?"

"Nothing I can tell you."

"Understood."

Callie tapped at the door to let him know the food was ready, and he rang off with Vince, promising to call as soon as he could.

They ate sitting on the black leather couch in front of the enormous flat-screen television. Mac had turned on CNN, which was running their story—complete with video of the burning boat, though not the explosion itself, that some tourist had taken from the shore—almost nonstop. The anchor announced breathlessly that both French and US officials had become involved in the search for Callie and Mac. Nikki's dual citizenship, her American marriage, and the fact that both Mac and Callie were US citizens accounted for the involvement of the American authorities. But Nikki carried a French passport. A French landowner, she'd been murdered on French territory, which put the case squarely in the hands of France's legal system.

No evidence connected either Mac or Callie to the dead officers aboard the gendarmerie craft, and by a stroke of luck no one had caught the Jayhawk on camera. The news station, however, tied the murdered heiress and the bombed police boat together with a big red bow under the headline Violence in the French West Indies, and the anchor revealed—with yet more breathless excitement—that a source inside the gendarmerie had let slip that the officers aboard the destroyed powerboat were investigating Nicole Lewis Brody's murder. The two couples Nash had dropped aboard the *Lady* claimed to have watched in horror as a small helicopter without markings flew in, bombed the boat, hovered for a minute, and then took off.

"It all happened so quickly," said one of the men, his bright orange shirt making Mac wince. "I'm pretty sure they looked us over, though not for long. Thank goodness, they must have realized we weren't a threat. This isn't exactly the relaxing vacation we had planned."

"He should get an Oscar," Callie remarked. "Role of totally innocent American tourist, or whatever."

"Nash's people are well trained. If they came out of the

DEA with him, they'll be chameleons. Take the outfit that guy has on. When people talk about him tomorrow morning over the breakfast table, they'll remember his shirt more than his words, and certainly more than his face."

Callie turned her dark gaze on him. "They planned to wear those clothes because they knew they might end up on TV?"

"They're costumes. Not only overwhelmingly bright enough to draw attention away from the men's faces, they also play into the 'stupid American tourist' stereotype, so they serve purposes for both French and American audiences.

"Nash thought it out that carefully?"

"Good strategy is all about details, and whatever else he may be, Nash has always been an excellent strategist." Mac gathered their plates and stood. "You cooked; I'll clean."

He carried the dishes to the kitchen and rinsed them before sliding them into the dishwasher. When he turned around to ask Callie whether he should make coffee, he saw she'd fallen asleep, her head resting on arms she'd crossed on the sofa back. Her hair had fallen over her face in a wild tangle—the combination of the racing boat and the helicopter hadn't been kind. She'd tied it up, but most of it had come loose.

He should wake her. She'd washed her hands and face earlier, but she would want to shower, tame the wild hair before she crawled into bed. Perversely, he wished she'd leave it. He no longer saw the similarity to Nikki when he looked at Callie, no longer imbued her with his former wife's lying ways, but even so he preferred the inherent honesty of the slightly ragged look to the polished, professional demeanor she'd worn when they'd first met. He refused to consider why such a distinction should concern him.

A shower sounded good, though, so he decided to let her nap a while longer while he, himself, cleaned up. Muting the television, he headed for the bathroom. He hadn't shaved in days, and hoped Nash had provided a razor.

CALLIE RAN. WHITE sand sucked at her toes, bogged her down, held her back, but ahead she could see her house. Just outside the door, her parents stood, laughing, chatting with Erin and Tommy. Erin's hand rested on the doorknob, her key in the lock. Any minute, she would open the door, invite them in, and turn on the kettle for tea.

And the house would explode.

Callie tried to call out a warning about the gas leak, but her throat closed over the words. She gasped for breath, running flat out, but no matter how hard she pushed herself, she got no closer to the group. And they did not see her, could not hear the choking grunts that were all she seemed able to produce.

Callie came awake with a start when Mac laid a hand on her shoulder. He crouched beside the sofa.

"You okay?"

"Yes." She sat up, trying to clear her head. "It was a nightmare. Or . . ."

He settled beside her, chafing one of her hands between his own, and she saw the myriad little nicks and scars on his skin. "Or?"

"I think . . ." She swallowed, reorganizing her mind, admitting what the dream had been trying to tell her. Unconsciously, she laced her fingers through Mac's, seeking stability. "I think this guy has tried to kill me before."

She explained the fireplace malfunction and how Erin's highly tuned chef's sense of smell had alerted them to the gas seeping into the house before any of them could be harmed.

"We could both have died."

"But you didn't." Mac dropped her hand and drew her close, wrapping a strong arm around her shoulders, and she let him. He had showered, she noticed, and he smelled of soap, shampoo, and something faintly musky. His black T-shirt and dark jeans were clearly new, from whatever stock the unflappable Nash had supplied, but they fit perfectly. Even the knowledge that she only focused on such minute details to avoid considering her own situation couldn't prevent the tiny, hormonal hum that trilled through her when he slid one large hand beneath her hair to rub away the tension at the back of her neck.

"It always bothered me that he let you get as far as St. Martin, knowing you'd run into Nikki's friends and family. This explains why. He didn't intend to; you slipped through. No police report, I take it?"

Callie shook her head. "It was a bad valve. Or so we thought. The plumber said it could happen to anyone. And since there were no damages, I didn't even have to file an insurance claim." But she hadn't slept that night. And she'd spent the next day, while packing for St. Martin, assuring herself over and over that she didn't actually smell gas.

"You don't remember anything like that happening in the past? Any narrow escapes or close calls?"

"No. But, then, this whole thing just started, right? Debbie and Diane were killed a few months ago. And it's only been a month since Robin's murder. And Nikki . . ." She looked up at him. "I'm afraid I've been wrapped up in what's wrong with my own life. How are you holding up? Now that you know for sure?"

His fathomless green gaze caught hers, held. "I'm handling it. But I've known practically from the minute she disappeared—it's the one thing John and I had in common after the mystery woman washed up; we both hoped it would put pressure on the police to find Nikki's killer."

"Why do you dislike each other so much?"

His lips twisted into a self-deprecating grin. "Right from the start, he thought I was after Nikki's money, and never made any bones about that belief. Kind of hard to get along with a guy who treats you like a fortune hunter. Plus, he's a pompous ass."

A smile tugged at Callie's mouth, though she'd have considered it impossible mere minutes earlier. "He is a bit, isn't he?"

"I didn't realize you didn't care for him. You certainly acted bowled over by his charm."

"Dealing with John is . . . easy." She looked away so Mac couldn't see the corollary in her eyes: *Unlike you.* "I've been around his type my whole life. Born rich, made himself richer, used to being admired. He's far from the most arrogant man of his class I've ever met, but I can see how he might not make the ideal brother-in-law."

"No. Unfortunately, the fact that he didn't consider me good enough spurred me on rather than deterring me."

"Oh, dear." She laughed, glanced up, and found herself trapped in the sudden heat in his eyes. He, too, seemed paralyzed, his fingers stilling on her neck muscles. Gradually, the smile faded from his lips. His eyes dropped to her mouth, then returned. The hand at the back of her neck urged her forward.

A tiny, tinny voice in the back of her mind tried to lodge a protest in the name of common sense, but the moment his lips touched hers it was drowned in a wave of sensation. Heat swamped her, rushing through her veins, along her nerves, under her skin, and all she could hear was the sound of her heart pounding in her ears. Of its own volition, her mouth opened beneath his. His tongue swept in, tangled, teased, coaxed, invited.

He shifted, pulling her with him until they lay pressed together on the sofa, her on her back with his heavy, taut body half covering her. God, he was big. She ran her hands across his shoulders, over his chest, tracing his muscles through the thin cotton of his shirt. His hands were moving, too, and she felt him tug her shirt free of the waistband of her pants. He muttered something incomprehensible against her mouth when his fingers found her bathing suit rather than bare skin. The slick Lycra of the maillot effectively transmitted the heat from his body, as his hand slid up to cup her breast. She heard her own whimper as his thumb brushed over her nipple. She opened her eyes, trying to get her bearings, only to find herself staring at a full-screen televised photograph of Nicole Lewis Brody.

Mac's wife.

The fire drained from her, leaving her empty, hollow.

To his credit, Mac stilled almost immediately, then slowly removed his hand from beneath her shirt and levered himself up slightly. He looked down at her, followed the line of her sight, then cursed softly.

"I'm sorry."

That seemed to startle him, and he laid a finger beneath her cheek and turned her to face him. He studied her. "For what?"

"I don't know." Nor did she know why she suddenly felt like weeping. "For not being her, I guess."

⁓

Mᴀᴄ'ꜱ ɪɴɴᴇʀ ᴄʏɴɪᴄ attempted to analyze the statement. What game was this? What was Callie after? She hadn't pushed him off, but she'd turned her head away again, staring at the television, though Nikki's picture had been replaced by an advertisement. He'd had plenty of experience with Nikki's manipulations—giving sex, withholding it, teasing until she got whatever she desired. He should be able to work out Callie's, but he couldn't see her angle. Of course, that could have something to do with the fact that the majority of his blood was still considerably south of the border, and his brain wasn't functioning at full capacity.

"Why in the hell would you want to be Nikki?"

He felt her shrug, and she still wouldn't meet his eyes. When she spoke, he could hear the effort she expended to make her voice light. "It would have been nice to be able to give you what you wanted."

Fishing, his inner cynic stated, but for once Mac didn't pay attention. Nikki would have been fishing. Callie was honest, which meant he had to consider her words in a way he never had with Nikki. He took her chin between his thumb and forefinger and forced her head around, waiting until she looked directly at him.

"You think this is about her?"

"Of course." She smiled, even tossed her head as much as she could in her position, but he was learning to read her and knew the actions were as false as her lightness of tone. "You told Claudine I was a fat, boring imitation of your wife."

"I never said that."

Her glare was a challenge, and he pushed himself to think

back to that first day, those first few moments when they'd met. He couldn't remember his exact words, but he knew they hadn't been kind. He'd been furious.

"Tell me what I said."

She did.

"Fuck. I'm an ass, Callie. That day, Billy had called me from the gate. He said some woman who looked just like Nikki had shown up. You were on his reservation list, and you showed up right after she disappeared. It was like I'd been worried sick and she was just fucking with me. So I was angry. To put it mildly."

"She was your wife. You make it sound as if you didn't even like her."

"You're going to make me admit every ugly truth, aren't you?" And he was going to let her. Why, he couldn't say. Maybe because she was facing the ugliness of her own reality with such stoutness of heart. He shifted away, stood, and walked to the giant glass window. Outside, the river was quiet, blanketed in darkness. He turned his back on it to examine the woman who now sat on the sofa, knees drawn up in a way that was becoming familiar, watching him through wide, dark eyes.

"Did I tell you that when I was with the PD, I worked Narcotics?"

She shook her head.

"Well, I did. Most of the guys I came up with wanted assignment to Homicide, but that never held any appeal for me. I was an adrenaline junkie. I wanted the undercover ops, the edge, the scent of danger that hung in the very air around dealers and the vermin they ran with. I craved it.

"After the knife fight, when I couldn't work the street anymore, I went to see Travis because I couldn't figure out what else to do. And, God, I was so damned bored. Whatever I'd been hoping for, it wasn't living on a boat in the middle of nowhere doing nothing. I was about ready to leave when the security job at the Paradis came up. The money was decent, and I didn't have anywhere else to go, so I took it. But I was still . . . jonesing. I needed the rush." Even thinking about those days disgusted him. He'd been so far gone. How much longer would he have lasted among the pushers and pimps before crossing a line?

"And Nikki provided it? The rush?"

"Yeah. She was dangerous. Don't ask me how I recognized it. Experience, I guess. I got the same sense when I was with her I'd once had in Atlanta."

"You loved her because she was dangerous?"

"No. I *needed* her because she was dangerous. I was an addict looking for a fix. Even then, I never mistook the emotion for love, and by the time she disappeared, I'd already filed for divorce." He wondered what was going on behind that dark gaze of hers. She was weighing, considering, but giving no indication of the direction of her thoughts. "Like I said, the truth isn't pretty."

"Does all this"—she gestured vaguely around the room—"does it give you the fix you need? Boats exploding, climbing ladders into moving helicopters, shooting and being shot at . . . Does all that give you the rush you were looking for?"

"You don't like the easy questions, do you?" But she didn't return his smile, so he moved back to sit next to her on the couch, waiting until she faced him before continuing. He needed to have her completely focused on him if he was going to lay himself bare. "Living with Nikki wasn't the same as going undercover. It was more like playing in traffic with no one there to pick you up when you get hit. And you *are* going to get hit. Because when you're playing field hockey on a five-lane superhighway, it isn't about being fast enough, smart enough, strong enough or, well, *good* enough to avoid the cars. You may make the goal, but sooner or later, you're going to get crushed.

"So I'm working at not needing the rush so much anymore. I'd be lying if I said I didn't prefer the life Nash lives to the one Travis does, but this particular situation . . . No, I'm not enjoying it."

"Why not?"

She was so earnest, trying so hard to understand what he couldn't explain, that he couldn't help himself. He laid a hand along the side of her face and brushed his thumb over her full lower lip.

"Because you're not Nikki. And you're not me. You didn't go looking for trouble, and I'd have preferred if it hadn't found you. That being said, if it was going to find you anyway, I'm more than happy to have been on hand to help." He slid his thumb along the seam of her lips. "And, in case I haven't been perfectly clear on this point, sugar, don't be sorry about not being Nikki on my account. What I want has nothing whatsoever to do with her."

CHAPTER NINE

OH, YEAH, HE'D been perfectly clear. But he'd also left the ball in her court, and she wasn't at all sure what to do. The slow drag of his thumb stroking her skin rekindled the flames running along nerves all through her body. It would be easy to succumb to the heat, to let the fire burn away all her fears, all her memories, even if only for a short time. He could make her forget the world.

The telephone jolted her out of his sensual spell. Both she and Mac whipped around to stare at it where it lay on the kitchen counter. She stood first, and was reaching for the receiver when the doorbell rang, three short, sharp bursts followed by the sound of a heavy fist banging on the security door.

"I've got that." Mac headed for the entry.

"Miss Pearson," said a crisp voice when she answered the phone, "this is Lexie. Nash is on his way up to your apartment. We need to move you."

"He's here."

"Ah, he elected not to stop, then. Good. I'll let him explain." She hung up, leaving Callie with a dial tone buzzing in her ear. Nash followed Mac into the apartment.

"Time to go," he said the minute they reached Callie. "Someone knows you're here."

"How is that possible?" Callie asked at the same time as Mac asked, "What happened?"

Nash addressed Callie. "It's my fault. It never occurred

to me to check you for tracking devices. I didn't realize what we were dealing with." He pulled a handheld scanner from his pocket and ran it up and down Callie's body, like a doctor examining a patient in a science fiction movie. "Not in your clothes. It'll be in your purse, then."

"But how . . . who . . . ?" A tremor shook the building, accompanied by muffled crash. The lights went out. Red emergency lights popped on, and a siren began to wail somewhere in the distance.

Callie was terrified, but Nash appeared unfazed. "Boom-Boom was right," he said.

"Seth's working for you, too? Did you leave anyone to do government work?"

Nash shrugged. "HSE can afford the best, and Lindsay fits the bill." He looked at Callie, read the confusion on her face. "Seth Lindsay worked as a demolitions expert when Mac and I were in the Army." The siren shut off. "Of course, now that his suppression design saved the damned building, I'll probably have to give him a bonus."

The floor had stopped shaking, but Callie had not. Mac slid an arm over her shoulders, pulled her close, and she wrapped her arms around his waist and held tight. Like Nash, he seemed to take the explosion in stride.

"Car bomb?"

"Indeed. He tried to jack the code to get into the garage, so we trapped him in the tunnel. Seth set it up. Baffles on top of baffles. You can't prevent the ground tremor, but you can keep the building from coming down around your ears. But we don't have time to chat. The insulation keeps the noise down, but this is a residential neighborhood. Someone will have called the police. So, Callie, if you'll get your purse?"

She reluctantly detached herself from Mac's solid stability

and retrieved the bag from the bedroom. Nash ran the scanner over it. A high-pitched whine indicated that it had found something, and he pressed a button on the device. A second later, the noise stopped.

"Useful," said Mac.

"Come to work for HSE and you, too, can play with all the cool toys. But we have to get a move on. There are wigs, hats, things like that in the bags of clothes Lexie left in the bedroom. Put something on. We have to take you out of the building, and I don't want you recognizable when you leave. There are also vests."

It took Callie a moment to realize he meant bulletproof vests. Once she did, her teeth began to chatter.

"D-do you really th-think we'll need those?"

Nash didn't meet her eyes. Instead, he shared a look with Mac, who grabbed her hand and tugged her into the bedroom.

"Come on, sugar," he coaxed, voice dark and soothing, "let's see what lovely Lexie bought for you."

He pulled some jeans and a T-shirt out of a shopping bag, then a pair of panties and a bra. The sight of the underwear—plain, practical, white cotton without a scrap of lace—in his large, dark, scarred hand sent a frightening shock of awareness through her. She swallowed hard and battled it back, concentrating on the mundane.

"How did she know my size?"

Mac laughed hoarsely, clearing his throat before he spoke. The sudden intimacy had obviously affected him, too. "I'd lay odds that was Trav's doing. He's a ladies' man. Probably had your measurements down before you set foot on *The Tramp*." He handed her the clothes, then dug back through the bag, coming up with two wigs. "You want to be black or blonde?"

Remembering Nikki's long fall of blond hair, Callie took the black wig and retreated to the bathroom.

She shucked off the clothes she'd been wearing for what seemed like a week, then pulled on the underwear and T-shirt. Unfortunately, no matter how she tried, she couldn't get into the jeans; Travis had sussed out her 34C bra correctly, but she hadn't worn size six jeans since . . . well, not since she'd broken off with Theo after her father's death. And wasn't that just the confidence builder she needed at this very moment? The memory of Theo, the perfectionist thoracic surgeon, who'd proposed to her despite constantly finding fault with her weight, her hair, her style of dress.

"Get a move on," she heard Nash shout. The regular lights flickered back to life, and she gave up on the jeans. Poking her head out the bathroom door, she asked Mac to pass her the shopping bag.

Inside, she found a loose, ankle-length bohemian-style skirt with an elastic waist. It wouldn't be as easy to move around in as pants, but at least it fit and didn't rub against her bruised hip. She pulled her hair into a tight knot at the base of her skull and yanked the wig over it.

She emerged to find Mac holding out a bulky black vest in one hand and a blue nylon windbreaker with a big New York Yankees insignia on the back in the other. He was already wearing a similar set of clothes, along with a Yankees baseball cap pulled low over his forehead. She slipped the vest over her head and tightened the straps around her waist.

"It's heavy, I know," he said, "but you'll get used to it." She doubted the truth of his statement but settled the awkward covering on her shoulders as comfortably as possible. He helped her on with the jacket, and they rejoined Nash in the foyer.

"You know the city, right?" She nodded. "Good. Lexie got you two a room at the DoubleTree Suites in Times Square. You're registered as Joshua and Kathleen Marsh." He handed each of them a credit card with the Marsh name. "You do the check-in. Even with the hat, the scar makes Mac's face too memorable.

"A crowd is gathering, so it's time we joined the party on the sidewalk." Nash handed Callie a MetroCard, the ticket to the New York City subway system. "Slip away when you can. If you can get a taxi, it'd be safer than the subway, but have them drop you at the TKTS booth or something, not the hotel, just in case anyone asks." He led them out of the apartment and down the hall. They jogged down the stairs, Nash's voice echoing slightly as he spoke to Mac.

"Call me when you get checked in. Before this guy showed up, we found an interesting connection between the Steeles and your in-laws, but I don't want to get into it until we have plenty of time to hash it out. Despite Seth's setup, I'm not certain we can hide the fact that the explosion came from here, so I suspect I'll be tied up for a while."

Callie stumbled, her sore hip knocking into the railing, but Mac caught her before she fell. "The guy who did this," she coughed, almost unable to voice the words. "Is he alive?"

"Unfortunately not." They reached the landing for the second floor, the public access area, and Nash pulled the door open. "Step off here for a minute. We can't talk privately in the stairway." When the door closed behind them, he held up a hand to silence Callie's questions.

"Guy breaks in, expecting to park the car under the building, get to a safe distance, then detonate. No idea yet how big a blast he expected. Maybe the bomb was designed to bring down the whole building, maybe just to send all the residents running into the street, where you'd be easy prey. Either way, when the gate came down behind him and the one at the bottom of the ramp didn't open, trapping him in the tunnel, he panicked. Lexie has that part on video. When I came to get you, he was standing outside the car, trying to figure out what to do. That tunnel has other . . . features. If he'd been alone, he'd have been unconscious in a couple minutes and we'd have gone in after him. Unfortunately for him, he had a partner, or an employer, who was willing to sacrifice him so he couldn't answer our questions."

"The partner smelled the trap and detonated with him still in the tunnel," said Mac.

"Looks that way."

Callie could feel hysteria bubbling through her system, emerging as a tiny squeak of sound in her throat.

Mac grabbed her shoulders, turned her to face him. "Look at me. Callie. Look at me." She did, focusing on his eyes. Once searing hot, they were now utterly cold. "That man would have killed you, killed every innocent person in this building just to get to you, to us, without hesitation. You have to remember that."

But she couldn't seem to. "W-what if h-he h-had a w-wife? A f-family?"

Some of the chill left Mac's gaze, and his voice went low, soft, persuasive. "Then they're better off without him. A man who'd blow up an entire city block for money, he couldn't be a good husband, a good father. He wouldn't have it in him. Right?"

She found herself nodding.

"So shut him out. We have to concentrate on getting you somewhere safe, where we can figure out exactly what is going on."

She nodded again, which Nash took as his cue to open the stairway door and begin hurrying them downstairs once again. They exited the stairway into a small lobby, no different from hundreds of others in Manhattan. A man in a doorman's uniform stood chatting with a young couple near the street entrance while several others milled around. Police cruisers and fire trucks had pulled up outside, and multi-hued flashes of light strobed through the plate-glass windows.

"Any problems, Ted?" Nash asked the uniformed man.

"No, sir." Pale green eyes flashed over her and Mac in a single, comprehensive glance. Doorman, my ass, Callie thought. Ted was another HSE operative.

Lexie approached them. "Seth is still in the tunnel," she said with a brief nod of greeting. "There's no damage visible from the street, so if we can keep people out of the building, no one has to know this was the source of the blast. With enough manpower, Seth can get the damage hidden within six to eight hours, completely repaired with no trace left behind within a couple of days."

"Good enough. Get him whatever he needs. Let's go outside and make ourselves available. Mac, Callie, hang behind and take off when you can. I'll catch up with you later."

Nash opened the front door, and everyone in the lobby began to drift outside. Mac took Callie's hand and towed her along, exiting the building behind the couple who had been with Ted when they'd arrived. Mac kept them close to the building, moving from one cluster of people to the next. Callie spoke a few words every time they shifted groups, Mac remaining silent, his right side toward each new group to prevent his scar from drawing unwanted attention.

Minutes seemed hours, but eventually they reached the subway entrance. Even sitting on the train, however, Callie could not relax, and when a transit officer entered their car, seemingly intent on memorizing the faces of all the passengers, panic welled up in her chest. Mac had seated himself to her right so he could hide his ruined cheek by facing her, but the window behind their seats acted as a mirror—should the officer glance at it, he'd notice the unmistakable scar.

As nonchalantly as she could, Callie raised her right hand and laid it along Mac's face, carefully masking the scar tissue. His body tensed as she used her hold to urge him toward her. His mouth met hers and she whispered "Cop" against his lips, hoping the single word would suffice as explanation.

Whether it did or not, she had no time for more, as Mac took control of the kiss, and the same hungry heat she'd felt earlier rushed back through her. The man could kiss. His left arm, which had rested along the seat back behind her shoulders, now cinched her against him, his hand cupping the back of her head. His right hand mirrored her own, sliding along the side of her face, both hiding her features and holding her in position. He sucked her lower lip between his teeth and bit down gently, and Callie felt a rush of wet heat soak her new panties. She wanted to climb into his lap then and there, take the ride all the way to the end, but he drew away.

"Our stop, I think." His voice was as low and uneven as the rumble of the train itself. How he'd managed to catch the announcement she had no idea.

Shaking with embarrassment and need, unable to look at him or any of the other passengers, she allowed him to take her hand and help her off the train.

As Nash had recommended, Callie checked them in while Mac ducked into the men's room in the hotel lobby, where he would not be noticed. By the time he met her at the bank of elevators, Callie had managed to regain some of her composure.

"We're in 706," she said, handing him a key card as they let a crowd of tourists sweep them into the elevator car. They remained silent while the car rose, disgorging passengers on both the fourth and fifth floor before opening onto the seventh for them.

The moment they entered the room, Mac used his cell to call Nash, who would ring them back, Callie assumed, from yet another prepaid cell so no record would exist tying him to the hotel.

"Why don't you take a shower," Mac suggested as he hung up. "It's been a long day."

"It has. I just wish we'd brought the new clothes your friend organized for us."

"He'll bring them. Checking in with only shopping bags looks too suspicious, and we didn't have time to round up suitcases." At her puzzled expression, he explained. "We talked it over while you were changing."

"So he'll be here tonight?"

"If he can get away. With the escalation, there doesn't seem to be time to waste."

Callie shook her head. "Don't you ever sleep?"

"Adrenaline." Mac smiled wryly. "You may be exhausted, but if you were to lie down on that bed right now, I doubt you'd be able to close your eyes."

"I'll just hop in the shower, then," Callie replied, hoping he wouldn't notice the blush that had begun to rise the moment he'd said the word "bed." What was wrong with her? So the guy was sexy as hell. She had more important things to worry about.

WHEN THE BATHROOM door closed behind Callie, Mac drew in a deep breath and let it out slowly, trying to ease the tension in his muscles. What the hell was the matter with him? He'd lost control on the train, so intent on the woman in his arms he'd barely heard the conductor announcing their arrival at Times Square.

And that after he'd admitted to her things about himself—and his relationship with Nikki—he'd never admitted to another person. He'd barely recognized the thrill-seeking behavior that had drawn them together himself. He paced the room for a couple of minutes, flipped on the TV, then sat at the desk to make a list of the things he wanted Nash to get him.

The knock at the door came sooner than he expected, not even twenty minutes after their arrival. Callie was still in the bathroom, though the shower had cut off and he could hear the hair dryer buzzing. He took the sack of women's clothes Nash had with him and tapped on the bathroom door. When Callie peered out, shielding her towel-wrapped body as much as possible behind the door, he handed her the bag.

As well as clothes, Nash had brought a laptop-computer setup complete with printer, and two large thermoses full of coffee. While they waited for Callie to finish up, Nash poured mugs full of the steaming brew for all three of them and laid them on the table in the sitting room of the suite, and Mac set up the laptop on the desk.

When Callie emerged, she was wearing the same outfit she'd had on earlier, minus the vest, which reminded Mac to take off his own. Some cops he knew complained that the things were hideously uncomfortable, but he'd never noticed. Perhaps it was because of the Army training, where he'd become accustomed to wearing and carrying far bulkier, more awkward items.

Nash settled in the armchair next to the small coffee table, leaving Mac and Callie the couch.

"So tell me about the Steeles and the Lewises," Mac said as soon as everyone was seated. "What kind of deal did they have going?"

"Do you remember what the press dubbed Ed Steele before he was arrested?"

"The gift rapist," Callie said promptly.

Nash looked at her in surprise. "Do you remember why?"

"Because he told the women they should be happy that he'd selected them, that he was a gift from God."

What a sick fuck. Mac hadn't had a chance to read through all the papers himself, and he'd forgotten that aspect of the rapes.

"Ed Steele grew up believing himself to be special. His parents repeatedly told him he was, literally, a miracle child, a gift from God. Financial records show payments to three separate fertility clinics before his conception, including—at the end—Mark Lewis's Miami office."

"Hell," said Mac, a sick feeling settling in his gut, "I know where you're going with this."

"Mark Lewis wouldn't have been the first fertility doctor to use his own sperm to inseminate a woman if her husband's wasn't doing the trick, nor would he have been the last. Probably the most famous was Cecil Jacobson, in the eighties. He was convicted of many crimes, but there was only one case where they found the genetic evidence he'd substituted his own sperm for a patient's husband's. In most of the cases, the women had signed up to receive sperm from anonymous donors. Since he claimed that one instance to have been a lab mistake right to the end, never admitting that he did it on purpose, we have no way of knowing the psychology behind the act."

"You're telling me that Mark Lewis might be my biological father?" Callie's voice was strained, and lines bracketed her lips. Without thinking, Mac reached for her hand and warmed it between his own.

"It's a good possibility." Nash kept his tone matter-of-fact, but Mac could see the anger seething below the smooth mask. He knew his own expression mirrored Nash's.

"John Lewis said his father was a name-dropper," Callie offered. "If he wanted famous clients, he'd have to keep up a good success rate."

"And Lewis would be reluctant to tell a famous client like Ephraim Steele that his sperm wasn't viable, which is likely what the other doctors the Steeles saw said. So when Polly got pregnant, they called Ed their miracle baby."

"And Lewis their miracle doctor," Mac remarked, slotting the various pieces into place. "The Masters family hasn't spoken to the police about fertility treatments," Nash continued, "but the incidence of fraternal twins is high in IVF, as it is when women take fertility drugs."

"What does any of this matter, though? Mark Lewis is dead." Callie shook her head. "So he was a criminal, and he conned a lot of people; his good reputation might have been enough for him to kill for, but surely not for anyone else to?"

"If you're all his biological heirs, you all have claims against his estate. Unlike ours, the French legal system specifies exactly how much of the estate has to be held for biological heirs. And when an estate is worth hundreds of millions of dollars, which Lewis's was by the time he died, that's a damn good reason for murder."

"So John Lewis could be killing off his father's other children." Mac watched Nash closely. "But you don't think that's all there is to it, do you?"

"No."

"Finish it, then."

"Thirty years ago, adoption services focused on 'matching' a child to parents of the same religious, ethnic, and cultural background, and they liked to keep track of adoptees. So your parents, Callie, with their traveling and the fact that they came from different backgrounds, much like the Corys, would have been considered unstable and bad bets as far as legal adoption went.

"Your mother died of ovarian cancer?"

Callie nodded.

"There's a long history of ovarian cancer associated with fertility drugs. I suspect that the problem for your parents wasn't on your father's side. If your mother couldn't conceive, even after the drugs, even with IVF, and adoption was out of the question, Lewis may have offered a . . . slightly less legal alternative."

"You think my parents . . ." Callie's voice trailed away, and Mac's heart broke for her. He'd heard in her voice that night on the beach how much she'd idolized her father.

"I think they bought you. Possibly, they believed they were going through a surrogate, that the egg and sperm were their own, but I doubt it. Not only because the idea of legal surrogacy didn't become popular until after your birth, but because had the transaction been legal, there would have been no need to dummy up a birth certificate that claimed your mother gave birth to you."

"And by then, Lewis had moved to the island," Mac agreed. *Stick to the topic, keep away from the personal aspects.* "He was operating outside the US legal system. He had the birth mother with him there. Your father must have taken the picture of you with your mother when they picked you up. You said your father was familiar with boats; chances are they came over from, say, Miami, collected you, and sailed home. Restrictions were a lot looser in those days. If they drove from New York to Florida, they'd never have to pass through an airport, through any kind of official channels. Using the private dock at the hotel and another private dock in Florida would have made them virtually invisible. Sure, their boat might have been searched for drugs, but that's about it."

"But why not bring my birth certificate with them? Put an earlier date on it, not a later one?"

"Maybe you were premature," Mac suggested. "They had everything planned out, organized the birth certificate and had it done up in advance so your parents could bring it with them to St. Martin in case anyone checked on their way back into the US, but you came early."

"That would do it," said Nash. "Lewis wouldn't want the birth mother to keep you—she might get attached to you."

"Even if I accepted all this, and I am not saying I do, parts of what's happening still don't fit for me." Callie pulled free of Mac's grip and walked over to the window overlooking Times Square. "You think John Lewis killed all these people to protect his inheritance. But would a man like him even know how to hire a killer? How could he find someone to stab Ed Steele in prison? And why try to blow up my house before I got to St. Martin, but then attempt a kidnapping once I was there, rather than just killing me outright?"

"I don't know," Nash admitted. "We're a long way from having a perfect theory, and a longer way from proving it, certainly from proving it to the satisfaction of the court system either in the US or in France."

"So even if you knew for sure John was behind this, you couldn't make him stop." Callie still hadn't turned around, and Mac wished he could see her face, rather than those tight shoulders, that stiff back. She was taking the whole situation remarkably calmly, at least on the surface, but without a glimpse of her eyes, he couldn't tell how much was an act.

"Not yet. We've put his name out through channels to see what we can dig up, though. HSE has resources, Calliope. We will get John Lewis. You just have to give us a little time."

Callie nodded but remained where she was. Nash shared a glance with Mac, then rose.

"I'm heading back downtown. I'll call you as soon as we hear anything. Try to get some sleep."

After bolting the door behind Nash, Mac walked over to the window. Callie had not budged. After a minute, he slipped his arms around her, pulling her back against him. She stiffened even further, every muscle strung tight, then relaxed. In silence, he rested his chin on the crown of her head. Outside, lights flashed, giant videos played on electronic billboards, and tourists in T-shirts made merry in the warm summer night. Times Square was still alive, bustling with movement despite the late hour.

"When we were on the island," Callie said at last, "and you suggested trying for a DNA match between me and the woman they thought might be Nicole, did John object?"

"Not much. He probably knew it wasn't Nikki, so he didn't worry about the results. I never mentioned wanting to send the results to Vince, or he might have put up more of a fuss."

"Do police check international databases of DNA? Do such things even exist?"

"I'm sure every country has their own that other law-enforcement agencies could theoretically get access to if they were willing to go through the necessary hoops, but the fact is that not every local PD even has the necessary equipment to connect to CODIS, the Combined DNA Index System for the US. I never heard of anyone in our department, or even in the GBI—the Georgia Bureau of Investigation—trying to find a match through an international database. Why?"

"Because Mark Lewis bought the Paradis from Andre Charbonnet after helping him and his wife conceive. How many other European clients might he have had? I can't help wondering whether any of their children have turned up dead or missing recently."

Mac reached for his cell phone with one hand, using the other to keep Callie anchored firmly to him, and dialed Nash. "Can you talk?" he asked when the other man answered.

"Yeah. I'm driving, though. What's up?"

"I have a project for your geek squad. We need an untraceable website with an e-mail drop box, dedicated to finding former clients of the Lewis clinic. And it has to be publicized as quickly and widely as possible, in papers worldwide. The kind of people who used Lewis's services don't surf the dark corners of the web, so we need to advertise in the *New York Times*, the *International Herald Tribune*, the *London Times*, the *Wall Street Journal*, places like that. If we can get enough evidence of Pop Lewis's misdeeds, maybe John will see the futility of trying to erase them."

"Just one problem. We can't be sure any of the people involved is related to Lewis. His DNA we don't have."

"Fuck. How could I have missed that?"

"We all did. Lexie was just pointing it out to me on the phone when you called. When I get downtown, I'll see what I can find out about Lewis's family, whether there are any brothers and sisters willing to submit samples for analysis. Exhumation's a possibility, if Lewis is buried in the States, though if the kid has half a brain—and he seems to—he'll have had dear old dad cremated."

A couple of unconnected bits of data coalesced into an ugly whole, and Mac cursed again. "Don't bother. If there were relatives, John's eliminated them. He couldn't afford to have them hanging around, because they would have proved he wasn't Lewis's kid."

"What?" Nash and Callie spoke as one.

"It's the only thing that makes sense. You never met Nikki, Nash, but I guarantee she and Callie are related. If they have the same father, and that father is Mark Lewis, then Callie and John should share DNA, too. But I'll bet anything you like they don't. It's the only reason he wouldn't have objected more strenuously to testing Callie. He knew no matter what happened, she couldn't be connected to him."

"Well, hell."

"Exactly." Callie tried to squirm out of his grasp, but he hung on to her. "Get your guys working on the Lewis clinic stuff. Call when you get something set up." He flipped the phone shut, shoved it back into his pocket, and, taking Callie by the shoulders, turned her to face him. Her dark eyes brimmed with tears.

"This is good news," he said, the ferocity of his own words surprising him. "You don't want to be related to a mass murderer."

"I don't want to be related to a con man who sold black-market babies or a serial rapist, either," she replied, shrugging him off and stalking across the room, "but no one asked me." She plopped down on the sofa and looked up at him. "What am I supposed to do now?"

"I wish I had an easy answer. It's late. Maybe Nash's night owls will have something for us in the morning."

"I don't think sleep is on the agenda." She glanced away, then back at him, then patted the cushion next to her. He accepted the invitation. "You told me you grew up in Atlanta," she said once he was seated. "What was your family like?"

"Small. Most of my life, it was just me and my mom. My dad couldn't hack the responsibility of a wife and kid, and hit the road when I was four. He sent money off and on for a couple of years, then disappeared altogether."

"That must have been tough."

"For my mother, it probably was. But most of my neighborhood was single-parent families, with mothers who cleaned houses like mine or worked as cocktail waitresses or worse. Many of the guys I ran with had never met their fathers, so I had it pretty good." Jesus, he sounded like a sap. What was it about this woman that made him open up like a fucking book?

"Your mother, is she still alive?"

"No. She died while I was in the Army. Massive stroke." It still hurt to think about her dying alone with him half a world away, but the doctors had assured him she hadn't suffered. "I'm sorry." Callie touched the back of his hand, and he flipped it, twining his fingers with hers. "Why the sudden interest in my parents?" He figured he knew the answer, but it would be better for her to admit it herself.

⌐

CALLIE STARED DOWN at their hands, her pale, small fingers meshed with his large, brown ones. How could she explain to him what she didn't even understand herself? Since her father's death, she'd felt unmoored, adrift. The discovery of the picture had compounded the sensation, and the events of the past several days . . .

"I'm not sure I know who I am."

"Of course you do. You're Calliope Elizabeth Pearson. You've lived all over the world and speak, what, four languages? You share a house with a chef named Erin and write articles for travel magazines. Nothing about you has changed. Your biological family is just a little different from what you believed."

"That biological family doesn't frighten you at all? I guess Mark Lewis isn't technically a rapist, but he certainly inseminated a lot of unwilling women, and he obviously passed along his bad genes to Ed Steele."

"Did he? I'm no scientist. I can't say definitively there's no genetic component to evil. In fact, I'm pretty sure there is one; one bad seed in a family of great people—what other cause is there? I saw it all the time in Narcotics. But biology isn't destiny. Humans are capable of tremendously unselfish acts, and there's no biological reason for them. Robin Cory, Deborah and Diane Masters—they were Lewis's kids, too, and they contributed to charity projects that benefited hundreds, even thousands of people.

"You were the one who said Ephraim Steele traded in his faith for profit. Doesn't it make sense he'd raise a kid without a conscience, even if that kid wasn't biologically predisposed not to give a damn about anyone else?"

"I suppose." Callie took a deep breath, tried to let Mac's assurance release some of her tension.

"And John Lewis, whose parentage we know nothing about—though I'm certain Nash is digging into it even as we speak—could have turned out completely normal if he hadn't been raised by Mark Lewis."

"His mother committed suicide." Remembering his telling her so, she realized she might have spent an evening looking through family scrapbooks with a killer. Shouldn't she have been able to tell?

"Yeah. Nikki told me about it. The first Mrs. Mark Lewis locked herself in their garage with the car running. Makes you wonder if she suddenly realized what she had married."

CHAPTER TEN

John Lewis hated to sweat, avoided it whenever possible, but he was sweating now. Luckily, the man on the other end of the phone couldn't see the moisture beading around his hairline or smell the fear and frustration oozing from his pores.

"I told you, she doesn't know anything. That picture was all she had. There was no need for your stunt in Grand Case. You brought the fucking gendarmes down on me for no reason whatsoever. They're crawling all over the hotel. I don't dare move the crates. Not now."

"You imagine I care about some provincial French law enforcement? Do you have any idea who helped your brother-in-law evade us? Who took him to the US and hid him there?" The smooth, cultured voice was sharp with fury.

A drop of sweat rolled down John's face. "Why don't you tell me?"

"Are you familiar with Harp Security Enterprises?"

"No."

"Then you are a fool. Dwight Harper would like nothing more than to get a man inside my organization. He and his private army, recruited from your country's three-letter agencies, have caused me no end of trouble. I've spent countless dollars, missed out on lucrative opportunities, lost good men, all because of him. And you, you bring him right to my door. Dwight Harper served with Brody in the Army. You should have known that."

"Don't lay this on me. Your man in New York was supposed to take Callie Pearson out of the equation before she even met Brody." John twitched, imagining Callie's body going up in flames. How could he have ordered such a thing? What a horrible waste it would have been, especially since he'd had to dispose of Nicole's body before he could get much out of it. The drugs, the booze, the freezing, something had damaged her beyond utility. And Callie, Callie was the youngest of the girls. She would have been his father's greatest creation. With every day, he was more certain she held the cure.

"And he has seen the error of his ways."

John shivered at the implied threat, again thankful Henry Falcone couldn't see him. John had beaten the odds for almost twenty years, using a playboy socialite persona to keep his reputation as clean as his hands were dirty, but Falcone, though close to him in age, had been in the game twice as long and more than twice as deep.

At fifteen, John had overheard a conversation between Mark and Ava Lewis that gave him his first clue as to the source of his father's wealth. He'd only had vacations to search, so it had taken three years to find Mark Lewis's secret records, but the payoff had been more than worth the effort. His respect for Lewis—lost upon discovering that his mother had conned Lewis into marriage by claiming another, far less respectable man's baby was his, which she'd told her son in a fit of drunken regret when he was seven—returned. That admiration had grown with the realization that Mark Lewis had manipulated his first wife into committing suicide when her drinking and wild moods had threatened to become an embarrassment.

Upon graduating high school, John had insisted on inclusion in all aspects of his father's business. He'd gone to college for hotel management but had spent his summers at the

Lewis fertility clinic in Miami. Between the two, he acquired a firm grasp on both international finance and the psychology of victimization. He could smell desperation whenever it entered his orbit, and never hesitated to take advantage of it. By twenty-five, he'd amassed a small fortune, carefully secreted in offshore banks, by selling drugs through the clinic behind Mark Lewis's back.

But after a while, running the clinic's illegal sideline became too easy. No one suspected such an upstanding citizen, and John became restless. He'd been searching for something to bring the heady taste of risk back into his life when a fire swept through the property in 2001. Like most people, Mark Lewis was underinsured. He sent John out to find new financing, but traditional investors had no interest in the kind of terms Mark Lewis—who insisted on retaining control of the hotel—was willing to offer.

John had tasted failure for the first time, and in the quiet wretchedness of it he could hear his mother's voice and her laughter. She expected him to come to a bad end. She sneered at his pathetic attempts to save his father and the legacy they had built together.

You're no better than your father. And I don't mean that shit with his fancy car and his fancy degree. I mean your real father. You know what he was? He was a high school football coach. I screwed his brains out the night after I lost my virginity to your precious daddy. He was a total loser, your biological father. He fucking cried afterwards. Said he had nothing to offer me. Like what? Marriage? He was already married. That's why I fucked him; his wife was my English teacher and she was a bitch. He was nothing. Nothing. Just like you're going to be. You're going to lose that goddamned hotel, and I am going to laugh and laugh and laugh.

Which was how John had come to an agreement with Henry Falcone.

For more than ten years now, Falcone had been paying to use the Paradis's private docks, its storage facilities, and the occasional bungalow to conduct his business under the aegis of the Lewises' sterling reputation. The relationship provided numerous benefits to both men, but the hotel was John's, and he'd always considered himself in charge of the operation.

Until today.

"Look," he said, forcing a conciliatory note into his voice. "Mistakes were made, obviously. But Calliope Pearson's no threat to you."

He'd asked Falcone for help to eliminate a few threats to the Lewis estate, claiming that undiscovered heirs endangered their business dealings. Falcone had lent him a hit man for the Masters sisters and another to blow up Callie's house. Thank goodness that one had failed.

"You assured me your sister's husband wasn't a threat."

"He wasn't. Isn't." At the angry silence on the other end of the phone, he rushed on, the next words tasting foul. "I could have been wrong about that. But you never told me to look for connections to Harp Security. I never even heard of them." Falcone growled, and John pushed on. "Nothing ties you to me. Nothing. We've made certain of it. So relax. Even if Callie Pearson manages to figure out what my father was up to, she couldn't connect it to you. Hell, she couldn't even prove her own paternity. You have nothing to worry about, regardless of what friends Mac Brody may have."

Still, John would be happier if Callie were under his control. He'd enjoyed killing Robin Cory even more than planning the deaths of the Steeles and Mark and Ava Lewis. Doing the deed himself had been so much more fulfilling.

Nicole's death, hurried and completely contrary to his plan, had been less than satisfying. Not that he liked killing people. He wasn't a monster, after all. He just preferred to solve problems in the most efficient way possible.

And while Callie Pearson was a solution, she was also a problem. Not to Falcone—he hadn't lied about that—but to the Lewis family name and therefore to John. If Brody had the kind of resources Falcone implied he did, Callie could turn over some rocks John would rather remain undisturbed before providing him with a permanent solution.

"If there's nothing to worry about," said Falcone, his ominously slick tone dragging John back to the conversation, "you should be able to deliver my merchandise."

Falcone's merchandise. Two hundred pounds of explosives, six grenade launchers, and three crates of grenades, along with one locked silver suitcase, all stored in a hidden four-foot-by-six-foot alcove John had built into the wine cellar during the post-fire renovations. He was damned proud of that room. He'd hired an architect from Paris to design two plans for the wine cellar, one with it and one without. John had filed the plans for the cellar without the extra space but given his contractor the set that included it. Both the contractor, a local, and the architect, had died in unfortunate accidents—a hit-and-run and a mugging—within months after the project was completed. And thanks to Falcone, those tasks had been undertaken by men with no connection whatsoever to either John or the hotel.

"Maybe in a few days. I told you, the place is infested with gendarmes."

"Thursday night."

"Jesus, Falcone, you're not listening to me."

"You have your priorities; I have mine. Eduard will be by

Thursday night at the customary time. I expect you to have the arrangements made." Falcone hung up, and John slammed the phone into the cradle. What the fuck was he supposed to do now?

He stalked over to the window and looked out over the midnight landscape. Past the driveway, a path wound toward the sea. His little yacht, a weekend cruiser named *Espresso*, was docked at the pier extending out into the water there. He had forty-eight hours to take it over to the Paradis docks and transfer the items from the cellar, then bring the boat back. Between three and four on Friday morning, Falcone's men would remove the merchandise.

Normally, John threw big parties when he had to move product for Falcone, either at his home or at the hotel, so boats would cluster along the shoreline. It was part of the logic behind expanding the hotel operations: the more people who came and went, the less suspicious any activity would seem. But this had been an emergency shipment. Falcone needed it to disappear for a couple of weeks when the original deal had gone wrong. He'd shown up with it two days after Nikki's death, reserving a bungalow for one of his men without advance warning.

Too many damned torches to juggle. John settled behind his desk and reached underneath for the button that would unlock the secret compartment where he kept his journal. Smoothing his fingers over the fine, leather cover, the uneven edges of the handmade paper, he let a plan begin to take shape in his head. He drew a fountain pen from the display case on the desk and began to write, setting out what he needed to complete his strategy. Once he had finished, he picked up the phone to call Falcone back. He was going to require assistance.

CHAPTER ELEVEN

Callie woke slowly, her brain adjusting to her surroundings with less than its usual agility. She'd been in too many hotels in the past week. This was the DoubleTree, she reminded herself. Times Square. New York City. The shades were drawn, but daylight seeped around their edges. The clock read 9:43.

From the other room of the suite, she heard the tapping of computer keys, the same sound she'd fallen asleep to. Had Mac been to bed at all? He'd gotten a phone call from Nash in the middle of their conversation about the Lewis family history and, following Nash's instructions, had used the new laptop to log securely into Harp Security's system. He'd urged Callie to get some rest and promised to wake her should anything of consequence occur.

That must have been around two. Could he really have stayed up all night? She grimaced at her reflection in the bathroom mirror and opted to take another shower before facing the world. What she really wanted was a bath—long, luxurious, and relaxing—but she didn't envision getting home to her soaking tub in the near future, so the sweetly scented hotel soap and the oddly soothing act of shaving her legs would have to suffice.

Once the hot water had rinsed away some of her weariness, she toweled off, forced her unruly hair into a tight French braid, and slipped into a fresh black T-shirt and the same skirt she'd worn the night before. The shopping bag hadn't provided much else in her size. Whatever Nash and Mac might be planning, she'd have to insist on stopping somewhere for a decent pair of jeans.

Stepping into the living area of the suite, she noted the linens piled haphazardly on the sofa and immediately felt guilty for hogging the bed.

"You shouldn't have slept out here," she said. "It can't have been comfortable. We could have shared the bed."

Mac glanced up from the computer, his jade eyes searing her skin. "No, we couldn't."

O-kay. Nowhere near ready to go there, Callie squelched her body's immediate reaction and changed the subject. "What are you up to?"

The hotel had provided only one desk chair, so in answer, Mac rose and moved the laptop to the coffee table, where both he and Callie could see the screen by sitting on the couch. She dumped the previous night's blankets and pillows on the chair, trying not to be flustered by the peculiar intimacy of the act, and sat beside him.

Mac had logged into a popular genealogy site and was in the process of buying advertising space in their sidebar. The ad copy requested anyone associated with the Lewis clinic contact "Jackson Ardmore," with an e-mail address. He filled in the credit card information for Ardmore, which Callie assumed Nash had provided. She wondered whether Mr. Ardmore existed at all and, if not, how many others like him — bodiless individuals with excellent credit scores — Harp Security kept on hand.

"Lewis probably has an electronic alert set to notify him whenever new information about his family or the Lewis clinic turns up on the web," Mac explained as he clicked the button to submit the advertising request. "I've spent most of the morning posting on adoption and fertility forums. I want to flood the guy's inbox. The harder we push, the more likely he is to panic."

"I take it Nash got the site you wanted up and running?"

"Yeah. He'll be here in half an hour or so. He called while you were in the shower." Mac's cell rang and he eyed the display. "Speak of the devil," he said, a crease forming between the black wings of his brows. He flipped open the cell and held it to his ear. Callie couldn't hear Nash's words, but the urgency of his tone and the deepening frown on Mac's face created a sick feeling in her gut.

Mac shot off the sofa and began pacing furiously. Twice he started to speak, but Nash cut him off, evidently not in the mood to be questioned. When Mac hung up, he returned to the couch and took Callie's hands in his own, and her nausea coalesced into a hard knot of dread.

"There's been a . . . development," he said. "It's not good. Last night, Nash promised to put a man on your roommate. His guy, Hal, got to the restaurant where she works at midnight, but Erin had already left. He went over to your house and hung around for a few hours, but she didn't show, so he drove over to her boyfriend's apartment, figuring she'd spent the night with him. Her car was there, so he parked behind it and called in."

No, no, no . . . Callie wanted to put her hands over her ears, to tell Mac to stop.

"When Trey got there this morning to replace him, he found the place roped off with crime-scene tape. Hal just turned up in New York–Presbyterian Hospital with two gunshot wounds. One in the head, one in the chest. He's in surgery but not expected to survive. Tommy Lowell's dead, and Erin is missing."

"Dead?" Tommy couldn't be dead. He couldn't be. She'd just spoken to him the night she called from St. Martin. And

Erin … *Please, God, not Erin, too.* "What do you mean, Erin's missing?"

She'd done this. She'd pushed and pushed, and Erin and Tommy had suffered. Erin had told her to let it go, and she'd been right.

"She wasn't at the apartment when Trey got there this morning. Obviously, he hasn't been able to speak to Hal, but Nash's contacts in the police department say the cops are looking for her, too. Tommy's neighbors called nine-one-one this morning when they heard screaming and what sounded like shots fired in his apartment, but by the time the police got there, she was gone."

Mac's voice was perfectly calm, controlled, and even. Callie wanted to scream at him, to scratch and claw and punch and, conversely, to curl up against the bulwark strength of his body and hide. Her face hurt, and tears blurred her vision.

No falling apart. Erin needs you. She'd gotten Tommy killed, and she couldn't let that happen to Erin. Someone had taken her for a reason. Callie had to get her back. Then she could spend the rest of her life making up for her mistakes.

"What are we supposed to do now? Why would they want to hurt Erin? She wasn't even home. They had full access to the house if they wanted to search it again."

Mac retrieved his phone from where he'd laid it on the table when he'd sat beside her. He placed it into her hands, wrapping her fingers around it when she didn't take it from him.

"You need to call her cell. Leave a message. Tell her to call you on this phone, not yours. Hang on." He strode to the desk and scrawled something on a piece of paper, then settled beside her again. "Here's the number, though it will probably show up on her caller ID."

"What good will leaving her a message do? She didn't run off somewhere!"

"I know she didn't. Someone took her. And they did it to get to you. They'll be listening to her messages. Once you've told them how to contact you, we'll go over what you need to do when they call you back."

"John Lewis?"

"Still in St. Martin. I underestimated him." He turned his opaque, green gaze on her, and she could feel the force of his emotions, though she couldn't interpret their meaning. "I should have realized he wasn't just another arrogant prick. He's connected to something much larger than just his father's baby-selling operation."

"But you still think he's involved?"

"Yeah. I do. We'll talk about it once you've called Erin."

"Right." Callie swallowed hard and called her friend, tears choking her at the sound of Erin's happy-go-lucky voice mail message. She left the number of the disposable cell, as Mac had instructed, but when she hung up she didn't return the phone to him. Instead, she went into the bedroom and dug the business card John had given her out of her purse, then dialed the number on it. Mac, who had followed her, realized too late what she planned.

John picked up on the third ring. "Callie," he said brightly when she introduced herself, "how are you? Where are you? The gendarmes say you never left the island, but they can't find you. Have you been watching the news?"

"I've been watching. And I'm not on the island. But you knew that."

The tears in her throat, the stiffness in her face burned away in a sudden flame of fury, leaving her voice rock-steady.

The false cheer faded from John's tone. "I have no idea what you mean. What's happened?"

"Don't lie to me. You——" Before she could accuse John of plotting Erin's abduction, however, Mac's hand closed around hers, snapping the phone shut and ending the conversation.

"Are you out of your mind?" Mac forced the words through gritted teeth, and Callie jerked reflexively away from their violence, pulling her hand from his. "That man killed his own sister or, at the very least, arranged her murder. And you just call him up like he's Joe Average you met at the coffee shop?"

Again, that sudden, violent urge to smack, to punch. But hitting Mac wouldn't get her anything. He'd just stand there and take it. Instead, she turned on her heel and stalked out of the bedroom. Calling John had been an impulse, a reflexive response to her need for action. No, it probably hadn't been the smartest move in the book, but for a moment she'd felt——for the first time she could remember since finding that damned picture——as if she knew what she was doing. As if she had a plan. And if Mac hadn't cut her off, she might have learned something useful.

She could sense him looming behind her. "Look," she said, doing her best to keep her breathing even as she faced him, "you said to leave a message for Erin. I did. But why be so indirect? You're certain John's involved in this, so why not go straight to the source?"

Mac scrubbed a large hand across his face and ran long fingers through his hair. Despite the black shadow of stubble beginning to color his jaw and the overtly masculine build, Mac Brody appeared disarmingly childlike with his hair in cowlicks, and Callie twisted her fingers together in order to resist the urge to reach out and smooth the disordered waves back into place. Damn him, anyway. He'd turned her life upside down.

"There's too much we don't know," he said, clearly struggling for patience. "Lewis didn't kidnap Erin himself, and until we know exactly who and what he's mixed up with, it's better if he believes you don't consider him a threat. Right now, my main concern is keeping you safe."

Which was hard to argue with, even if it did piss her off.

⌒

MAC WATCHED CALLIE'S face carefully, trying to gauge her reaction. He'd worked damned hard to modulate his tone, but he was practically shaking with fury. And—though he didn't like to acknowledge it—fear. John Lewis wanted her dead, and if she continued to act without thinking, or asking, he would get his wish. No way was Mac letting it happen on his watch.

The cell in her hand rang. She glanced down at the number, frowning when no identification came up. "It's probably John calling back," she said. "If he's still on the island, it would be long distance and wouldn't show up on the caller ID." Her eyes met his, red-rimmed and dull, and while he appreciated that she'd turned control over to him, he wanted the spark back, even if it was merely the fire of anger. "What should I do?"

"Answer it. Tell him you got cut off and you're on the road, about to go into another dead zone, so you'll call him back when you can. Then hang up." More than anything, they needed time to work through the permutations and possibilities to come up with the best strategy.

Callie did as he instructed, assuring John she was fine, that she'd call him as soon as she could, even going so far as to thank him for his concern. The whole time, her cocoa-colored gaze never left Mac's, as if she were using his strength to shore up her own. Not that he thought she really needed it. She amazed him, remaining composed in a situation that would have shattered most women. Most men, too.

She shut the phone, and the composure vanished. She simply broke. Her arm shook visibly as she held out the cell, and rather than taking the phone from her hand, Mac slid his fingers around her wrist and tugged her toward him, then closed his arms around her.

"This is my fault," she said, her voice muffled against his T-shirt, her breath hot against his collarbone. "I had a good life. Erin told me so. Why couldn't I just have left that stupid picture alone?" Her hand, still clutching the phone, pounded against his chest as she railed. "What does it matter where I was born, or whether my parents were totally honest about how they got me?"

"Don't," Mac said, smoothing a hand up and down her back. "You can't think that way, sugar. This is on Lewis and whoever he's involved with, no one else." But he knew the words wouldn't be enough. Self-blame and other flavors of what the shrinks called "survivor's guilt" ran rampant in both the police force and the Army. He'd borne plenty himself, including the weight of Nikki's murder. If anyone should have recognized John Lewis for what he was, Mac should. But he hadn't. And now Nikki was dead, Callie's roommate was missing, and Callie herself was in danger.

"What do you think they're doing to her?"

He didn't have to ask who. He put a finger under her chin, forcing her to look up so she could see the truth in his face. "Nothing. Erin is their ace in the hole. Without her, they have nothing. When they call back, you're going to insist on speaking to her. If they won't let you, you're going to hang up."

"I can't—"

"You can. You have to. They want you, not her. Their only reason for keeping her safe and sound is that you insist on it. If they think they can fool you, can bully you into accepting their word for her wellbeing, they won't need her."

A tear dripped slowly down Callie's cheek, the sparkling drop filling him with a combination of vicious rage and savage frustration, both of which he forced down. She didn't need his anger. He brushed the droplet away with his thumb, but another followed it.

"I can't do this." In the whispered words, he heard both guilt and shame. "I'm not strong enough."

"Yeah, you are."

"How can you say that? You haven't even known me a week."

He had no answer. In five short days he'd completely revised his opinion of her. Granted, his first impression had been less than charitable, based on her similarity to Nikki, but the woman in his arms was light-years different from the one he'd married, and not just in looks. The soft curves pressed against him masked a strength of character and depth of feeling completely foreign to Nikki Lewis.

～

CALLIE COULD FEEL the slow, steady beat of Mac's heart beneath her cheek. His solid warmth was comforting, and she pressed herself even closer, amazed that he thought her strong. Under normal circumstances, she would agree, but now . . . she'd never felt less competent, less in control. Without him, she'd be dead. And now she was relying on him to save Erin as well. She pulled away slightly to ask him how long he thought it would be before they heard from the kidnappers, but when she looked up into his face, the words dried up and her brain short-circuited.

In her need for stability and comfort, she'd somehow managed to forget the man's overwhelming sexual impact. The eyes that met hers were alive with desire, and a shock of heat so intense it was almost painful speared through her. He took the cell from her suddenly nerveless fingers and laid it on the television next to him. Moving slowly, he slid a hand beneath her hair to stroke the nape of her neck with one, calloused thumb. The caress echoed through her entire body. She drew in a shuddering breath, and his gaze fixed on her slightly parted lips.

"Callie," he murmured roughly, her name both plea and warning.

She leaned in, rising to her toes, and pressed her mouth to his as she ran her fingers up his torso to tangle in the waves of his hair. With a groan that sounded almost like surrender, he dragged her closer still, wresting control of the kiss, devouring her with lips, tongue, teeth. She could feel every muscle of his chest through the thin cotton of his T-shirt, and through the denser fabric of his jeans the evidence that his desire matched her own. Instinctively, she wrapped one leg around his waist, trying to draw him even more tightly against her. Without removing his mouth from hers, he anchored her with an arm about her waist, then reached down and urged her other leg up, so that he supported her totally. The skirt bunched around her middle, and for a moment, reality intruded—Callie was no lightweight; how could such a position possibly be comfortable for him?—but then he shifted, cupping her nearly bare butt in one hand as he began to walk toward the bedroom, and conscious thought was sucked away on a wave of sensation.

He laid her on the bed, then stood looking down at her. His breathing was ragged, his eyes bright, but he didn't join her.

"Are you sure?" The words were harsh, sibilant, spoken with a locked jaw and clenched teeth. It cost him, that nobility, and if Callie hadn't already been certain, it would have been the clincher. In answer, she rose to her knees and reached for the button fly of his jeans. She fumbled awkwardly with the stiff material, managing to loose only the top button as he shed his shirt.

With hands both rough and gentle, he pushed her back, then strode to the living room. She saw him reach for something on the desk, but before she could make sense of the move, he had returned, a small packet in his hands. He tossed the condom to the nightstand and joined her on the bed, rolling so she sat astride him. Unclothed, his shoulders and arms seemed impossibly muscular, wide chest covered with only a slight dusting of hair that arrowed down, irresistibly drawing both her eyes and hands.

As her fingers trailed his skin, he shuddered and reached up to tug the elastic from her hair. He slid his fingers through the braid, unraveling it until her unruly hair hung completely loose and free.

"Better," he murmured. "God, I love your hair."

She could feel the heat of a blush stain her cheeks.

"Oh, yeah, and that, too." He ran a long finger down her throat. "Let's see where that starts." He gripped the hem of her shirt and quickly stripped it over her head. Her bra followed in short order, at which point he reversed their positions, pinning her beneath him.

His mouth found hers again, but this time he didn't linger there, moving on to her jaw, her neck. When his bristled chin rubbed her nipple, every muscle in her body tensed and a mewling cry like nothing she'd ever uttered escaped her throat. What was he doing to her? She'd never reacted this way to anyone. Not ever.

His tongue soothed the abraded skin of her breast, and she found herself sobbing, begging for she knew not what. His mouth, wet and feverishly hot, moved to her other breast while he hooked his thumbs through the waistband of her skirt and panties and, in a single, fluid move, dragged them from her body. Once again she reached for the buttons of his jeans, but once again the heavy fabric defeated her. Impatient, he pulled away and shucked them — and the briefs beneath them — himself.

She had only a moment to marvel at the sheer, masculine perfection of his body before it once again covered her own. He pressed against her, trapping her legs between his own, holding them together, but she wanted more. She wanted him inside her, immediately, if not sooner. When she twisted, trying to separate her legs, to draw him in, he chuckled softly, the rumble passing from his body into hers.

"Slow down, sugar," he murmured against her lips. His drawl was thick and honey-sweet, but the underlying rasp excited every nerve ending in her skin.

"Please," she whispered. "Mac, please."

In reply, he kissed her, fast and hot, then reached for the packet. When he ripped it open, the prosaic sound brought her halfway back down to earth. What was she doing? How did he happen to have protection handy? But she was too far gone to heed the concerns that seemed so distant, and the moment he had the condom out, she stole it from him and shoved him to his back. Her hands shook as she rolled the thin sheath down his hot length. It was an act she'd never performed before, and the sight of her own fingers sliding down his body transfixed her.

⟳

M AC LAY PERFECTLY still, almost afraid to move. The sensation of Callie's delicate fingers on him was bad enough, but the expression on her face could be his undoing. The rapt attention laced with greedy anticipation almost had him coming in her hands. He'd had no shortage of lovers, but he couldn't remember a woman ever looking at him in quite that way.

When he could take it no longer, he reversed their positions. She was panting, her body twisting beneath his, pushing against him. The wild mix of desire and innocence gave him pause — she was clearly running on instinct, not experience. But her long legs parted, and her hesitant fingers positioned him, and he could no more prevent himself from plunging into her than he could stop the world turning on its axis. She drew in a sharp, hissing breath, which she let out on a little sob, and he took her mouth again, mingling breaths as they mingled bodies.

He was completely attuned to her, his body mirroring her every tremor, every inhalation, every stroke and clench and arch. When he felt the convulsions begin deep within her, he tried to hold back, to control his reaction, but it was impossible. He followed her over the edge.

It seemed hours later he came back to himself and slid from her body, then from the bed to clean up. When he returned, she had drawn the covers up. Her eyes were closed, her wildly curling hair covering most of her face. She wasn't asleep; she was hiding. He rounded the bed and slipped in beside her, pulling her close and positioning her head on his shoulder.

"Too fast," he murmured against her hair. "Sorry, sweetheart, next time will be better."

BETTER? CALLIE ALMOST choked. For him, maybe. For her, she couldn't imagine better. She was wrung out, destroyed. Better would kill her. Callie had never imagined herself capable of the kind of passion Mac inspired. He made her want in ways she'd never believed possible. She couldn't help but wonder whether that was a good thing.

And the fact that he just assumed there'd be a next time . . . She wasn't at all sure how to take that, either. The guy was a self-confessed adrenaline junkie; would he even be interested in her if buildings weren't blowing up around them? Would she want him if she didn't need him? He'd been married to her half-sister, for crying out loud. How could she ever believe he saw her for herself?

The phone beside the bed rang. She reached for it, but Mac beat her to it. "Be right there," he said after listening for a moment. When he hung up, he told her to get dressed, that Nash was on his way up. She started to climb out of bed, assuming he'd do the same, but he held her fast for a moment, then kissed her roughly before letting her go. She escaped to the bathroom on shaky legs.

CHAPTER TWELVE

MAC YANKED ON his clothes in record time and went to wait for Nash in the suite's outer room, closing the bedroom door to give Callie some privacy. She'd locked herself in the bathroom, and he could hear the shower running. Again. He hadn't had a chance to shower once, and probably smelled less than appealing, but there was nothing to do about it now.

Down the hall, elevator doors opened, and Mac saw Nash coming toward him, a grim set to his shoulders and mouth. He stepped aside to let Nash into the suite, then checked the hall before locking the door behind him.

"Hal's dead," said Nash.

"I'm sorry."

"Yeah? You don't look sorry. You look like you spent the time he was bleeding out on the operating table fucking the woman responsible."

Mac didn't think; he just reacted. His hands fisted in the collar of Nash's white, button-down shirt and slammed him into the wall. Nash made no effort to stop him, his gray eyes narrowing but remaining cool.

"This is not Callie's fault," Mac said once he was sure he had Nash's attention. "She didn't ask to be hunted, and neither one of us asked you to get involved. You want out now? Take off. We'll figure it out on our own."

"Stop it!" The door to the bedroom swung wide, and Callie stormed out. Mac loosed Nash and stepped back.

"What the hell is going on?" She glanced from one man to the other.

"Nothing," Nash assured her. "Just a little difference of opinion."

She snorted in disbelief and turned her eyes on Mac for clarification.

"Hal died," he said. "We're tense. It's nothing. Really."

Callie scowled, obviously unconvinced, but let it go. "I'm sorry to hear about Hal. You had him watching Erin?"

"Yeah." Nash rubbed a hand over the back of his neck, then twisted his head to the side until the bones cracked. "I had word from some of my other contacts, though, and I'm beginning to get a sense of the shape of this thing. It's not pretty."

"Not pretty?" Callie's voice was hard. This was changing her. She'd been the softest, most honest thing Mac had ever known when he sat with her that night on the beach, but that woman was disappearing before his eyes. "Don't you think 'not pretty' is an understatement? My best friend is missing, and her boyfriend and your friend Hal are dead. Women have been murdered. Your building was almost blown up."

"The world's a brutal place," said Nash.

"Why don't I order us some coffee," Mac interrupted before Callie could explode. "I suspect we could all use that and a bite to eat."

"Before you do," said Nash, his voice casual, his eyes on Callie anything but, "tell me what you know about Henry Falcone."

He expected the name to mean something to her. Mac could see it in his expression. But after a moment's thought, Callie shook her head. "I don't know him."

Nash studied her for a long moment.

"He took Erin? He's working for John?" Callie asked.

"I suspect it's the other way around. At least, I suspect he's provided the funding and some of the manpower. I've been chasing him for more than a decade."

More than a decade. Nash had been aware of Falcone while still in the Army. Had Falcone been involved in the assassination of their commanding officer?

"Your Moriarty? Are you certain you're not just imagining his involvement? It seems terribly coincidental. This is my best friend's life we're talking about. I can't let you blow this because you're seeing something that isn't there."

Mac would bet good money it was the first time anyone had dared question Nash's intel in a long time.

Nash, however, appeared unfazed. "Food," he said. "Let's order before we start talking, because this is going to take some time."

Mac called down an order for sandwiches, coffee, and assorted snacks, and they all settled in the living room. Mac didn't speak, letting the silence grow until Nash felt its weight and broke it.

"Henry Falcone is an arms dealer. I can tell you that, and swear it to be true, but I can't prove it. He's forty-seven years old and has been providing weapons to various parties for at least twenty-five years. He's sold to groups on terrorist watch lists in every country in Europe as well as to more traditional buyers, like several factions in civil wars in South America and parts of Africa.

"Falcone was born in Italy. His mother was a Florentine prostitute who hooked up with an American businessman of some sort in the 1960s. They settled in Miami, where both he and his mother became involved in drug trafficking. By the time he was eighteen, Falcone had been arrested twice for dealing, and had gotten heavily involved with various Colombian interests.

"He moved to Colombia for good in 1990 after he graduated college and took up with a man known to the DEA as a major player in the drug game who posed as a coffee plantation owner. Before Falcone turned thirty, his mentor died, and Falcone took over the whole operation. According to rumor, he was tired of employing people who used the products they were supposed to be selling, so he began shifting the drug portion of his business over to a lieutenant, focusing his own interest on weapons.

"There was plenty of opportunity for him at home in Colombia, and that kept him busy for a good five years. But his mentor was already on the CIA's list when he died, and despite his care, Falcone ended up there, too. Especially once he began selling weapons to various Middle East interests."

Afghanistan. That had to be where Falcone had run afoul of Nash. Hard on that thought came another. *Was Nash really Army when they were stationed together? Or was he CIA?*

"How on earth is someone like that connected to John Lewis?" Callie asked.

"We're not sure. We're never a hundred percent positive of anything where Falcone is concerned, but here's the little we've sussed out: in the past ten years, three men we have pegged as top people in Falcone's organization have stayed at the Paradis. All of these guys have legitimate positions in society as wealthy businessmen. There's no reason they shouldn't stay at any resort they want to, but they've all chosen the Paradis, repeatedly. And virtually every time they stay at the hotel, some gala or event brings boats from all over the Caribbean. For all intents and purposes, it's a foolproof cover. No one can even track, let alone search, all that traffic.

"HSE has connected two of the three definitively to weapons sales, and we'd pass along the information we have to any government interested if we could tie them to Falcone. But as important as they are, they're middlemen. There's no point in taking them out of the game; it's better to be able to watch them.

"That's connection one. Connection two comes in the form of a contract killer who turned up in the East River Monday with a bullet between his eyes. He's an Argentine national, Hugo Americh, known to have done many jobs for Falcone over the years. He flew into JFK airport two days after you reported Nicole missing. No one knows where he spent the next week."

"The gas leak," Callie murmured. Mac nodded and passed along the details to Nash.

"That works. Quiet kills were Americh's specialty. Ostentatious ones, on the other hand, are Sonny Juarez's. Juarez operates out of Miami. Again, lots of unproven ties to Falcone, mostly through the Colombian population in Florida. Juarez flew into New York Monday, probably with orders to kill Americh for his failure. A simple miss wouldn't be a problem under normal circumstances, so we have to assume that either there was some outstanding friction between Americh and Falcone to start with, or he's having control issues generally and wants people to see what happens to those who cannot fulfill their contracts with him."

A knock signaled the arrival of their food. Mac stood, reaching for the pistol on the coffee table and tucking it into his jeans at the small of his back before he walked over and peered through the peephole in the door. Satisfied that nothing more dangerous than bad coffee had arrived, he pulled the hem of his T-shirt over the weapon and admitted the waiter.

CALLIE COULDN'T QUITE get past Nash's matter-of-fact tone as he recited the information he'd uncovered. How had she gotten mixed up with people who took for granted that contract killers operated along a spectrum from quiet to ostentatious? Nash's employee, possibly his friend, had been killed, but he'd somehow managed to put that away after his initial outburst. She, on the other hand, could devote only half her attention to the picture he was painting, the rest of her mind consumed with Erin's abduction and Tommy's death. Emotions washed through her, and she found herself battling them back constantly, forcing herself to focus on Nash and Mac, who seemed her only hope of taking back her life and her friend's.

The waiter rolled a cart into the room. Mac signed for the delivery and ushered him out, then poured three cups of coffee, handing one to her. She wrapped her hands around the mug, letting warmth seep into her veins. The air-conditioning in the room was not particularly strong, but the conversation had chilled her.

"Even if John is involved with Falcone, what interest would a man like that have in me?" she asked after a couple of sips.

"I was hoping you'd have an answer for that. Lewis probably called Falcone and asked him to lend a hand getting rid of you. If the Paradis is functioning as a transfer point for illegal weapons, the last thing either man wants is for it to pop up on law-enforcement radar, even for something like a previous owner's peccadilloes. Despite Americh's failure, Falcone probably thought he had everything under control until you escaped his men in St. Martin."

Nash sighed and rubbed the back of his neck again. He took a drink of coffee, then pulled a club sandwich off the tray of food, took a bite, and chewed it slowly. He seemed disinclined to speak until Mac prompted him.

"What aren't you saying?"

"I pulled you out of there. And as much as I've followed Falcone, he's followed me. If he wasn't sure whose helicopter chased his men off, a quick check of the records of ownership for the building his man bombed in Tribeca would give it away. I've caused him a fair number of problems over the years, both during my stint with the DEA and in my work with HSE.

"Falcone doesn't have friends. He had a wife and daughter, but they were killed in a DEA op gone wrong. His allegiances are . . . temporary and expedient. It wouldn't occur to him I might have sent someone to get the two of you without having been in touch all these years. He'll assume Mac's been working for me, that I somehow organized his placement at the Paradis in order to poke around in the arms business. He no doubt considers the two of you far more dangerous and knowledgeable than you are."

"Well, that's just fucking great," Mac muttered.

"You'd rather I'd let him blow you to smithereens out there in the middle of the Caribbean?"

Again, Callie wondered at the apparent tension between the two men. It prickled along her skin, a nagging reminder of how little she really knew about either of them. She needed both, but they were operating with diverse agendas. Could she trust either of them?

"We appreciate your help," she said in as diplomatic a tone as she could muster.

"You do," Nash corrected, but the left side of his mouth lifted in a half smile. "But I am not insensitive to the fact that I've complicated an already difficult situation. Still, I don't see any other way to have handled it."

"No. But what do we do now?"

"Unfortunately"—the half smile disappeared—"all we can do is wait for them to call."

"What do I say when they do?"

Mac took over. "First, you tell them you want to speak to Erin. You tell them you will be asking her three questions that only she can answer. If the answers are wrong, you'll know it's not her and you'll hang up."

"It doesn't need to be such a production. I'll recognize her voice."

"The questions are security," he explained. "You have to have an interactive conversation, not something they can pre-record or get someone to imitate her voice for. But it's more than that. You need to show them that you have some idea of what they're up to, that they can't fool you. I know you feel powerless, but you can't afford to let that feeling show. They have to believe you'll hold up your end of whatever deal they propose; that will only happen if you let them think you think you're in control. They won't mind dealing with a difficult negotiator, but if they consider you some kind of emotional wildcard, they may . . . choose a different path."

"You mean they'll kill her."

Mac didn't answer, but when her hands started to shake, he pried the mug from them and laced his fingers with hers, lending her his strength. She couldn't look at him but held tight as she turned to Nash.

"You think this Sonny Juarez is the one who took Erin?"

"It's possible, though kidnapping is out of his usual comfort zone. The real question is who gave the orders. There's no doubt in my mind Falcone's men—whether Juarez or someone else—did the actual work, but he may have lent them to Lewis. If we could figure out who was pulling the strings, we'd have a better idea what they might want. And if we had a handle on that before they called, we'd be in a better position."

The prepaid cell sitting on top of the television rang. Mac retrieved it, looking at the caller ID, and handed it to Callie. "It's a local cell. Maybe Erin's."

Callie recognized the number and nodded. With a deep breath, she accepted the phone and hit the button to answer the call.

"Hello?"

"Hello, Miss Pearson." The faintest hint of an accent colored the man's voice.

"Where's Erin?"

"All in good time."

"No." Callie steeled herself, remembering Mac's words. She had to appear in control, no matter how she felt. "I want to speak to her now."

"It doesn't matter what you want, Miss Pearson."

"Yes, it does, or you wouldn't have bothered to call. So put Erin on. Or I'll hang up."

A short silence, and then Erin's voice came on the line.

"Callie?" At the subdued, tremulous quality of Erin's voice, so out of character, Callie's eyes prickled with tears.

"Erin! Are you okay?"

"I don't know what these guys want."

Mac mouthed the word "questions" at her, and she nodded.

"Erin, I am going to ask you three questions. It's for security. Tell the guy who called that I am going to ask you three questions every time we talk so I know it's really you and you're okay, all right?"

She heard Erin repeating her words to someone in the background.

"What flavor do I hate?" she asked once Erin's captor had agreed to the stipulation.

"Curry," Erin replied promptly.

"What do I always order at the Indian restaurant?"

"Tandoori salmon."

"And what do you always tell me?"

"That you're boring, and should try some curry on your tandoori."

"Erin, I promise—" But she heard a scuffle on the other end of the phone, and the man came back on the line.

"You have asked your questions, Miss Pearson. Miss Campbell is well. If you follow the instructions we give you, she will remain so. My employer requires some information from you. He would have preferred to avoid involving your friend, but since you seemed determined to hide, it was necessary to take certain measures to find you."

"Look, I'm happy to tell you whatever you want."

"My employer requires ... assurances. We will allow Miss Campbell to go free once you come to us. Don't call the police. Don't talk to Brody or Harper. If you do, your roommate's usefulness will come to an abrupt and very painful end. We will be calling back with details." He disconnected, but Callie hung on for a long moment, the dial tone buzzing in her ear.

"What did he say?" Nash's question pierced the fog creeping across her mind.

"Nothing." She considered the conversation. "Really, it's weird. He didn't say much of anything—they had Erin, they wanted me, they'd trade, and they'd call back with more details later. Why wouldn't he just go ahead and tell me what he wants now?" She left out the admonishment about withholding information from Mac and Nash, unsure how far she planned to obey it.

"Stalling," Mac said slowly. "Maybe he's waiting for his boss? Where does Falcone live?"

"Anywhere he wants to," replied Nash with a grimace. "He has a villa in Tuscany, a private island in the Grenadines, the coffee plantation in Colombia, and a pied-à-terre in Miami. He's also part owner of a horse-training facility outside of Brussels. He's been active this summer, in and out of the US, though he usually spends summers in Europe. Let me check something."

He walked over to the desk and sat down at the computer, his fingers racing over the keys as he used some program Callie had never seen—probably written by his own people, she thought—to connect to the mainframe at HSE.

"Your buddy Lewis is on the move," he said after a couple of minutes. "Bobby, who took over for you two on the *Lady*, has been doing his best to keep an eye on him, but he says Lewis left his house late last night and never came back. Travis went back to the island, and he's asking around, since it's easier for him to do so without looking suspicious, but hasn't heard anything yet about where Lewis might be headed."

"Is there any question? Obviously, that's what the guy who called is waiting for."

"Nothing's ever obvious in cases like this," Mac said. "Jumping to conclusions leads to mistakes. But if we run with the idea that Lewis is headed to the US, the next question is: Where? It's certainly easy enough to get into the country, but getting into New York itself is a little harder. He'd probably take the same route we did—quick hop to Puerto Rico, which gets him into the country, then some kind of transport from there. Or maybe he goes through

Florida. It's not such an easy trip from St. Martin, but it could be done. Chopper to a boat anchored offshore somewhere, then smuggled into the country by some rich friend of Falcone's?"

"Possible," agreed Nash. "If he's using Falcone's allies, he'll go through Miami rather than Puerto Rico. Falcone has an enormous network in Florida; he's practically untouchable there. It's, what, a thousand miles from Miami to St. Martin? If Lewis left last night, took a speedboat out to a bigger boat somewhere nearby with a helipad, he could have been in Florida early this morning. Plenty of private jets fly between Miami and New York on legitimate business every day, so Lewis wouldn't have to go commercial; he could borrow one of Falcone's partner's planes."

"What could John possibly want to ask me? The man I spoke to said he wanted 'assurances,' that that was why he was insisting on meeting me in person. And why bother sneaking into the country when he could just fly into JFK and meet with me?"

Mac and Nash shared a glance, totally in sync for once. "The only assurance Lewis wants," Mac said, "is that you won't live to reveal his secrets. Before he kills you, he would prefer to find out just how much you've uncovered and how many people you've told so he can estimate how much damage control he has to do, but that knowledge isn't essential. What's essential is that he prevent you from learning or telling anything more than you already have."

Nash spoke up. "Which is also why he won't fly commercial. He wants you for some reason, but he can't afford to leave a trail back to him once you're gone.

"I assume the man you spoke to threatened Erin's life if you consulted me?"

Callie stared. Mac hadn't been kidding about Nash's ability to know everything.

"It's only logical," he explained. "The whole object of this exercise is to limit the scope of what must—to both Lewis and Falcone—appear as an impending disaster. HSE has formidable resources, so you have to be cut off from them."

Fine. If he wanted to put it all out there, she would. "Involving you could get Erin killed."

"Not involving me will almost certainly get both you and her killed." Nash's gray eyes reminded her of ice floes on the Hudson in winter. No warmth, no softness showed in them, just implacable chill. "If you hope to survive this, you'll inform me and Mac of your every move before you make it." He glanced at his watch. "In fact, Lexie should be here soon with tracking devices and some items Mac requested last night. We'll get you outfitted with them soon enough."

"Not that you'll need the GPS," said Mac, "since there's no way in hell you're meeting with these guys, but it's best not to take chances."

Callie took a deep breath and called on the diplomatic skills she'd absorbed listening to her father negotiate day in and day out to keep her manner calm and relaxed despite the churning in her belly. "I appreciate all you two are doing, have done. But it's me they want, so you can't keep me out of this altogether. I'll wear whatever electronics Lexie brings, but I doubt the men who have Erin are going to turn her over without at least seeing my face."

Nash cut off Mac's incipient protest. "She's right."

Mac propelled himself from the sofa and stalked over to the window to stare down at the insanity of Times Square. Callie wondered what was going through his head. She poured herself another cup of coffee and picked up half a ham sandwich. Nibbling it, she waited out the two men's silence. Mac finally broke it.

"You said Lexie was coming here?" Nash nodded. "Then I'll shower while we wait for her. If you have a phone, I'd like to call Vince, see whether he's heard anything from the feds, though he says they're keeping him in the dark."

"You can call through the HSE switchboard. If they are tracking your partner's calls, they'll be able to trace it back to HSE, but no further. He can tell them I called to ask about you. In fact, I'll make the call myself in case he's not the one who answers."

"That'll work."

Callie thought "Thank you" might have been a better response, but whatever was between the two men seemed to inhibit gratitude. With a brief nod, Mac disappeared into the bedroom, leaving her alone with Nash.

"Travis didn't have a high opinion of Nicole Lewis," he remarked the moment the bedroom door closed. "I believe the term he used was 'skank.'"

"It's not polite to speak ill of the dead," Callie replied automatically. What was Nash's object with this line of conversation?

"Oh, she wasn't dead at the time. He called me the day she and Mac got married. Of course, by then it was too late for me to check up on her. Not that it would have done much good anyway. Mac doesn't listen particularly well, especially to me, and Trav is too honest not to tell him where the information came from."

"What happened between the three of you?"

"A . . . breach of trust." He shrugged, as if the topic were of little importance, but would not look at her. When he did, his pale eyes were carefully blank. "Aidan Macmillan Brody is not a forgiving man. If your relationship is important to you, I suggest you don't lie to him."

"We don't have a relationship." But her cheeks heated. *Aidan.* She'd slept with a man without even knowing his first name. She turned the conversation back on Nash. "Is that what you mean by a breach of trust? You lied to him?"

His smiled lacked even a trace of humor. "I lie to everyone."

Before Callie could process the statement, Lexie knocked and identified herself. Nash opened the door and she swept in, an enormous backpack dwarfing her slender frame. She'd applied her makeup strategically, but nothing could hide the red rims of her eyes. Had she and the dead Hal been friends? Lovers? Callie could not come up with a suitable way to express her sympathy, so she ignored the remnants of the other woman's distress, allowing herself to be drawn into a discussion of the items Lexie was removing from the pack and laying on the coffee table.

"Is that what you're planning on wearing for the next couple of days?" Lexie's bloodshot eyes swept over her, leaving Callie squirming like a guest on the television show *What Not to Wear.*

"Actually, I need to buy some jeans. I planned to do that today. The ones you got for me were too small."

The other woman snorted, the sound a startling con-trast to her professional air. "Told you," she said to Nash. "Moreland gave you the sizes he'd want to see her in, not the ones she'd want to wear." Her expression brightened and she winked at Callie. "Travis is such a guy."

"You know him?"

The grin disappeared. "I did. Years ago. He was a friend of my brother's." She focused on the items on the table. "If you're going to buy jeans, we won't sew a transmitter into the skirt. Do you have any experience with firearms?"

"Guns? You want me to carry a gun?"

"Only if you know how to use it." The voice came from behind her. Mac had emerged from the bedroom, shirtless, hair still shower-damp. She couldn't help ogling just a bit as he reached into the shopping bag he'd left next to the desk and withdrew a clean T-shirt, but by the time he'd pulled it on, she had herself back under control.

"My father taught me to shoot when I was in high school. He believed in physical activities, so he took me hiking, riding, waterskiing, target shooting, whatever was popular where we were living. I kept up the shooting—both guns and archery—through college, but I haven't picked up a bow or a pistol in more than five years."

Mac grunted. "Fair enough. At least you won't shoot yourself in the foot. Target shooting—were you using a revolver or a semi?"

"Revolver."

He cocked an eyebrow at Lexie, who nodded and dug a weapon out of the backpack, along with a carton of bullets.

"It's a .357," she explained as she handed it to Callie. "I brought .38-caliber loads for it. Plenty of stopping power, but it won't kick too hard."

"It's not exactly a purse pistol." Callie turned the gun over, getting a sense of the weight, then loaded it, relieved to feel the muscle memory of the actions returning.

"Snub noses aren't accurate enough. And a .22 won't do anything but piss off a serious attacker. Besides, no gun is small enough to hide if someone's searching you. The idea is to keep them at a distance, and for that you need heft. If you're going to be wearing jeans, you can use a belt holster." She passed one across, and Callie snapped the revolver into it. "Just buy a peasant blouse or something to wear over it."

"The holster is tagged," Nash said, "as is the gun. We'll also put trackers in your purse, shoes, and clothes. The more devices we can stash on you, the more likely they are to miss one in a search, if it comes to that."

"Which it won't," Mac growled.

CHAPTER THIRTEEN

A half hour later, Callie had been outfitted with multiple tiny electronic trackers. Mac had consented to wear one himself, and he suspected Nash had slipped a second into the handgrip of the Sig Sauer P228 he'd turned over to Mac and probably a third in the grip of the knife he now wore strapped to his ankle. Nash preferred to keep track of all his assets, human and otherwise. Tracking software had been installed on a fresh sat phone Nash had brought for Mac's use, and the bugs registered to it. The same software resided on the computers at HSE.

Nash and Lexie had headed back down to HSE headquarters, leaving Mac and Callie alone. Mac would have preferred to stay in the suite, but Callie claimed she needed jeans. Which he guessed she did, as the skirt she was wearing would trip her in a chase. Besides, just looking at her in it reminded him of how her skin had felt beneath his hands as he'd stripped the skirt from her body. Not conducive to concentration.

Nash had brought a shoulder holster for Mac, which was his preferred carry, but in the August heat he couldn't very well wear a jacket. At the moment, he had the pistol stashed in a holster at the small of his back, which was great for concealment but made for an almost impossible draw. He'd have to pick up a T-shirt big enough to hide the gun if he wore it at his waist.

Mac considered shopping torturous, even without the

added stress of knowing they could be attacked at any moment. The crowds thronging Times Square hid them but could also hide their pursuers.

"How can you stand living here?" he asked after a few blocks. Callie had explained that in New York City, the north-south blocks ran twenty to a mile and that, since the store was only half a mile from the hotel, walking was the best option. But in the last quarter mile, he figured he'd seen—and been seen by—more people than lived on entire Army bases. In the high season, St. Martin had been crowded, but this, this was intolerable.

Callie slanted a look up at him, managing to keep one eye on the street before her. "I keep forgetting you're not from here. Chappaqua, where I live, is nothing like the city. Most of the state isn't like the city, and even most of the city isn't as bad as this." Still moving forward, she waved a hand at the crowd. "A good half of these people are tourists. Penn Station, where the trains come in, Times Square, the Port Authority bus terminal—there are all kinds of draws for this area.

"And then, this is the garment district. FIT—the school for fashion—is just a few blocks down from here, and there are actual manufacturers and designers as well as students, professors, shopkeepers . . . all people who don't keep nine-to-five schedules. And they all smoke, so they have to stand out on the street for at least ten minutes every couple hours. Foot traffic here is much heavier than it is in other parts of town."

"If you say so."

"I do. You didn't see swarms like this down in Tribeca, where Nash's office was, did you?"

"It was late." But he hadn't. As they'd driven through the neighborhood, he'd noticed only a few stores. Most of the buildings seemed residential, with some galleries, a couple of offices, and the occasional bodega. "Is that the kind of neighborhood you live in?"

"No. My house is on half an acre of land. The people around me have fenced yards, barking dogs, fruit trees, fancy gardens, the whole suburban package."

Mac had a hard time imagining such a thing existing mere minutes from where they wound their way through the human traffic jam.

Inside Macy's, which Callie insisted was the most efficient place to go, since they could get everything they needed in one place, the situation was worse.

They started in the women's department, where Callie wanted to find a particular brand of jeans.

"If I get the ones I usually wear," she explained, "I don't need to try them on. We can just buy them and go." But she couldn't find her size and couldn't find a salesperson. Other women, acting as if Armageddon was approaching and they needed just the right outfit, pushed by them, twice jostling Mac so hard he put his hands on his back, letting his fingers rest on the Sig.

Finally, Callie got her jeans, and they headed to the men's department, where it took him all of ten seconds to find a T-shirt. While he was paying, however, the cell in Callie's purse rang. She walked away to take the call in private, pretending to sort through a rack of fall jackets about ten feet from Mac and the salesman, her head ducked down as she listened to the caller. A man approached her, and Mac automatically reached back for his gun, but the guy seemed intent on the clothing and didn't follow when she moved away.

The salesman took Mac's money and handed back his change and the bagged shirt. Mac glanced down to complete the transaction. Only a second, but when he looked back,

Callie had disappeared. Every muscle in his body tensed, locking him into place, only his eyes able to move, scanning the area.

The man who had taken Callie's spot by the jackets had been joined by his wife, and they argued quietly, the wife waving her arms. A teenaged shoplifter fingered a slinky nylon shirt with a skateboarding logo on it, glancing surreptitiously from side to side. A woman held a sweater up to check the size against the shoulders of her harried-looking son. Two Japanese men peered into a glass case whose contents Mac couldn't determine from a distance.

Where the hell was Callie? They couldn't have found her, taken her, in the scant window his distraction had afforded. He strode toward the spot he'd last seen her, his scar itching like the devil. Black shadows danced at the edge of his vision. He paused by a rack of sweaters and drew his gun, draping the new shirt in its white plastic bag over his hand to conceal the weapon.

He stepped back into the aisle and saw her. She was kneeling next to a shelf of jeans, apparently tying her shoe. But as he strode toward her, he realized her hands were shaking too badly to maneuver the laces. He pushed her fingers aside and made quick work of the mangled knot, then rose, drawing her close and wrapping his arms around her. She clung, and he could feel the trembles running like chills through her body. He didn't speak, letting the physical contact assure them both that she was safe.

"She was crying," Callie said after several breaths, and he could hear the rasp of tears in her own voice. "Erin never cries."

Mac stroked the silky waves of her hair. "We'll get her back. I promise." She nodded against his shoulder. "What did they want?"

She didn't answer, and he could feel her decide to lie to him. He refused to let her, pushing her slightly away from him to stare down into her tear-damp eyes. "Don't. Whatever they said, whatever their threats, you're better off with my help. With Nash's, too. You know it."

When he stood as he did now, a bulwark between her and danger, she absolutely believed him. But she believed Sonny Juarez, too, when he described with gusto how he planned to cut off Erin's fingers, cauterizing each wound so she wouldn't bleed to death too soon. This would be Erin's fate, he promised, should Callie bring either Mac or Nash to the meeting John Lewis would arrange.

Remembering Lewis, at least, gave her something she could safely tell Mac.

"He said it was John Lewis who hired him, who wanted to meet. He didn't set a time or anything, but told me to gather any evidence my father might have left, that John would want all of it, along with the picture I showed him in St. Martin, in exchange for Erin."

"You know that's an excuse, right? Lewis couldn't care less about a photo you could have copied dozens of times or some nonexistent evidence. It's just a way to force you into killing range."

His harsh tone stiffened Callie's spine. "I'm not an idiot."

"No." Mac's voice lost its cold edge. "You're not. But you're frightened for your friend. The guy who called — did you find out who it was?"

"Sonny Juarez. He seemed to think I should recognize his name."

"Because he knows you've spoken to Nash. Remember

what Nash said about Juarez specializing in over-the-top killings?"

How could she forget? She nodded.

"Message murders are terrorism in its most basic form. And terrorism works, which is why it's always been part of human societies and always will be, no matter how hard we try to eradicate it. Scared people, no matter how smart they are, don't act rationally, or even in their own best interest. You're not an idiot, but you're also not used to dealing with the Sonny Juarezes of the world."

"And you are."

It wasn't a question, but he inclined his head in response. Staring at his dark features, Callie realized anew how far out of her depth she was. Standing in the men's department of an enormous department store discussing murder, kidnapping, and terrorism hadn't been in her life plan.

"What if I make the wrong decision?"

"You won't." Mac's opaque eyes revealed nothing, but there was a solidity to that, an obscure comfort. "Lewis and his men are going to try to rush you. It's another terror tactic—isolate the subject, then remove time for consideration and reason. To combat that, you have to get ahead of them. Plan your reaction. Work out what path you'll take, what lines you will and won't cross, regardless of what they do."

She understood the inference: the line she should never cross would be the one that separated her from him. But she couldn't make that promise, so she looked away, excusing the move by leaning down to pick up the shopping bag with her new jeans and red empire-waist shirt. She didn't like the style on her, but the fabric fell loosely to her hips, providing inconspicuous cover for a weapon at her waist.

Mac let the lack of response pass. "Let's get back to the

hotel," he said, plucking the bag from her hand and consolidating her purchases with his own.

"Yeah, okay." Callie started to move toward the exit, but he laid a hand on her shoulder. When she stopped, he let his fingers trail lightly down her bare arm, sparking fires beneath her skin, until he could lace their fingers together. Then he brought her hand to his mouth and brushed his lips across her palm.

"We'll get her out."

He couldn't guarantee Erin's safety, and Callie recognized both the promise and the physical contact as forms of manipulation designed to ensure her cooperation, but the steadiness of his gaze added force to the words, and in spite of the nagging, logical voice in the back of her mind, the constriction in her chest eased a bit.

Outside the artificially maintained environment of the department store, the weather had shifted to match Callie's mood. Storm clouds hung low, and heavy and damp air muted the sounds of passing cars and people. Pedestrians peered upward as they rushed along, hoping to reach their destinations without getting soaked, their contagious anxiety infecting others. Even Callie, who quite liked the rain, found herself hurrying, and noticed Mac's strides becoming choppier as well. Thunder rumbled in the distance.

The first drops fell when they were half a block from the hotel, quickly increasing to a deluge. Lightning shot through the gloom just as they stepped into their suite. Callie jumped, tension getting the better of her, and Mac gripped her shoulder briefly in reassurance.

"I'm gonna nuke myself a cup of coffee," he said. "You want one?"

"Sure." Maybe the caffeine would kick her brain into gear,

because she had some serious thinking to do. As of Juarez's phone call, she had four hours to ditch Mac, at which point Juarez would call back with instructions.

The microwave pinged, and Mac handed her a steaming cup of coffee. His own he set on the desk while he booted the laptop and logged into the program allowing him access to the HSE system. He didn't speak, and Callie wondered whether he was deliberately giving her space and time to consider her options. She settled on the couch and watched him work.

After a few minutes, he seemed to forget her entirely. His focus on the computer deepened, and his coffee sat untouched as he muttered, tapping keys and clicking furiously through page after page of information. He'd run a hand through his hair, as was his custom, and it stood up in ragged clumps. The muttering and the hair gave him something of a mad-scientist appearance, negated by the muscles bunching where his neck and shoulders met and the preternatural concentration he exhibited.

Although he ignored her, Callie couldn't avoid the knowledge that all his effort, the danger to which he'd subjected himself, was on her behalf. He could have left at any time. Sure, he'd have some awkward questions to answer from the gendarmes regarding Nikki's murder and his own disappearance, but they would cause him no real difficulties, especially with Nash on his side.

A bell sounded on the computer, and a message window opened on Mac's screen. Callie couldn't read it from her position, so when Mac cursed at its contents she rose and pulled a chair over to the desk.

"NICOLE LEWIS DNA SHOWS SAME PATERNITY AS OTHER VICS. BOTH PARENTS SAME AS CALLIOPE PEARSON."

"How in the hell is that possible?" Mac muttered. "We know Ava was Nikki's mother."

"No," Callie said slowly, remembering the pictures of a slender and gorgeous Ava mere months after Nikki's birth. "Ava left the island, remember? Maybe she got her child the same way my parents did. The whole affair and separation story gave her an excuse to disappear so no one would notice she never got hugely pregnant or gave birth. She came back with an infant she claimed as her own, and no one thought to question it."

"Okay, but why fake an affair? Why not just argue a lot, then separate? Wouldn't you think Lewis would want to claim his own kid, not allow people to think his wife had cheated on him?"

"There's still something missing," Callie agreed. She stared at the words on the screen. "She was my sister."

Mac shut the laptop and turned to face her. He didn't touch her, but the steadiness of his gaze had an almost tangible weight.

"We've always known the two of you shared a heritage."

"Yes, but to have both parents . . . It seems so much closer, somehow. Like we could have been raised together." What would it have been like to have had a sister, someone close to her own age with whom she could share all the joys and sorrows of her life?

"But you weren't. For which you should be damned grateful. Christ, it's no wonder Nikki was so screwed up. A mother who claimed her as her illegitimate daughter but never actually carried her, a father who knew she was his but didn't recognize it publicly, and a brother who probably hated her for having the genes he didn't and for taking half his inheritance: the ideal family. No surprise Nikki couldn't tell the truth to save her life."

"You think you failed her."

"I know I failed her. I always wondered why the hell she married me, but I never asked. I figured it was at least half to piss off big brother, but it never even occurred to me she might have been afraid. I should have listened better, watched more carefully."

"Juarez gave me a deadline." The words were involuntary, but she felt no regret when they popped out. Whatever might happen, Erin had a better chance with Mac's help, and Callie couldn't stand the idea of becoming another "should have" in his future.

"A deadline." He didn't sound surprised.

"By six, I'm supposed to shed you and any trackers." She remembered Juarez's description of what would become of Erin if she didn't and couldn't repress a shudder. Mac reached for her hand, twining his fingers with hers. The sensation was becoming too familiar, far too easy to accept, but she needed the comfort too much to pull away. "He'll call back then and give me specific instructions."

⌐

HER HANDS WERE shaking. No doubt she already regretted telling him about the meeting. Mac couldn't imagine why she'd confessed. He'd just finished admitting how completely incompetent he'd been with Nikki, how he'd been unable to protect her, and Callie chose that moment to trust him with her own life and that of her roommate? He'd never understand women.

But whatever twisted female logic lay behind the decision, Callie had put her faith in him. And he wasn't about to let her down. He checked his watch.

"That gives us a little under three hours. Can I call Nash?"

She swallowed, weighing her options. "Do you think that's

the right move? Juarez was . . . adamant about not involving anyone else."

"I do. Nash has the manpower, and he knows Juarez. More important, he knows Falcone. This setup is too elaborate for Lewis to manage on his own, which means Falcone is involved at least peripherally, and I have no idea about the scope of his influence. But this is your ball game; you call the shots."

Callie examined him, her dark eyes giving no indication of her thoughts. He'd never met a woman so hard to read. As he waited, he found himself recalling the expression in those coffee eyes when he'd lain naked beneath her. He forced the image away—she needed to see him focused on the case, not sidetracked by memories of pleasure. But he couldn't prevent his body's reaction, the tiny zing of anticipation. He wasn't done with Calliope Pearson. Not by a long shot.

Evidently, he succeeded in masking his thoughts because after an interminable moment, she nodded. "Call him, then. In for a penny, in for a pound."

"Give me an hour," Nash said once Mac explained the situation. "I'm in the middle of something that may prove useful."

"No problem." Mac hung up the sat phone and met Callie's eyes. "He's in, but he's working on something and can't get here right away."

"Okay." She rose and collected the shopping bag from by the door. "I'm going to change. Be right back." She stepped into the bedroom and shut the door, and Mac's mind followed her, imagining her stripping off the skirt and tee, until he yanked it back.

He reopened the computer and logged into HSE's databases. Nash had provided him with a password that could be used only from the laptop. When Mac logged in, the system automatically generated a second password, which was sent to the sat phone. He had to use yet another code to collect it from the message bank on the phone and enter it on the laptop in order to gain access.

Once he'd finished entering all the appropriate codes, Mac began checking on properties owned, or used, by Falcone. Nash had mentioned the man's homes, but he wasn't looking for houses. If Falcone or one of his men had Erin stashed somewhere, it wouldn't be in an upscale residential area. It would be a factory, an office park, a half-deserted slum.

Falcone didn't own any properties like the ones he was looking for, but Cauca Café, a boutique coffee roaster with five shops in the New York area, owned a small roasting and packaging plant on Long Island in a building behind the original café. HSE had flagged Cauca because the owner, one Paul Rivers, bought the entire output of Falcone's coffee plantation every year. Rivers also picked up coffee from other small plantations in Brazil, Colombia, and Africa, just like other boutique roasters.

Nash's files revealed nothing unusual about Rivers's business or his personal life. He traveled extensively in all the countries from which he bought coffee and lived well off the profits from his enterprise, which included packaging specialty coffees for several high-end hotels as well as his shops. Mac clicked over to a list of the hotels serving Cauca coffee, hoping to find the Paradis. No such luck. All the hotels were in the United States, in New York, Florida, Massachusetts, and Washington, DC.

"Cauca Café?" Callie came up and peered over his shoulder, her body too close for his comfort. "There was one of those near my father's house in Montauk. What do they have to do with anything?"

"Small world. The owner is connected to the coffee

plantation Falcone owns. The business ties could be legitimate, though."

"I thought people used coffee to smuggle drugs, not guns."

"People still try that, though it's never hidden the scent of the drugs from dogs. But I doubt Falcone is actually shipping arms with the coffee. More likely, the coffee business serves as a money laundry. Falcone claims to grow and sell more coffee than he does; Rivers—the guy who owns Cauca Café—claims to buy and sell more coffee than he does, and everyone shows a nice, healthy profit. The government gets their chunk in sales tax and income tax, and no one looks too closely at the business."

"But what would that have to do with us?"

"Maybe nothing." He explained his search for a building where Juarez could hold Erin, then pointed at the address of the Cauca roasting building. "Do you know where that is?"

"Atlantic Beach. No, I don't." She glanced at the aerial map he had opened, then leaned over his shoulder and pressed the keys to zoom out. "Okay, that's Nassau County. An hour or so from here, maybe more depending on traffic."

"I wonder how soon Nash could have people there."

Callie laughed, surprising him. "Nash may be a miracle worker, but you're talking New York traffic. If they leave now, right this instant, they have a chance. But all those people you were complaining about on the street? Come four o'clock, they all start heading out of the city, and most of them in the direction of Atlantic Beach. The non-beachfront towns in Nassau County are primarily bedroom communities, places where people live when they work in the city. The Long Island Expressway, the main artery out of the city and down the whole length of the island, isn't called 'the longest parking lot in the world' for nothing, and the other highways clog just as badly. And during the summer, traffic is at its worst because people want to squeeze in every second they can get at the shore, and it looks as if Cauca Café's building is right on the beach."

"Damn. If the area's that crowded, maybe he wouldn't keep Erin there."

"He might." Callie tapped an area of the screen near the thumbtack icon that represented the Cauca Café. "I've been to this town. Point Lookout. It's not low rent, but it's not the Hamptons, either. People mind their own business, and when the beach day is over, it's over. Cauca seems to be on a boardwalk. I bet half an hour after sunset, it's deserted.

"But why use a place connected to him at all? Why not rent a moving van or panel truck and keep Erin in the back of that?"

"Because it's not secure. If he's driving, he could be pulled over if his taillight goes out, his turn signal malfunctions, a rock breaks someone's windshield behind him. He could get a flat, and a helpful officer could stop to help him. If he's parked, Erin could attract attention by banging on the walls. If these guys had more time to set up the op, I wouldn't even bother with the property search because they'd have found something untraceable. But the way this went down, the schedule will have forced them to use the best thing they had at hand."

"Which you think is Atlantic Beach."

"Possibly."

"Let's assume for a minute you're right. What happens next?"

"Nash's men pull Erin out of that building before Juarez calls you back. Let me talk to him, see what he's got on the location and who's available to check it out." Without waiting for her reply, he called HSE.

"He's on the way to you," Lexie explained.

"Then how about while we wait for him, you tell me what's not in the file on Paul Rivers and Cauca Café?"

Lexie hesitated. "I don't know what you mean."

"Yeah, you do. The file's just facts; it has to be, so current speculation doesn't taint future investigations or send them in the wrong direction. But I've read the facts. Now I want the dirt, even if it can't be proved."

"Ask Nash."

"We can't afford to wait. You came from DEA with him, and you run HSE. What he knows, you know."

Another long pause, and Mac clamped down on his tension. He couldn't remember the last time he'd had to beg someone to trust him. Had his steady decline since the knife fight stole his peripheral vision and his career had taken such a visible toll? Could Lexie tell he wasn't as powerful, as trustworthy as he'd once been? Could Callie?

"Paul Rivers started Cauca Café in 1990," Lexie said, and Mac let out his breath as quietly as possible. "The first couple years, it was your average local coffee boutique. Rivers had a thirty-year mortgage on the property, which he paid regularly, and a substantial ten-year small-business loan, which he couldn't keep up with. In 1996, he suddenly switched from buying exchange-grade coffee through the New York Coffee Exchange to buying premium grade coffee, single-origin stuff he purchased directly from plantation owners, primarily in Colombia. This track he found considerably more profitable. Enough so that in 1998 he paid off his entire small-business loan, which brought him to our attention."

"'Our' meaning the DEA?"

"We tracked his shipments, set dogs on his containers when they came into port, put people in his shops to watch sales volume—but he always came up clean."

"Still, you suspected him."

"Yes. The best coffee grows from soil seeded with coca plants, often soaked with blood and tilled with scythes of political unrest. None of the plantation owners Rivers buys from care much for human or civil rights. At some point, he may get dinged by the fair-trade movement among folks willing to pay his ridiculous prices for a cup of coffee, but at the moment he's doing very well. His contract with Falcone kept us on him after we might have given up."

"What's their history?"

"Rivers is a second-generation American, but he has strong familial ties to Colombia. His second cousin, Diego Rivera, manages Alegría Verde, Falcone's plantation, has since before Arturo Rodriguez, the previous owner, died. The connection could be as simple, as legitimate as that."

"Or Diego could hold a more integral position in the organization."

"Yes."

Everything Lexie said reinforced his belief that Falcone's men would stash Erin at the Cauca building. Even if Rivers wasn't dirty, he might cooperate because of his family's financial dependence on Falcone.

"There's a good chance Juarez is holding Erin at Rivers's building in Atlantic Beach. Do you have anyone who can check?"

"I'll look into it, but you don't give the orders here, Mr. Brody. Have Nash call me when he gets there."

"Of course." He rang off, then relayed what he'd learned to Callie.

"So when Juarez calls, he'll tell me to rent a car and drive to Atlantic Beach?"

"No. Whatever you mean to Lewis, Cauca Café is far more

important to Falcone than either you or Erin. He won't let Juarez risk such a valuable asset by revealing its location just in case you manage to survive the meeting. They'll take her some place else for the meet, which gives us even less time to get eyes on that building."

A sharp rap at the door signaled Nash's arrival. Once again, Mac went over his analysis. Before he finished, Nash pulled out his cell and called Lexie.

"Get Dylan and Nick out to Atlantic Beach. Do we have anyone else uncommitted? Do we know anyone out there?" Lexie spoke for some time, Nash commenting only occasionally, while Mac rubbed at his scar, which itched as badly as it had the first few weeks of healing. Twice, when Nash ordered Lexie to leave men where they were, Mac swallowed protests. What could take precedence over a woman's life? But as Lexie had reminded him, he wasn't in charge.

"Dylan, who drove us home the other night, has family in Valley Stream," Nash said when he hung up. "He'll find someone to watch the building until he and Nick can get to the place."

"I take it that's close by?"

Nash shrugged. "Closer than we are, assuming usual amounts of traffic."

"So what do we do in the meantime?" Callie asked.

"Script," replied Mac. "His questions, your responses."

"How do you know what he'll ask?"

"We don't. So we decide what you need to say, then figure out how to maneuver the conversation to allow you to get your point across regardless of what direction he chooses."

CHAPTER FOURTEEN

By the time Nash's phone rang at four thirty, Callie felt as if they'd devised a strategy for every possible scenario, though Mac assured her more rehearsing remained yet to do.

"It's Dylan," said Nash once he'd checked the display. "I'll put him on speaker."

"Smart money says she's here," Dylan informed them, "but we can't get into the building. It looks like a renovated warehouse, with the ground floor as a garage or loading bay. First set of windows is maybe fifteen feet up."

"Is the shop open?"

"Nope. According to a sign in the window, they're closed due to a leak they are trying to fix. It thanks customers for their patience."

"Imagine that. Vehicles around?"

"According to Lexie, the business owns a panel van. We didn't see it in the neighborhood, but it could be parked inside the building. In Juarez's position, I'd bring her out in that, then find a nice, quiet spot to switch over to a rental, give the van to a partner, and have him bring it back to the shop and clean it."

"Agreed. How many exits from the roasting plant itself?"

"There's the garage entrance on one side, and a regular pedestrian door on the other. Nick and I will stay on the garage side. My brother-in-law and his partner are keeping an eye on the front."

"Dylan's sister is married to a Nassau County sheriff's

deputy," Nash explained. "They're off duty, so nothing they do is official, but they've got the skills and experience to help watch and tail."

"So you're not going to do anything?" Callie wanted to scream; her words came out hoarse from the effort she expended to keep her tone even. "You know he has Erin there, now, but you're going to leave him be?"

"We have no proof. And, unfortunately, while we do, occasionally, bend the rules, it's best not to do so in broad daylight. The best possible outcome is that Juarez continues to stall until true dark. At that point, we can send in a team and get her, and you won't have to leave the hotel. But until then, yes, we wait. My guess is that they will move her out, bring her to meet you, which will make picking her up a hell of a lot safer and easier. I've already lost a friend today and so have you. I'd prefer to keep the numbers down."

MAC COULD FEEL Callie's anger, taste his own frustration. And he wanted to slug Nash for reminding her of Tommy's death, though he doubted she'd forgotten for even a minute. But he did understand Nash's position. It was the eternal law-enforcement dilemma: the good guys had to play by the rules; the bad guys made it up as they went along. If Dylan and Nick broke into the warehouse, they'd be the ones who ended up in jail. And if Juarez had the place booby-trapped, which in all likelihood he did, they could end up dead. Without a warrant, Dylan's sheriff's department connections couldn't help him, and the loose tangle of associations, enough to satisfy Mac, Nash, and Dylan, wouldn't satisfy a judge.

To her credit, though, after her single outburst, Callie stifled her anger, though her fingers clenched together so hard her knuckles turned white. She listened to the conversation, let them plan. And when Dylan hung up, she went back to running scenarios without complaint.

At five thirty, Dylan called back.

"They're moving," he said. You want us to follow, or cause a little accident?"

"Follow. I don't want to take him out of the game yet."

Mac felt Callie tense beside him. Obviously, Nash saw it, too, because he explained his reasoning. "If Dylan wrecks Juarez's van, and Erin's not in it, we've tipped our hand too soon, and we may lose them forever. If she is inside, maybe we save her. Or maybe Juarez panics and starts shooting and everybody dies. Either way, we haven't eliminated the threat, just postponed it. We have to take Juarez alive if at all possible, and get him to turn on Falcone. Better yet, we wait until Falcone himself, or at the very least Lewis, is on hand."

A satisfied grunt came from the phone. "Got him. We tagged the truck with a transmitter. Lonnie, my brother-in-law, has a receiver. We have another, and I am setting up the feed to go back to HQ as we speak so you can access it. We can hang back a little this way."

"You tagged a moving vehicle? Without the driver noticing?" *Impressive.*

"The RC heli?" Nash asked.

"I told you it would come in handy."

"Dylan has a thing for radio-controlled planes." Nash sighed. "He's always telling me they're not just toys, and I guess he's proved his point."

"Had it hovering at the corner, since the street's one way. When Juarez passed underneath the streetlight, we planted the tracker on the roof. The trackers only a couple inches square, and the chopper's not much bigger, so the only people who might have noticed would be kids, who would just think it was cool to see a tiny helicopter land on a car. Of course, I lost the chopper. No way to bring it back unobtrusively while we're on the move. You owe me for it, Nash. It was a good one."

"I'll buy you a dozen. Can you tell where they're headed?"

"At the moment, they're getting on the Nassau Expressway, but that could take them anywhere."

"Yeah. Keep in touch."

"Will do."

No sooner had Dylan signed off than the other cell rang. Callie's face went white, and she looked at it with fear and hatred before lifting it from the coffee table.

⌒

"Have you rid yourself of your companions?" The sound of Juarez's smooth, almost oily voice caused Callie's stomach muscles to clench, but she forced her own tone to mirror his.

"I have. Let me speak to Erin."

"That's not possible at the moment."

Mac had warned her that Juarez would test her limits, try to withhold proof of Erin's welfare, and he'd given her instructions. She followed them, though it was the hardest thing she'd ever done. "Call me back when it is," she replied, and hung up.

Minutes passed. A cold, clammy sweat broke out all over her body. She brought her knees up and ducked her head to rest her forehead against them, wrapping her arms around her calves, the phone still clenched in her fist. Mac stroked her back, then hauled her onto his lap, surrounding her with his strength.

"Hang in there, sweetheart," he murmured. Although acutely aware of Nash's presence, Callie couldn't bring herself to pull away. The phone buzzed. With a deep breath, she flipped it open and held it to her ear. Erin's voice brought tears to her eyes.

"Callie?"

"It's almost over, Erin. I'm coming to get you. I swear. But first, you know the drill, I have three questions."

"Of course you do, nosy." The spark of humor lifted Callie's spirits — doubtless Erin's intention. God, she would kill Juarez, Falcone, and John Lewis herself if they injured Erin.

"Who's the most overrated celebrity chef?"

"Trick question: they're all overrated."

The speed of the reply reassured Callie even more than Erin's earlier bravado. She wouldn't be up to such a snappy comeback if they'd hurt her. "What area of the world would you most like to visit?"

"Tuscany." They'd often talked about taking a trip to Italy. *I promise, Erin, we'll go. Just as soon as this is over, I'll make it happen.*

"What country makes the best beer?"

"Belgium. And one day you'll acknowledge it."

Callie heard a scuffle of some sort, then Juarez came back on the line. "As you can see, your friend is fine. Follow directions and she will remain so."

"I have a message for your employers." Callie could see the script in her head. "I'll come to you, trade myself for Erin, but I am not stupid. The information you asked for won't be with me. When I see Erin walk away, I'll take you to it."

"That will do." As both Mac and Nash had predicted,

Juarez sounded almost amused. The requirement that she bring any information she'd gathered had been a ruse; he'd agreed to her terms because he planned to kill her on sight.

"Not so fast. I suggest you mention a few details to your bosses so they don't assume I'm bluffing."

"Certainly."

"John Lewis has nothing to fear from me. I don't want his inheritance, even if his father did routinely impregnate patients with his own sperm and sell black-market babies. I also don't care about his business with Henry Falcone, or Falcone's dealings with Diego Rivera and Paul Rivers. Several government entities, however, both here and elsewhere, might feel differently about the picture I've put together. You should probably get your hands on my files before putting a bullet through my brain and dumping me in the East River." They'd chosen to use the reference to Hugo Americh's death to create a personal stake for Juarez. Allowing him to believe Callie had proof he'd done the deed could help keep her alive.

"You've been busy."

"I have a keen instinct for self-preservation. And you told me to bring my father's papers. You can pass along to John Lewis that asking for them was a mistake—my father had contacts better even than Nash Harper's, and an intricate understanding of politics, especially personal ones. He kept track of his enemies. Until Lewis asked for the information my father had gathered, it didn't occur to me to examine anything not directly related to my birth. Imagine my surprise at finding so many names in his files that coincided with those in Mr. Harper's database. I suggest you discuss that with your employer. I doubt he wants Nash Harper to get his hands on my information. Consolidation of my father's data and Nash's could prove . . . detrimental . . . to Falcone's operations."

Juarez ignored the threat.

"You have just under an hour to get to Grand Central Station," he said. "You will take the 6:43 Metro-North Hudson line train, buying a ticket for Garrison. We'll phone you once the train leaves the station and tell you where to get off."

"I won't get off without talking to Erin, so be sure she's with you when you call."

Juarez hung up without answering. Only when Mac gently pried the telephone from her hand did Callie shake herself free from the conversation's thrall. She buried her face against Mac's neck, inhaling his musky, masculine scent for three long, deep breaths before scrambling off his lap to pace the room. Neither he nor Nash spoke, content to give her room to organize her thoughts.

"The geography's wrong," said Nash when she finally gained enough control to repeat the conversation. "Why would they send you northwest when they're south and east of us?"

"Hang on." Callie sat in front of the computer and brought up the Metropolitan Transit Authority's site, checking the routing for the Hudson line trains. "I don't know this line at all. Maybe that's the point. They couldn't send me out on the Long Island Rail Road when I spent all those years in Montauk, and the Harlem or New Haven lines are too close to where I live now. But I've never even heard of Garrison, New York."

"Is that the last stop?" Mac asked.

"No. Poughkeepsie is the end of the line. Garrison's most of the way, though."

"So they could plan to take you off anywhere. Maybe the line doesn't matter so much as the fact that they can get you onto a busy commuter train in an unfamiliar area."

Nash called his office. "Tell Carlos I want him on the 6:43 train to Poughkeepsie out of Grand Central. He needs to be on board as soon as they open the doors, in the last car of the train, near the final set of doors. Tell him to go with the construction look and a paper-bagged bottle." He walked over to the desk and brushed Callie's fingers off the keyboard, then entered a series of programs and passwords, finally bringing up a photograph of a man in his late thirties with shaggy blond hair and a deep tan.

"This is Carlos Herrera. He'll be on your train, probably covered in dust and looking disreputable enough to discourage the business types from sharing his seat. He'll be carrying a paper bag, and he'll smell a bit beery. It's rush hour, so the trains will be packed, but if you can sit next to him, do. If you can't, pick a spot close by. He'll be looking for you."

"And you and Mac?"

"I suspect Mac will want to be on the train."

"Damned straight."

"So he'll be a couple of cars up. We can't risk whoever Falcone puts on the train recognizing him, and unfortunately New York City isn't the best place to be anonymous once your face has made the news. The MTA cops are pretty careful, and Grand Central's always crawling with security." Nash studied Mac. "Wear the ball cap. There are newsstands inside the station. Buy a *Daily News* and bury your face in it. And use one of the machines to buy your ticket. Buying tickets on the train attracts attention from the conductors."

Nash turned his attention to Callie. "I'll drive Mac to Grand Central, then head to the West Side Highway and start north, try to follow your signal once the train gets moving. You should probably take the subway from here. The S will take you across town, drop you right below Grand Central."

"She shouldn't be alone."

"I'll be fine. They have no idea where I am coming from, and as Nash said, security at Grand Central is really tight. The subway is a nightmare this time of day, so they couldn't pick me out of the crowd even if they wanted to." She could see him struggle with the idea of her being out of his sight. His protectiveness was comforting, but now that the endless waiting was over, a peculiar calm had settled over her.

"One more thing." From his jeans pocket, Nash withdrew a hair tie and a small, flesh-colored torus a few inches in diameter. "These are what I was waiting for."

"What are they?" Callie asked as she took the scrunchy and the odd piece of foamy rubber from his hand.

"They're tracking devices, but unlike most really small units, they turn off."

"Why does that matter?"

Mac touched the black scrunchy, feeling for the bug, and frowned as he answered. "Because the way most bug detectors work is by looking for signal. A tracking device is bouncing signal off a satellite or cell tower for location all the time. Even the ones that only check for location when they're triggered, like the car security systems, have to remain on to be found by the tracking system. That means they are vulnerable."

Nash nodded. "The handheld scanner I used on you the other night looks for signal or electrical current, then essentially targets the bugs it finds with an electromagnetic pulse. It will work on any active electronic device. The nifty thing about these trackers is that neither of them is actually on. They can't be detected or disabled that way."

"So how do I turn them on if I want you to be able to find me?"

"The tracker sewed into the hair tie has a physical switch.

Feel for it." Callie did, finding the button in the hard spot in the band. "When the button is depressed, it's off. So you put that in your hair and be sure the switch rests against your hair tightly, that it's wrapped inside. That will keep it turned off while he's scanning you."

Callie handed the second tracker to Mac and pulled her hair into a tight, high ponytail, positioning the button in the hair tie between layers of wrapping so it remained depressed. "And the other?"

Nash appeared uncomfortable, staring at the device Mac was rolling between his fingers rather than looking into her eyes as he spoke. "Something entirely new. It's a heat switch. As long as it's kept above eighty-eight degrees, it will remain off."

Callie plucked the bagel-shaped bit of foam from Mac's hand. "How am I supposed to keep it that hot?"

Nash pulled a folded square of paper out of his back pocket. "Instructions," he said.

Callie glanced at the piece of paper and realized why he hadn't given her the details verbally. "Lovely. I'll be right back."

In the bathroom, Callie examined the device. Under the fluorescent light, she could see the vague, gray outlines of electronics beneath the rubber skin. She washed the thing thoroughly before looking over the instructions, which seemed to have been copied, almost word for word, from the instructions for inserting a contraceptive sponge.

A vaginal tracking system. What kind of lunatics did Nash Harper employ? And how was she supposed to turn the thing on? What if they handcuffed her? Watched her constantly?

On the other hand, once inserted, the blasted bug felt really secure. However they'd come up with the idea, Nash's engineers had developed a smart product. Still, she felt horribly self-conscious when she returned to the living room, and she couldn't meet Mac's eyes.

"Ready to roll?" asked Nash.

"Not quite. How do I . . . activate that second tracking device? I mean, unless I'm dead, my body's not getting below eighty-eight degrees, and I sort of want to survive this."

"It's a last-resort backup. Ideally, we'll be able to retrieve Erin safely before you even get off the train, and force Juarez into a confession. At that point, I'll let Carlos and Mac know and they'll bring you in. You should never have to use any of the trackers.

"But of course, nothing's ideal. So if Juarez just continues to drive around until you get picked up, we want a way to track you.

"The final tracker is in case we lose you completely. We're good, Callie. Very good. But we're not perfect. In that case, I trust you to find a way to remove it from your body. That's all you have to worry about. Do that, we'll find you no matter what.

Yeah, okay. She could do that. "How soon will you try to rescue Erin?"

"As soon as it's prudent. I wish I could give you a more specific answer, but I can't. Do not worry about her. I have men on her, and they won't let anything happen. If you get another phone call, be sure to insist on talking to her. The longer you can keep that up, the better chance we have."

"I guess that's it."

"Good. Get going, then."

"No." Mac put a hand on her shoulder. "We need a minute, Nash." He slid his palm down her arm to capture her hand, and tugged her into the bedroom, shutting the door behind them.

"I'm going, Mac," she said before he could speak, before he could begin to try to keep her safe while others risked their lives on her behalf. "You heard him. I have to show up. Having everyone in the same place gives us the best shot at finishing this once and for all. Otherwise, these guys can just keep doing this until they succeed. I can't live that way. I won't."

"I won't try to stop you. But I need you to swear to me that no matter what Juarez says or does, you won't deliberately try to lose us. You have to trust me on this, Callie. Please." The intensity of his green eyes overwhelmed her, yet she could read nothing of his thoughts in them. "We can protect you, but only if you let us."

She laid a hand along the sharp plane of his stubbled cheek, feeling the peculiar urge to reassure him. "I do trust you. Absolutely."

He covered her hand with his own, holding it in place, then turned his head to press a hard kiss into the center of her palm. Fire rocketed through her body.

"Good." He let go of her hand and pulled her against him, sliding muscular arms around her waist and dipping his head to nuzzle her neck. "Because we have unfinished business, you and I."

He bit her gently where her neck met her shoulder, and her knees went weak. "Mac. I have to go."

"Yeah." His mouth covered hers, driving all rational thought from her head. She wrapped her arms around his neck and held on as his tongue tangled with hers. One of his hands slid from her waist to cup her butt, pressing her intimately against him, and she couldn't prevent a moan welling up from her throat. She ran her own hands blindly over his back, memorizing every line, then over smooth biceps and back up to his jaw. Her right fingers found the scar and traced it gently.

A knock at the door had him backing away from her.

"That will be Nash. Time for you to hit the road." But his eyes held hers.

"Yes. I ..." She didn't know what to say. "I trust you, Mac."

His lips quirked in the sexy half smile he so rarely exhibited. "That's my girl."

CHAPTER FIFTEEN

CALLIE ARRIVED AT Grand Central Station at 6:32. She stopped at the first ticket machine she saw and purchased her ticket, no more anxious than Mac for a conductor to recognize her face from the news. The monitor showed her train at one of the lower-level tracks, so she took the escalator down. Passing through the food court, her stomach rumbled, but even if she had had time to buy something, she was far too nervous to eat. She did grab a Coke, counting on the sugar and caffeine to keep her going.

People streamed toward her train. She stepped into the first car, spotting Carlos Herrera without a problem. His disreputable appearance hadn't dissuaded a teenage girl from squeezing into the window seat next to him. The girl wore an iPod, the music blaring out beyond the edges of her headphones and assaulting Callie even as she settled across the aisle. Callie shared a bench with an elderly gentleman who'd propped his cane against the seat next to him, probably to discourage anyone from sitting there. But rush-hour trains, even as late as this one, didn't allow for empty spots, and when Callie asked him about the cane, he removed it with a remark muttered so quietly she couldn't hear it.

Before sitting down, Callie took a minute to study the occupants of the four rows of seats behind her own. Tired, irritable businesspeople, for the most part. No one who looked suspicious, but the spot between her shoulder blades itched beneath the body armor Mac and Nash had insisted she wear, and she slouched into her seat, trying to make herself as small as possible.

In front of her, commuters clustered around the first set of doors in the train car. Beyond them came dozens more rows of bench seats, then a second set of doors, and another short run of seats. More business types filled the seats and the aisle, along with a couple of families, a few men who appeared to be day laborers, some teens, and the obligatory nutcase, who stood in the vestibule, eyeing every person who came through the doors and commenting under his breath.

The doors closed with warning bells, a few commuters squeezing aboard at the last possible moment, and the train lurched forward. The conductor worked his way through the throng, most of whom—Carlos Herrera included—carried monthly passes rather than tickets. Did Nash keep train passes for whoever needed them? It seemed a ridiculous expense, but worked to prevent Carlos from appearing suspicious. The conductor, a slight, gray-haired man, paid far more attention to both the teenager and Callie, who carried tickets, than he did to any of the pass holders. Even the vestibule lunatic, wearing his pass on a chain around his neck over his ratty and moth-eaten sweater, didn't merit a second glance.

The train squealed to a stop at 125th Street. A few more passengers crowded on, but no one got off. Callie checked her cell phone, which had shown no signal inside the station. Four bars. Good. Juarez could contact her. She twisted the cap off her soda and took a long slug, trying to calm herself.

More jerky starts and noisy stops, and slowly the car began to empty. At Riverdale, Callie's seatmate left, his spot taken by a dark-haired woman in a severe pantsuit. Two stops later, at Yonkers, both she and the teenager next to Carlos exited. He looked over and smiled, just another stranger passing the time on the way home from work. Under normal circumstances she'd have made some kind of joke, asked if he were deaf from the teen's music, but talking to him might make anyone watching her suspicious, so she nodded but remained silent.

A few minutes later, just as the train started to pull away from the platform at Greystone Station, it halted, and the engineer's voice came over the intercom.

"Sorry about that, folks." He maintained an almost jocular tone, but Callie could hear notes of stress beneath it, even over the scratchy sound system. *Or maybe you're projecting your own nerves onto him.* "We're having a little technical difficulty. If you're in the front three cars of the train, I'd like you to walk back, because we're going to have to off-load everyone. I know it's going to make you all late to dinner, and it's hot and still drizzling, and no one's in a good mood, but it can't be helped."

Around her, people grumbled and gathered their possessions, most appearing irritated but unsurprised. Then the lunatic began to pound on as yet unopened doors and shout.

"Terrorists! Let us out! There's a bomb on the train!" And all those people who'd watched him with bored distaste and thin tolerance suddenly found gospel in his words. The aisles filed in a rush, and a mob formed in the vestibule.

A man in the seat behind Callie tapped her on the shoulder, and she jumped.

"Help me get the window open," he said, his eyes wild. "We can get out that way."

"You can't be serious." Callie tried reason, though she didn't have much hope it would work. "That guy's nuts. This is a train breakdown, not 9/11."

Another man shoved past her and reached for the safety

latches on the window. "If you won't help, get out of the way," he snapped. "I'm not dying on this fucking train."

Callie slid out of her seat and into the packed aisle. She tried to push through to grab the seat beside Carlos, but the doors opened and she was carried along on a panicked wave of commuters. On the platform, the single-minded surge continued as the mob headed for the stairs to the catwalk that arched over the tracks, leading toward the street. Frantic, Callie searched for Mac or Carlos but saw neither.

Something hard jammed into her waist just below the hem of the bulletproof vest.

"Keep moving, Miss Pearson," said the lunatic. He'd removed his torn sweater and lost the ragged backpack and now fit right into the swarm. He shoved a blue waterproof poncho into her hands. "Put it on. Pull up the hood."

Not good. Fear permeated the crowd. One scream, one shouted "Gun!" and they'd panic, which could give her the opportunity to escape. On the other hand, it could also allow him to escape—after shooting her. After a brief hesitation, she dragged the poncho over her head as she mounted the steps to the catwalk, deliberately slowing both actions to give Mac and Carlos as long as possible to find her without resorting to the GPS trackers. Despite Nash's assurances that they wouldn't lose her, she felt a whole lot better when his men were close enough to touch, or at least see.

Neither man appeared in the interminable trip up the stairs, across the walkway, and down the steps on the other side, but as she stepped off the curb into the parking lot for the train station, she thought she glimpsed Carlos. Her heart picked up speed—how could she attract his attention? She pretended to stumble, and her captor yanked her back to her feet. A blue van pulled up in front of them, and the back door opened, but before the man beside her could force her in, someone shoved him away. He fell forward, his head slamming into the metal side panel of the van with a crunch and a thud. As she turned to run, Callie caught sight of Carlos attached to his back like a limpet, scrabbling for the guy's gun.

"Go!" he shouted.

She went. She took the stairs up from the station to the street two at a time, her hurry increasing the nervous tension in those she passed. "What happened?" she heard people call out. "Where are you going? What's going on?"

Which was a damned good question. Carlos had told her to run. Did that mean they had already rescued Erin?

Cars zipped by along the street at the top of the steps. Where to now? Apartment complexes lined the far side of the street, while her side, the station side, where the land fell away sharply toward the Hudson River, was completely barren. She dodged the traffic and crossed to the lighted apartments, then stood in front of one and pulled out her phone to call Nash. Before she could flip it open, however, the blue van squealed to a stop next to her. The door slid open and two men jumped out.

Callie ducked into the street and fled against the flow of traffic, hoping the oncoming drivers would realize what was happening. Headlights blinded her, and she heard a man curse as he passed. A driver slammed on his brakes, his car fishtailing wildly. A second slammed into him, almost knocking his car into Callie, who leapt to the hood of a station wagon parked alongside. She looked up and down the street, but the blue van was gone.

The two drivers exited their cars, both yelling. The first one pointed toward her, and she clambered down off the wagon. She couldn't afford to stick around and be recognized by the police. She had entered the country illegally, and her presence would implicate both Mac and Nash, who had done nothing but try to help her. She slid into the shadows as the two drivers progressed from words to shoves.

Just before she reached the safety of the well-lit atrium of a large condo building, she was yanked into an alley. Something sharp pierced her neck, and she looked up into empty black eyes as the light faded from her view.

GASPING FROM HAVING run up the stairs at top speed when he realized—too late—that Callie had taken that route, Mac watched in frustrated fury as the van disappeared around a curve in the road. *Fuck.* Sirens approached and instinctively he stepped back into the shadow of the trees lining the sidewalk. He needed to get the hell out of Dodge before the media arrived and began filming everything—and everyone—in sight. He began walking down the road in the same direction the van had gone, keeping his pace slow, just another bored commuter, but his hand shook as he yanked the sat phone from its clip on his jeans and speed-dialed Nash.

"I'm two minutes from you. Carlos already called in. He tied up the man he knocked out with the help of a couple of good Samaritans and is waiting for the police. He'll tell them he saw the guy trying to manhandle a woman into a van and stepped in to stop it. He got the vehicle's plate number, but these guys are pros; they'll have new plates or a whole new van in minutes."

"You think they changed plans when you got Erin?" Mac

had been headed toward Callie's car to tell her that her friend was safe when the train stopped.

"No way to tell. I thought we'd handled it smoothly, but it's possible Juarez called in before he pulled over and told them there was a problem."

As Mac rounded the bend where he'd lost sight of the van, Nash's black town car pulled up across the street. He'd given Nash grief about the sedan, hoping to get a rise out of him, but Nash had merely grinned and said that no vehicle was more anonymous in the New York area than a fleet car. No one paid them any mind in either rich neighborhoods or poor ones.

"Are you tracking her?" Mac belted himself into the passenger seat. With barely a glance out the window, Nash pulled back out into traffic, then pointed at a screen set into the dashboard, where a bright red dot traversed yellow roads.

"Yeah. The van must have gone around the block or something. There's a huge traffic snarl, and her trackers all stopped for a couple minutes, then started moving again. They're not that far ahead of us." He pushed a button beneath the screen, and the image zoomed out, erasing roads but revealing a second red dot. "That's Dylan."

"He's not moving."

"Nope." Satisfaction oozed around the words. "That's how we got Juarez. Nick and Dylan rear-ended him when he got stuck in traffic. They're in Westchester, not Nassau County, but a couple Nassau cops happened to be passing by and stopped to lend a hand." Right. Dylan's family. "Erin seems to be okay, but she's on her way to the hospital under guard."

"Where were they headed?"

"Westchester airport. Lexie has been watching flight plans and alerted me to a private flight that came in from Miami.

That was the direction Juarez was headed, so we took him out before he could get there. I've got a half-dozen guys headed in that direction right now in case either Lewis or Falcone are on hand."

Mac's eyes hadn't left the red dot that symbolized Callie, and when it split, one, dim light breaking away to remain still on the map while the brighter part continued, he cursed.

"They found one of the bugs. Probably tossed it out the window."

As if on cue, Nash's cell phone, sitting in a cradle hooked into the dash, rang. He pushed a button, said "Go," and Lexie's voice filled the car. "That was the shoes. Fair assumption if they found one device, they found them all. At least, all the traditional ones. If they have enough men mobilized, they can send them all off in different directions."

"With any luck, they'll have kept the op too small for that. Find out what's going on with Dylan and call me back." He disconnected.

The little dot took a left. Moments later, so did Nash. Frustrated, Mac wished he had a better grip on New York's geography. In Atlanta, he'd have known where the van was headed and how to get there first, but here he was lost. Gray stone and cement buildings lined the street they traveled, but unlike those he'd seen in Manhattan, these maxed out at about five stories. Gas stations and bodegas brightened the drab residential landscape, though the deepening dusk and thick clouds leached the vibrancy from even those splashes of color. Night, which stacked the deck against the hunter, was approaching.

The red light turned right. It dimmed, blinked, then went out entirely.

"Shit," said Nash.

CHAPTER SIXTEEN

CALLIE WOKE WITH gritty eyes, a throbbing head, and a tight, unfamiliar collar around her neck. The plastic pinched her skin, and drops of sweat formed beneath it, making her itch. She was lying on a cot in a large, dimly lit space she took to be a basement. Faint illumination leached into the area around the half-open door of a room a few feet away. From the angle at which she lay, Callie could see a sink beyond the door, and she assumed the light came from a bathroom. With that recognition came the urgent need to pee.

She sat up, the pounding in her head increasing as she inched toward vertical. She moved her legs and realized that her left ankle had been cuffed, attached to the leg of the cot by a cable. Lightweight, but very solid. Was this what had happened to the woman from Plum Bay Beach? Could the same cuff have caused the abrasions Mac had described on her ankle? And if so, had Callie returned to the island? Could she have been unconscious so long?

Determined not to suffer the same fate as the Plum Bay victim, Callie squinted into the dim grayness. The faint light limned a neat stack of perfectly even loops of cable at the foot of the bed. Stretched straight, it would easily reach the bathroom. First things first. As she stood, hair fell across her face and she reached back, feeling for the tie containing the tracking device.

Gone. Either they'd found and removed it deliberately, or it had fallen off at some point. She still wore her jeans and shirt but assumed her captors had disabled the bugs sewn into them, as Nash had destroyed the one he found in her purse. The gun and its holster, along with her shoes, were missing, which left only the tracker she carried inside her.

Still woozy, she stumbled into the bathroom. The dim light brightened as she crossed the threshold. Motion sensors? Was someone videotaping as well? Did she dare remove the tracker, or would they see?

She peered around the bathroom, searching for hidden cameras before lowering her jeans. She should have kept the skirt. True, it was harder to run in, but it would have provided a modicum of privacy. *You have more to worry about than perverts watching you pee.* But still she pulled the hem of her shirt as low as she could and huddled over, shielding herself from the view of any potential cameras.

The light remained bright as she washed her hands and splashed water onto her face, but the moment she stepped out of the room, it dimmed. Not motion activated, then. Her fingers traced the collar. Could it be a trigger? Keeping her upper body back, she kicked a leg through the door. No reaction from the lights. Planting her hands one either side of the jamb to stabilize herself, she leaned forward slowly, letting the top of her head, then her face, pass the threshold. The moment her neck crossed into the bathroom, the lights popped back to their brighter setting.

And wasn't that just peachy? Almost certainly, the collar had other functions, too. She glanced toward the shadowed area farthest from the cot, where she thought she could determine the outline of stairs. The cable wouldn't reach that far, but even if it did, the collar would almost certainly trigger some punishment, like the "invisible fence" her neighbors had that kept their Labrador retriever from leaving the premises. She shuddered.

She explored the room as far as the cable allowed. Cinderblock walls and the lack of windows declared the spacious, rectangular room a basement. The bathroom, along with dusty boxes stacked just out of her reach, argued for a residential space despite its size. *Must be a helluva house.* She wished she had a clue how long it had taken to reach the spot, but her watch had stopped at 7:13 p.m., probably as a result of whatever they'd used to kill the tracking devices.

Mac would be frantic by now. Whether he cared about her or not, he would take her capture personally. Especially since they'd been so close to a win. And she had to believe that. Had to believe Erin was safe, protected by Nash's men.

She took a deep breath and held it for four counts before letting it out slowly. An odd note registered beneath the musty smell of old cardboard and unused space, and she sniffed again. Salt. The house's climate control seeped into the basement as well, so the air was cool and dry, but the salty tang convinced her that her captors had brought her back to St. Martin.

Again she thought of the unidentified drowning victim. In the madness of the last few days, Callie had come to think of her as a clue rather than a person. But she'd been an individual with dreams and ambitions, friends and family. Had her life ended here, chained to this cot? Her killer had strangled her, which gave Callie a little hope. She'd taken plenty of courses in close-quarters fighting. She'd never tried to engage an opponent with one leg shackled, but the long cable might not interfere too badly. She stood and threw a few tentative kicks. Yes, it could work, though she'd have to take care not to trip.

Of course, her first two half-sisters—how weird did that sound?—had been shot. And there was the collar. Who knew what that could do?

If, as she believed, she'd been brought back to St. Martin, it would take Mac hours to get to her, even with Nash's connections. She needed to get the tracker out, activate it as soon as possible. But what if this wasn't her final destination? What if she activated the beacon, Mac and Nash got under way, and then John and his cronies shipped her somewhere else? Suddenly cold, she drew up her knees and rocked on the cot, trying to decide what to do.

Footsteps overhead ended the debate. She hustled into the bathroom. When she'd shoved the door shut as much as possible over the cable, she yanked down her jeans and panties and huddled over as if suffering a bout of nausea. Hooking the device with one finger, she pulled it out. She made a production of flushing, then washed her hands in water as cold as she could make it, hoping to activate the bug more quickly. She palmed the device as she headed back into the main room. There weren't many places to hide the thing, so she pretended to fuss with the shackle on her ankle in case hidden cameras followed her movements as she tucked the bug behind the leg of the cot.

"Hurry up, Mac," she whispered into the dim, gray space. "Please."

⌒

"They've taken her back to the island," Mac said. "I know it."

"Doesn't make sense," Nash countered. They'd returned

to HSE headquarters, and Nash had recalled every available agent to work sources and technology. Depressingly few, to Mac's eyes. They had abandoned Nash's plush office suite for the seventh floor and a utilitarian warehouse of a room that literally hummed with technology. The low buzz of the computers and the cooling systems didn't interfere with conversation but added an urgent undercurrent to everything.

Dylan, still tied up with Erin and the NYPD, texted in as often as he could, and they had an open line to Travis in St. Martin, who said John had been locked up in his own house, so no one could be positive he hadn't left the island. The gendarmes had questioned him in depth when Nicole's body had turned up and had found nothing incriminating, but he still topped Mac's shit list.

Two women had responded from the Internet posts and sites Mac had instigated. Both had used the Lewis fertility clinic. One had discovered when her husband had needed a bone-marrow transplant that her daughter was not a match, not, in fact, her husband's daughter at all. But her daughter had never been harmed; she lived in Virginia with her husband and two children of her own. The other woman hoped Mac could help her—her daughter had disappeared five months before off a cruise ship in the Caribbean.

"It doesn't seem strange to you that this woman's daughter, Nancy Rossetti, that she disappeared from Nevis? The e-mail says Nancy told everyone where she was going, that she was over the moon about it. It would have been easy for John to snatch her there. It's no time at all from St. Martin."

"You still haven't explained why he would want to. I'm not buying the inheritance angle, especially if we can't prove he isn't the doc's biological kid. And as for Callie, if she's down there, she can't get her hands on the evidence she threatened

Juarez with. Why would he take her, knowing all that could become public?"

Mac understood the arguments, heard the logic. But his gut screamed at him to get in the air ASAP. Despite the cool indoor temperature, he could feel sweat trickling down his back. Years undercover, years in the Army, and he never remembered perspiring from fear. He had to find Callie, had to get her back before something terrible happened.

"I think he's right," Lexie said from behind him. When Mac turned, he saw she was reading from one of the screens. "Falcone's company has five cargo flights flying out of New York area airports between seven tonight and midnight tomorrow. Two of them are headed for San Juan. But I've also got reports that two of Falcone's associates have been staying at the Paradis. They landed a couple days ago. Came in commercial. It took us a while to figure out when they bought the tickets, but it turns out they were both last-minute purchases, which I don't like."

"Where's the great man himself?"

"Last seen in Italy, but he's gone under." The response came from a man Mac hadn't met, seated at a computer in the far corner.

"Fuck," said Nash. "When?"

"Ten days ago."

"Find him."

"Working on it."

"So he's got something going down on the island. Maybe he's involved himself, maybe not." Nash rubbed a hand over his face. "Either way, we need to be there." He checked the clock on the wall. "Airfield's closing. Lexie, get us a pilot and a flight plan for San Juan. Notify Trey we're coming in tonight and we'll need the chopper to go back to the island."

"You get out of there by midnight," Travis's voice came across the speaker, "you'll hit PR at four, the island around five in the morning. Let me know, and *The Tramp* will be waiting far enough out to avoid notice. You'll want to do a water drop. It's quicker, cleaner, and harder to track. Your people can climb aboard."

"You're sure you're not being watched after the last incident?" Mac asked. "We can't afford the scrutiny."

"Nope. Nash's crew handled it. The gendarmes detained them for twenty-four hours, but that's it. At the moment, they're running around making asses of themselves and keeping law-enforcement attention focused on them. I should be able to collect you with no problem. If not, I know a couple guys I can trust to do it."

"Flight plan is filed," said Lexie. "I'll drive you to the airport since Dylan's not available. Saul's fueling the Cessna."

"I take it you modified the fuel capacity," said Mac. He didn't know much about planes, but he'd never heard of a small jet that could fly so far without stopping for gas.

"Never know where you'll need to get to," replied Nash. "I told you we have good toys here."

Mac ignored him, addressing Travis on the speakerphone before following Lexie out of the room. "We're heading out. Catch you in a few."

Mac had seen the beacon tracker in the town car when they'd followed Callie, but the forty-five minute trip to the airstrip in New Jersey brought new surprises. As soon as the car cleared the underground garage, Nash—still on the cell phone he'd been using nonstop to pressure various contacts—depressed a button to reveal a computer.

"Hang on," he said to the man on the phone. He popped open the laptop, logged in, and passed it over to Mac. "We hook up to a cell network," he explained. "It's already connected to the office. In a minute, they'll get a feed going so we can see what they find out."

Nash returned to his conversation, and Mac watched the screen fill up with information about both Henry Falcone and John Lewis. The two men staying at the Paradis had hot links next to their names, so he clicked them.

Falcone, it seemed, was an equal-opportunity scumbag. The first man, Muhammad Rahim Jahangiri, came from Pakistan, where he'd worked his way up the ranks in Falcone's freight company.

The second, Joey Shriever, had played semipro football before a steroid scandal had ended his career. He'd gone on to become hired muscle in the American arm of the shipping company, providing "security services." According to the notes, he often accompanied suspect shipments into and out of the UAE and Africa as well. What he was doing in St. Martin was anyone's guess. Whatever his plans, they didn't bode well for Callie, and Mac wanted to howl, to shake the driver of the car until he hit the gas. But getting pulled over for speeding wouldn't help their cause, so he sat silently, every muscle clenched to hold himself together.

CALLIE TRACKED THE footsteps overhead back and forth a few times before the door at the top of the stairs in the far corner opened noiselessly. It should squeak, she found herself thinking. A place like this, it should have horror-movie squeals from the hinges, groans from the timbers. But here evil made no sound. She checked to be certain she'd tucked the tracker fully out of sight yet close enough to grab if they tried to move her.

She watched the door, but for long seconds, no one came through. She almost called out. What if those were the good guys up there? The gendarmes? But she suspected they would have identified themselves, so she remained on the cot, her eyes trained on the empty rectangle of light. At last, loafers came into view on the top step, followed, as their wearer descended, by suit pants, a dress shirt, and finally John Lewis's patrician features. She had expected him, had discussed his motives and involvement with Mac and Nash, but still the sight of him came as a shock.

The two bruisers behind him were even more surprising. Time to stall.

"What's going on, John?" She aimed for puzzlement, but her voice came out a croak. She swallowed and tried again. "Why have you brought me here? Any business we might conduct can't be completed without access to my father's files."

Rather than answering, he clucked his tongue against the roof of his mouth.

"You're dehydrated. I'll just get you some water." He spun on his heel and jogged back up the stairs.

Callie studied the two left behind. Both wore black designer T-shirts of some silky material that stretched around bulging necks and biceps. The taller had fair hair, a boxer's nose, and squinty eyes, while the shorter looked to be of Middle Eastern descent. His black eyes, lizard-like, darted constantly around the room. Callie wondered whether the movement was natural or drug induced. Neither spoke.

"Who are you?" she asked after a minute. "What do you want with me?"

"Why don't we wait for Mr. Lewis's return?" The taller

man's voice matched his expression — cold, empty, and perfectly flat. Where was John? How long could it take to get a glass of water?

"So you guys work for him?" To use her diplomatic training, which she considered her best hope of surviving long enough for Mac and Nash to find her, she needed to understand what was going on. Any little drop of information she could squeeze out of these two would help, if only they'd cooperate.

The two men exchanged a glance, and Lizard Eyes smiled with sly humor. "Oh, yeah, that's it. He's the boss."

So they were Falcone's men. She'd guessed as much but hadn't figured out how to use that fact to her advantage. Why couldn't they be Bond villains, crowing over their nefarious plans rather than staring impassively? Maybe henchmen didn't crow. A hysterical giggle rose in the back of her throat, surprising her. Concentrating on the practical aspects of her situation had hidden the level of her fear even from herself. She shoved away both the terror and the hysteria.

The upstairs door reopened, and John appeared with a bottle of Perrier. Perrier? The giggle rose up again and almost escaped before she could slam it back. As John approached, she imagined attacking him when he handed over the bottle. He didn't seem particularly strong, though looks could deceive — after all, he appeared sane. She could break the bottle, assault him with it. Would Falcone's men even care?

Lizard Eyes pulled a remote control from his pocket. "You wouldn't want to try anything funny," he said. "That collar you're wearing has some unpleasant functions."

Well, that answered that question.

John passed her the bottle, which turned out to be plastic, and remained standing over her. "Drink up. I'll bring you some food in a little bit. You must be hungry."

Callie saw her own confusion and discomfort reflected on the thugs' faces before they returned to their customary disinterest.

"Why am I here, John?" she asked again. "The information I have, the information my father collected on yours, is in New York."

This time, he seemed to hear her. "Your father? You mean Arthur Pearson? I need nothing of his. The man was a weakling. Couldn't father a single child. Not one."

"Fatherhood—and strength—are more than biology. You of all people should understand that. Mark Lewis raised you as his own, even after Nikki, his biological child, came along. Or did he believe you were his natural child? Did you hide the truth even from him?"

"He is my father. He recognizes me for who I am and what I need. That's why he provided you."

"W-what?" Fear strangled speech, and Callie began to shake. Sweat dripped from her nape in a cold trickle down her spine. She searched John's face for clues but saw the same serene, completely rational expression he always wore.

"You're going to help me. I just have to get everything ready first. While I do, these men want to ask you some questions. But don't worry. They've promised not to permanently damage you."

"D-damage? What are you talking about?" She reached out a hand, willing it to remain steady, and laid it on one of his, hoping the connection would reach him. "Help me out here, John. I don't understand."

"You're no use to me with your mind clouded or your soul stifled by drugs. Or, Father forbid, dead. I need it all—your body, your mind, your spirit, your blood." He looked as if he actually expected her to approve.

"You're completely insane."

He belted her across the face so hard she fell sideways on the cot. He was stronger than he looked. Way stronger. And she hadn't expected the reaction, though she should have. Her words had popped out, driven by shock, beyond her control. There was no reasoning with madness.

He leaned over, bracing one arm on each side of her supine body. "We'll see who's crazy in a few hours. We'll see who's the loser, you old bitch." His hot breath fanned her face, scented with wine and herbs as if he'd come from a meal, and her stomach threatened to revolt. He levered himself off the cot and stalked out without another word.

Cautiously, Callie sat up and faced the two thugs left behind.

As soon as the door shut behind John, Lizard Eyes took the steps two at a time and stood guard at the top while his companion pulled a headset from his front pocket and donned it.

"Base, this is Cougar One." He waited for a reply, then spoke again, abandoning the militaristic lingo. "Yeah, we're in the house with her. But we may have a problem. We need to get the product out, and Lewis has gone over the edge. Totally fucking batshit crazy. Doubt he'll be any use at all in getting it out clean." He waited again, then nodded to his companion, whose eyes were darting between him and Callie. "Copy that. We'll be ready."

"Look." Callie tamped down her terror and forced the desperate note from her voice as the man peeled off his headset. "Lewis is insane. Your boss isn't. I have information he wants. I had a deal to trade it for my friend Erin. Falcone knows it's legit."

"Did I say anything about anyone named Falcone?" Blond goon looked at Lizard Eyes, who shrugged.

"Okay, so we won't talk specifics." That suited Callie just fine, since she didn't actually have any. She ran over the little information she'd gleaned from conversations with Nash in her head. "Someone—anyone—might be interested in what I uncovered in Nash's files pertaining to a DEA operation that went badly, resulting in casualties. Particularly casualties of women and children."

"Yeah, right," scoffed Blondie. "Like anyone's interested in some drug bust." But Lizard Eyes took two steps down the staircase and focused on her.

"Give me the information. I will evaluate it."

"No deal. Get me out of here, and I'll discuss it with your boss."

He pointed the remote and pushed a button.

Pain ripped through her. Her jaw snapped shut as her muscles convulsed, catching the inside of her cheek, and the coppery taste of blood filled her mouth. For a stuttering heartbeat, the agony seemed to lessen, allowing almost a full breath, but then a second wave crashed through her. She fell forward off the cot, knees slamming into the cement floor just before the current switched off.

She stayed there, gasping for breath, spitting out her own blood, until she could drag herself back up to the cot. She wanted to stand, to defy them, but her muscles wouldn't cooperate.

"Tell me."

Her body still quaking with aftershocks and fear, Callie shook her head. She could live through this. They wouldn't kill her.

But the second jolt was worse. Fire tore down her spine and blew apart every nerve. She felt her head slam into the wall behind her as the violent spasms took control. In her mind, she screamed, but her jaw had locked tight. When the pain subsided, both Falcone's men stood over her, their outlines blurred by the tears streaming down her face.

"Tell me what you know."

Callie's brain had stopped functioning. Clouds rolled through her thoughts. The dark man's command barely registered. What did he want? She could not quite grasp his meaning. The inside of her mouth had swollen, both tongue and cheeks, and she was certain one of her teeth had broken. Surely he didn't expect her to answer when he'd never be able to understand a word? She closed her eyes.

"Shit, man," she heard the blond, the American, say. "You hit her too hard. I told you the traditional way is better than all those high-tech gadgets. Give me a chance at her when she comes around."

"She knows nothing," said the dark one. "She would have given it up if she did. Leave her for Lewis."

"What's the plan?"

"We need to get the shipment out of storage. Falcone is sending assistance in case things do not go as planned."

"How long do we have before they get here?"

"Eight."

"Three hours is plenty of time for me to see what I can get out of her."

"I tell you, she knows nothing. First, we try removing the shipment ourselves. If that fails, you can come back and have your fun."

CHAPTER SEVENTEEN

MAC HATED NIGHTTIME water drops with a passion. He'd learned to do them without flinching like a good soldier, but as he leaned out of the chopper and stared at the black surface of the Caribbean, roughened to white peaks by the rotors, he couldn't help remembering all the deadly creatures who made their home beneath the waves.

The sun would rise shortly, after which they'd be able to see what lurked in the clear, blue water, but Mac couldn't wait. The beacon had been activated mere minutes after they'd landed in San Juan. It was broadcasting from John Lewis's home. She was there, on the island, in the presence of at least one killer. And an hour ago, she'd been alive.

Mac suggested calling Michel Vichy, believing Callie would be safer in police custody, but Nash disagreed. The gendarmes, he pointed out, were army. And Henry Falcone dealt with armies all over the world. Vichy would likely not be able to get into the Lewis home without the equivalent of a warrant, and while he was getting one any bad actor on Falcone's payroll would have a chance to remove her. Better to go for a covert recovery, then turn to the police with a fait accompli.

"Go!" Nash shouted, and both he and Mac pushed their overboard bags from the Jayhawk, then jumped after them. It sped away, headed for St. Kitts per its original flight plan. Each man grabbed a floating duffel filled with clothing and weapons and began swimming for *The Tramp* bobbing a few feet away, its lights doused. Travis guided them in using the beam of a flashlight. Nash climbed aboard first, Mac close behind, and Travis opened throttle to head back to St. Martin.

"What's the word?"

"They're holding her at Lewis's place. We should head for his private dock."

"No can do." Travis shook his head. "He brought in private security on Tuesday morning. Said the gawkers and paparazzi were getting to him. The island's been packed with them ever since Nikki's body was positively identified. There are boats anchored as close in to the Paradis grounds as they can get. I'm going to have to drop you off down the beach and have you go in via the road. It's not convenient, but it's safer than trying for the dock or the beach."

"How much security?" Nash asked.

"No way to tell. I've seen four on the property. Big 'n' dumb, which is probably what he wants if he's holding a hostage inside the house. You can't have anyone too honest or too smart—they might ask uncomfortable questions."

"Fan-fucking-tastic," said Mac. He stripped out of his wet clothes, toweled off, and dragged on fresh jeans and a clean shirt. Pulling his Sig from the bag, he checked to be sure no liquid had seeped into the waterproof bundle during the brief swim. Next to him, Nash went through the same motions. Nash handed him a headset from his duffel, and Mac slid it into place. A brief sound check showed the headsets hadn't suffered from the impact with the sea.

Adrenaline raced through Mac's system as he watched the shoreline approach, but even so there was a comforting famil-iarity to the setup. How many times had he, Nash, and Trav moved in concert, headed into danger as a single unit? How many high-stakes games had they played together?

But the stakes here were higher than any he'd faced in the past. *Hang in there, sugar; the cavalry's coming.*

Travis guided the boat into its slip and handed over a backpack, along with a couple of small keys and helmets he pulled from a storage locker. "Pack has standard necessities. I rented you motorcycles. Easier to get around, faster, and the helmets hide your faces from local law. Mac, I know you're good on one. Nash?"

"Can do."

Travis gestured to the parking lot at the top of the marina. "There they are, under that streetlight.

Get going. And good luck. Call if you need anything."

Mac nodded and gripped Travis's outstretched hand in his own for a moment. Then he took off at a jog for the motorcycles, hearing Nash's footsteps right behind him on the macadam.

He didn't dare drive all the way to the private road that led down to the Paradis and the Lewis homes. Instead, he and Nash pulled into the parking lot of a small strip mall a half mile down the main thoroughfare.

The sun had risen, but the roads were still almost deserted. Both he and Nash checked to be sure their T-shirts covered the guns holstered at their backs; then they continued on foot. A few yards before the turnoff, Mac stopped and Nash went on to see whether the guard would let anyone down the road. He wouldn't. With a glance in either direction to be sure no one would see them, Mac dropped to his stomach and began to crawl through the wild tangle of bush and brush that lined the road. He'd kept the helmet on, which helped him move considerably faster. He couldn't see, but he didn't need to. He just forced his way through the underbrush in the right direction. Sooner or later, he'd come up against a fence, the private road, or unfenced backyard. Any of the three would do.

"What's the Lewis place layout?" Nash's voice crackled in his ear.

"Place faces pretty much due south, on a private road off the road to the Paradis. Wrought-iron fence around all sides. Nothing we can't handle. Front faces the road, and the driveway's only maybe twenty feet long. Hot tub on one side of the house, with entrance into the kitchen, small yard on the other. Back's the biggest problem because he's got a massive, totally flat lawn with nowhere to hide."

"Where would he keep her?"

"Probably the basement. I've been in that house. I can't think of any place else safe."

"Windows?"

"No. Fully below ground."

"Entrance?"

"Through the kitchen."

"Kitchen at the back of the house?"

"Yeah. So we go in that way if we can."

Nash assimilated that, then spoke again. "Bugs the shit out of me I can't figure out what he hopes to get from keeping her alive."

"Right there with you." Because if Mac could believe Lewis would keep Callie alive, he could focus. As it was, he didn't feel as if he'd taken a full breath since she'd left him at the hotel in New York.

"We will get her out. When you run an international security company, you do a fair amount of hostage recovery. We prefer to do straight ransom delivery on a K and R case, but sometimes the kidnappers decide not to turn over the hostage."

It was Mac's turn to consider. "Getting all soft and touchy-feely on me?"

Nash snorted, but his tone remained serious. "I'm not your commanding officer on this one, Brody. Your woman, your op."

"She's not my woman." But the response was automatic, and both men knew it. Callie had reached something inside him he hadn't even known existed, and he wouldn't let her down, no matter what.

"Hold up," said Nash. "Something's coming through."

Mac waited while Nash unhooked his cell phone, which he'd set to vibrate, from his belt holster and read through some text messages.

"There's a big-ass yacht anchored offshore near Anguilla. You know where that is?"

"Ferry ride away."

"Okay. Yacht is owned by one of Falcone's known associates, and Lexie thinks Falcone is either aboard or came to St. Martin after being aboard. It would have been easy enough to get there from his island retreat in the Grenadines." Mac began crawling forward again. "Which means there's something here that's important to him. The weapons shipment?"

"Looks like."

"Fuck. This is gonna get real ugly real quick."

Mac could feel Nash's familiar, grim smile beneath his reply. "Only if we let it."

GET OUT OF *here!* The thought cut through the fog in Callie's mind. How long had she been lying on the cot, staring up at the broad beams of the ceiling since Lizard Eyes and Blondie had departed? Time tangled, stretching out and snapping back. Her body ached, and a throbbing pulse emanated from the swelling in her cheeks and tongue where she'd bitten them, breaking the skin.

She examined the contraption attaching her to the cot but found no weakness. The supplies—a simple combination lock and length of coated stainless cable—could be bought at any hardware store or bike shop, but their ubiquity in no way cheated them of effectiveness. The shackle itself she couldn't figure out. Had he had it made specifically, or was it merely adapted from something else? It fit loosely around her ankle, snapped shut and locked with the same lock that attached it to the cable. She pulled off her shoe and tried to squeeze her foot out of it. No luck. No matter how hard she pointed her toes, she couldn't force the cuff down over her heel.

Fear rose as acid in the back of her throat. They would kill her. Either John, for some insane reason she couldn't fathom, or Falcone's men, who believed her intimately connected to Nash Harper's organization.

Could she play them against one another? For whatever sick reason—and Callie forced her mind away from any consideration of what that might be—John had instructed the goons not to hurt her. If she pretended a more severe injury, would he wait for her to heal? How bad would it have to be? And how bad could it get before he would decide she was no longer useful and kill her on the spot.

She studied the cot. Most of the edges were rounded, but the feet were sharp and square. She could get her shoulder under the frame, pick it up, then let it down so the corner of the foot sliced her leg.

Would it be enough? And what if the cut went too deep and John did not return in time?

She heard movement overhead, and the door reopened.

John skipped down the stairs, his gleeful appearance more frightening than the goons' dour coldness. In his hand, he held the remote control for the collar.

"All ready," he said to her. "Now, let's go upstairs. I am going to tell you what the combination for that lock is, and you are going to come along quietly." He held up the remote. "This has some very nifty capabilities, and you won't like them. So just do as you're told."

As soon as she'd freed her leg, Callie stood. "Falcone's men have gone after whatever you're holding for them." Her speech came out a bit garbled from all the swelling in her mouth, but she could see understanding in John's eyes. "They intend to get it without you, then come back here and kill you."

John frowned. "They can't get it without me. They have no way into the storage compartment."

"That's not what they said. Why do you think they're not down here questioning me? They decided I wasn't so important after all."

"You're lying."

"Why would I lie?" She kept her tone non-confrontational. "As you said, our father, Mark Lewis, left me here to help you. And they . . . hurt me." She touched her face.

"You don't believe in Father's work."

Okay, so he was crazy, not stupid. "I believe we have a better chance fighting Falcone's men together than we do apart. I heard them talking; they'll kill both of us the minute they have whatever you're storing for them. That's not belief; it's fact."

His gray eyes narrowed on her, evaluating, and she allowed herself a moment to hope she'd gotten through. But then he shook his head.

"Once you help me, I'll be able to handle them." He

backed away from the foot of the stairs and gestured for her to ascend. He remained several steps behind her on the way up, and were it not for the collar, she'd have made a break for it.

On the main floor he directed her to the office. Of their own volition, Callie's eyes went to the couch where she and John had sat flipping through photo albums. How could she have been so completely deceived? How could she have missed the insanity in him when he was so close?

Lewis, it seemed, was remembering the same evening.

"Your friend Brody was here that night, you know. I checked the monitor on my cell phone when it went off during dinner, and again while I was pouring our wine. He was hiding in the closet, waiting to come to your rescue. I could have called the gendarmes on him the minute he tripped my secondary alarm system, but I didn't feel like interrupting our fascinating conversation. Besides, he might have piqued their curiosity. I assume he was looking for Nicole?"

What was the best answer? What would keep him talking the longest? "Actually, he said he was going to the Paradis that night to check for evidence my parents had been guests. He didn't mention breaking in here. If he had, why would I have agreed to come over?" She swallowed. "But now that you mention it, was Nikki here that night?"

"Naturally. I didn't move her until after I brought you back to Port de Plaisance and checked the security cameras to be sure Brody had taken off. I'd arranged for you to be safely out of my hair for the rest of the evening, so I showed my face down at the hotel, had a drink with the night manager, then took Nicole home."

"Without one of her hands."

He shrugged. "It was worth a try. And the ring, at least, proved useful. But the freezing—or some other factor—worked against me. I won't make the same mistake with you." He sidled over to the bookcase and removed several books, revealing a lever. He cranked the lever down, and a section of the bookshelf shifted back, then slid sideways.

"Inside."

As slowly as she figured he'd let her, Callie inched toward the gap in the bookcase, simultaneously fascinated and terrified. Might there be some sort of weapon in the hidden room she could use against John? It would have to be long, like a broomstick or mop, something she could use to attack him quickly, disabling him or at least making him lose his grip on the remote before he could hit her with another charge.

What she saw shocked her to a standstill. The small space had obviously once been a security room and still had monitors on the back wall where video feeds of various parts of the property ran silently, casting a flickering light through the space. But the rest had been converted to an operating room, complete with tiled walls, a drainage grate in the floor, and a table with gutters on both sides. And stirrups. *Stirrups. What the hell?* She'd seen enough CSI shows to know that some of the other devices laid out on tables along the sidewall shouldn't be used on living patients.

She turned to run, but John stood behind her, pointing the remote.

"Inside," he said, a little smile playing about his lips.

No way in hell was she entering that room.

"Go ahead and zap me. Your buddies already did it a couple times, though, so you'd better be careful. Whatever freezing did, I can't imagine an overdose of electricity could be that much better for your long-term plans." Her muscles tensed, anticipating the pain, but it didn't come. Instead, a damp, sweet-smelling mist surrounded her head. She choked, sucking the drug into her lungs before she could stop herself, and the world disappeared in a rushing cloud of black-winged butterflies.

THE BITCH HIT the floor hard, but he wasn't worried. A soft Persian rug he'd bought on a trip to Morocco covered the hardwood, so her body wouldn't be overly damaged. Falcone's boys should have stuck around to help him shift her to the lab, though, instead of running down to the Paradis to try to retrieve their precious cargo themselves. They'd pay for that once he had her safely stored.

He bent over and pulled her into a sitting position so he could wedge his shoulder under her arm and hoist her into a fireman's carry. *Cow.* He felt a moment's fear as he strained beneath her weight.

What if her slovenly lack of care for her appearance infected him? Could a woman who exhibited such lack of restraint in her eating habits really be the one? He hadn't had time to research her thoroughly. What if she had an addiction or some form of illness?

And she'd doubtless been fucking his former brother-in-law. God knows what she could have picked up there. The man was total scum. Could he have passed her something so quickly? Something that might lurk in her blood?

Then you'll be well and truly screwed, won't you, buddy boy? You'd better hope she's not tainted like the one your precious daddy kept for himself. Weak genes. Pretty enough, but flawed. Just like him.

"Shut up!" John stumbled, pitched forward, almost lost his footing. "Shut fucking up! You're dead. Dead!"

But laughter echoed in his head even as he made his way into the secret lab.

THE GROUND BENEATH Mac's hands went from dirt to grass in an instant, and he called a halt to their progress. Nash inched up next to him, and both men pulled off their helmets. They'd reached the edge of Lewis's property. A wrought-iron fence lay between them and the expanse of manicured lawn. The fence, at six feet high, presented no problem. The lawn might. Or, more accurately, the two guys with machine guns patrolling it might.

He could shoot them, of course. And if he were certain they'd been assigned here as part of Falcone's organization, he might. But if they were just hired muscle, working for some European or American security company like Nash's, they didn't deserve to die for doing their job. Too bad he and Nash hadn't brought tranqs, but Mac rarely found himself in need of such exotic weaponry.

"I'll circle around, create a diversion, then meet you inside."

Mac shook his head. "They're heavily armed, and we don't know how many there are. You can't take them on, and these two may not budge if there are more up front already."

"Have I mentioned how much I hate ops without adequate intel?"

Despite the knots in his gut, Mac couldn't help but grin. "A time or two."

Nash grunted. "All right, then, what do you suggest?"

Mac watched as the two guards met in the center of the yard, spoke briefly, and continued along their individual paths. One paused at the northwest corner of the house, his head swiveling to watch the back and side of the property, while the other continued patrolling, passing out of view around the northeast corner. A few minutes later, the walker returned and the one who had paused disappeared and walked up the west side, where he seemed to stop and speak to someone beyond Mac's line of sight. Then he returned.

"So three at least. Probably four. Concentration on the front." Nash's words echoed Mac's thoughts. "Wonder how many he has in the house."

"Probably none. Maybe some of Falcone's inside guys, but no low-level hired help. Not if he's holding Callie prisoner." Please, God, let her just be a prisoner. As long as she was alive, they could deal with anything else.

"Your op," Nash reminded him. "How you want to do this?"

"Work our way around. As I recall, Lewis has a hot tub on the west side of the house with palms around it. Papa Lewis planted them for privacy with his model bride." He remembered using the tub with Nikki in the early days of their relationship. She'd insisted they sneak in, though John would have given them permission. It was all part of the game to her, part of what gave him the rush he got from being with her. In hindsight, he wondered how he could have imagined such a passing adrenaline high could last a lifetime. How he could have wanted it to.

"The trees will give us some cover, especially at this hour when the sun's still low enough there will be plenty of shadow.

We can take out whatever guard John has on that side. We won't have long, though, because these guys check in with each other on every pass."

"Let's do it."

Lizards and rodents scurried away as the men continued pushing through the growth, heading east. They rounded the corner, and Mac sent up a prayer of thanks for the brush that continued to hide them as they made their way toward the grove of trees around the hot tub. But while Lewis had left the tangle of plants between his property and his neighbor's alone for a measure of privacy, both men had erected fences, leaving only a narrow strip for Mac and Nash. The plants would move with their passage, and any alert guard would notice.

And if said guard started shooting, they'd be dead meat. Nowhere to run.

They had to go over the fence.

⌒

JOHN WINCED AT the sight of the cow's pale, fat flesh as he stripped her. Looking at her lying there on the table brought all the doubts back. She was so far from perfect. How could Father have meant her to perfect him? But then, he didn't need her outside. He'd tried that before.

He'd read her résumé. She was smart and didn't have any apparent vices. If she'd gotten lazy about taking care of herself, if her body was unattractive, that served his purpose. It meant she'd probably polluted herself less than others like Nicole with her perfect figure and flawless skin, who'd had men trailing in her wake since her early teens.

He pushed the cow's unresisting feet into the stirrups, then grabbed a roll of duct tape and taped her legs to the metal extensions from ankle to knee. He couldn't have her trying to get out during the surgery. After testing the strength of the tape, he locked the stirrups to keep her legs open.

Satisfied with her legs, he moved up her body and wrapped tape tightly around her hips. He'd have preferred to coat her head to toe in the stuff, but he couldn't afford to. He was no gynecological specialist, and he had to leave himself other ways into her body if his first attempt went awry. Not that he expected it to. He'd been studying for a long time, ever since he realized that as his psychological weakness came from his mother during the months he spent in her womb, he would need to perfect it with uterine cells as well as brain matter from the chosen one.

Still, he didn't want to cut her open too soon. Abdominal surgery was risky if you cared about keeping the patient's blood flowing to the brain. Better if the uterine tissue could be extracted vaginally, so her brain would remain perfect right up to the moment he cut into it.

He'd wanted to try the process with Nikki, but he'd been forced to kill her too soon. The hand, well, that had been a last-ditch effort to make lemonade. No, this was the way it had to be. Living tissue, dying breath.

He snapped her wrists into restraints.

Callie woke to hell. Bright lights blinded her, but when she tried to shift her head to the side to avoid them, she realized that what she'd first felt as a bandage around her temples was actually some kind of restrictive device. In fact, she couldn't move any of her limbs. She'd been strapped to a table, her feet in those stirrups she'd found so shocking. And she was naked.

A gag had been stuffed into her mouth, but she tried to scream around it.

"I thought you might do that," said John, appearing above her. "Which is the reason I had to gag you. The room's sound-proof, so screaming when you're not even in pain won't do anything but make me angry. I would rather do surgery without it, so if you promise to behave, I'll take it out."

Behave? This lunatic wanted her to behave?

"Nnn-hnnn" was the best she could manage behind the gag. The headgear prevented her from nodding, though she could still shift her upper body a bit. Too bad she didn't need to shrug.

"Good." He stood over her and pulled a piece of duct tape off her mouth. She almost screamed again, this time from the pain, but she held it in. Instead, she pretended to be coughing, choking on the gag. But the ruse didn't work. John took long forceps and grabbed the cotton wadding. She'd been hoping he would use his fingers, giving her a chance to bite them off his hand. That have would put an end to his surgical dreams for a while at least.

"What do you want from me?" Her mouth was parched, all liquid absorbed by the cotton, but talking was the only weapon left to her. "You could have asked. Are you sick? You need an organ transplant or something?"

"I'm not sick!" John snatched a scalpel from the tray and held it over his head, aiming down at her chest. She shrank back into the cold metal table as best she could. "She made me weak. It's her fault! Now you're going to make it right. That's why he created you. Why he created all of you."

"She?"

But something happening on one of the monitors on the wall behind her head had caught his eye. He laid the scalpel back into the tray with a frown.

"I'm afraid I have a few things to take care of before we can get started," he said, suddenly calm. She followed him with her eyes as he moved toward the door and left, carefully sliding the panel back into place, closing her in.

⌁

AS THE PATROLLING guard reached the corner of the house and paused to speak to a second man, Mac and Nash hoisted themselves over the wall ten feet apart in perfect synchronicity, each landing in a patch of thick shadow. The guard turned, casually surveying the yard, and Mac tensed.

But the man's eyes skimmed over the shadowed areas without pausing. He'd had time to grow bored, to tell himself his employer was overreacting to some threat. Unlike the two guards in the back, this one carried his gun strapped to his back, not at the ready, which told Mac everything he needed to know about the man's character. Up for a good fight, but slightly resentful of the luxury he had been hired to protect, the guy wouldn't think a rich, cultured man like John Lewis could have serious enemies. He'd underestimated Lewis, just as Mac himself had.

Which was a big fat plus as far as Mac was concerned. He slipped forward a few feet in the shadows to hide behind the trunk of a palm. The guy didn't notice. Nash, who had a more complicated path to reach the cluster of palms, remained in position.

The guard paused by the kitchen window, peered inside for a second, then turned to saunter back toward the corner of the house. Mac waited. One step. Two. Three. Then the man was in range, and Mac was on him.

Killing him would have been easy. Disabling silently, as always, was more difficult. He took the guy from behind, hoping to lock his arm around the man's neck. But at the last moment, the guy must have felt something, caught a movement from the corner of his eye. He turned, started to call out a warning, and Mac punched him instead, spinning him around. The guy stumbled backward, right into Nash, who wrapped an arm around his neck and choked him out.

Within seconds, they'd disarmed the guard, trussed him with duct tape ankles to knees, gagged him, and hidden him behind a freestanding bar by the hot tub. Without a word, Nash headed toward the front to deal with the guard there, while Mac pressed his back to the wall of the house and darted a look around the back.

Two guards, walking away from one another. Not ideal, but workable. The approaching guard's steps were audible in the early-morning hush, and Mac counted them off to himself. When the guy reached the corner, Mac stepped away from the wall, grabbed his arm, and pulled him forward, shoving his palm up beneath his chin at the same time to knock him out. Not a sound escaped to alert the other man, and Mac quickly dumped him with the guy they'd left behind the bar, using the same binding and gagging method to keep him still and silent.

Mac assumed Nash had dealt with the guard at the front of the house, which left the other man he'd seen in the back, who was probably returning from his round up the west side, if Nash hadn't gotten to him. Mac headed for the west side at a run. But the guard must have realized there was a problem—he was waiting, gun drawn, when Mac rounded the corner.

"Stop right there!"

Mac stopped. Held up his hands in the most reassuring manner he could. "What's going on? Where's John?" he asked, aiming to confuse the guy a bit. If the guards had been given even a vague description, it wouldn't work—there was no hiding the scar—but if not, it could provide him an opening.

"Where did you come from?"

"Down the street."

The guard narrowed his eyes. "How did you get onto the property?"

"I walked, man. I come here all the time. I was hoping to use the hot tub, but when I knocked on the kitchen door, there was no one there. So I came around the back." Mac saw Nash's head pop around the corner, but the guard glanced back over his shoulder, so Nash withdrew.

The guard pulled out a walkie-talkie and tried to radio his companions. When he couldn't raise any of them, he pointed the gun at Mac's head and ordered him to the ground.

"Dude. Seriously?" Mac protested. Consistency was key.

"On the ground!"

Mac complied.

"Face in the dirt, hands on the back of your head!"

"Shit, man, Lewis is gonna be pissed. I bring him fish and stuff all the time."

"Shut up!" Mac heard the guy pull zip cuffs from his belt and felt the man's fingers on his wrists as he leaned over to attach them.

The problem with cuffing, as Mac knew, was that it was damned hard to do with a gun in your hand. And the guard had no backup. So when Nash came flying over the lawn to tackle him, he was down in a second. A minute later, he was unconscious and cuffed with his own zip ties, arms behind him and a belt and more zip ties used to attach him to the trunk of a slender palm.

Mac and Nash took off for the kitchen door, which they figured would be less well guarded than the front. Nash retrieved a set of lock picks from his bag and made short work of the deadbolt, and they were in. Mac headed straight for the basement, but as he laid his hand on the knob, movement flickered in his peripheral vision and Nash shouted, "Gun!"

Mac hurled himself backward, diving for cover behind the island, where Nash had already taken a spot just as the corner of the door where he'd been standing splintered away.

"She's not downstairs, Brody." Lewis's reasonable tone grated against Mac's already raw nerves. "You'll never find her without my help, and if I don't get back to deactivate the bomb she's wearing around her neck, she'll die."

Bomb? What could he possibly want badly enough to tie explosives around Callie's neck to be sure she didn't escape? But at least she was still alive. As long as she stayed that way, they could get her out.

"What do you want, Lewis?"

CHAPTER EIGHTEEN

THE MINUTE THE panel clicked into position behind John, Callie began to rock the center of her body, the only part she could move, from one side to the other. Long minutes passed as tiny vibrations along the table became visible unsteadiness. She rocked harder, pushing the right side, next to the instrument tray, more forcefully than the left. And then she was falling, the table crashing to the ground, bringing the tray with it.

The sound deafened, paralyzed. Surely, he heard it. He would come back. She'd seen him in a fury when she'd accused him of being crazy. What would he do when he saw she'd disrupted his carefully laid-out laboratory? But he didn't return and her muscles unfroze. The soundproofing of the room had protected her. *Score one for the good guys.*

Now what? Her forearms, like her calves, had been duct-taped into place on sidebars attached to the table, but her hands remained free. Unfortunately, while the impact had snapped the locking mechanism on the leg extensions, allowing her legs to meet, her hands were still too far apart to use one to free the other.

A variety of surgical instruments lay strewn nearby. The scalpel was the obvious choice, but no matter how Callie stretched her fingers, she couldn't reach it. She picked up a pair of curved forceps and tried to grasp the scalpel's handle. On the third try, she got it, only to have it slip out again when she tried to lock the forceps, the force pushing it even farther away. She could have cried. Almost did. Then she tried again. This time the forceps held the scalpel better, and she didn't risk trying to get a lock.

She eased the scalpel toward her until she could touch the handle with her fingers, then began attempting to find a way to slice through the duct tape without accidentally puncturing a vein in her wrist. Nothing doing. The blade skated across the slick surface of the tape, and the only motion she could achieve was horizontal, nothing that would cut against the tape's fibers and enable her to free herself.

She pulled up hard against the tape, trying to create a space between the table's extension and her arm where she could insert the scalpel. Nothing happened near her wrist, but Lewis must have become a little more casual by her elbow. Unfortunately, the handle of the scalpel wasn't long enough to allow her access to that spot.

Once again, she reached for the forceps. Careful not to allow the handle of the scalpel to slide out, she locked the jaws of the forceps around it, giving her extra length and a measure of flexibility. She slid the blade of the scalpel into the tiny space between metal and skin and pushed down.

And screamed in pain.

Ohhellohdamnohfuck. Somehow, she'd gotten it wrong. She'd cut into her own flesh rather than into the tape. She could feel blood oozing, dripping, and she began to shake in reaction. Gritting her teeth, she twisted the forceps so the scalpel's blade would face the tape and once again dragged it forward, applying as much pressure as possible. When it broke free, she pulled up on her arm as hard as she could and heard the satisfying rip of duct tape.

Of course, that, too, was accompanied by pain, and when she brought her newly freed arm up to her face, she saw that the tape had taken large swath of skin with it, leaving raw patches behind.

Her second arm came free more easily, as did her legs. Pushing the table away, she looked around the room. She needed clothes and some kind of bandage for her arm. She'd missed any veins, but the bleeding didn't seem to be slowing down, and she felt nauseous and light-headed. She located a roll of gauze and a tube of antibiotic in a cabinet and awkwardly dressed the wound. She doubted any of John's "patients" needed such things. He probably kept them around in case the women fought back.

Her clothes she found in a trash can in the corner. Unfortunately, though her sneakers and socks were whole, he'd cut the rest of her attire from her body, so there wasn't much point in putting it back on. She reached up to slide her fingers beneath the collar she still wore but hesitated before attempting to rip it off. She'd seen several of its capabilities. Might it not also be booby-trapped? What if attempting to remove it caused another electrical shock—or something worse? She couldn't afford to be incapacitated. Not now.

Her fingers found a narrow band of metal at the back of the collar, resting against her neck. So that was how they'd shocked her. She grabbed the roll of duct tape from the counter where John had left it, pulled off a strip, and did her best to cover the metal. Then, remembering the knockout gas, she went further, covering as much of the collar as she could in tape.

She had to get out of this room, but first she needed a weapon. John had brought her up from the basement alone, but that didn't mean he hadn't ordered guards to the door once he'd left her. And her nudity made her more vulnerable, both physically and emotionally. Her best option appeared to be a large pair of shears, so she took them in her right hand, grasped the lever of the door in her left, and cautiously stepped out into the library. She was alone.

Where to go? The front door was mere steps down the hallway, but she had no idea what lay outside. She needed clothes. Her best bet for that was upstairs, so she pressed herself against the wall to keep the steps from creaking and headed up.

The first door at the top of the stairs led into a guest bedroom. The bed had been made up, but no clothes hung in the closet or lay folded in the drawers. She moved on. Three steps down the hall, she stopped, heart in her throat, when an old board creaked under her weight. Oh God, that was loud. He would have heard it anywhere in the house. He'd know she'd escaped. She tried to listen for him, but her pulse was pounding too loudly in her ears.

Nothing for it but to keep going. Maybe whatever had attracted his attention had taken him outside.

The next door opened into John's room. The thought of putting his clothes on her body after what he'd done sent a shudder through her, but she couldn't afford to be fastidious. A thick carpet covered the floor, so she moved quickly, without fear of being heard. Dress shirts filled the closet, but she found workout attire in a drawer in the massive dresser opposite the bed. She dragged on a black tee and a pair of gray cotton sweatpants, grateful for John Lewis's slim build. Automatically, her mind flashed to Mac's broad shoulders and long legs. If the clothes had been his, she'd have swum in them, but these were tight across her hips and breasts. At least the pants had elastic at the bottom of each leg, so she didn't even have to worry about tripping over the excess length.

She tucked the shears into a pocket and searched the room for another weapon to add to her arsenal.

JOHN STIFFENED AT the creak of the floorboard above him. Someone was upstairs. But who? He darted a quick glance into the kitchen, then strafed the room with gunfire to keep Brody and his buddy from following him. He slammed the kitchen door shut and ran through the dining room into the living room and took up position behind a heavy leather couch where he could keep an eye on the front hall and anyone coming down the stairs while tracking his former brother-in-law if the man came out of the kitchen.

He had to think. He should have stayed in the lab with the woman. They'd never have found him in there, and he could have dealt with them once he'd completed the work, completed *himself*. But he'd been afraid of Brody from the minute Nicole had brought him home. He'd treated the man with disdain to cover up the sour quaking Brody inspired, but he'd always worried someone would see through the facade. Glimpsing Brody and his companion on the security screens, watching them disable one of the guards, had brought all that back, and he'd reacted irrationally.

He poked his head around the edge of the sofa. Could he make it across the entry hall to the office and into the laboratory without anyone seeing? What if they saw the door open? They'd know where she was. No, better to let her stay hidden until he needed her. He patted the reassuring bulk of the remote control in his front pocket.

CALLIE WAS STANDING at the top of the steps when she heard the shots.

Now or never. Whoever John had seen on his security screens—she refused to allow herself to dream it might be Mac, not this soon—was keeping him occupied. Trying to keep a balance between speed and silence, she headed down the stairs.

She'd almost made it to the bottom when the front door crashed open. The thugs had returned. With friends. She turned to flee back up, but the smaller one tackled her on the top step. She wedged her heel into his groin and kicked back like a mule, knocking him down a few steps. He came back up angrier, but a clatter indicated he'd lost his gun. Still, he was blocking her path. If she stayed upstairs, sooner or later he'd find her.

"Brody's here! In the kitchen!" John's shout drew Lizard Eyes' attention for a moment, and she launched her body at him like a rocket, taking him down the rest of the stairs even as her heart leapt with the knowledge Mac had come for her.

More shooting downstairs, but she couldn't focus on it, too busy grappling with Lizard Eyes. As they rolled, she felt the shears in her pants pocket and cursed herself for forgetting them. They thumped down a stair, and as his arm came around her neck she got her hand on the scissors. She couldn't release them from the pocket where they'd tangled, so she didn't bother, merely pushing them backward into her assailant's leg.

"Bitch!" His arm tightened while his other hand went to his leg to try to remove the shears. But she kept her grip on them, despite the panic threatening to rise as he cut off her oxygen. She slammed her head back as best she could. It didn't give her much space, but he flinched slightly, giving her room to twist.

Then, miraculously, he let her go and sprang away from her. Too late, she realized his intention. The gun he'd lost in their first scrap rested on the floor a few feet away, and he grabbed it. She turned, intent on getting out of the way, but he was on her in seconds despite the blood dripping down his leg.

"Enough!" He shifted the gun briefly, aiming down to the base of the wall, and fired, showering them with plaster dust. Then he aimed it once again at her head. Movement on the floor below ceased. One man lay dead, facedown in a spreading pool of his own blood. The air smelled foul, rank with blood and plaster and gunpowder and odors she couldn't define and didn't want to think about.

Mac stood frozen in a grappling hold with the big blond goon. He, too, was bleeding, both from his arm and from his face. As soon as he saw her situation, he raised his hands and stepped back. The blond used zip ties to cuff his hands behind his back, then forced him to his knees and zip-tied his ankles. The Hispanic thug—the one left alive—held a gun on him the whole time.

John stood off to the side, watching.

"Lewis," said Lizard Eyes, "you want the woman alive. Our deal hasn't changed. You will escort Pablo to the hotel and help him acquire the merchandise. Once it is safely in our possession, we will release her to you."

"What a load of crap," Mac scoffed. Callie admired his nerve but wished he'd shut up. His husky voice scratched with pain, and goading the men seemed an unwise choice. Especially when Blondie took the opportunity to kick him in the side, hard enough to bring tears to Callie's eyes. "You can't believe they'll let you—or Callie—go. You screwed up, Lewis, and now you're only useful as an object lesson. Falcone's got plenty of guys on payroll who'll be happy to show the rest of the organization what happens to those who can't get their shit together."

"Shut up, Brody." Blondie kicked Mac in the ribs this time, and Callie heard a distinct crack. Mac's face went white, and he fell over onto his side. He scooted back out of the man's way until his back rested against the wall. "You're lucky the boss has a hard-on for your buddy Nash, or I'd put a bullet in your brain right now. If you're smart, you'll give him up sooner rather than later. I know you Army types are all about honor, but you have no idea how dedicated some of Falcone's enforcers are. And it's usually not the primaries they go to work on." He jerked his chin at Callie and her stomach clenched.

Incredibly, Mac laughed. "You think I give a damn about either of them? Nash Harper deserted me in the middle of a fucking firefight. Typical fucking executive officer. Hundred percent pure bureaucratic candy-ass." He struggled to a kneeling position, every move a visible agony.

"Yeah? Well, what about her?" John countered. "You came all the way back here to rescue her."

"Damn, Lewis, you always were a moron. I don't care about this one any more than I cared about your sister. I wanted in on the action. Do I look like the kind of guy who's cut out to spend the day catering to the whims of trust-fund babies at some fancy resort?"

It had to be an act. Had to. She couldn't have misjudged him so badly, could she? But, God knew, her judgment sucked. She'd misjudged her father, misjudged herself, misjudged John Lewis . . . Why should Mac be any different? He'd told her about his addiction to adrenaline, how he'd married for it, lived for it. He hadn't lied in that respect. And yet, she'd allowed herself to believe he might feel something for her, even if it was just responsibility. *Stupid, Callie. Stupid, stupid, stupid.* She forced herself away from that line of thought to pay attention to the men.

"I'd never have let you in on my operation!"

"Let me? Boy, who do you think you are? You're entirely expendable. I married your sister. Once I'd made contact with Falcone myself, I'd have knocked you off and inherited both the hotel and the side business."

"In that case," her captor interjected smoothly, "why don't you tell us how to access the secure space in the wine cellar in which Mr. Lewis is keeping Mr. Falcone's merchandise. I am sure it would be seen as an act of good faith." John's face reddened and Callie tensed. If they didn't need John, they didn't need her.

"I wish I could," said Mac, and her heart settled a little. "I'd hoped to spend some time cracking it, but Nikki disappeared and the gendarmes were everywhere and then Miss Pearson showed up and caused all sorts of new problems. Still, I am sure I can come to some kind of agreement with Mr. Falcone regarding employment."

"Dream on," Blondie snorted. "All he wants from you is Nash Harper."

"And I want my life. And a job. Sounds like a match made in heaven." Mac grinned and Callie had to turn away. If it was an act, it was a damned good one. But it couldn't be true. She couldn't have been so wrong, no matter how badly her judgment sucked. She had to stay alive, stick it out until she could find out the truth.

"Right." Blondie turned to the man standing next to John. "Pablo, take Mr. Lewis down to the Paradis. Get the merchandise stowed and safe, and stay with it. Call in and we'll come to you."

"Joey, are you sure this is a good idea?" Lizard Eyes prodded her in the back with the gun, and she stepped forward.

"Who's in charge here, Rahim? I say they go, so they go." He turned to John. "I said, 'Go!'" Pablo and John left, John sputtering the whole time about how they'd better keep their word and how important he was to Falcone's business.

"Bring her over here," Joey ordered Rahim. "I have a few questions for her. You can take this asshole to the kitchen while she answers."

"She's taped over the collar," Rahim warned. He moved the gun from her forehead to her back and began prodding her down the stairs. "Some of the functions may not work."

"I told you, you rely on technology too much. Besides, Lewis has the remote." He smiled, and Callie's stomach turned over. "The lady and I are going to have us a good, old-fashioned party, and she's going to help us out."

When they reached the ground floor, Rahim pushed her forward. Joey reached out and tucked his fingers into the front of her sweatpants to pull her close enough for him to slap a pair of zip cuffs on her. He ran the gun down her chest, then untied the drawstring of the pants.

"Go on," he ordered Rahim, "take him to the kitchen. See if you can contact the boss and let him know where we stand." For a moment, Callie thought she saw a spark behind Mac's eyes, but then it disappeared, replaced by the same bland cruelty visible in Joey's.

"C'mon, man, you're not going to let me watch? I was hoping to get a piece of her myself, but you kept us too busy for that kind of fun, so you could at least let a brother get a vicarious thrill."

Crudely stated as it was, the message came through: Mac was lying. And if he was lying about having slept with her, chances were he was lying about the reason he'd come to the island as well. Maybe she hadn't misjudged him so badly after all.

⌒

Mac watched expressions flit across Callie's face out of the corner of his good eye, thankful both Rahim and Joey had focused their attention on him instead of her. She'd never make it as an actress, which was why he'd kept his gaze fixed on Joey while lying about his reasons for returning to St. Martin. The words would hurt her, and he couldn't afford the distraction of witnessing her pain. This was bad enough, this inability to reach for her, to reassure her.

Joey appeared to be in charge, though Mac bet Rahim had orders to let him believe that to be the case. He turned his body slightly to appeal to both men, ignoring the grinding pain that reminded him one of his ribs was broken. He'd heard the damned thing go and was just happy it hadn't punctured a lung when it did. One among many things he owed Joey for.

While he spoke, he kept his hands perfectly still, not wanting the movement of the muscles in his arms to show that he was slowly cutting himself free of the restraints they'd applied to his wrists. Thank goodness for fancy kitchens with paring knives no one used or allowed to get dull. He'd secreted the little weapon in the waistband at the small of his back, hoping not to stab himself with it accidentally. A cursory pat-down hadn't revealed it.

"C'mon. You guys have me trussed up like a damn goose. What harm can I do? Let a guy have a little fun."

"Look," Callie said, her eyes wide. Mac feared her shaking

might be a bit over the top, but Falcone's goons seemed to eat it up. And when they looked at her, he began sawing away once again at the bindings. "I'll tell you whatever you want. You don't have to—"

Joey laughed. "I know I don't have to. But, see, I want to." He tossed his weapon to the couch behind him and reached out, grabbed the neck of her T-shirt, and tore it straight down.

Mac's hands clenched so tightly he nearly snapped the handle of the knife, but he forced himself to remain still. Tears dripped down Callie's face, and he beat the rage back with skill and determination of years of undercover work. He could not let it show. His hands were still bound, and if he acted too soon he'd lose his shot.

Callie tried to curl over herself and turn to the side, but Joey slapped her across the face. Then he reached out and grabbed her breast. When she tried to pull away, he slammed her up against the wall next to where Mac knelt and twisted her bare nipple between his fingers. Rahim kept the gun pointed at Mac, barely glancing at the violence.

"You get much primo American white meat like this where you live?" Joey pulled the torn shirt from Callie's body, inviting the other man to look. "I can't imagine choosing to stay where women keep all their goodies hidden."

Rahim switched his focus—and aim—to Callie, examined her critically for a moment, then shrugged. "My wife is not to be seen by other men. But even in my country, there are plenty of whores like this one who can be viewed by all who wish it."

Mac felt the last bit of plastic give on the word "whores," pressed his feet into the wall, and launched himself forward on the word "it". His shoulder connected with Rahim's breastplate, and he heard a gasping exhalation and a clatter as the gun went flying. Behind him, he heard Joey scream "Bitch!" and assumed Callie had gotten in at least one good strike.

Rahim rolled to the side, hand reaching for the gun, but Mac landed on him. He'd intended to grab the man's head and slam it into the floor, but Rahim forced his palm up and into Mac's broken rib. Black spots danced before his eyes as he gasped for breath. Damn the man for paying attention to which side Joey had kicked. Still on top of the smaller man, Mac took advantage of his greater weight to keep Rahim from going after the gun. He rolled slightly to the side, which—while it put pressure on the broken rib—trapped Rahim's arm and prevented another strike.

Rahim reached up with his free arm, aiming a punch at Mac's temple. Mac angled his head away, then slammed his forearm down on Rahim's throat. He felt cartilage crush, heard the trachea collapse, and the man began to suffocate.

Mac turned his attention to Joey and Callie. She must have attacked the man the instant Mac had lunged for Rahim, or else Joey would have gone for his gun. Now, though he had her in his grip, she struggled forcefully against him, not allowing him to gain enough control to reach for the weapon. At the moment, he was holding her off the ground, one arm around the plastic collar, the other around her waist, as she kicked backward at his knees and shins and twisted her head to bite at every inch of exposed flesh on his arm.

Mac leapt over the back of the couch and scooped up the Glock. Aimed it.

"Drop her."

"Like you're going to shoot me while I'm holding her?" Blood streamed from Joey's nose, and his words came out fuzzy. "I don't fucking think so." He began dragging Callie in the direction of Rahim's pistol.

Callie dropped her head forward, then propelled it back, smashing him in the nose. He jerked away, but she rapped him solidly in the chin. Mac grinned. She was a fighter, his girl.

"Me, I can wait all day," Mac said. "Doesn't look as if you have that kind of time."

With a grunt, Joey thrust Callie toward Mac and dove for the weapon on the floor.

Mac shot him in the head before he could reach it, then turned to Callie.

⌒

Oh, god. Mac had killed him. Killed him. Just like that.

Callie couldn't take her eyes off the carnage, the remains of a man. Another she'd heard choking to death mere minutes before. He was silent now. A third had died within seconds of entering the house. Was this the truth of Mac Brody? She forced herself to look at him.

Blood dripped down the side of his face, and his eye had swollen nearly shut. He put down the gun and walked to where the shears she'd stabbed Rahim with had fallen, and for a split second, images of horror-movie villains lumbered through her head. *Run!* screamed half her brain, but the other half would not obey. He had saved her. Whatever other truths the day might reveal, he had saved her from both Joey and John Lewis.

"Turn around, sugar," he said, his tone soft, persuasive, gentle. "Let me cut those things off you." A single snip released her. She closed her eyes, breathed deeply, trying to ignore the acrid smell of death. Then she turned to face him again.

He was pulling his shirt over his head. As he did, she saw, beneath the smooth, sexy movement of muscle and sinew, the displaced awkward sharpness of broken bone. When he reached out to hand her the T-shirt, his face had paled beneath the island tan.

At first, she didn't even realize what he wanted from her. She'd become so caught up in the violence and its aftermath that her own nudity meant nothing. As soon as she remembered it, however, she felt a fierce blush rise to her cheeks, and she looked away from him as she accepted the shirt and pulled it over her head.

When she was covered, he drew her close.

"Your ribs—" She tried to resist, but he refused to let her.

"I'll be fine. I need this, sugar. Just for a minute. Okay?"

What could she say? She needed it, too, needed to be reassured that there was more to the man than the killing machine responsible for the bodies strewn about the floor. She slid her arms about his waist and pressed her ear to the steady thud of his heart.

"I have to patch myself up and then go help Nash," Mac said after far too short a time. "Let me get my pack from the kitchen; then we can see what Lewis has in the way of first aid."

"I'll show you." After they retrieved the leather satchel from the kitchen, she took him by the hand and led him to the office, then into the lab.

"Oh, hell," he said as he surveyed the damage. This time when he reached for her, his hands shook. "Oh, sugar, I am sorry. We never should have let you go with him. I never should have let you go with him."

Callie looked up at him, hearing the questions he was afraid to ask.

"It wasn't your decision to make, Mac; it was mine. And I got away." She rested a hand on his cheek, turning his face away from the table and the bone saw and other implements that lay scattered around it. "I got away, and you came for me. That's what matters."

He swallowed, then nodded. As she watched, the sorrow on his face transmuted to rage. If she were a better person, she thought, she'd try to damp that anger. But the sight of the table brought back all her fear, all her helplessness, all her pain, and she couldn't force herself to care if— or how— John Lewis died.

"Let's get this show on the road," he said.

Callie pulled out ACE bandages and followed Mac's instructions on how to bind his ribs. Then she cut away the blood-soaked leg of his jeans below the knee.

"It's just a graze, but I'll get it cleaned up and stitched properly later on," Mac said, hearing her gasp. "For now, just slap some antibiotic and gauze on it. No time for anything else."

When she had done as directed, Mac led her out of the house to the driveway, where two Jeeps marked as belonging to S&S Security had been parked angling away from the house. He pulled a couple of tiny tools from the satchel and went to work on the door.

"Where are we going?" "I'm taking you down to the docks so I can drop you with Travis and you'll be safe. Nash got his hands on the plans for Lewis's new wine cellar, so he went to try to liberate the merchandise Falcone had stored there. What he has is far too dangerous to allow it to be sold on the black market." The door popped open, and Mac leaned through to unlock the passenger side.

"You're saying he really did desert you in the middle of a

firefight? I just figured he was never here." Callie couldn't get her head around it.

"He—we—prioritized. You, me, neither of us is as important as that shipment. We figured if all the action was up here, he could get in and out of the hotel with relatively little fuss. He doesn't need to retrieve the weapons; he just needs to move them so they won't be where Falcone expects them. As long as Falcone can't get to them, Nash can send a retrieval force in for them later. Plus, there's only one that really matters." Mac hustled her around the other side of the Jeep. "But he wasn't counting on Lewis and Pablo arriving late to the party."

"Then you go. Leave me here. I'll find my own way to the dock. I know Travis's boat. You need to move fast."

"Like hell. Yeah, I want to get over there, but Nash is a big boy. He's been taking care of himself a long time." Mac pulled her to him for a quick, hard kiss, then raised his hands to her shoulders and pushed her down into the passenger seat. "But I am not leaving you alone. Not now, not ever. Got it?"

"Then we go to Nash together. He saved my life. Saved Erin's life . . . didn't he?"

"Yeah, he did. She's in the hospital in New York, but she's going to be fine."

"Then I owe him. So I'm not going to hide out on Travis's boat while he's in trouble. I couldn't live with myself."

"Callie—"

"Don't. I want to see this through."

"Yeah, okay." He slammed the door and tore around to the other side to hop into the driver's seat.

He connected a couple of wires beneath the steering column, and the engine rumbled to life. The road remained empty, the sound of the Jeep jolting along far too fast exceptionally loud in the morning air as they drove, until a man in the uniform of the gendarmes stepped out of the Paradis gatehouse, aimed a wicked-looking weapon at them, and shouted for them to halt. Mac ignored him.

"Get down!" He shoved Callie down into a crouch beneath the dashboard as the Jeep crashed through the ornamental wrought-iron gates to the hotel. The gendarme—or whoever he was—followed, shouting and shooting, but they lost him when the driveway curved. Callie pushed herself back up into her seat and held on to the roll bar as they tilted at an alarming angle.

"Jesus!" Mac slammed on the brakes and swerved to avoid a couple in matching jogging suits exiting the Paradis's main building. The man shouted and raised his fist, but Mac ignored him, maneuvering the car around the side of the building. "I hate ops with civilians. These people are going to get themselves killed, and there's fuck-all I can do about it."

Callie started to answer, to reassure him, but her head hit the roof of the Jeep, cracking her teeth together, as Mac jumped the curb, ignoring the path in favor of cutting across land to reach their destination more quickly. They rounded the corner of the hotel and found themselves confronted by an olive-skinned man holding an AK-47. He aimed at them and Mac gunned the engine. The solid *thunk* of flesh against metal turned Callie's stomach as the guy flew up and onto the Jeep's hood. His face pressed for a minute against the windshield, dead eyes permanently open in a kind of shocked horror, before Mac braked and he slid to the ground.

Mac jumped from the vehicle, tucked the pistol he'd taken from the house into the back of his jeans, and retrieved the machine gun from the guy's twitching body. "C'mon," he said, "he won't have been alone. We have to find Nash."

Callie slid from her seat, the Glock that Mac had given her

at the house an unwieldy weight in her hand. But the body lying before the Jeep put paid to any thought she might have had about leaving it behind.

"Stay close." Mac edged forward, staying pressed up against the wall of the hotel, and she followed. He ducked his head around quickly, then pulled back. "Door's clear. But I wouldn't expect more than one outside anyway. Inside's more practical for an ambush. Wait here."

He ran back to the Jeep and retrieved the leather bag he'd brought with them. When he returned, he slung the machine gun over his shoulder and dug around inside the bag, coming up with a pair of binoculars. He used the glasses to study the wall of the building.

"What are you doing?" she whispered.

"These show me the heat signatures of anyone in the cellar. I need to know what we're up against."

After staring through the glasses for a minute, he grunted and drew a square in the sandy dirt beneath his knees.

"Here's what we've got. Two guys in this area, here." He put a couple marks on the drawing. "Then one here, by this door, another on the opposite side, which I assume is the door from the kitchen and dining room, and a third off to himself over here." He made appropriate marks for each.

"The first four are moving. Not doing jumping jacks or anything, but moving around. The last one is staying very still. I'd wager that's Nash. Either he's been captured and tied up or unconscious, or he's trying to avoid that fate by remaining hidden."

"What do we do?"

"First, we get every innocent person out of Dodge. Claudine can handle it. I'll give her a good reason to do it quickly." He reached into the bag again and withdrew a phone.

"Claudine," he said when the woman answered, "this is Mac. Yes, I know. I don't have time right now. Listen, you have to round up my team and have them evacuate the hotel. There's a bomb in the wine cellar. Yes, yes, call the gendarmes, but get the people out first. Get them far away from the building. That's the important thing. Be careful."

"She'll be able to handle that?"

"She and Andy and the rest of the staff and security team. Between hurricanes and high-profile clients, we have drills several times a year. After a drill, we apologize to the guests with special incentives — spa treatments, water-sports excursions to Pinel Island — make them feel extra pampered. It gets the job done."

"Impressive. Too bad I'm not really writing an article about the place. I could advise them to come when they thought a drill might be imminent in order to get access to the goodies."

The spark of humor in their situation impressed him, and he grinned down at her, hoping to prolong the moment. "Why no article? You don't think Vacation Spots for Serial Killers and Arms Dealers is the sort of thing your readers would enjoy?"

"Nope. To them, a 'sick puppy' needs doggie detox."

"Tell me you're kidding."

"I wish I could." She gave him a strained smile and returned her attention to the building, all levity gone. From around front, they could hear a rising babble and ruckus as people exited.

"So what now?"

"Let's see what goodies we have." He dumped out the satchel and began sifting through the items.

The colors of death are steel blue and charcoal, matte metal and black rubber. She glanced away to get her bearings.

"Okay," Mac said, after hefting a couple of the objects. "Here's what we're going to do. You are going to set up behind that palm." He pointed to a tree some fifteen feet opposite the door and handed her a pistol. "You can use that? You don't have to be precise." She nodded, then checked the gun to be sure it was loaded, proving her point.

"Good. When I left, I . . . retained some keys. I thought we might need them. I doubt they've had a chance to change the locks, but they will be listening for anyone trying to break in. By now, they have to have heard the exodus and have some idea what's going on.

"I am going to unlock the cellar access door over there, open it, and get the hell out of the way. You are going to fire. Aside from the guard, no one should be in the path of the bullets, and from this angle, it's unlikely you'll hit him. The stairs go directly down from the doorway, so you're too far above and outside to do much damage.

"Give it six shots. Count them. When you're done, I'm going to roll in a flashbang. At that point we'll both run like hell for the front."

"A flashbang?"

He held up a canister with a loop-and-pin lock at the top. She'd imagined the word to be jargon, but the device actually said FLASHBANG in large letters on the side. "I can't throw it in—you don't want this baby hitting anyone, believe me— but I can roll it. It explodes, with a lot of light and sound, just as the name suggests. It also generates a fair amount of heat. It will temporarily blind them, especially given the dimness of the wine cellar and the fact that they'll probably be look- ing in the direction of the door, and create a distraction. By the time they get sorted, I want to be around front and in through the other door."

"Do you really think we can run that fast?"

His mouth tilted up on one side. "Nope. But I think six shots and a three count before a flashbang will alert Nash that we're coming. I'm hoping he'll provide the rest of the distraction. I don't suppose I can convince you to stay behind?"

Callie examined his long legs, compared them to her own, suppressed the flash of heated memory at how well they'd fit together. "I'd slow you down if I tried to follow."

"Okay, then." He glanced around, eyes coming to rest on a squat, square cement building about thirty feet from the palm-tree vantage point from which Callie would be shooting. "That's the laundry building. When I roll the flashbang into the cellar, squeeze into the vegetation next to it. Stay close to the building. There's a lot of scrub, which will keep you hidden, but the cliff drops off pretty quickly, so watch your step. I'm not going far, so if anyone comes after you, shoot and shout. Ready?"

Was she? Did she have a choice?

"Let's do it."

He pulled her close, kissed her hard, and led her to the palm tree, where he had her check to be sure she could see where she was supposed to shoot. Then he pulled a set of keys from his pocket and crept toward the cellar door. He eased a large bronze one into the door. In that moment, Callie's hearing sharpened and silence fell as if the very air had stopped moving, and every footstep on pebbled ground, every jiggle of the key, every snick of the lock was magnified. How could the people in the cellar not hear? Not realize they had an enemy poised to invade?

Mac turned the handle with excruciating deliberation, then slammed the door open hard and fast, simultaneously pressing himself against the outer wall of the building. Callie could see no movement from within the cellar. She hesitated.

"Go!" Mac shouted, and she fired, counting off the shots under her breath. One, two, three, four, five, six. Then, hanging onto the gun with her finger outside the trigger guard, she ran for the laundry building. Behind her, she heard the enormous, crashing explosion that signified the flashbang's deployment.

She shoved her way into the dense foliage next to the laundry building, ignoring the scratching twigs and occasional thorn. Though she hugged the wall, the three feet separating her from the cliff's edge seemed mere inches. And no sooner had she found a spot where she felt secure than tires crunched across the gravel at the front of the building and she heard a French-accented voice calling Mac's name.

⌒

MAC ROUNDED THE corner of the hotel and hit the front door of the Paradis at a dead run, doing his best to ignore the grinding pain of his broken rib. Once inside, he slowed slightly, watching for guards. None appeared, however, despite the shadows fluttering at the edges of his vision. The door to the wine cellar—a stout, darkly stained affair custom-crafted to match the hotel's furnishings during the remodel—blocked all sound. Mac swung it wide and launched himself through it in a somersaulting leap he could only hope didn't get him killed.

Shots sounded, and he felt the spit of splintering stone strike his skin, but he landed safely in a deep crouch, his enemy before him. He kicked out, heard the satisfying crunch of bone and cartilage signifying a direct hit to the knee and an equally satisfying scream of pain. The man went down but didn't lose his grip on his gun. He squeezed off a shot that tore the air a breath from Mac's neck. Mac's own bullet found its mark a second later, puncturing a neat hole in the bridge of the guy's nose and spattering the back of his pulverized skull over a tall rack of red wines.

Nash had also dispatched at least one man, Mac realized as he stepped forward and almost stumbled over the body. Now he faced Lewis, who stood in front of the entrance to the secret compartment. He'd evidently opened it before Mac's arrival. Mac, approaching at an angle, stilled at the sight of the object in Lewis's hand. In the sudden absence of gunfire, Lewis's words ran out over the others' harsh breathing.

"One more step and I'll kill her." He held up the small, utterly innocuous remote control. None of the five buttons on it bore labels, but Mac had no doubt that at least one would cause Callie's death. If the device operated on simple infrared, Lewis would need a direct line of sight to get to her, but the men who'd created the subtle evil he held so casually wouldn't have gone for something so straightforward. Nor would they have chosen radio waves, not when any passing boat might interrupt the signal. And Mac, no electronics expert, had no clue what other forms of linkage might exist between the control and the bomb.

"Come on, now," Nash coaxed. "No need for that. You don't want to kill her, or you'd have done so already. And we couldn't care less about what happens to her. If we did, why would we be here, with you, instead of back at the house helping her? All we want is the bioweapon."

"That's not what he said." Lewis jerked his head at Mac. "He said he planned to betray you and go into business with Falcone."

"Did he now? Well, as you may have noticed, Mr. Brody's

loyalties display a certain flexibility. Liberal applications of cash have always kept him in line in the past." Nash cast an evaluative eye over Mac, who grinned. Oh, yeah. He'd played this game before. Never with Nash, however, which increased the danger, as they'd had no chance to practice timing or signals.

"That'll work just fine," he said, ostensibly replying to the cash comment.

"So you say. But I'd just as soon not take any chances." Nash swung around, aimed, and fired.

Mac fell sideways, deliberately landing in the blood pooling on the floor from Nash's previous kill without letting go of his gun. His lungs burned and his ribs shot pain through his body, but he stayed perfectly still.

"Jesus Christ!" Lewis's horrified outburst indicated their ruse had succeeded. Mac cracked one eye open to get a position on him.

"One problem solved." Nash spoke with perfect calm. "Now we need to discuss your little weapons stash."

The sound of a male voice heavily accented in French calling Mac's name distracted Lewis. Mac took advantage of the moment to shift unobtrusively, bringing his gun arm down to aim at him. But Lewis was moving.

"Take it," he said, gesturing toward the cache. "Take all of it. You won't get anywhere. Falcone won't let you." Every step he took away from the alcove brought him nearer to Mac, whose eyes tracked him though he didn't move a muscle.

"Go home to your girlfriend, then." Nash moved toward the alcove, forcing Lewis back yet another step, right into Mac's line of fire. Mac emptied the magazine into Lewis's head.

Gritting her teeth against nerves and pain, Callie retraced the path she'd just carved, then poked her head around the side of the building just enough to see, not enough to break free of the foliage. Mac's friend Vichy stood beside the Jeep. He touched the driver's seat, and Callie saw his hand come away bloody. The bandage on Mac's knee must have come loose when they were driving. She hadn't noticed it when he'd been explaining the plan to her, nor had he given in to a limp when he'd run for the front of the hotel after dropping the flashbang. Remembering the beautiful grace of his walk, she hoped he hadn't crippled himself abusing that knee.

Vichy raised his hand, showing his companion that the driver of the Jeep had been injured, and Callie suddenly realized the other man was not Vichy's gendarme partner. This man was younger, with dark, slicked-back hair, sharp cheekbones, and a slim build, and he wore a pair of slacks and polo shirt rather than a uniform. He was almost pretty. Almost.

Could this be Henry Falcone himself? Both he and Vichy had machine guns slung over their shoulders, but Callie had traveled enough to know that was not unusual for police forces in countries other than the United States. And Vichy had seemed friendly enough with Mac. He'd even provided assistance with the DNA testing.

Again, Vichy called Mac's name, and Callie almost stepped out of hiding to tell him to stop, that he would get Mac killed. But her mistrust of that second man held her in place. Instead, as the sound of gunfire erupted within the cellar, she checked to be sure her own weapon still had bullets.

Vichy ran toward the cellar door. The other man remained with the vehicle. Just as Vichy reached the opening, Mac flew out, a silver briefcase in his hand. Callie had a split second to exult in the knowledge he'd made it before Vichy aimed his weapon at him. Mac lowered his head, dove for Vichy's legs, and the gendarme's weapon went flying. Without thought, Callie aimed at the other man and began firing from her hiding place.

The attack clearly came as a shock to him. He took a single step toward the men scrabbling on the ground, then retreated, climbed into the vehicle, and took off, tires shooting gravel in every direction. He'd be back, she was sure, and with reinforcements. Did the case contain the weapon Mac and Nash were determined to protect? She crept out, keeping her gun pointed at the two men rolling in the dirt, hoping she could get a clear shot at Vichy, and grabbed it.

The movement, or the sunlight reflecting off the metal, caught the men's attention. Freeing himself from Mac's hold momentarily, Vichy lunged at her. She backed away, but he grabbed her hand and tore the gun from her grip. Dismissing her as little danger, he turned to fire at Mac, who already had hold of him around the waist and was pulling him to the ground.

In desperation, Callie swung the briefcase at Vichy's head. It connected with a weird, hollow sound, at the same moment as the gun went off. The two men fell backward simultaneously, separating from one another. Callie spared a glance at Vichy to be certain he was unconscious, then stepped over his body to kneel beside Mac, who was cursing and attempting to sit up.

Blood poured down his left arm from a wound in the shoulder, soaking through the bandage she'd wrapped around his ribs. Callie pressed her hands desperately against the hole, but the blood kept pulsing out between her fingers.

"Harder," Mac ordered through gritted teeth. "You have to press harder."

Movement caught her eye, and she grabbed in panic for the gun only to relax when she registered Nash staggering out of the cellar. One side of his face had been scraped raw, and he was favoring his right leg, but when he saw Mac's condition he hurried toward them, dragging his shirt off over his head.

"Christ." He took Callie's place, pressing his shirt to Mac's shoulder. "We have to get him out of here. Travis has *The Tramp* down at the dock, but this place isn't exactly accessible. And *The Tramp*, for all it's not huge, isn't a speedboat, either. Trey's in the air; I radioed him when I left the Lewis house, but I won't be happy until we're back in the US. We need to get this show on the road." He slid an arm around Mac's chest and heaved him to his feet. Both of them swayed, and Callie was afraid they'd go right back down, but they steadied themselves.

"Grab the weapons," Nash ordered. "And that." He jerked his head at the metal briefcase. For the first time, Callie wondered just what kind of evil it contained that so many had to die for it. That so many were *willing* to die for it.

They made their way around the front of the hotel and past the pool to the path leading down to the beach. Callie kept watch behind them, becoming more concerned as she recognized the increasing density of the blood trail they were leaving. Still, no one followed. Almost to the sand, Nash paused, holding up a hand. A moment later, Callie heard voices.

"Friend or foe?"

Callie listened to the French, translating the parts she could catch. "Gendarmes. I'd say they're honest ones from their conversation, but that doesn't make them our friends."

"No," Nash agreed. "So we keep moving. Fast." He started forward again.

When they stepped off the paved path onto the beach, Callie could see *The Tramp* anchored out about thirty feet from shore, but there was no sign of Travis. With the gendarmes so close, she didn't dare call out, but she didn't see how they could get Mac, who'd begun to sag heavily against Nash, out to the boat without help. Then Travis's head popped up from one of the small, sleek water-sports boats tied to the dock, and he waved them over.

They stumbled across the sand toward the dock, driven forward by the increasingly loud voices behind them.

"This will be faster," Travis said as he helped them aboard and fiddled with some wires he'd pulled loose from the boat's dash. The engine choked, caught, and they pulled away from the dock as three gendarmes appeared on the beach. Shouting, the men ran toward them, weapons at the ready.

"Everybody down," Travis shouted. He whipped the boat into a steep curve, sending up a huge wake.

Mac's face had gone gray. Callie and Nash pushed him to the floor and took up positions on either side of him, crouching as low as possible. A bullet *thunked* into the frail fiberglass side of the boat and Travis turned again, sending his passengers tumbling.

"We're almost out of range. If we'd been any closer, that would have come right through. But they're getting on the other boat. I didn't have time to scuttle it before you showed up."

"I'm not killing cops," Nash said. Callie raised her head and peered back at the beach. Several more gendarmes had joined their pursuers, and as she watched, four of them boarded the other speedboat at the dock.

"No worries," said Travis, tapping his headset. "I'm on with Trey. He's only a couple minutes out.

Take the wheel a sec." Nash did, and Travis pulled a small electronic device from his pocket. The second speedboat fired up and pulled away from the dock. Just as it passed *The Tramp*, however, Travis pushed the button on the device he held and the larger vessel exploded, sending a shockwave through the water and capsizing the speedboat.

A grimly pleased smile transformed Travis's features, and he nodded in satisfaction before taking the wheel back from Nash. A moment later Callie heard the sound of helicopter rotors over the engine, and the Jayhawk appeared around a curve in the coastline.

"You're first!" Nash shouted over the noise. The rope ladder dropped.

"How are you going to get Mac up there?"

"Don't you worry; it's under control. Just get up there before the cavalry arrives from Marigot!"

Callie got. When she reached the top of the ladder, Joseph helped her into the aircraft, then turned around to steady the ladder again for Travis, who'd hoisted Mac into a fireman's carry and was carefully making his way up. Nash held the bottom, but the rope still swayed alarmingly, and Callie's stomach knotted. Only when Joseph was hauling Mac into the chopper did she realize she hadn't breathed since Travis had started his ascent.

Nash joined them, pulling the ladder up behind them as Trey headed out to sea.

She sat cross-legged on the floor of the chopper and positioned Mac with his head in her lap. The bleeding from his shoulder had slowed; the impromptu bandage was holding. Or maybe he just didn't have enough blood left inside him to force its way out. She stroked the hair away from his face.

"Don't you dare die on me, Aidan Macmillan Brody." It

was as close as she could come to saying the words welling inside her. *I need you. I love you. Please don't leave me. You promised.* None of them appropriate for this time and place.

His eyelids twitched. "Wouldn't dream of it." The words slurred slightly but still brought hope. She turned to Nash. "We need to get him to a hospital."

"Screw the hospital." Mac shifted and she could tell he was trying to get up. She held him down. He subsided but continued to argue. "The first thing we need to do is get that damned necklace bomb off you. For all we know, it has a timer built in."

"The two are not mutually exclusive," Nash snapped, interrupting her incipient protest. "You'll both be taken into police custody the minute we land. No way around it. But this"—he tapped the silver briefcase—"should suffice as a get-out-of-jail-free card. I have to go up front and let Lexie know who to call to make arrangements. He stood, but Mac reached out and grabbed his leg.

"Get Boom-Boom to Puerto Rico to get that thing off Callie's neck."

"It'll be quicker to let the local bomb techs handle it."

"Right. Because San Juan sees so many sophisticated explosive devices."

Nash nodded. "I'll see to it."

"Try not to worry," Callie said once he had moved off. "John wouldn't have let them put something on me that might accidentally blow up. He needed me alive."

"Why? What did he plan to do with that operating-room setup?"

Callie shuddered, then tried to keep the remembered terror from her voice as she spoke. "From what he said, I'm pretty sure he recognized something was wrong with him.

But he was crazy. Utterly insane. He believed he could use pieces of Mark Lewis's true children to correct the lack in himself."

"Jesus." Mac shifted position, and she resumed smoothing his brow, running her fingers through his thick, springy hair.

"It's over. You killed him, didn't you?" She'd known from the minute Mac had emerged from the cellar; he wouldn't leave her attacker alive. And although she didn't consider herself particularly bloodthirsty, she'd felt no guilt for the brief surge of satisfaction she'd felt.

"Yeah. But he died far too quickly."

"He was insane, Mac. And, I suspect, miserable." Amazing how forgiving she felt now the man was dead and no longer a threat.

⌒

"We're landing," Nash said far sooner than Callie expected. Far sooner than she wanted. Mac needed help, but she wasn't ready to let him go. As if he heard her thoughts, he reached for her hand, drew it to his lips, and pressed a kiss into her palm.

"Don't worry, sugar, Seth's the best there is." It took a minute for his meaning to penetrate.

"I'm not worried about me, Mac! You're the one who's been shot!"

"No problem. I'm hard to kill." His voice, and his grin, had lost considerable strength, however, and she felt the press of tears behind her lids as she tried to return his smile.

"He is," Travis assured her. He'd been so quiet since coming aboard she'd almost forgotten his presence. But then, she'd been focused on Mac.

The helicopter landed on the hospital's roof, and before the rotors even stopped moving, men swarmed around it. Men wearing scowls and suits, men with uniforms and guns, and men in scrubs.

They lifted Mac out first, placing him on a gurney. Medical personnel rushed him away, followed by police, while others kept Callie, Nash, Travis, and Trey in place. Once Mac had disappeared, a dark-suited man stepped forward and called Nash's name. Nash hopped out, conferred briefly with the stranger, and came back for Callie. And the suitcase.

"Trey, take her back to the airfield," he ordered. "Travis, you can either go with him or stay here. You're both to give your names and cell numbers to the officers before you head out, and make yourselves available for questioning should the need arise, though I don't expect it will."

"I'll stick around," said Travis before Callie could beg him to do so. The police would want her and Nash—someone had to be at the hospital when Mac woke up.

⌇

MAC OPENED HIS eyes, winced at the light, and promptly shut them again. It was far from the first time he'd found himself in a hospital bed upon waking, but he couldn't remember another instance being quite as painful. And then his brain caught up with his vision, and he looked again to be sure he wasn't dreaming.

But there she was, curled into the chair beside his bed, feet tucked beneath her and her neck blessedly free of the bomb she'd worn when they'd wheeled him away from her. She'd showered while he slept, and her hair hung in a damp fall of curls over her shoulder. Someone had given her a pair of scrubs decorated with balloons so bright her fair skin turned ghostly in comparison.

Even the alarming outfit, however, couldn't leach the color from the bruises beneath her eyes or along her left cheekbone. A surge of impotent rage overwhelmed him; he'd gladly have gone back and killed the men who'd hurt her a second time.

She shifted in her seat and her lids fluttered. Gradually, her gaze focused. "You're awake!"

"Told you I was hard to kill."

She rewarded his feeble attempt at humor with a brilliant smile. "I do believe you mentioned something to that effect."

"Has anyone every told you that you have a gorgeous neck?"

This elicited a full-on laugh. A more beautiful sound he'd never heard. "You're crazy."

"I guess you met Seth?"

"Yes. He's very efficient. He took the bomb away to study. He said it was intriguing."

"Naturally." She obviously wanted to gloss over the incident, so Mac let it go. He'd watched the removal of a similar device from around the waist of a kidnapped executive in Atlanta. The man had almost collapsed in terror midway through the operation, though the bomb tech had kept up a reassuring drone of chatter designed to keep his mind off the possibilities.

"What about the police?" he asked. "Nash is working on it. Some guy from Homeland Security already interviewed me, as did another, who could have been his brother—or maybe it's just the suits that make them look so much alike—from the Department of Justice. You'll have to talk to them, too, no doubt, but they seem a lot more interested in the contents of that briefcase than in our many misdeeds."

"You've been busy. How long have I been out?"

She checked her watch. "I'm not sure when we got in, but it's almost nine. So about twelve hours?"

"Twelve hours?"

"Mac, you were shot. And lost a lot of blood. And had major surgery. No one really expected you to wake up before morning."

"What about Falcone?" Jesus. He'd been unconscious half a day while she sat alone, possibly unprotected. Where were Travis and Nash? The machine next to his bed beeped angrily.

"Calm down," Callie ordered, "or the nurses will come in and tell me I have to leave for upsetting you."

"Falcone. What happened to him?"

"He's in the wind." Nash's disgusted statement drew both Mac's and Callie's eyes to the door. "As usual, we can't even conclusively prove his involvement with the bioweapon shipment. We're tracking the rest of the items Lewis had stored, but I don't have high hopes for those, either. Falcone insulates himself well. He probably has a dozen witnesses at hand to say he never left his buddy's yacht in Anguilla."

Mac cursed and Callie shivered.

"I doubt you have to worry." Nash rested a hand on Callie's shoulder, and Mac felt a growl rising in his throat. When the hell had he gotten so possessive? He stifled the sound before it emerged. "You were Lewis's project. Now that he's gone, you can get back to your life."

The words slammed into Mac with the familiar punch of a bullet. As usual, Nash had cut straight to the heart of the matter; Callie no longer needed their protection. In fact, Mac's presence in her life could only hurt her by potentially rekindling Falcone's interest. The responsible thing to do was to let her go. So he gritted his teeth and forced a smile.

"Erin will be happy to have you home."

She didn't return his smile. In fact, all expression disappeared from her face. "Yes," she said. "I spoke to her on the phone. She's staying with friends in the city until I can get back to the house; she's not up to being alone. We're both very grateful for your help getting her away from those men."

"I'm so sorry she got involved in all of this," Nash said. Mac tried to recall ever hearing the man apologize before and failed. Clearly, however, Callie didn't recognize the significance of the words.

"That's it, then?" Although her face was still emotionless, anger seeped out in her words. "Go on home and play with your dollies while the big boys clean up the mess?"

Mac tried to intercede. "Be reasonable, Callie. You have a life, a home. Your roommate needs you. Yes, Nash is—I am—asking you to leave the mess to us, but not because we don't respect your strength or intelligence. Just because it's not your job to deal with men like Henry Falcone."

"And is it yours?"

"I don't know. Maybe." He glanced over at Nash, who nodded. The promise of work, real work, not ferrying drunk tourists on fishing trips or overseeing security at a glorified playground, held more healing power than any IV drip. "Yeah, I guess it is."

Callie unfolded herself from the chair, the movement stiff. Because he'd upset her? Or just from the abuse her muscles had suffered over the past few days? "I suppose that is it, then," she said, her voice as expressionless as her face, as stiff as her posture. "It's been . . . interesting." The door, swooshing quietly shut behind her, held a finality no slam could equal.

SHE WOULD NOT cry. Dammit, she would not. What had she expected? That they'd get married and live happily ever after? That he'd move into her house and share pancakes on a Sunday morning in her sunny kitchen? Not likely. Did she even want such a thing? With a man like him? A self-confessed adrenaline addict?

She liked her life just fine, dammit. She had her work, her friends, her house. She didn't need some man to complete her.

"I'm sure you don't."

A smile hid behind Travis's words. She hadn't realized she'd been muttering on her way down the hall. A hot blush rose up her face.

"Sorry about that."

"Not at all. Mostly, we're a pretty useless lot, unless you want to open a jar."

She forced herself to smile. "Some of you aren't so useless." Travis had stayed by her side while Seth Lindsay had carefully cut through first the duct tape, then the plastic shell, and finally the wires of the necklace bomb. She'd wanted him to go to Mac, but he'd refused. Mac, he'd claimed, would be unconscious for hours. And if he woke to find she'd gone through her ordeal alone, Travis's life would be over.

So much for that idea. Their adventure at an end, Mac had dismissed her like a book returned to the library once the story had been absorbed. Not a keeper.

The teasing grin disappeared from Travis's angelic features. "Give him some time, Callie."

"Don't worry about it, Travis. I'm not." *Liar.* "I just wish I could go home, but I haven't had a chance to talk to anyone about how I am supposed to manage that. I don't have a license, let alone a credit card, so I can't buy a plane ticket."

"Let me see what I can do," he offered. "Grab a seat in the

waiting area—I'll be right back." He gave her a gentle push, then disappeared down the hall in the opposite direction.

Out of options, Callie obeyed the command, curling up on a couch in the foyer at the end of the long hall beyond the nurses' station. In her head, she began composing a list of the things she'd need to do to get her life back. A new driver's license, passport, bank and credit cards, keys to her car and house ... She drifted off imagining the reams of red tape.

When she woke, Travis had not yet returned. How long had she slept? Minutes? Hours?

The nurses, who'd become used to her while she waited for Mac, nodded to her as she wandered down the hall. The guard who had originally sat beside Mac's door had disappeared, but she could hear voices from inside.

Despite herself, she sidled up and pressed her ear to the door.

⌒

MAC ITCHED TO put his fist through Travis's face. Which didn't make any sense, really, since Trav was his closest friend and was only doing the right thing by offering to see Callie home safely and to ease her way over the bureaucratic hurdles she'd face when she got there. Still, he couldn't keep the sarcasm from his voice when he responded.

"Why don't you just move in with her while you're at it?"

Travis cocked his head. "Might not be a bad idea. Just to be sure she's okay. Plus, I haven't got a place to stay yet."

"Stay the fuck away from her," Mac spat.

"Dog in the manger, Brody. Either you want her or you don't."

"It's not about what I want. It's about what she should have.

She deserves better than a scarred ex-cop who barely finished high school and can't possibly support her."

"We haven't even discussed salary yet, and you're already angling for a raise?" Nash asked.

"It's not about money!"

"You just said it was. HSE pays well."

"This whole conversation is ridiculous! She left. Walked out. Went home. She doesn't want anything more to do with any of us. For God's sake, you've all seen it before—adrenaline and fear make for strange bedfellows. Give her a week or two and she'll be happy to be rid of everything having to do with the island and her trip there!"

The door squeaked slightly. Great. Doubtless his pissed-off attitude had triggered something, and now they'd poke him again. But at least the nurse would make Nash and Travis leave him alone.

But it wasn't a nurse.

‚

"OUT. BOTH OF you." Callie pointed at Travis and Nash, who rose quickly from their seats by Mac's bed.

On his way out the door, Travis kissed her cheek and whispered "Give him hell, kid" in her ear.

"Callie," Mac started before the door even finished closing.

She held up a hand. "Don't. I don't need excuses, Mac. I just need you to answer one question for me."

He studied her, then nodded. She swallowed hard, determined to keep her voice level and not to play the tears card.

"Do you think I slept with you because I was afraid?"

"That's not what I said."

"'Adrenaline and fear' were your exact words, I believe."

"Yes. But I didn't mean them that way. I meant . . . the excitement . . . It seeps into every aspect of experience while you're living it. Everything seems bigger, sharper, more colorful, more potent. That wears off eventually."

"So you don't have any feelings for me. Just chemicals in your bloodstream that will fade in a couple of weeks." She was proud of the flat, unemotional tone.

"Stop putting words in my mouth! I lo—"

Callie thought her heart might literally stop. She reminded herself to breathe, then said in as offhand a manner as possible, "You what?"

"I love you. Dammit, Callie, you know that. I could barely fucking breathe the whole time Lewis had you on that island."

"It might have been nice of you to mention that before now." She blinked hard, trying to stifle the welling tears. "As it happens, I love you, too."

"No—"

"Yes. It's not fear or gratitude or any of those things. It's not even the great sex, which you seem to think could get better."

Heat flared in his eyes, but it wasn't the heat that practically melted her into a puddle right there on the cold hospital floor. It was the hope. She walked to the bed and lowered herself onto the edge.

"You hardly know me." But his hand gripped hers, sending a conflicting message.

"What's to know? Your favorite color? Your favorite food? Your favorite television show? I'm partial to blue, but if you want to paint the house red, that's fine. I'll eat just about anything except curry, and I have a DVR so we can both watch whatever we want."

He chuckled then, a low rumble from deep in his chest. "You're a stubborn woman."

"But you love me anyway."

"I do. I really, really do." He pulled her down and settled her head into the curve of his good shoulder.

CHAPTER NINETEEN

MAC WAS STUBBORN, too. He insisted upon getting an apartment of his own so he and Callie could date before making long-term plans, and no matter how much she tried to wear away his resolve, he stood firm on the issue. He took the job Nash offered him, and although they had no further word on Falcone—which he and Nash both seemed to take personally—Mac frequently talked about how much he enjoyed the other aspects of the job. Callie began to realize he needed to prove to himself that he could be successful, so she stopped pushing him to move in with her.

She did, however, insist on Christmas. She invited Travis, who'd found a home on Long Island where he could keep a boat, and a few of the other folks from HSE who didn't have families, including Nash and Lexie. All but Travis declined, however. Erin cooked, and her brother flew in from California with his roommate, and the six of them ate and drank well into the night.

"I was worried about the holidays, you know," she confided to Mac once they'd climbed into bed in the wee hours of the morning.

"What do you mean?"

"My mother was big into decorating the house, and cooking and presents, and even after she died my father and I kept it up. For the past couple of years, he came here and spent Christmas and New Year's with me and Erin and whatever strays we brought in. When he died, and I found that picture, everything changed. And when Erin started talking about Christmas, which she did as soon as she got home from work on Thanksgiving night, I wasn't sure how I would handle it."

"Because it's supposed to be about family."

"Yes."

"From where I stood, you handled it just fine. But if you were uncomfortable, next year we can go somewhere, spend the holidays out of the country."

Next year. It was the first time he'd said anything to indicate that kind of permanence. And yet, even without the words, she'd known.

"No. Today was wonderful."

"Sugar, of all people, you should know family's not about blood. You didn't lose all of yours when your dad died." He tightened the arm he had around her shoulders, pressing her closer to his body. "On the other hand, maybe your family did get a bit too small. Maybe we should think about making it bigger."

He couldn't be saying what she thought he was saying; she'd only just adjusted to the idea of keeping their relationship relaxed. *Shouldn't have had so much wine.* She pushed slightly away so she could look him in the eyes. "Bigger?"

He grinned and rolled them so he was atop her, arms braced on either side of her head. He bent his elbows and brushed her lips with his own. "Bigger," he said huskily, "as in, a husband and a couple kids bigger. Does that work for you?"

Tears sprang to her eyes. "Yeah," she said. "That works for me." She looped her arms around his neck and pulled him down so the heat and strength of his body surrounded her, pressing her into the mattress. He tried to roll away.

"I bought you a ring."

"It can wait."

"I meant to give it to you as a Christmas present."

"It can wait, Mac."

 And that argument, at least, she won.

ACKNOWLEDGMENTS

Every book is made better by its editor and that has never been truer for me than with this book. Without Leis Pederson taking charge of development and copyeditor Matthew Patin riding herd on the timeline, both the characters and the details would have suffered immeasurably.

Although Paradis de la Mer was created specifically for this novel, most of the other places were not. I've altered the geography of the island slightly to make room for the new hotel on the French side. I've also altered the time a bit; by 2015 when this book was published and set, the rotting remains of the cabanas on the Mullet Bay property were gone, but when I began writing they remained as blots on a lovely landscape and they seemed so appropriate as a foreshadowing that I left them in the story even when the actual property began to get cleaned up.

I have been visiting the island of St. Martin for most of my life, and I've never been subjected to any violence. It's important to me that you, my reader, understand that. The violence and pervasive corruption I write about here are entirely fictional though the landscape is real. The Princess Port de Plaisance, where Callie's friend has his time-share, is a real place. It has a lovely marina and a tacky casino and the people who take you to your room could not be nicer or more helpful. Calmos Café is a real beach bar and the people there are also as helpful and friendly as any you'll meet anywhere in the world. And yes, there really are goats who run through the shopping center in Marigot of an afternoon.

I hope you all make it to the island yourselves one day to check it out.

ABOUT THE AUTHOR

Laura K. Curtis gave up a life writing dry academic papers for writing decidedly less dry short crime stories and novel-length romantic suspense and contemporary romance. A member of RWA, MWA, ITW, and Sisters in Crime, she has trouble settling into one genre. She has published four romantic suspense novels (*Twisted*, 2013; *Lost*, 2014; *Echoes*, 2015; and *Mind Games*, 2015), two contemporary romance novels (*Toying With His Affections*, 2014; *Gaming the System*, 2015), and a host of short stories, many with a supernatural bent.